THE BLACK TOWER

BOOK FIVE OF THE FIVE TOWERS

THE BLACK TOWER

a novel by

J.B. SIMMONS

This is a work of fiction. Names, characters, and incidents in this book
are products of the author's imagination or are used fictitiously.

ISBN 978-1-949785-12-8

Published in the United States by Three Cord Press

www.jbsimmons.com

"But when some spirit, feeling purged and sound,
Leaps up or moves to seek a loftier station,
The whole mount quakes and the great shouts resound."

— Dante Alighieri, *Purgatorio*

"The innocence is now enriched by all the bitter experience;
the evil is not simply blotted out, it is redeemed."

— Dorothy Sayers, *Introductory Papers on Dante*

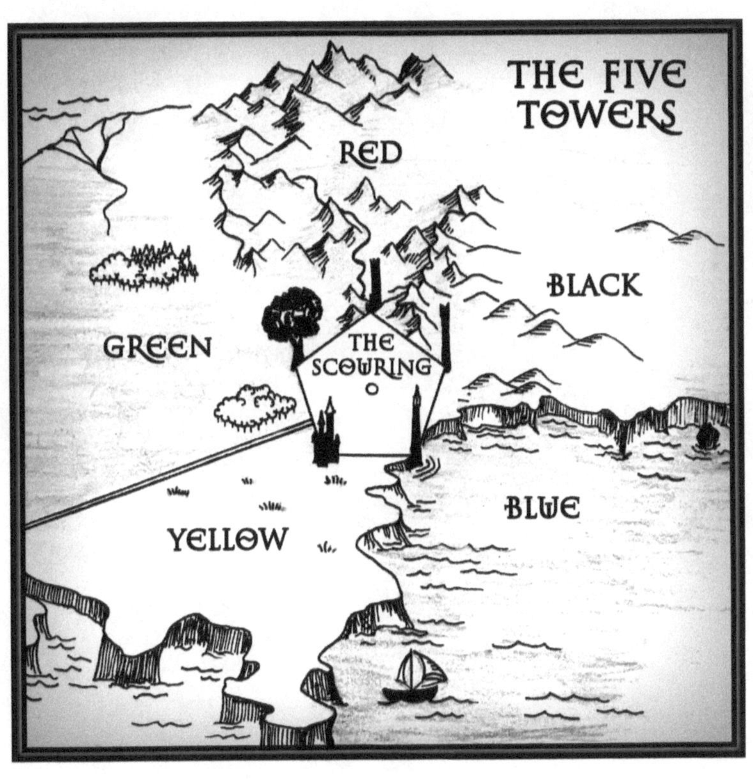

THE FIVE TOWERS
RED
BLACK
GREEN
THE SCOURING
BLACK
BLUE
YELLOW

1

FLAT ON MY back, body still, all black. Breaths come slow and easy. The air is stale. I feel like I've slept a thousand years. Nothing hurts. Nothing feels good.

I could stay here another thousand years. I could sleep, maybe dream. But there's *something*—small and distant as a star—that won't let me rest. This *something* opens my eyes.

Darkness and nothing more.

I try to move. Walls are tight around me. My head lifts and bumps against the ceiling—an inch above me. I swallow.

I yearn to stretch, to stand. I prod around with my fingers, feeling smooth metal everywhere. No gaps. No seams. No cracks. But that can't be right. I had to get in here somehow. If only I could see. I just need to let my eyes adjust.

I maneuver my arms in the cramped space to press my palms up against the hard surface above me. Then I push. I push harder. As hard as I can. Nothing bends, nothing gives.

Okay. How did I get here? Who am I?

Deep breath. There's still *something*. These thoughts, from a mind in a body, mean I'm alive. That's something.

So don't panic. Or…panic just a little.

I kick at the bottom. I slam my knees into the top, then out against the sides. The metal thuds mercilessly. It hurts.

That's something. Pain, it's called.

A coffin, it's called. But coffins are buried in graves…

I form my hands into fists and knock. It sounds hollow, echoing outside and in. That means there's no dirt around me. Not a coffin. No, can't be a grave. I'm alive. Heart beating. Mind thinking.

I lay still again. I breathe fast, shallow breaths. My hands clasp over my chest. I feel rough lines of skin at the center of each hand. My fingers trace the blemishes. Two matching scars. Scars come from living. They form when blood congeals to seal a wound, scabbing over and healing into quiet reminders of pain. How do I know that if I don't know how I got these scars?

Wait. Was that a sound outside?

"Help!" The shout rattles my parched throat. "*Help!*"

There's no answer.

I shout again. Then I remember: the brain needs air. Is this box sealed? What if I run out of air?

I beg for anyone to come. I start to cry. I sleep.

When I wake, trapped in the same box, I hurt all over. Knuckles banged raw and scabbed. Legs ache from bruises. I'm stiff as wood in the metal case.

Okay. It can't get worse. Don't panic.

My mind is working. Think, think, think. I pore through my mind, trying to grab onto a memory, anything. It feels like being suspended in a cavern, unable to see walls or floor or ceiling, unable to guess at the mysteries and secrets hidden in the distant nooks and crannies. Yet, even in the complete darkness and silence, there is still this *something.*

Colors. That's it.

I have memories of them: blue, red, green, and yellow. They exist between black and white, a spectrum of light, and I can distinguish them. So there is more to life than this darkness. There is color. There is hope.

I lay still, resting, thinking. There must be a way for air to enter my box, because I'm still alive. But what about food, water? Even if I'm motionless, the brain consumes energy. It requires fuel. How long could I survive?

Doesn't matter. I have to preserve my energy.

These thoughts keep me calm for a time, spinning in circles and going nowhere, remembering nothing. Then my legs cramp, desperate to move. They kick as if with a mind of their own, slamming into the bottom of the black box.

"Let me out! Help!"

No answer.

A while later I plead and beg. I cry again.

It's a waste of energy and oxygen. People think you starve to death if you're buried alive, but the problem is air. How can anyone get enough oxygen under six feet of dirt? I'm getting oxygen. So I'm not underground. I have that going for me. The oxygen and the scars and the faint memory of colors.

I sleep on and off. Think on and off.

There's a sound. It's a tap, tap, tap, on the outside of my box, just above me.

I surge up in shock, only to slam my head.

I shout: *"Help! Please help!"*

The response sounds like it's from another world: laughter.

It's a girl's laughter.

She sounds young. She sounds positively giddy.

"Who are you? I'm in here! Help me!"

The laughter stops and I start to hope. Then comes the tapping again. It's regular—tap, tap, tap—then irregular—tap...tap...tap, tap. My shouting doesn't change it. Only when I start to scream does the laughter start again.

I cry, wasting more energy and oxygen, but so what?

The girl and her giggling grow distant, then fade away. I lay in quiet for a long time, listening, thinking, sinking. Fear is a quick slide down to anger.

What kind of person was that? To know I'm trapped in this box and laugh? Maybe she can't open it. But she laughed! Like it's a game! Does she know how long the box has trapped me—no food, no water, no light, nothing? Is she going to leave me to die? It might be better to be left in here than to meet *that* kind of person. No names or faces come to me, but dark ideas hover over my mind like shapeless specters of people who do despicable things.

I drift in and out of sleep, over and over. I count to one hundred, then a thousand, then give up. There's no use tracking time, if I even could.

There is no more tapping.

The scabs on my knuckles and knees harden. My throat goes dry. I'd do anything for a drop of water.

Then, with no warning, the lid opens.

I leap out like an escaping frog. I stand, totter weakly, then collapse to my knees. I struggle to take it in. It's an open space, a cavern. The ground is flat and sandy. I lift a handful of sand in my palm. It feels supple as a feather after the box. I glance back at the black container. It looks just like a coffin.

A faint sound draws my gaze up. There's a ledge overhead, and a girl out of reach. She wears a black robe, even blacker than the rough cave walls and ceiling around her. She throws her hood back. Hair spills down like red silk, like blood, over her robe. Her skin is pale and freckled, her eyes green and deviant.

"Welcome to Black," she says, her lips curling into a snarl. "It's about time."

My scabbed fists clench at the amusement in her voice. She sounds like the girl who laughed.

"Who are you?" My voice is raspy.

"I almost wish you remembered."

"Give me a name."

"I shouldn't…but for you…" Her smile is haunting. "You *should* know my name as you suffer. I'm Samantha."

This isn't good. I have to get out. I ask, "What is this place?"

"Are you disappointed? Most are glad to leave the coffin…"

The *something* in me grows. The hours in the box, the ache in my weak body, the tone of her voice—it all courses up through my heart and mind like a swelling flood, a wild rage of energy.

Blue threads shimmer in the air. I grab them. I *move* them.

Wind whips past me. The force blasts at the girl, but slams to a stop against her outstretched hand. Black smoke swirls around her and suffocates the blue threads of air. The smoke drifts down and over me like fog.

"I can't blame you," she taunts. "You don't remember."

"Remember what? Tell me."

"Let me make this easier: you have no power here. I shut down everything you have."

I have power. That was the force, the blue threads.

"You will fight like an animal to survive," the girl says. "And I will watch you die, over and over."

Metal scrapes against metal behind me. I turn away from the ledge and notice another box for the first time. It's on the opposite side of the room from mine. The lid slides away and falls with a dull thud on the sandy floor.

A boy surges out, fists shaking, face frantic.

He spots the girl and shouts at her. She does not respond. She holds out her arms, palms up, and torches light up along the walls. The light reveals dozens of faces around the rim of the room, level with the girl and high above the boy and me. Their expressions are intense and hard as iron.

"The Black Tower," the girl says loudly. "Where all may rise by the will to power!"

The onlookers stomp and pound and find a steady rhythm, like drums of war. They begin to chant. "Black, Black, Black!"

"Now which of *you* will rise?" the girl glares down at us. "Only one leaves alive. The other goes back into the coffin. The strong shall rise!"

2

THE BOY CROUCHES, all skin and sinew. He advances toward me. He looks more predator than human. The onlookers chant and stomp above. The sound booms in the cavern. The girl still stares down at us, amused.

It's hard to think. The boy moves closer. I back away from him. Sand squishes under my toes. I almost trip over the metal box that held me. I feel cold as I glance at it.

The other goes back into the coffin, the girl said.

I look up at the boy. His eyes are locked on me.

I hold out my hands innocently. "Hey, no need to fight. Do you know what's going on here?"

He doesn't acknowledge the words. He doesn't slow down.

"Black, Black, Black!" the crowd chants above.

"Wait, please," I say. "Do you understand? Who are you?"

The boy stops. He kneels down on the sand, then rises with something in his hand. He inspects it as I do—a dark shaft and a gleaming, wicked point—a spear. He grips it firmly with both hands, sharp end aimed at me, and advances again.

"Wait…"

But he is charging now. His body tenses. He pulls the

spear back, ready to throw.

Instinct takes over. I crouch and grab the coffin lid by my feet. It takes everything I have to lift it. I hold it up like a shield just as the spear flies.

The impact knocks me back. The shield falls. I stare at the spear shaft on the sand at my feet. It would have killed me.

The crowd above us roars with approval. Words emerge from the rhythmic chants: *The strong shall rise.*

The boy comes at me again, crouched like a hungry lion.

I scoot back along the sandy ground. I hold up my hands in an offer of peace. "Wait, there has to be some way—"

The boy steps over the coffin lid. He grabs the spear off the sand. The sharp point gleams. He wipes the hair from his forehead, leaving a smudge of sand. His dark eyes look up, taking in the crowd's approving shouts.

The strong shall rise.

The boy's gaze lowers to me. He has me now. He knows it. I know it.

"Why are you doing this?" I ask. "Why…"

His only answer is a blur of fierce motion, straight at me.

* * *

Flat on my back, body still, all black. Breaths come slow and easy. The air is stale. I feel like I've slept a thousand years. Or was I dreaming? A nightmare?

No, it wasn't a dream. I was trapped here before. The black box. The parched throat. The girl who laughed and taunted me. I shudder at the memory of her green eyes and red hair like blood over a black robe.

You will fight to survive, she said.

I will watch you die, over and over, she said.

So it will happen again. The lid will open and I will be in the cavern. The girl will be on the ledge. The others will cheer. A boy will attack. And I will die.

My body shakes, trembling with the cold sweat of fear. How do I remember this and nothing else? Who was I before? And how did I get to this terrible place?

I do not struggle long inside the coffin. Just enough to confirm: there's no way out. But I do not hurt. I have no wounds from the fight, only the odd crisscross scars on my hands and feet. I will save my energy for when the lid opens.

I drift in and out of sleep. Hours pass, maybe days.

Once, as I stare into the motionless darkness, my mind drifts to the color of the fires in the cavern, to the girl's red hair, to the blood that spilled out of me. So many hues of red, like visions parading through the darkness.

I've known this living death before. The scars on my hands and feet prove it. As my fingers run over the scarred flesh, thinking of red, something appears. It's small, seen through the narrowest of lens, but clear as day.

I stared into a fire. In the fire there was the girl with the vivid green eyes, except she was older. I was older, too. Who was I? Where was I? Her name…it was Samantha.

The girl here said her name: Samantha.

She wanted me to know that. She knew me, but how?

The flame of memory, lit by her name and the color red, flickers out. It's too dark. There's too much black.

I sleep. I stir. I calm myself and doze again.

The next time I wake, the lid is grinding open.

3

I LEAP OUT of the coffin into the cavern. The other box is still closed. But this time I'm ready. This time I'll fight.

Just like before, the girl stands on the ledge above me. Black robe. Red hair. Green eyes ready to devour.

"You rise again," she says.

"Samantha? Why are you doing this?"

She is silent a moment. "How do you know my name?"

"You told me last time."

"I see. And what else do you remember?"

"There was a fight."

"And before that?"

"I—don't remember anything before the box."

"Yes, good," she says, sounding grimly satisfied. "You will fight and die as many times as it takes. It is your fate."

The girl's smoke comes as before, obscuring the blue threads that I saw before. If only I could find a way to use this. She admitted it last time: I have power. But her smoke stops it.

"The Black Tower…" she begins. As she repeats the same words as before, the torches light up on the walls and the crowd chants.

I pay them no attention. I focus on the cavern floor, where another boy has emerged from his coffin. He looks big, but confused.

Last time there was a spear under the sand. I spot it—a speck of dark wood—and race for it. I kneel and pick up the spear. I stand my ground with the point forward.

Samantha has stopped speaking above us.

The boy eyes me dangerously. He scans the surroundings. His gaze stops on the coffin lid.

He picks it up and hoists it overhead, then faces me. He lowers the lid like a shield, thick metal defending him almost head to toe. He's stronger than I am. He advances toward me.

Only one leaves this room alive.

I panic.

"Hey, look!" I lower the tip of my spear to the ground. "I'll drop the spear if you drop the shield."

He answers by charging.

The shield looks like a hammer, ready to slam into me. But his feet are exposed.

I kneel. He plants his foot to smash against me. I jab the spear down. Blade slices flesh. Metal hits me like a train. We're both down. My head spins. He writhes on the ground, screaming and grabbing his foot.

Rush to stand. Raise the spear. Approach him cautiously.

"Don't fight," I say. "I won't hurt you."

He lunges up and jabs the shield at me. I'm not ready. The edge of it crashes into my shoulder, knocking the spear loose. He dives for it. I dive for it. We struggle on the sand.

He gets a hand on the wooden shaft, and so do I. We're on our knees, facing each other, both clutching the spear. It's the only rope out of here.

The crowd's chants shake the air. "Black, Black, Black!"

I catch the boy's eyes. "I'll let it go if you will."

For a split second, he sees me. There's something innocent and knowing in the hazel reflection of myself.

He nods. "You first."

I barely hear the words over the chanting, but we have agreed. We do not have to fight.

My grip releases. His doesn't.

He yanks back. The shaft spins and takes me in the temple. The boy surges to his feet. He's a blur of motion, jabbing down.

It's the last thing I see.

It happens again, and again. The coffin, the girl on the ledge, the chanting crowd, the boy who kills me. I lose track of how many times. The eyes of the boys spin through my memories. What will it be this time? A wiry brown-eyed boy or a bulky hazel-eyed one? The coffin lid or the spear's point?

Each time that I die and wake again a new layer of hardness grows around me, like the rings of a tree trunk earned by another year of survival. Except I don't age. I don't have any wounds from the fights. Only the same four scars.

The times in the box offer a sort of comfort. There is no chanting, no attack. In the quiet I explore the fringes of my thoughts. They lead ever inward, blindly roaming the brain as if seeking the center of a labyrinth. Somehow I know the maze's tiniest details—neurons passing from cortex to hippocampus—but I see no full picture, no way out. Vast darkness lays over every memory beyond this box and cavern.

The next fight is against a skinny, blue-eyed boy who looks almost dignified. He seems as reluctant as I do, but uses his coffin lid well. We both grow tired of circling each other, and as the fatigue makes the spear heavier and heavier in my arms, he comes at me and…wins.

The box welcomes me back, tight as the embrace of an old friend. I gaze into the pitch black and imagine vivid colors.

Every color starts with light. The light enters the eye, where millions of tiny cells send signals to the brain. Cells and neurons make colors. There's no color without the brain. There's only light. So it's my mind that reveals these bright hues. It's memory.

I focus on one color: red.

Blood dripped on the sand. Flaming torches lit the walls and cast flickering shadows. But no red was as sharp as the girl's hair. For some reason her hair stands out, like a small, broken shard of stained glass. I've seen it before this place.

The memory flashes. In a flame. At the top of a tower.

I looked into a fire and saw myself, in the past, on Earth. I was Paul Fitzroy—a messed up neurosurgeon and husband and father. I died and somehow showed up here.

This is the Five Towers.

It all comes flooding back. I arrived blank and alone, treading water beneath the Blue Tower. The tower's leader, Abram, came with a blue light on his staff. Blue like the boy's eyes.

And Emma's eyes.

I captured her in the Scouring. The brilliant girl with the golden hair, the healing power, and the valiant heart.

We went through so much together as we rose to lead the Blue, Red, and Green Towers.

Now Emma leads the Yellow Tower. She bears scars, too. We are two of the five marked ones. We were together on Yellow's wall when she wove light into me—into a memory we shared. She told me it would help me remember. She was right.

The memory was from the flame atop the Red Tower. Emma was there. So was my mother, before she escaped through the White Tower. She was the last one to leave.

Now we're stuck in this place. The White Tower went dark.

That's why I came here.

The Black Tower.

Kiyo, another marked one, warned me about this darkness. Black captured her in the Scouring. She lived through this…suffering. No wonder she became so cold. Yet she was my first friend here. She was the first to ask my name, and I told her it was Cipher. Like a secret code to be unlocked. After four towers I've unraveled so many of this place's mysteries—the towers' leaders and powers and methods. I've also seen the pit below and our true enemy.

The Colorless One.

It's his taint that makes this tower black. It's his power that blocks the White Tower and traps us here.

The leaders said the Black Tower was once Purple, and that one of its leaders is missing. The Colorless One blocks the other leaders from entering, but it's different for me. I was brought here as a prisoner. I can work from the inside, just as Emma and I did in Yellow. We found Yellow's leaders and set them free. We restored light to the Yellow

Tower.

I have to do the same in Black.

This box will open again. I have to survive and find the missing leader. I have to get past the girl with the green eyes.

Samantha.

Her name sets off another spark—a blaze of passion from our past. The Red Tower showed what we did on earth. Maybe I'm the reason Samantha is here. No wonder she hates me.

But I've changed. I'm not the same Paul Fitzroy she knew on Earth. I've been wiped and cleansed and restored. I'll get through to her somehow. She can change as I did.

We'll all be scoured. It's the only way out.

4

WHEN THE LID opens, I stay perfectly still. No smoke clouds the faint light of torches on the wall. Samantha speaks the usual words from the ledge above, ending with, "The strong shall rise."

The crowd chants. "Black, Black, Black!"

They expect me to leap out. They expect the other boy to face me. They expect us to fight.

I will not do what they expect.

Subtle currents of air swirl over the box. In the Blue Tower I learned to weave the wind. My power has only grown since then, but Black's power—Samantha's smoke—is stronger. She will shut down my power the moment I reach for it. She will stare down at me with her vivid green eyes and...

Green. I have more than just the wind. In the Green Tower I learned to go invisible. If I can do that, I could avoid the smoke. I could escape. All I need is a memory of joy, of contentment.

But time is short. And I'm on my back in a coffin.

"Black, Black, Black!"

Think. Focus.

A memory comes. I'm the doctor named Paul Fitzroy, sitting in a car beside my wife, Susan. The car is bitter cold.

Snow lays heavy outside. Susan puts her hand over mine, tender and warm. We drive away from a mansion together, leaving a dark weight behind. We drive toward the light.

I feel the Green threads gather around me. I raise my hand before my eyes. It's invisible.

Holding to this vision, I rise slowly and silently. I weave as I move, matching the interlaced strands of light with the colors around me—the sandy ground, the rock walls.

Samantha stands on the ledge above with her arms crossed, like she is waiting for me to rise from the dark box. A boy approaches from the opposite wall. He already has the spear. He moves warily to my coffin, leans over and gazes into it with his spear raised. He lowers the spear. He steps away and looks up to Samantha.

"No one's there," he says.

"Impossible!" Samantha shouts. The word is barely out of her mouth before the smoke comes. It billows out from the ledge like a predator, a sleek black panther.

I can't stay invisible for long. Her smoke will find me.

The crowd's chanting fades. The cavern goes quiet.

The boy prowls around, ready to stab his spear into me like all the boys before him. I could fling him against the wall. I could grab the spear with the air and turn it against him.

But this is the Black Tower. I won't play by its rules.

I use the wind to grab the boy and fling him up like a leaf in a hurricane. He flails helplessly as he soars straight at Samantha. He slams into her with a loud crash.

The smoke vanishes.

This is my opening. I lift myself on the air. I rise twenty feet in a breath and land silently on the ledge. Samantha and the boy are still in a tangle, struggling to rise. Her red hair swings wildly as she scans around.

"Find him!" she shouts. "Guard the exits!"

There's an open doorway past her. She'll find me soon. It took almost all my power to get here. I won't be able to hold much longer.

I dash quietly around her and out the doorway. It opens to a dark hall, going left and right. Footsteps pound from both directions.

I guess and go right. Pairs of guards charge toward me—some boys with spears, some girls in robes. I press against the wall and use everything I have to hold onto the fading power, like trying to hold my breath as my lungs scream for air. The guards race past me. The power slips. They rush into the room with Samantha without looking back.

"Find him!" she shouts. "Find him!"

I turn and run from them. My legs struggle at the effort, still weak and stiff from their confinement in the box. But the hope of freedom propels me. The shouting continues behind me.

I pass door after door on the right side of the hallway. The left wall is solid and dark as iron. The hall bends around, as if it's a circle that will lead me back to Samantha and the guards. Every door looks the same, plain black, until one stands out. It's twice as wide as the others, with the shape of a shield imprinted at the center. Maybe it leads out.

With my ear against the door, I hear nothing on the other side. Footsteps echo from the hallway around me.

There were doorways like this in the other towers—sealed until touched with power. I focus and manage to funnel a tiny wisp of wind into the shield. It's enough. The edges begin to glow, brighter and brighter, almost purple in hue.

"There he is!" someone shouts.

The door swings open. I rush through and slam it shut behind me. Ahead a spiral staircase coils up with no end in sight. I charge up as fast as I can. Shouts erupt beneath me, closing on me, like lava surging up through a volcano. I climb faster.

Finally I glimpse the top of the stairs. They open into the tallest room I've ever seen. It seems to have no ceiling, only darkness above.

"Who's that?" a girl asks.

She stands twenty feet from me, robed with a hood covering her face. Already black smoke emerges from her.

"Is that…?" A boy asks behind me.

I recognize the voice even before I turn and meet his granite eyes, gazing out from a black knight helm.

"It *is* you," he says. "Cipher."

It's Baron. It's John D. Rockefeller. We fought against each other in Green, but he changed. He saved me in the Scouring. He sacrificed himself…to Black.

Shouts echo loudly from the staircase below.

"Baron, can you help me?" I ask.

"I knew you would come," he says, expressionless. "I have been waiting. But how do you remember?"

He draws a spear and moves toward me.

The girl's smoke covers me. Now there's no chance of using my power, even if I had any energy left for it. I turn to run but boys with spears surge up from the stairs.

In seconds they surround me.

I hold up my hands. "Look, I can explain this."

"No." Samantha steps through the ring of guards. Her

hood is flung back, her green eyes furious, her breathing heavy. "Silence him. Then kill him."

Two boys step forward, spears raised. Another grabs me from behind and ties a gag tight over my mouth.

"Stop," Baron says, stepping between them and me. "He made it out. He is one of us now."

"He broke the law!" Samantha shouts.

"The Judge's only law is power," Baron replies coolly.

A few guards mutter agreement. Samantha looks around the group, eyes ablaze. She shakes her head, then steps to me. I move backward, but a spear at my back stops me. She leans closer and presses her hands to my temples.

"You will never disobey me again," she says.

Darkness settles over my mind, like oil dripping into the wrinkles of my brain, smothering every trace of color. No more blue ribbons of air. No more green threads that could make me vanish. No more light. Colorless.

My power is blocked. But I still remember.

"Now, that's better." Samantha releases me. A twisted smile lifts the corners of her lips. "You'll be back in a coffin soon, and next time you won't escape." She pulls her hood over her head and turns away.

"So he's with me?" Baron asks.

"No, Deputy. Put him in one of Karl's troops," Samantha says. "Let's see how long he survives."

5

BARON DRAGS ME by chained wrists toward a tall, black doorway. Guards escort us with spears and grim faces. The four of them shove against the door, iron grating against stone as it opens. We march out and descend narrow, steep stairs with no rails. My heart tightens in my chest as I take in the view.

The sky is lifeless gray. Crows caw and soar ahead of us, swooping over a line of wooden stocks. At least ten boys stand there, locked up, their limp heads and hands hanging out of the devices. Beyond the stocks there's a makeshift village around the base of the Black Tower. It looks like a war camp.

Let's see how long he survives, Samantha said. Are they going to lock me up? Send me into battle? Who will we fight? They send only twelve to the Scouring.

Baron stops at the bottom of the stairs. He points to a large sign nailed to a pole rising from the dirt. "Better learn these," he says. "They're from the leader himself."

I feel a surge of hope. It could be the missing leader.

Baron studies me, then unties the gag over my mouth. "Why so excited about the rules?"

"The leader," I say. "Where is he?"

A grin touches Baron's eyes, not his mouth. "They say

he's up there, at the top."

I follow his gaze up along the Black Tower. Its edges extend like sharp barbs at the top. Baron's black helm has matching barbs at the crest. A weapon if he charges.

"Who is he?" I ask.

"All you need to know is the rules," he says. "Learn them."

His tone quiets me. He sounds like the Baron who once led the Wolves in Green, the one who knocked me off a cliff. What has Black done to him? Without my power, I have to proceed cautiously. I tuck away my questions and look to the sign. It lists five rules:

1. *Obey your superior, for his will is your law.*
2. *Fight only when and where commanded.*
3. *Leave every battle with your shield or on it.*
4. *No contact with the enemy outside the tower.*
5. *The strong shall rise.*

"Your troop will tell you more," Baron says, walking away toward the encampment.

"Heeellppp!" A groan comes from beyond the sign, where a boy in the stocks has raised his head and spotted us. No one else pays him any attention. A crow is perched on the wooden frame above him. His young voice croaks out, distant and broken, "Mercyyy, pleeease…I'll do anything…let me out!"

I try to step toward him, but one of the guards swings his spear to my throat.

"No. Follow." He points toward Baron.

I spare a last glance at the boy, then trail after Baron. *Obey your superior, for his will is your law.* I wonder which rule the boy in the stocks violated. There will be a time to fight back, but not yet.

Baron leads us past low, canvas tents around the tower. Each one is long and straight, the color of charcoal. Their entrances face out from the tower and show painted numbers: "1" then "3" then "5". They are set in perfect order, each extending from the tower like spokes of a wheel from an axle.

Only a few boys scurry around. They wear black and steer clear of us, keeping their heads down. One carries a bundle of wood in his arms. Another balances a stack of three shields on his head. They look heavy enough to crush him under the weight. We pass a forge where a boy hammers like a blacksmith. Sparks fly from the metal on the anvil. Beside him another boy fits a sharp spearhead to a long shaft of wood. They all look serious. No one is idle.

We are almost halfway around the tower when Baron stops at one of the tents. The flap of canvas at the entrance is painted with a black number "9".

"Troop nine," Baron calls out toward the tent, like it's a command. He crosses his arms. "Troop leader. Baron here!"

A lanky boy with olive skin and curly brown hair steps out of the tent. He yawns and rubs the back of his neck. He eyes Baron, then his gaze settles on me. He frowns with disappointment as he mutters, "another champion…"

"Take him," Baron says. "He's stronger than he looks."

The boy sighs with contempt. "So why don't you take him?"

"I would," Baron says, "but the Council's leader told me I couldn't. Besides, I already have my nine grunts."

"All the first picks. All the helmets." The boy glances at Baron's guards, rolls his eyes. "Fair as ever for the Deputy…"

"The Judge rewards power. The strong shall rise." Baron salutes formally, and the boy gives his own lackluster salute back. Baron marches off with his four guards in rigid formation.

The boy turns to me. "Get in, grunt, before they throw you in the stocks and the crows peck your eyes out."

He ducks into the canvas tent.

I hesitate, and he peeks out again.

"Waiting for something?" he asks. "Nothing will save you out there. Join us and at least you get a fighting chance."

This doesn't sound good. "A chance for what?"

The boy laughs. "To stay alive and out of a box."

He slips inside, and this time I follow. He goes straight to a cot, lies on his back, and closes his eyes.

I stand alone at the front of the tent. It's low and narrow and crowded with boys. Cots line the canvas walls. It smells like sweat and metal. At the back of the tent is the hard, black outer wall of the tower. An orderly row of spears leans against it, beside a stack of shields. Ten each. There is no other furniture, no decoration. Only grubby boys eyeing me with the interest a cow gives a gnat. I count nine of them.

"Hello, I'm Hugh," says a boy who approaches me. He's skinny, with blue eyes and a dignified demeanor.

I almost cringe. He fought me below the tower. He won.

But he looks friendlier now, like he's greeting a stranger. It's close enough to the truth.

"I'm Cipher."

He shakes my hand formally. "We are troop 9, in Karl's brigade. That boy who walked you in, the one with the girly curls, he is our leader, Crispus." Hugh eyes the boy on his back on a cot. He talks about him like he isn't even there. "Rumor is, he was a famous Roman, some Caesar or such, 'til his own father ordered him put to death. No wonder he cares little about our quandary here, but he is still fast as a snake. You will see."

Another boy steps up beside Hugh, with freckles and big ears and a shock of red hair. "Whew, look at this un! What a hero…"

"Oh yes, a legendary warrior of old." Hugh's shoulders slump as he turns away and falls onto one of the cots and covers his head with his arms.

"Don't pay him no mind," says the freckled boy. "I'm Shucks."

He holds out his hand and we shake. He glances at the scar on the back of my hand and doesn't let go. "How'd you get that?" he asks. "Didn't you wake up in the box?"

"Take a spear through the hand before you won?" asks another boy.

Some of the boys circle closer around me. They wear identical black tunics and bleak expressions.

"How did you all get here?" I ask.

"Same way as everybody," Shucks says. "Wake up in a box under the tower and fight yer way out."

"So you all killed someone?" I ask.

No one answers. No one meets my eyes.

"It's the only way," a boy mutters. "The strong shall rise."

Shucks adds, "Don't matter much. We out now, ain't we?"

"For a day," a boy says.

"What do you mean?" I ask.

"Now our troop's got ten so we gotta fight," the boy says. "And we gonna lose. Again. Last time we lost half the troop."

"What kind of fight?" I ask.

"Aw, you boys get some rest," Shucks says. "I'll get newbie here some food and tell him what's what."

"You'll die, that's what," a boy says, "and I'll tell ya—"

"Enough," Crispus demands. He hasn't budged from the cot. He speaks with his eyes closed. "Shucks is right. No use talking. Rest now. Tomorrow we fight."

The boys nod like disciplined dogs and shuffle toward their cots. Shucks leads me outside. The sky has grown darker. He starts going back the way Baron and I came.

"Wait," I say, pointing the opposite way, toward the other side of the tower. There are more identical tents, but the boys in the distance sit in groups around campfires. It almost sounds like they're singing. "What if we go that way?"

"No can do," Shucks says. "They'll lock ya in the stocks. Or kill ya. That's the rival side. Troops 2, 4, 6, 8, and 10. Ya saw the rules, right? No contact with the enemy."

"But we're all in Black," I say. "Why are they the enemy?"

"Hey, I'm just tellin' ya the rules. I don't make 'em."

Shucks continues past troop 7's tent until we reach a fire with a black cauldron hanging over it. He grabs a dark metal bowl off the ground and scoops out two spoonfuls of mush from the pot. He gives me the bowl and motions for me to sit on the ground near the fire.

We sit together. It's quiet other than the distant voices on the other side of the tower. The mush is overcooked gooey rice, but it's the first thing I've eaten here and it tastes better than nothing. Shucks tells me that the rice comes from the hills around the Black Tower, and that I should consider myself lucky to have joined a troop instead of a village.

"Farmers starve," he says. "Believe me, that's worse than a spear through the gut cuz at least the spear pain ends fast. Why, the boys in the troop tell me last time I only got a jab through the foot. It probably woulda got better with some salt and rest. That just ain't Karl's way. He came and finished me off himself, real quick. At least that's what the boys tell me. All I know is I woke up a box and fought my way out. Air's better out here. Enjoy it while you can."

What I gather from Shucks, as he talks and night falls, is that every boy starts in one of the boxes and has to win a duel to get out. Weaker ones can be down there for countless fights before they manage to win. Once a boy makes it out, he's assigned to a troop like ours, or to some other task. Shucks says there are ten troops, with ten boys each. They fight each other constantly. The strongest move onto the Scouring. Some boys rise fast. Win a duel, join a winning troop, and a day later they're in the Scouring. Others languish. Shucks has never made it to the Scouring. He has no idea how he got here.

"No memories at all?" I ask.

"Not since wakin' up last time in the box."

"How about the other boys, do they have memories from before this place?"

"Well, a few, like the commander…"

"Who's he?"

Shucks' freckled face goes pale in the firelight. "Karl,

the head honcho. You'll meet him. Big dude. Some say he was the Holy Roman Emperor, whatever that means. All I know is he's brutal. He'll send you to a coffin without a flinch."

An emperor. Quite a title. "So how did Karl get memories?"

"I figure he survived a Scouring. Girls reward those who do. They control the Black Council, and the crown."

"What crown?"

He shrugs. "Heck if I know. I just heard they control it."

"What are the rules for the girls?"

"The rule is: stay away! Ya won't catch me talkin' to one. Some boys say they control the smoke. Terrible stuff. It takes dead bodies, sometimes living ones, straight down to the coffin. They say you don't remember nothin' when you wake up after the smoke takes you."

"Is that how girls control the Black Council? What is it?"

"The Black Council makes the rules. There are twelve of them. Ten girls, two boys. The two commanders. You don't wanna piss them off."

I set my empty bowl down, thinking. It's the opposite of how Black fights in the Scouring, when they take two girls and ten boys. It privileges the girls. I need to learn more about how Samantha has power here.

"Who decides which girls are on the Council?" I ask.

Shucks looks from side to side as if making sure no one is listening. He lowers his voice: "I hear there's an old man up high in the tower."

"An old man?"

"Yeah, ya know how the rest of us is 'bout the same

age, same size, and such. Well a boy told me he heard a girl say there was a leader. I figure there's an adult up there, decidin' things."

I can't suppress a grin. I remember feeling the same way as Shucks when I learned about Blue's leaders, Abram and Sarai. But the grin quickly fades. I need to get to this leader.

"How do we get to the top of the tower?" I ask.

"No way," Shucks says. "Ain't no grunts going in the tower, much less to the top. Only the Council goes there. They decide everything that matters. They pick who fights in the Scouring, who wears a collar, who works in the rice paddies, and…well, you get the idea. They even pick the commanders of the two brigades. Right now it's Karl and a boy named Napoleon. Troop leaders like Crispus and all the rest of us grunts obey them."

"*The* Napoleon?" I ask, remembering the one from Earth. Just like Baron is *the* John D. Rockefeller, and I am *the* Dr. Paul Fitzroy.

"That's his name," Shucks says. "But it'll change. Everything changes fast here, quick as a nose pick."

"Gross. How does it change?"

"Ain't no grosser than blood, and you'll be seein' plenty of that," he says. "It's always the same. *The strong shall rise*, they say. *The Judge rewards power*, they say."

"Who is the Judge?" I ask.

"Gee, some god or somethin'. Don't matter much. Just live by the law, die by the law."

"What's the law?"

"Eh…" he scratches his head. "I reckon it's whoever wins."

6

WE RETURN TO our troop's canvas tent in the dark. The other boys lay quiet, sleeping. More than one of them snores. Shucks points to a plain cot with no pillow, right by the tower's iron wall. I shudder as I lay so close to it, but at least I'm outside. The cot is a lot better than a coffin.

Cawing crows wake me before dawn. Flat on my back, eyes closed, I prod for any gap in the block Samantha laid over my mind, hoping something has changed. The threads are there, but obscured by smoke. A mirage of water in the desert. Forever out of reach.

The other boys have begun to stir when the flap of our tent opens. A huge boy steps inside and looms in the doorway, two guards at his back. He has sandy hair, large eyes set in a large round head, and a thick, short neck. His broad shoulders and rotund belly make him look almost like a grown man.

"Up, up," he grunts, before biting off a loaf of dark bread.

The other boys hurry to their feet and grab a spear and shield and stand facing him. I follow their lead, standing in the back. The spear feels like a curse in my hand.

"Time to train." The boy takes another bite and tosses the half-eaten loaf into our group.

Our troop's leader, Crispus, snatches the bread, takes a bite, and passes it on. The rest of us follow him. There's no crumb of the bread left for me.

"That's Karl," Shucks whispers beside me. "Gotta do what he says or else." He drags his thumb across his throat and makes bug-eyes.

"Obey your superiors," I grumble.

Fog lays heavy on the encampment outside. All we can see is the dirt under our feet and each other. We form a double-file line and march after Karl, spears held upright. Soon we hear another troop marching beside us, only a few feet away. They emerge from the fog like ghosts.

There are ten of them. Boys like us, but not. They wear helmets that cover the brow and have a line of gun-gray metal over the nose, leaving only eyes and mouths exposed. They wield spears like ours. They also bear heavy shields the same color as their helmets. I catch the granite eyes of the boy at the front. His helmet has two barbs rising at the crest. It's Baron.

He chants something, and the troop chants back, "Hooah!"

They drop smoothly into formation, with shields raised like a unified wall in front of them. They bang their spears against shields. It sounds like war.

They shout "Hooah" again and jab their spears out from the wall of shields. The group advances toward us with a forceful, unified step.

"Hooah!"

Karl almost looks impressed. "Well Deputy, they look ready."

"Yes, sir." Baron salutes, his eyes intense.

"I'll lead 'em in. You fix this sorry lot." Karl turns from

Baron back to us. His expression sours. "Crispus, form 'em up!"

Crispus tries to organize us into formation, a single line like the other troop. Two boys trip over each other and fall to the mud. Karl lumbers toward them. As the boys rise, he grabs one of their spears. The spearless boy is Hugh. He keeps his head down.

We are in line now. We stand straight, silent.

Karl glares at Hugh. He holds out the sharp point, a foot from Hugh's belly. "What happens when the enemy gets this?"

No one answers.

Karl growls, "*This* happens."

He lunges and the spear goes clean through the boy, out his back.

Hugh barely makes a sound. His face goes mottled white and gray, like a sycamore's bark, as he falls.

No one else budges. But there is a sudden motion. Smoke streams out of the ground and wraps around Hugh like black vines. The cloud darkens until it fully covers his lifeless body. Then it dissipates and he is gone, leaving only a pool of blood.

A crow caws in the distance. I feel sick to my stomach.

"Hooah!" Karl shouts. "I *said*, Hooah!"

Half of our troop lunges immediately, and the rest of us hurry to follow their lead. We jab our spears into the air. They are not aligned like the other troop, but not a single spear drops.

"It's a start." Karl spits. "Crispus, you make a fine fighter but a slack leader. I expected better after the Scouring. Deputy, work these grunts. Crispus, too. Make 'em all sweat. And if they don't sweat, make 'em bleed.

They'll see more blood soon, just a question of whose."

"Yes, sir," Baron says with a salute. He steps out of the line of shields toward us. His granite eyes study our group. He turns toward Karl. "Bow to your Commander. He goes to battle."

We bow toward Karl as he leads the other troop away. They vanish into the fog with a faint shuffle.

Baron drops his spear and shield to the ground. "Spears down!" he says.

None of us obey.

"Good. You learned. Commander Karl requires this." Baron picks up his spear and paces before the line. "Karl takes our best to battle for the Scouring. He and Napoleon lead the two brigades. Napoleon, shrewd as he is, usually gets the honor. But lately Karl has been winning with those nine boys you saw right there. And here's why: discipline. Those boys don't budge an inch. Not in their group, not in their stance, not in their minds. They are iron. They are strength. And even a sorry lot like you can learn to be like them. It might take you a while. You might die a dozen times. But you *will* be strong. Discipline demands it. *I* demand it. Now, let me show you how it's done." He steps toward me. "Starting with the new boy."

"You know me," I say calmly. "I'm Ci—"

The punch comes out of nowhere. It hits me square in the jaw. I spin, legs crumple. My cheek is on the dirt. My fist is clenched around the hard shaft of the spear.

"Get up," Baron says. "And keep your mouth shut."

I rise to my hands and knees. I wipe at my face and my hand comes away covered in blood. I look up at my old enemy. "I know who you—"

His boot slams into my side. It knocks the words and

the breath out of me.

"Get up," he says. "Mouth shut."

This time I don't say a word as I struggle to my feet.

The point of Baron's spear aims at my neck, only inches away. The other boys are staring from me to Baron with fear in their eyes.

"Your grip is wrong. It's like this." Baron shows me how he holds the shaft. "Back hand here. Front here. Then shift like this when you lunge." In a blur of fluid motion he steps forward and jabs the spear into the air, flashing past my cheek. He stands straight again. "Now you try."

I still see stars as I adjust my grip, the way he said.

He steps closer, making me clench.

"Rotate this hand." He moves my back hand's grip slightly. "You need all the torque you can get."

"Torque," I breathe out, meeting Baron's eyes and thinking of John D. Rockefeller and his oil drills. Torque earned him a fortune. Torque put him above me in yet another tower. "Torque…"

"Yes, try again," he demands.

I follow his instruction. My grip tightens and my front leg extends and plants firmly in the dirt. I jab the spear out.

"Again, faster!"

I do it, over and over, at his command. On the sixth lunge, Baron grabs the shaft of the spear, holding it in place.

"Stay there," he commands. "Steady as a rock."

I swallow my pride and my pain and do what he says, feeling the weight of the spear. Then Baron picks up his shield and loops the straps around my left arm. It feels like an anvil. My arms shake under the weight. Sweat drips into my eyes.

"Get used to the weight," he says. "And don't you dare move. Lose this stance, lose your life."

Baron moves to Shucks beside me. He goes through the exact same steps, with no trace of resistance from Shucks. How to hold the spear. How to lunge. How to hold the shield. Shucks moves into position. Baron pushes him so that Shucks' shield bumps into mine with a metallic thud. I strain to hold it up.

"No gaps," Baron says, "unless you're lunging, then you part them just like this. Lunge."

We step forward, not quite in unison, but better. The shafts of our spears are nearly parallel.

"Too wide a gap." Baron pulls our shields closer by a handspan. "Stab through there. Do it again."

Shucks looks to me and I nod and we stand straight and lunge again and the spears go through the gap. It's not bad, I think, and Baron moves on to the next boy. He adds each boy from our troop until we are all lunging and stabbing in a unified line. There are no chants, no "Hooahs." Just sweat, heavy breaths, grunts. The pain in my arms and legs makes the headache from Baron's punch fade away. The weight of the shield is impossible. If only I could use a little blue thread of wind, but Samantha has shut it down, like a wall in my mind. I lunge again, wondering if this will be the one that breaks me. Then I lunge again, and again. I refuse to drop my spear.

"Enough," Baron suddenly calls out. "To attention."

Four boys emerge from the fog, with Karl at the front. He has sweat on his brow, blood on his spear, and a slight limp. "It was a draw," he says. "Napoleon's got some good ones."

"So there will be a full melee?" Baron asks.

Karl's large head nods up and down. "Soon enough. Ready or not. Show me what these grunts can do."

Baron turns to face us. "Hooah!"

My legs shake with the effort, my grip almost slips, but we manage. Shields just so wide apart. Spears stabbing through, shafts parallel, points steady.

"They'll die by the law," Karl mutters. "Or you will. But I, I will live…" He limps away without another word.

"He's right," Baron says. "But I've taught you what I could. Remember torque and discipline. All is equal and just in the fight, against each other, even against Napoleon. You earned your chance. Now get some rest."

He stalks off. I try to get to him, to talk, but two guards—strong-looking ones—block my way. They escort our troop back to our tent. Apparently we haven't earned Karl's trust. Crispus leads the way with his head down, curly hair hanging.

I fall into step beside him. "You okay?"

"Same as ever," he mutters. "No end to this hell."

His tone, dire as it is, makes me respect him more. I prod gently, "You look like you know where you came from."

"Yeah, Rome."

"Someone said you were Caesar."

He sniffs dismissively. "Doesn't matter."

"I met the mother of a Roman emperor here."

He turns as if seeing me for the first time. "How would you remember that?"

"Not sure. I just do." I shrug. "Her name is Helena. Her son was Constantine."

Crispus's face goes white, like he's seen a ghost. A false half-grin slowly covers his shock. "Impossible. Quit screwing with me."

"It's true. I swear. I first met her in the Blue Tower. She was in Green, too."

He looks at me in disbelief. "Did she mention me?"

"No, sorry."

"I don't know who you are," he says. "But if you see her again, tell her that her grandson forgives her."

"*Grandson?*"

He waves off my question. "I've said enough. Don't need more torments…" He moves ahead, clearly not wanting to talk.

I walk forward in a daze. Was he Helena's grandson? Why is he here? Another boy said his own father had ordered his death. Whatever happened, the past haunts Crispus. The Black Tower seems worse for him than for the boys with no memories.

We reach the tent and leave our shields and spears inside. No one stabs us for it. No one pays us any attention at all as we gather around a black pot over a fire. A boy fills our bowls with rice mush. The fog still hasn't lifted.

I sit beside Shucks and shovel in a few bites. Shucks is unusually silent, huddled over his bowl.

"You okay?" I ask.

"Yeah, tired, that's all."

"It's not right," I say, "what happened to Hugh."

He idly stirs his mush with a dirty finger. "It is what it is."

"No, it's what we make of it."

"Eh, or what the smoke makes of us."

I shiver, remembering it. "How did it…take Hugh like that?"

"Ain't no wastin' here. You die and go back to the

bottom. Don't matter how."

"So it's happened before?"

He nods and stands and steps away. "Sorry, still hungry. And mighty tired." He refills his bowl and sits on the other side of the fire, opposite from me.

I finish my mush in silence. My thoughts go to Baron. He remembers me. He's a marked one, with scars like mine. But something about this tower has changed him for the worse. Was it the fighting? The helmet? Or is he just playing a part until the right time to speak with me? I need to figure it out. The leaders said we marked ones have to work together to fight the Colorless One. He's the one who has trapped us here. He's the real enemy. I have to talk to Baron, away from training, away from the others. Maybe he can help me find the missing leader.

But again the grim-faced guards escort us back to our tent without any chance of a detour. As if I could escape. I have no power. I can barely lift my arms after the day's training.

We enter the tent and sleep.

A while later rain wakes me. I sneak quietly to the door. A dim line of light shows through the canvas. It might be morning again. It's hard to tell dawn from dusk.

I peek outside. Two spear points greet me.

"Back in," a guard commands.

I freeze, trying to figure a way out.

A spear jabs forward, pricks my shoulder. "Back in."

I wince as I step back. The canvas flap falls closed. My hand goes to my shoulder and comes away with a small drop of blood. Baron can wait. I go back to the cot and sleep again.

I'm dreaming of spear thrusts when I next wake.

Crispus stands at attention by the tent opening. He faces a dark silhouette with a wide belly. Karl.

Guards shove a boy inside. He falls to his knees at Crispus's feet. Crispus helps him up. He stands a head taller than the newcomer.

"You sure this grunt won down there?" Crispus asks.

Karl huffs in faint laughter. "Your troop has its ten again."

Crispus runs a hand through his hair. "Why so soon?"

"Because you're weak," Karl says. "You'll fight at dawn."

7

BLACK CLODS OF MUD sink and rise and squish under each step. My boots wrestle to get free. I want to think it's rain that stains the wet spots of the battleground before us, but I remember Hugh. It could be blood.

"Line up!" Crispus orders.

We halt in our formation, shields raised. Adrenaline fuels my sore muscles. Across from us is the other troop in a line. The enemy. They wear helmets. We don't. So much for a fair fight. Their shields bear a crudely painted "1" in black. Ours bear "9".

To our left Karl stands with two black-robed girls by his sides, and at least twenty boys flanking them. They look relaxed, like spectators out for a show.

Karl raises his arms. "For Black!"

"For Black!" The other boys shout.

The troop facing us responds: "Hooah!"

Then they charge.

None of us musters a word. We inch forward. The other troop's spears pump at their sides as they run.

"Shields!" Crispus's voice is steel.

We raise our shields like Baron taught us. We form the wall. I'm on the left edge. Shucks to my right, Crispus beside him. No gaps. Solid as we can be.

The charging troop hits us like a tsunami against a straw hut.

We fall back. Shields knock loose. A boy takes a spear through the throat. Shucks vomits at the sight of it.

It's all chaos. The only way to tell who's with me or against me is the helmets. Most of our team is already down, but somehow, Crispus is pressing ahead. He spins in a wild blur, spear like a lethal extension of his arm. I watch in awe as he blocks a blow, stabs an attacker, rolls forward, yanks the spear out, and rises again. But now five fighters surround him. They press in with their shields. He can't spin away. A moment later the five fighters turn toward us, leaving Crispus face down on the mud. No time to mourn.

A grunt makes me turn.

A spear flashes from the side.

Instinct takes over. I duck. The attacker misses, barely. I rise and swing my shield, aiming at a purple scar running down his cheek. It hits his helmet with a painful crunch, knocking the shield off my arm.

He goes down, hands to his head.

I glance around, shieldless, spear gripped with the fear of death. Two boys wrestle on the mud. Another stands over Shucks, who's curled up in a ball.

I dash forward to help, shouting.

The boy turns, spear and shield ready. Granite eyes peer out from under his barbed helmet. Eyes the same color as the metal. Baron grins and steps over Shucks. The look on his face tells me I'm going to die.

I lunge in desperation. His shield deflects my spear with ease. He raises his own, drawn back, vicious.

"Rockefeller," I say. It's a greeting, a plea, a final word.

My old foe hesitates. He eyes me cold as ice, shakes his

head, and moves forward to finish me.

But his eyes pop wide open in shock.

There's a sharp intake of breath. His shield slips off and falls to the ground with a thud. A spearpoint juts out of his gut. He drops to knees. Collapses. Granite eyes gone still.

No. No… He was a marked one. He *is* a marked one.

"Did I…?" Shucks rubs his hands together, can't take his eyes off Baron. "I just jabbed like he said…but…"

"Hold!" Karl shouts, moving toward us with his entourage. "It is done."

A dozen bodies are on the ground. A few moan in pain. Most are motionless, silent. Shucks and I are the only ones still standing without helmets. Five from the other troop surround us. The boy with the scarred cheek stares at me with controlled fury. They would have killed us if not for Karl stopping the fight.

"Bravo! Bravo!" Karl strides toward us with his hands clasped behind his back. "A fine display. The just prevail!"

He stops beside Baron's body. Nudges it with his foot.

A girl steps from behind him, kneels, and places a hand on Baron's neck. She looks up at Karl and nods. "Gone."

Karl smiles like a hungry wolf. "About time that upstart got his turn. He knew too much, got too close to taking my place." He scans the others along the ground. "And Crispus's gone. Both leaders, hm…" He stops over a moaning boy, stabs his spear down, then turns away. "Girls, remove the dead."

The smoke comes in a rush, like steam out of the muddy ground. It takes Baron, and many others, leaving only their armor and spears and blood.

"Boys, gather around," Karl says.

We form a rough circle with him at the center. Karl has

picked up Baron's barbed helmet. As he studies it he muses, "I'll need a new Deputy, but no one earned it today. Yet some will rise. Who will it be?"

Karl looks from face to face among the winning troop, pauses on a tall boy with a mop of blonde curls, then settles on a taller one, the one with the purple scar.

"Helmet off," Karl commands.

The boy lifts it. There's a welt by his temple, from where I hit him. He has a shadow of a mustache and eyebrows so thick they look like a single dark caterpillar above his stern eyes.

"Grunt, you've survived a while to earn that mustache and scar," Karl says to him. "What's your name?"

"Whatever you want, sir."

"Now that's a fine grunt!" Karl spreads his arms wide in approval. "We'll call you Scara. And it's got nothing to do with that mark on your face. When I was emperor, my elite bodyguard was the scara. I give you that honor. You'll lead troop 1."

The boy salutes. "Thank you, sir."

"Now, the rest of you, troop 9 needs grunts and a new leader." Karl points a thick finger at Shucks. "You killed the Deputy. What's your name?"

Shucks doesn't answer. He steps back, face pale.

"So…not you. We all get lucky sometimes." Karl turns to me. "You, name?"

It chokes out, surprises me: "Paul."

"Paul, then. Saw what you did. Charged, feinted, distracted. That's how Napoleon does it, too. Nothing comes as you expect it. Time we took a turn playing his game. You're a troop leader now. You, Scara, come with me."

8

KARL STOMPS STRAIGHT to the tower, up the steep stairs, and through the massive iron doors. I follow dutifully, numbly. This is what I wanted, to survive and enter the tower again. But at what cost? And what can I even do without my powers?

Inside, a large group of boys gathers around a long table. They still wear battle-worn black, with mud on their boots. They talk together like friends. Some even laugh, their voices echoing in the vast room. Baron is not among them. He's in a coffin far below us.

Karl moves to one end of the table. He tells the boys to sit, and they do. He directs me to sit at his right, and I do. There's a large loaf of black bread and a plate of butter in front of him. In the center of the table there's a metal tray with a small fire burning under a steaming, black pot. Smoke drifts up into the dark, hollow tower. The claws of living, scrambling lobsters grab for the pot's edge. The boys sitting close to the pot use wooden spoons to shove the lobsters back inside. They laugh like it's a game.

"Order!" shouts the boy at the opposite end of the table, and the others fall silent. He glares at Karl like an enemy. "Tomorrow we fight."

"And tonight we feast," Karl replies.

For a moment no one speaks. The fire crackles on the table. Claws scrape in agony against the pot. I count nine boys on each side of the table. That makes twenty of us, total.

"We feast as one, we fight as one." The boy lifts a dark loaf of bread high over his head.

Karl lifts his own loaf beside me. "The strong shall rise."

Each leader pulls their loaves apart and passes half to the ones who sit to their right. I take the half loaf, not knowing what to do with it.

The boy to my right leans close and whispers. "Split it and pass. Don't talk unless a Commander lets you."

I glance to Karl, who studies me with large, hungry eyes. My hands look ghostlike as they pull the dark bread apart. I put half on the table before me and pass the other half to the next boy. He does the same, and so on, until there's barely a crumb for the last two boys.

"So…" Karl eyes the boy across the long table, then he slaps me on the back, so hard I almost choke on the bread. "Frog, I got a new troop leader today. You won't last long next time."

The boy at the opposite end of the table looks at me. "My name is Napoleon," he says. "Believe nothing from Karl, whether he's your leader or not."

"*The* Napoleon?" I ask. "Bonaparte?"

Karl punches me in the shoulder. "Quiet, grunt."

"Wait," Napoleon says, "you know of me?"

"Of cour—"

This time Karl's punch hits square in the jaw, knocking bread out. I almost fall off the bench. Stars flicker in my vision.

Karl sounds like he's underwater as he says, "Impossible…this one's never worn the crown."

"Leave him be," Napoleon says. "I demand inspection!"

"Go ahead," Karl replies. "He's nothing special. No rule's been broken."

Two boys from Napoleon's end of the table come to my side and pull me to my feet. They escort me to Napoleon, who has stood to face me. He is shorter than I expected, with a slightly yellow complexion and lank hair. Every face around the table is locked on us.

"How do you know of Napoleon Bonaparte?" he asks.

I keep my voice steady. "Everyone knew about you."

He grins. "I suppose they would. But it could be a mistake. Many would have been named after me, no?"

"No, actually," I say. "Very few were named after you."

"Ah, a pity, a downside of unique power." He sighs. "But the benefits were worth it. I died and came here, didn't I? It's not quite what I expected of paradise, but close enough."

"*Paradise?*" I utter in shock. Drew and others said that about the Yellow Tower, and it almost made sense in those golden fields. But not Black. This place is closer to hell. "How could you think that?"

"A never-ending battle!" Napoleon says. "Immortal bodies. A clean slate for those who lose. And yet, I never lose. What could be better?"

"If I won," Karl replies coldly. "You've had your inspection. This is Paul. He led a weak troop to defeat Baron. He will lead my troops to defeat you. That is all."

"Many have tried…" Napoleon says, turning from Karl to me. "And all have failed. On Earth and in this marvelous tower. Now, I must insist, this inspection is not finished. How do you know of me, Paul?"

"You were a French general."

"Is that all?"

"No, there's a lot, actually." I glance at the table, wondering how to put this. No one has moved to stop me. Even Karl looks interested amidst his fury. "You rose from a meager beginning to lead the French armies to conquer most of Europe in the eighteenth century. You were a military genius. And your laws, your system of government, left a great mark on the world."

Napoleon studies me quietly, emotion in his face, moistness in his eyes. "This boy is amazing! He must have donned the crown. Did you?"

"No. I don't know what you're talking about."

"I see…so when did you live?"

"The twenty-first century, in America."

"Ah, America. She grew by our follies. A rowdy bunch, but tough enough. And how do you remember?"

All eyes are still on me. It's too much to explain. My treks through the other towers, my memories, my scars, how Emma sealed light in my mind through her power, how the colors helped me find the past on my own. I say simply, "I just did. I remember almost everything, except how I died."

Napoleon waves dismissively. "Knowing this thing is overrated."

"You died in exile, right?"

His face hardens. "Only after I had already won. Human battles are never over places or things, no matter what people say. They are about the spirit, and over that I *always* win."

"I don't understand."

"Ah, everyone wants to know how I win," Napoleon says. "They study my battles, no? Even you, living hundreds of years after me, know of my rise, my leadership. But still you ask, how? It is the wrong question." He turns to face the table full of boys. "All one needs to know to find a leader is the *will*. Karl here, legend that he is, has the will. This is why he leads opposite me. But I want it more than anyone. I yearn for power. I dream about power. I always have. It was my backbone, my lifeblood, on Earth. It drove me from nothing to more power than any of you can imagine. I would do anything for it. I would threaten. I would inspire any fear, with real or imagined violence. There will always be war and striving, for there will always be men with a will to power. But there were few like me." He glares at Karl across the table. "Not even the Holy Roman Emperor can rival me."

"I was the giant who carved your path." Karl's arms are crossed. "You're only a follower. A scion of history."

Napoleon scowls back at him. "Later in time, yes, but so much greater. I earned everything I built. You were born a prince. And when you died, your empire broke." Napoleon glances to me. "You heard the American. Everyone knew about me. So, Paul, what do you know of Charlemagne?"

I look to Karl, who glares at me, brooding and expectant. I feel caught between titans. And the truth is, I remember very little about Charlemagne, other than he was some famous old emperor who, apparently, is now my commander.

"He led the Holy Roman Empire," I say carefully.

"Anything else?" Napoleon presses.

"He was a legendary king."

"See, Karl?" Napoleon snaps his fingers. "Your memory is but a flash, a shallow legend. I, however, reign in history as I reign here, for I rose alone, in the truest and best spirit of conquest. Paul, you see these lobsters?"

Napoleon moves toward the center of the table. Karl rises from his seat and meets Napoleon. "This has gone far enough."

"One last lesson," Napoleon says.

The boys sitting near the pot lean away as the leaders hover over it. Napoleon holds his hand close to the pot's edge, dangles a finger. The crustaceans clamber over each other, claws trying to snap on any unshielded flesh.

"Know what's wrong with lobsters?" Napoleon asks.

"They're not human," I say.

Karl laughs with a roar, his jowls shaking. But Napoleon studies me with a fixed glare. Then his lips, too, began to curl, slowly, into a vicious smile. "That's good, Paul. The other problem is they have no order. Look."

He picks up a set of tongs and pokes into the pot. A lobster snaps up at him, but another snaps at it, causing a ripple of attacks to spread among them. He seizes one behind the head—safely out of claws reach—and lifts it. Two heavy claws and eight spindly legs dangle over the pot. It tries to snap at the closest lobster.

"See?" Napoleon says. "He's still going at these others, blind to the real threat. We are the ones who will be feasting on him."

Napoleon drops the lobster back into the steaming pot.

Karl steps forward. "You go too easy on them," he says to Napoleon. "Order requires pain."

Karl reaches out and grabs a lobster by the claw. He

holds it upside down, spindly legs flailing. He takes one of the lobster's smaller legs between his fingers. He pulls enough to make the lobster squirm.

"Pain reveals truth."

Karl yanks suddenly, jerking the thin leg clean off. The lobster writhes. He grabs one of the claws next and yanks again. A gray viscous juice splashes out of the lobster as it curls its body and fights desperately to get free.

"Stop!" I say.

Karl's grin flashes again. He reaches his hand, clutching the claw, toward the pot. This time the other lobsters back away from his hand. "They smell fear," he says. "But also weakness. Watch this."

He casually drops the wounded crustacean back into the pot. The other lobsters react instantly. They attack the injured one like it's a virus. It scrambles to get out but has no chance with a missing claw and leg. The other lobsters smother it and leave only a battered carcass.

There's a sharp crack. Karl has broken open the dead lobster's claw. He pulls out a hunk of raw meat and uses tongs to dip it in the simmering water. He grins at me as it cooks. "To the victor goes the spoils. And the orderly, the disciplined, will always be the victor." He pulls the cooked meat out, covers it in butter, and drops it into his mouth.

"You brute, this is the wrong lesson," Napoleon says. "All that showed is that forces are stronger when united. And this time you'll be the dead lobster."

Karl snaps back with some retort, but the words drift past me. The lobster's claw replays in my mind as we return to our seats. Napoleon and Karl argue over the rest of the dinner. Each claims to be a better general, to have fought more important battles, and won greater victories, on

Earth. The rest of us eat in quiet. The lobster and butter and bread taste better than the mush they serve outside the tower, but it goes down without a trace of pleasure. The only ones who seem pleased in Black are those with power. But I wouldn't want to be any of them.

We have mostly finished eating when a hush falls over the room, cold as a gust of wind before a storm. I follow the boys' gaze toward stairs along the tower's inner wall.

A group of figures descends toward us. Ten robed girls.

Everyone at the table rises. Even Napoleon and Karl look serious. They stand at attention, like soldiers ready to be inspected. I copy them, standing rigid, ready for anything.

The girls move into a line before us. Their shoulders touch. Their eyes smolder. They are like a black iron wall, a ballast at the base of the tower. They ask together: "What is good before the Judge?"

The boys answer: "Everything that heightens power in man. This is the will to power. The strong shall rise."

"What is bad?"

"Everything born of weakness."

"What is happiness?"

"Power that grows," the boys chant.

The words linger like toxic fumes. They are wrong. These are the Colorless One's lies, infecting the Black Tower. Weakness is not bad. Happiness is not power. Happiness is Emma's warm touch atop Yellow's wall. It's the wind in my sails on the open sea. It's the memory of my mother and my wife and my son on Earth. It's this chance to be scoured clean of my past mistakes.

A girl steps forward from the line of black robes. Samantha. One of my past mistakes. Her green eyes pass over me as if I'm nothing to her. I stand motionless in the line, reluctantly accepting that without my power any fight would be futile.

She approaches Napoleon. Her quiet words resound in the silence: "Are you content?"

"Never," Napoleon answers. "There is always more conquest. More victory. More strength."

Samantha nods as if satisfied. She begins to walk down the line of boys, speaking as she goes. "No one's place is secure. No one's past means anything, unless it can be used for power. Your Commanders know of their pasts because they've earned it in the Scouring. But they've let you grow too soft. We lost four in the last Scouring. We're not ready to conquer another tower. But we will be. We just need the right Commanders. So the Council has decided to hold a melee. A full melee. Ten troops of ten. Last troop standing wins." Samantha's eyes lock onto mine. "Put a spear through an opposing Commander and you might take their place. Then *you* will join our Council. You will learn your past. And you will meet our true leader."

Samantha spins away and moves back toward the other girls. I begin to follow her, to try to talk to her, but a boy grabs my arm, holding me back. It's the boy Karl named Scara.

"*No*," he whispers the demand. "*Obey.*"

I twist out of his grip but hesitate. Scanning around, I see Karl eyeing me, as if waiting for me to do something stupid. This is not the time. But the time will come. I will get past him and past Samantha. I will find the leader.

"Salute!" Napoleon commands.

One by one, each boy raises his hand to his forehead, saluting as the girls climb the stairs up the Black Tower.

9

WAKING UP AS a troop leader brings no light to the Black Tower. I'm on a cot, under a charcoal canvas tent, surrounded by boys called grunts. I barely slept. Karl came with guards four times during the night. Each time they brought a boy. Shoved him inside. No one joins by choice.

I rise and stand in the doorway to the tent, listening to crows caw outside, watching the troop wake. Troop 9. My troop.

A boy with a mop of blonde curls is the first to rise. He was against us in the fight against Baron's troop. Now he marches up to me like he knows what he's doing and says his name is Birger. He says Karl reassigned him to my troop. He looks about my age, but a head taller and blunt as a Viking warhammer. He reminds me of my friend Hank, except without the smile.

"Why were you reassigned?" I ask.

He gazes down at me. "You ever led a troop?"

I consider trying to fudge the truth, to tell him I'm a marked one, that I've led whole tribes in the Green Tower, that I've captured boys from Black in the Scouring. But instead I shake my head, "No."

His broad shoulders shrug. "Best to train in the morning," he says. "Then train in the afternoon until we get blisters. Then put some salt on the wounds, eat some slop, and sleep."

"How long have you been at this?" I ask.

"Long as I can remember."

"You were in Baron's troop?"

"Aye, a fine Deputy. Such discipline. Such power. Maybe we'll get him back."

The other boys have gathered around us. There are only five. One of them is Shucks, from my troop before, but I don't know the others. Their hollow stares look bleak. We'll need four more grunts to complete the troop. Karl will make us train and fight, but no one has commanded anything of us today.

"What's the plan?" asks Shucks.

The others eye me coldly.

As the troop leader, I decide what to do, as long as I follow the five rules. I have to survive to rise in the ranks and find the missing leader and learn how the Colorless One has infected this tower. So what will help us survive? Training won't be enough. We'll be stronger if we learn to work together.

"You've all fought before?" I ask.

They mumble yes. Out of the coffin or reassigned, either way none of them shows a trace of remembering Earth. I don't bother asking about that. Not yet.

"So you know how to use a spear and shield?"

More yeses.

"Then let's do something different today."

Shucks looks at me like I'm nuts, but he and the others follow me out all the same. They obey their superior. Until a boy stops me outside the tent, hand on my arm. There's something familiar about him. He has straight black hair down to his chin and gold flecks in his cold, dark eyes.

"What about our spears and shields?" he asks.

I force myself to smile. "We'll come back if we need them."

"We have to take them," he says. "It's the law."

He looks unflinching. It's a first test, a sign for my troop. I don't want to be like Karl. I can't make them take risks they don't want to take. "Fine, bring yours if you want."

The boy's hard expression softens, like steel bending an inch. He and the others slip into the tent and emerge with their arms a moment later. They look more comfortable that way. I'm more comfortable without the burdens.

I head toward a fire with a black cauldron of mush. We fill our bowls and move to the side and sit together on the ground. The boys are quiet as they begin to eat.

Another troop, with the number 5 on their shields, comes to the pot in a single file line. They manage to hold their spears even as they fill their bowls. They file off, scarfing down the mush as they go, looking ready to fight anything.

"Shucks," I say. "Would you tell us a story?"

His freckled face looks surprised. "Gee, what kind of story?"

"Anything you know."

"I reckon I could do that," he says. "Let's see…I heard this one from a boy who heard it from another boy who'd survived the Scouring. Once upon a time, there was a girl walking through the forest to visit her grandmother's house. She wore a bright red hood…"

He tells the whole story of little red riding hood. As the other boys listen, I see their hard faces soften. They even smile a little when Shucks get to the part, "My, what big teeth you have..." They slap their knees in approval when Shucks gets to the end, when the hunter comes into the house and cuts open the wolf to save the grandmother.

"Tell us another!" one of the boys says.

"Hey, I know one," Birger volunteers. He looks to me, like a bashful giant seeking my approval.

I never expected such a dark tale to make the boys lighten up. "I'd love to hear it," I say. "But first, Shucks, who told you that story?"

He glances down. "Crispus, our last leader."

"I heard mine from someone else, too," Birger says.

The stories spread like they did on Earth, told and retold. I ask the group, "Do any of you remember anything from before the Black Tower?"

The boys all shake their heads no.

"We'll try to fix that," I say. "Birger, let's hear your story."

"Once upon a time there lived a woodcutter and his wife," Birger begins. "Their early days were lived in bliss in a small wood cottage with their two children, Hansel and Gretel..."

He continues with the whole fairy tale, of the woodcutter later marrying an evil stepmother, of her sending Hansel and Gretel to be lost in the forest, of the evil witch who tried to trick them, and of their escape to live happily ever after with their father again. The story twists more than little red riding hood, and the boys seem to like it even more. Fantasy gives us not only escape, but also a way to explain our own strange reality.

We finish the stories long after we finish eating. Two boys take the cauldron away, probably to clean it or cook more. The fire has burned low. Other troops have come and gone, and we can hear the sounds of training—metal on metal, grunted commands, in the distance. The heavy morning fog has lifted, revealing dark clouds high overhead, like a storm always on the verge of breaking forth with lightning and wind and hail. It gives brooding energy to the still, humid air.

I decide we should explore. Shucks tells me he thinks it's a bad idea, but none of the boys can give me a reason why, only that their prior leaders never ventured far. They focused on training. I have a different focus.

I've already been around the tower and seen the low canvas tents like spokes from the metal axis. But I know there's more to the Black Tower than this. When I was in Red, Emma and I ventured through Black's surrounding lands. We climbed the steep, terraced hills. We visited a village. My old foe Max called himself Lord there, and Kiyo was called Rice. So there is more to the Black Tower than this warring encampment of boys. We just have to hike out to find it.

Without the fog, it's easy to see the way. The Black Tower sits in the center of a flat plain, like the bottom of a bowl. To one side there's the sheer wall between the Scouring and us. To the other side rise the terraced hills, stretching into the distance. Gazing out, I can see the steep ridge to the left, separating Black and Red, and the cliffs dropping to the sea to the right, separating Black and Blue. I lead our group straight out, toward the hills.

The land rises gently as we make our way. We pass a few other troops training. No one pays attention to us, much less tries to stop us. A few other boys in black tunics—without shields and spears—rush about doing chores. When I ask my troop why some get those tasks instead of fighting, the only answer is that the Council decides. Another question to tuck away for later.

As we approach the base of a steep hill, I notice a dark figure ahead. It looks like one of the girls, standing motionless in a black robe, hood up. We are only a stone's throw away. Her hooded gaze is toward us. She does not budge.

"What's she doing?" I ask the troop behind me.

The five of them look uncertain, maybe afraid.

"No clue," Shucks says. "But we know the leader's first law: *obey your superior.*"

"Have any of you actually seen the leader?" I ask.

No one answers.

"What if the Council is lying?" I ask.

"Ain't our business," Shucks says. "We oughtta, um, head back."

"Why?" I ask. "She might let us pass. Let's see what happens."

"No." Birger shakes his head. "I don't like this. We are troop nine. We are supposed to be training."

"I told ya about the girls," Shucks adds. "They control the smoke. Ain't no good come from messin' with 'em."

I study Birger and the others. We laughed together at the stories. They seem to have accepted my lead. I could lose their trust if I drag them into trouble, just like with their spears and shields. And they could be right...yet, if I'm ever going to rise up in the Black Tower, to change it, to rid it of the Colorless One's taint, I need to do more than fight and die over and over in its pointless muddy battles.

"Listen, you might be right," I say. "So stay here and

keep an eye out. I'll check it out on my own. If there's no problem, I'll wave for you to come. Sound good?"

They don't answer. Shucks nods, his fingers pale as they clutch his spear tightly. I figure it's the best I can expect from them. I walk away, toward the girl, and a boy mutters softly behind me, *"He's a goner…"*

The girl is motionless. Her hood shadows her face.

What if she's Samantha? No, I assure myself, it's very unlikely. Samantha is on the Council. She has always been in the tower. And this girl has no red hair spilling out over her black robe. There's nothing at all to hint at who she is.

The green hill behind her looks slashed in black, with its terraces of black water. A steep set of stairs rises through the middle of the terraces. The girl stands right at the base.

Each step is harder to take. My feet weigh me down, as if dragged by an invisible force. I stop twenty feet away to rest. I glance to the left and right.

There are more of them. Hooded black figures stand at distant intervals, easy to see from this angle, but barely within shouting distance. They look like sentinels guarding the way out of the plain around the Black Tower.

I force myself to take another step, and another.

The girl raises her arms. Her thin hands look pale as bones reaching out of her robe, extending toward me.

"Get back!" a boy shouts from behind.

I can feel the girl's eyes on me, though I can't see them. I glance to the side. The distant girls' heads have turned to me. Their arms are raised.

My heart clenches in fear. I take a deep breath. "Hi," I say, risking another step, hands out innocently. "I'm Cipher."

The first wisp of smoke swirls up out of the ground like a black rope. I panic and jump back. But there's more and more of it, billowing like the cloud of a bomb. It swoops over me and drags me down to my hands and knees. I reach in desperation for my power, but the block remains. I feel pressure sucking me down, dragging me down, down, down into the earth.

"Get up!"

I hear shouting. Distant. Darkness is close.

Something pulls at me, yanking so hard I feel like my arm will pop out of socket. And then, suddenly, a release.

I'm on my back. The pressure is gone. The ominous clouds come into focus overhead. Faces appear, hovering over me. It's my troop.

Shucks' freckled face starts to laugh. "Ya dang near died!" he says. "But we gotcha!"

"You were in the belly of the wolf, like the grandmother," Birger says, looking intense under his mop of blonde curls. "So we cut you out."

10

THE BOYS HELP me to my feet. I brush off the dirt and gaze back toward the girl. She stands still as a statue in the same place, with her arms by her sides. There is no trace of smoke. The green hills are taunting behind her, but I won't be trying to go there again. Not without my power.

So I'm stuck. The hills are off limits on one side. The Scouring wall blocks the other way. And we're not allowed inside the Black Tower except for feasts. So all that's left is the war fields and the troop's idea of training. This isn't the Yellow Tower where we could simply rest and sleep in peace. Here we'll have to fight soon enough.

We make our way back toward the tower and the tents. We pass a large group of boys, fighting. They struggle on a battleground so dark it looks covered in blood. Maybe it is.

Their leader, Napoleon, stands on a low rock with his back to us, hands clasped tightly behind him. Others stand around him. We move closer to watch. Napoleon barks out question after question as two troops stand facing each other, practicing their thrusts. He never stops speaking, offering instruction, questioning forms. His relentless energy and competence seem infectious. The group near him looks alert, as if ready to dive into the fight any moment.

"Enough!" Napoleon calls out. "I have chosen."

I expect him to name a winner, but instead he takes a helm from a boy beside him. When he lowers it over his head, he looks a foot taller. He takes a spear and approaches one of the troops.

"You," he says, pointing at one of the boys.

The other boys step away from him.

"You are not loyal," Napoleon says. "You do not fight with your all. We saw you holding back."

Napoleon turns toward the onlookers. His glance passes over me, with a moment of recognition, but he continues unaffected. "Those who hold back are not fit for my troops."

In a blur of fluid motion, he spins and stabs his spear into the boy he singled out. The boy falls, and Napoleon turns again, his face stoic. "In war we must use severe examples," he says. "Immediate and sharp consequences will save the blood of many. We fight with intensity, for this is the only means of making the battle shorter and thus less deplorable for us all. Now, I will take the fallen's place and we will have a proper fight."

Napoleon leads his troop of ten boys into a tight formation. The opposing troop does the same. The air is electric as each troop moves in unison. They approach each other like walls of shields, testing, parrying, falling back, and charging again. The three suns have almost set when the right flank of the troop against Napoleon flinches. It is only one boy, his shield dipping, probably from exhaustion, but that's all it takes.

Napoleon shouts and his troop stabs into the gap and separates the other boys like a wedge. Shields swing violently, spears stab, and in the end four boys from the losing troop are motionless on the ground, and the others have surrendered. A cloud of black takes the downed bodies away.

"Gather round!" Napoleon calls out. "Bring the helmets!"

The onlookers gather close around their leader on the fighting ground. The winning troop and losing troop line up and kneel before Napoleon. He walks down the line, saying something, too distant to hear. But the effect is obvious. For the winners, he places helmets on their heads. They stand looking proud as roosters. For the losers, he places a dark mark—probably of mud and blood—on their foreheads. They show a mix of shame and determination. The whole brigade, dozens of boys, chants something after that, ending with a loud "Hooah!"

The sky darkens as they march away, passing close to us. Napoleon spots us and approaches. His helmet is tucked under one arm. The other holds his spear. Sweat has matted his hair on his forehead. He looks like a skinny child, not a threat. But I've seen him fight now. I know better than to underestimate him.

"Scouting the opposition?" he says to me.

I force calm into my voice. "We were just passing by."

"Karl is foolish to let you roam like this." He steps closer. His voice lowers so only I can hear. "I see a spark in you, Paul, for I alone see the details, the personal, the visceral. A moment will soon come when your spark could ignite. You could topple Karl, the Holy Roman Emperor himself. And if you do, you'll become commander in his place. I promise you that." He steps back and salutes. "See you in the fight."

I salute as he stalks off, with his troops following him

dutifully. Most of them are bigger than he is, probably stronger. Something about Napoleon demands respect. And he's right. They're going to beat us.

Why did Napoleon tell me this? Would he rather face me than Karl? Or is he only a pawn, like the others? Whatever the reason, it's tempting. It might not be enough to simply survive. As commander I'd be able to learn more about this tower, maybe find a way to cleanse it. And even if the smoke took Karl, he'd come back, wiped clean.

I shake the thought away. It would be betrayal. These are Black's tactics. But still Napoleon's words linger.

We head back toward our tent and stop at one of the fires with a cooking pot of mush. The boys talk in hushed tones as we eat. One of them, the boy with the gold-flecked eyes, sits beside me. He still has his spear and shield.

"I doubted you," he says. "But today was…interesting. What you did took guts. Challenging the girl, then scouting the enemy."

"I'm glad you stuck with me," I say. "I might not have made it back without your help." I eye his spear. "No one punished me for leaving mine in the tent."

"You were lucky Karl did not see us." His white-knuckled grip does not loosen. "It is better to be safe. We are stronger if we obey."

"You're probably right," I admit. "I saw Napoleon's group. We won't be much of a match against them."

"Do not doubt. It is the enemy of victory."

Something about his voice and his eyes is still familiar. I ask him what his name is, and he flinches like I hit him.

"Whatever you want," he says.

He doesn't know his name. I remember how hard that

is. But he was in Baron's troop. They must have called him something. "What do the others call you?"

"Silk."

"Why that name?"

"My hair. They say it's like a girl's."

Boys will seize on anything for a name. But it's true, his hair is even longer than Crispus's and Birger's. "Was it that long at the start?" I ask.

He shakes his head. "I let it grow."

"That would take months."

"I have survived. I control myself. And stay away from the girls."

"Why does that matter? I'm not afraid of them."

"You should have learned better by now. They control the smoke. Most boys fear them. Even Karl. But not Napoleon or, apparently, you."

"You think I'm like him?" I ask, incredulous.

"You saw how Napoleon leads his boys. He's disciplined, with no thought of dying. He's seen how it plays out—dying, getting wiped, starting over, rising again. He thrives in the struggle and relishes the chance to rise. Karl uses his power only to protect himself. That's why we have more rules. You seem more like Napoleon."

"Thanks, I guess. How did Karl make it to Commander?"

"He killed the prior one. Thought he was too weak. Karl is ruthless in weeding out weakness. He finds the strongest boys to guard himself."

"But not you? Why are you loyal to him?"

"Loyalty does not always have to run deep. I want what all of us want. To rise. To remember."

"You want to be Commander?"

"Anyone who denies this is lying. Everyone wants power. It has always been this way."

"Always?" I study him—his calm face, the distant look, like he sees more truth than most of us. He knows more than he is telling me. I lean closer, lock eyes with him. "Who were you before this place?"

"Is that an order?" he asks.

"If it needs to be."

"I've seen something. I got to wear the crown once."

"What crown?"

"The Council controls it. The crown shows you things. Hard things. In the vision I was a boy named Omaki, in a country called Japan, on Earth."

Omaki. I've heard that name. Where? When? His eyes…his straight black hair…so much like Kiyo's. That's it. She said this name long ago in the Blue Tower. It tumbles back into my mind. "You're Kiyo's son!"

He looks confused. "Who is Kiyo?"

"Your mother. And she is here. I know this is a lot to take in. Trust me, I know. But I have been to the other towers. The first one was the Blue Tower, and there was a girl who looks like you. She told me she had a son named Omaki. She told me he—you—trekked with her through snowy mountains. You were trained to fight, but you were…killed. That's how you came here."

He studies his hands. "I see."

"I can help you find her. She'll help you remember."

"No, please, the memories are no good. They are terrible."

"What did the crown show you?"

"I was tied to a cross." He glances at my hands. "It was shaped like your scars. It was in the sea. The waves would come in, rising, rising. The salty water filled my mouth and my nose. It went down. It came back. Over and over. I do not need to see more of this…pain. It is better here."

"I'm so sorry." I put my hand gently on his shoulder. "You've probably seen the worst. Maybe the crown is tainted. Maybe…" But I can't tell him everything—about the Colorless One and the pit and the darkness. It would be too much. "Who gave you the crown to wear?"

His expression softens, his gaze focuses on me again, retreating from the cold, distant place of his memories. "Karl," he says. "He told me it was a reward after we beat one of Napoleon's troops or survived a Scouring. It was unusual but…"

"What was unusual?"

"Normally grunts do not get such rewards. Only troop leaders like you. But this time I did something different. I was on Napoleon's side…until Karl convinced me to betray him. It was during the fight. I switched sides. Ever since I have wished I died instead."

"Why?"

He shakes his head. "Napoleon hasn't always been a Commander here, but he should be. No matter how many times he dies and forgets, he will rise up again. He was a troop leader, like you, when he showed me how it's done."

"You mean fighting?"

"More than that. He got our troop together and lined us up and said, *Five more days, boys.* He paced before us and asked, *What do you say?* Well we didn't know what to say, but he showed us. *Hooah!* He shouted. So we shouted it back, *Hooah!* Then he pulled us into a huddle and we were all shouting it, this hooah of power, louder and louder until it took over us and we were like a single organism yelling at the universe. Then Napoleon turns and takes off at a sprint, shouting *hooah* as he goes. And guess what? We took off after him, single file, like we knew what we were doing. We stayed tight together, chanting as our legs relished the motion, the pace, the unity. That's all it was. That's why we followed Napoleon. Because he *willed* it. We'd heard that he was a fighter, a survivor. But he wasn't a Commander back then. It was his will that got him there. And I thought to myself, *I can be that strong.* I wanted power. So I helped Karl win. He gave me the crown, but the vision of my memories left me in despair. Karl did not honor his word. He said I was no longer fit to be a troop leader. He stuck me under Baron. Now I'm under you."

Omaki's story turns something in me, like a river finding a way around a boulder. Karl rose by betrayal. He can fall by it, too. "I will make this better," I say softly. "When I have power."

He nods, his knowing eyes cold like Kiyo's. "I will fight for you, and we will rise."

11

THREE NEW GRUNTS join us by the next morning. The first has matchstick legs and bug eyes. Shucks calls him Twig. The name sticks. The second is built like a frog, with hardly any neck. Somebody calls him Bowler. The third grunt has a mop of light brown hair and totters unsteadily a head taller than the rest of us. The boys call him Broom.

So we are nine, one short of the complete ten, as we begin to train. I lead us out to an empty space removed from the other troops. The ground is dry, the sky brooding as ever. The boys line up in front of me: Shucks, Birger, Omaki, Twig, Bowler, Broom, and two other boys from Baron's troop who haven't bothered saying their name or much of anything at all.

We focus on formations. Our shields have to be united to defend against attacks. We practice in a line, shields raised, spears thrusting. We form into a wedge to press into opponents. We form into a block with a solid wall of shields on four sides. We switch between the different forms as I call them out: "Block. Wedge. Line." We improve. We move quicker. It is almost smooth. But each time it starts to feel like pouring concrete into my tired legs.

The suns are low when I say it will have to be good enough. We take our spears and shields and return to our tent. We dine on bowls of rice mush.

I settle onto my cot, exhausted, when a large figure appears in the tent flap. Even with his face shadowed in the night, I recognize him as Karl. I rise cautiously. Salute.

"Present for you," he grunts. "Last one. Troop nine has its ten. Train tomorrow. Day after that is the melee, at high noon. Come ready."

He steps out and his guards shove a boy inside.

It's Crispus. Curly brown hair, olive skin, and no hint of injuries from our last fight. His face no longer carries the burdens of his Roman past. He doesn't even remember what happened here—how this very troop, and four of the boys still with us, killed him in a fight. No one tells him. Shucks and I exchange a glance. We know we need his strength.

"Crispus," I say. "Can we call you that?"

He bows his head. "As you wish."

I smile at his regal formality. "Welcome to troop 9. We know what you've been through to get here. No need to talk about that. We'll tell you what's what tomorrow. Your cot is over there. Everyone, get some sleep."

The boys do what I say. Acting like a leader seems to make people think I really am one.

The next day we move stiffly out of the tent, spears and shields at the ready. We eat our rice mush. We could shuffle listlessly over to the same training space, but this is our last day before our lives will be at stake. Other troops are nearby, having their own mush, preparing their own way to the fight. We have to speed this up.

I draw the boys into a huddle. I catch Omaki's eyes. "Boys, we have two more days. If we don't get strong, together, we're going to die. If I have anything to say about it, I'm not going to let that happen. Are you with me?"

They don't answer.

But I try it anyway, softly at first, "If you're with me, Hooah!"

"Hooah!" Omaki shouts back.

Another boy joins, then another. Our huddle pulls closer and we're chanting it, louder and louder. "Hooah!"

We break and I lead us charging across the training grounds in a run. I feel the group fall into rhythm behind me. Left feet strike the ground, and we breathe out, "Hooah!" Right feet, breathe in. Left, "Hooah!"

By the time we stop, sweat beads on foreheads. My heart thumps quickly, blood rushing and filling my body with energy, masking the pain. Now the pain brings strength. And strength brings victory.

We train hard in the morning, like the day before, but better. We break into teams of five and go at each other with the blunt end of our spears. It's good practice. It's exhausting. I decide to stop at midday. We have to preserve something for tomorrow.

We return to the cooking pot. More rice mush. I ask if anyone would like to tell a story. Shucks goes first. Birger tells one, then Omaki says he has a story. He's normally quiet around the others, so a look of curious anticipation spreads around the group.

Omaki tells us about a fisherman who rescues a turtle and is rewarded with a special trip under the ocean to visit the king who lives beneath the sea. The king thanks the fisherman for saving the turtle, and presents his daughter, the princess, to guide the fisherman. The princess's many kimonos blended the colors of all the fish of the coral reefs. Her sleeves reached the tatami mat. Her long hair, like black silk, was crowned by a royal headdress. She bowed before the fisherman and led him on amazing underwater adventures, until the fisherman began to miss home. The princess gave the fisherman a beautiful, black-lacquered box and promised that as long as he kept the box closed, he would have happiness.

Omaki pauses, studying us in the firelight.

"Well?" Shucks says. "I figure he opened it, didn't he?"

"The fisherman rode the turtle back to the village," Omaki says. "He was anxious to share his adventures with his family. But to his amazement, all was changed. He could not find his home. When he asked after his family, only the oldest men of the village knew of them, and they knew only old stories of the fisherman and his parents. He had no one to share his plans, and sadness filled his heart. Early one morning he took the chest to the edge of the sea and thought again of the beautiful princess and her enchanting world. Perhaps, he thought, she has left me some happiness inside the box. Ignoring her warning, he opened the lid. A tendril of smoke escaped from the box, swirled around the fisherman, and floated away on the gentle wind."

"Smoke? Like here?" Shucks asks.

Omaki shakes his head. "The fisher looked down at his hands. They were veined and wrinkled. As he turned in sorrow to walk back to the village, his steps were slow and halting. A young boy passing by noticed an old man with long white hair and a beard making his unsteady way along the shore. It was the fisherman. He had pursued happiness over obedience, so he had lost the magical protection against the effects of time. And yet we, it seems, have such a protection."

"I like it!" Shucks says. "But I woulda kept that box closed tight, sure would."

"You would have opened it before you got out of the sea," Birger says, and the boys all laugh. For a moment it feels like the Black Tower has lost its darkness.

We move to our tent, bone tired but somehow lighter than we started the day. When we wake up the next morning, I swear we look more alike. It's not just the identical clothes and arms. We wear the same look of grim determination. We are as ready as we can be.

All the troops in Karl's brigade gather for the melee. There are five groups of ten, fifty total, ready to fight to the bitter end. Around us a few girls look on. They don't have to be announced. They will be the enforcers if anything goes wrong.

"Boys of black," Karl says, surrounded by his robed guardians. "This is your final training. I will choose the ten best, the elite, to join me in the battle against Napoleon tomorrow. You fight until I declare it finished. The Judge rewards power. The strong shall rise."

We salute in unison, in order. Then we move to positions around the perimeter of the battleground. The girls raise their hands. When they drop, we will fight.

I step out from the line and face my troop. The boys look steady as steel, with pride in their stoic faces. Omaki. Crispus. Birger. Even Shucks' usual grin hides behind a set jaw. The Black Tower has forged us into weapons. We have no choice. We fight or we die. And we do it together.

"Hooah," I call out. "What do you say, troop 9?"

"Hooah!" they answer.

The girls' arms drop.

I give the command to march. We move all at once,

forming into a phalanx. Our steps fall into rhythm. Our chants spark off the battleground as we go. "Hooah! Hooah!"

Spears clang against shields before us. Two troops have already collided. The first boys drop to the mud. But the lines of both troops hold. Troop 1, the only troop with helmets, advances on the opposite side of the fray.

"Wedge!" I shout.

We flow into the formation. I'm at the front, Omaki to my right, Crispus to my left. We charge into the fight. We hit the two deadlocked troops from the side.

Lunge. Strike. Several fall.

The troops shift to face us. Omaki blocks a stabbing spear. It deflects and pierces into a gap between our shields. The point comes within inches of my eyes, close enough for me to see the dark wetness on it.

Over the rim of my shield I see the helmeted boy who attacked. A purple scar runs down his cheek. Scara.

He scowls as he yanks to get his spear free, but Omaki moves fast. He stabs. Scara blocks and then slams his shield into us. The force knocks me flat on my back. Shield and spear flung away, out of reach.

I bounce up to my knees, but too late. Omaki has turned to stop another attacker. Scara looms over me, spear raised. He stabs down. I dodge and roll. Grab my spear. Shield too far away. I think of blue threads, my power over the air, but that's no help to me now.

Scara raises his spear again. I stab low. His shield deflects easily. My spear jabs into mud and sticks. I don't have a chance. Scara shouts as he lunges at me.

A golden blur hits him on the right, knocking him down. Birger. He saved me. He wrestles Scara in the mud, writhing and punching. I rush for my shield, and when I turn back, the wrestling boys are lost in the melee's shuffle.

"Block!" It's Crispus, shouting behind me. "Block!"

I hurry back into our group, fitting within the tight formation. Our shields meld into a wall. The battle is more sound than sight after that. Clangs and crashes. Groans and screams.

"Wedge!" I shout through the chaos. "Left! Line! Back!"

I keep our troop moving. Fluid against the onslaught. We block. We lunge. We hold.

"Turn!" Shucks yells beside me.

Three shields marked with "3"s come at us. They've broken through our left side. Crispus, now spearless, charges into the gap and tackles one of the attackers. They go down, grappling for control.

I race to help but a boy gets in my way. He deflects my spear, but not completely. It takes him in the thigh. I yank it out and swing at his head. The wooden shaft hits him at the ear and he collapses. Our group finishes the last of the three, and when we look around, the fighting has stopped.

"...the just prevail!" Karl is shouting. I didn't even hear him announce the fight's end.

Somehow I'm still standing, along with five others from my troop. Omaki, Crispus, Shucks, Bowler, and Twig. But not Birger. Not the others. There are no troop 3 shields being held, and only eight from groups 1, 5, and 7 put together. A few boys tend to wounds. All of us are bruised and bloodied.

Karl proclaims our troop the winner. He walks down our line, studying us. "Time to name my Deputy. Who's your leader?"

Shucks points at me. "Him."

Karl studies me like he's never seen me before. "You're small. But your troop fought well. Your name, remind me?"

My throat is tight. For some reason it doesn't feel right to tell him I'm Cipher. "Paul," I say.

"Right, Paul. You're my Deputy now." He holds out a barbed, black helm. The five from my troop eye it warily.

I take it and bow in recognition, even if it should be Crispus or Omaki, not me. The boys can call me Deputy, like it's important, like it's permanent. The title didn't help Baron. All it takes is a spear through the gut and, like him, I'd be back in a coffin underneath the Black Tower, fighting for my life to get out. What matters is that I'm closer to Samantha and the Council and figuring out how to stop this brutal cycle.

<h1 style="text-align:center">12</h1>

"SIR, THIS ONE tried to run away last night."

The boy kneeling before Karl, like a criminal before a judge, is the third of the four accused. His troop leader stands beside him like an executioner. "It's the second time he's tried it."

"You," Karl says to the runaway, "anything you want to say?"

The boy looks at Karl like a scared rabbit, his lower lip quivering. "I—I'm sorry. I—won't do it again."

"Hmm…" Karl rubs his thick chin. "Deputy, what do you recommend?"

I hesitate. Karl asked that I join him for this, but it's the first time he's asked my opinion. The first of the accused was a runaway, too. It was only his first time trying. His troop leader recommended execution. Karl opted for the collar for him. He'll be a girl's slave. It doesn't seem fair to give the same punishment.

"He should be executed, sir," the troop leader says.

"Deputy?" Karl asks.

I keep my voice steady. "Let's make an example of him. Put him in the stocks for a day and a night."

"A fine idea," Karl says. "Do it."

"Yes, sir." The troop leader bows and walks away with

his soldier.

I marvel again at the obedience of the boys. They treat Karl, and even me, like we're gods. Put on the right hat and the world will bow down to you. But the helmet feels like a cage on my head. Hard and heavy iron. My neck strains. Hair matted down. Sweat on my forehead. The boys think the hunk of metal means something. The helmet doesn't seem to bother Karl.

The last of the four accused stumbles forward and falls to his knees. I instantly recognize his blue eyes and dignified face—Hugh, the boy who Karl killed and the smoke took. His blank stare shows no memory of this.

The troop leader shakes his head gravely. "He shared his mush with a soldier from Napoleon's brigade, who came as a spy. Contact with the enemy is strictly forbidden. And this was worse, giving food we need. Each soldier must take care of himself."

"Well?" Karl asks Hugh. "Anything to say?"

"Sir, I meant no harm by it. The other boy said he was hungry. I had no idea he was a spy. I am loyal to you, I swear."

Karl's gaze swivels to me. "Deputy?"

"What's your name?" I ask, buying time.

The boy looks at me like I'm an angel for asking such a simple question. "My troop calls me Hugh."

He has the same name as before. He fought me below the tower, but he was kind to me when I first arrived in a troop. He was wiped and now this? I believe him. He didn't know the other boy was from Napoleon's side. He was trying to help, and he shouldn't be punished for that. Stupid rules. Sharing food is a kindness, that much I learned in the Green Tower.

"You know the rule now?" I say to Hugh.

He nods vigorously, as if sensing my tone of mercy. "Oh yes, sir. No sharing food, sir."

"Let's put him in the stocks for an hour." I try to sound firm but mostly fail.

Karl studies me. "That all?"

"Yes, sir. We need our fighters."

"We never lack for boys here," Karl says, sneering as he turns slowly to Hugh. "This one's weak. Take him back to your troop and execute him."

"No, sir, please!" Hugh falls to his knees. "It's not fair…"

"Live by the law, die by the law," the troop leader says.

He and two guards seize Hugh and drag him away, kicking and screaming. Karl watches, bemused.

I'm furious as I glare at Karl. His guards stand between us. They would stop me if I tried anything.

"Justice done," Karl says. He gazes up at the darkening sky. "Let's get to the tower. Feast starts soon."

I follow him. He pauses as we pass the row of stocks by the base of the stairs into the Black Tower. One of the boys is the one Karl just sentenced, at my recommendation. Beside him another boy's wrists are bloody and scabbed from the rough wood. Karl leans his face close to the boy and says something I can't quite hear. The boy writhes and spits, but Karl moves away with surprising speed. The saliva misses.

Karl laughs as he turns to me. "Ah, there's nothing for the soul like the stocks. Public punishment does double work. How many accused do you predict tomorrow?"

I glance at the sign with its five rules. Such simple rules, except for the first one—*Obey your superior, for he is the law—*

which gives complete power to Karl. "One, sir."

He raises an eyebrow. "Only one?"

"The troops have mostly obeyed." I try not to sound defensive.

"Obedience comes in degrees." He holds up a finger as if lecturing. "I figure the bottom fourth always deserve to be punished, the top fourth to be rewarded. Keeps a troop honest. Keeps boys striving."

It's a terrible idea. It's not just. But I nod. "Yes, sir."

"You'll catch on, Deputy, or you'll die." He turns away and strides toward the Black Tower. I trail after him in disgust, like following in the slime of a slug. Napoleon's promise is more tempting than ever, to topple his rival. Even if Karl was the Holy Roman Emperor, he's tainted here. A reset could do him good.

We gather around the long table in the Black Tower as before, a couple dozen battle-worn boys between the two Commanders. This time I sit at the middle of the table, as far from Napoleon and Karl as I can. The lobster tastes better that way.

The boy beside me says he is a troop leader from Napoleon's brigade. He says he's been stuck in the same place for five Scourings. "Hard to beat Napoleon and Karl," he whispers.

"How did they become Commanders?" I ask.

"The Council picked them."

"And what if a Commander dies?"

"The Council picks another boy to take his place. Usually a Deputy." The boy eyes a lobster claw on my plate. "You going to eat that?"

My appetite has vanished. I let him finish the rest of my food. The others around the table eat like it's their final meal. How many times has each of these boys died and come back only to fight hopelessly beneath tyrants and the shadow of this dark tower?

The girls descend the stairs like before. They repeat their mantra about power and fighting and all that terrible stuff. It's enough to make me reach again for my power—to blast them away with the wind, or maybe disappear and run away—but Samantha's vow holds true. There's not a trace of power in my mind. Where blue threads once flowed, there's only smoke.

Before the girls leave, they ask the Commanders, Deputies, and troop leaders to step forward. Fourteen of us line up, leaving only a handful of guards behind. The girls walk around us, appraising us like cattle. We're not allowed to say a word. Then they leave, just like before.

"What was that about?" I ask to no one in particular.

"The next fight is twelve against twelve," Napoleon says. "A true training for the Scouring. Ten boys and two girls for each team. They are assessing which girls are going to join which Commander."

"That's right." Karl thumps his chest, stares down his rival. "The frog or the eagle."

Napoleon doesn't respond, but his face takes on a terrible expression—eyes flash fire, nostrils dilate as if swollen by an inner storm. Karl misses it, his attention already back on the pot of lobsters.

I hope Samantha chooses Napoleon. Better to fight against her than for her. But I also think of Omaki switching sides, betraying Napoleon for Karl. Tomorrow could be my chance to return the favor, to become a commander.

<h1 style="text-align:center">13</h1>

MORNING MIST BLURS the Black Tower's sharp edges as we march to the battlefield. We gather on a rocky outcrop, near where Napoleon trained his troops before. The black-robed girls approach with their hoods up. They look like grim reapers emerging from the fog.

Two of them split off to join us. Neither one is Samantha. One of them has large oval eyes that peer out from her hood like a mouse from a hole. The other girl is tall and strong, with short black hair, chocolate skin, and bright green eyes. Even in the mist, I instantly recognize her.

She's Jade, from the Green Tower. But now she has no eagle imprinted on her hand, no spear, and no buckskin clothing. A heavy black robe covers her lean frame, but I remember the sinewy muscles that lurk underneath. She was the leader of the Eagle tribe and, on Earth, an American like me.

When her eyes meet mine, she gives a slight, knowing wink. She remembers. A grin plays at the corner of my lips. Someone who knows me, finally.

"Remember the goal," Karl barks. "Touch one of their girls, and we win. Let them touch one of ours, and they win. Got it?"

No one answers. We got it. Karl has picked the boys he thinks are the strongest from each troop. There are four from mine—Crispus, Omaki, Shucks, and myself. Our team moves into formation. A wedge in front of the two girls. Crispus has the right edge beside me. Omaki is to my left.

Karl calls out the march. "One, two. One, two."

We advance into the mist. Then we hear something completely out of place: a song. It rings out from the opaque air before us. The other troop is singing, chanting. The low beat pounds into rhythm—low and joyous and deeply unsettling.

Karl raises his voice, "One, two! One, two!"

But it's no use. The other troop's song drowns out our chant. The figures emerge from the mist. It's like nothing we've practiced for. Instead of coming at us, as one, they come from both sides. They've split their force, making our wedge useless. They charge with such speed that we have only moments to react.

"Defend!" Karl shouts.

We stop and raise our shields and lift our spears. My grip slips from moisture—mist and sweat. There's so little I can control in this battle. Only myself. I steady my breathing. Ready for anything.

Napoleon leads the charge. His eyes blaze out from his helmet. Beside him is Baron. Hard gray eyes focused. Legs churning. Spear raised.

"Hold!" Karl shouts.

They slam into us like hammers from both sides. The impact shatters our line. But we don't go down. We're still between the enemy and the girls we have to protect.

"Hooah!" Crispus grunts beside me, pushing back.

My shield knocks a spear aside, but the boy's momentum hurls forward. We both crash to the ground. I manage to hold onto my spear. The boy rises to a knee. He stabs his spear down. I roll away just in time. Omaki is by my side, his shield trying to cover us both.

While the opposing boy struggles to pull his spear out of the thick mud, Crispus takes him. But an instant later, Crispus falls forward beside him, a spear through his own back.

No time to mourn. Another boy bursts through our troops. He charges past Omaki and me toward the two girls, his spear aimed at Jade. She stands still and stoic, with no defense, no smoke.

I throw my spear in desperation. It stabs into the boy's leg. He collapses a few feet short of Jade.

Karl is suddenly there. He stabs his spear down, pinning the attacker to the ground. Karl stands before Jade like a boulder, ready to stop anything from getting to her.

Fighting fans out around us. Duels and clashes ring out. Omaki duels with a boy a head taller then he is. Other boys are down, motionless. No girl has been touched yet.

"Troop, here, to me!" Karl holds a spear in each hand, retrieved from the boy he finished. He tosses one of the weapons to me. I catch the shaft. "To me!"

I hurry to Karl's side. He points his spear toward two boys coming at us. Napoleon and Baron.

They are within feet, in ready stance, when Napoleon suddenly stops. He keeps his weapon up, but there's a moment of stillness, his eyes locked on me.

"This is it," he says. "The spark ignites."

Karl ignores him and lunges. Baron moves in blur, his shield blocking Karl's attack. They strain against each other, vying for control.

"Now!" Napoleon shouts to me, with a nod toward Karl.

I understand. Karl's back is exposed.

The mist wraps around us, and in this world, the tainted Karl stands in my way, not Napoleon, not Baron. I need to be Commander if I'm ever going to get my power back, find the leader, and change this place.

It happens in an instant. Karl has just started to turn when my spear finds his thick, unshielded belly. He falls to his knees. "I'll…remember you…"

He topples over. He won't remember.

"Charlemagne falls again." Napoleon sounds almost wistful as he gazes down at Karl. "There can be only one emperor, old friend." He looks to Baron. "Finish this."

By the time I turn, it has already happened. Baron has a hand on Jade's wrist. He lifts her arm and shouts:

"Napoleon reigns!"

14

AFTER THE SMOKE has taken the fallen, the mist has cleared, and Napoleon's victorious troop has been recognized, ten black-robed girls escort us back to the Black Tower. They glide beside us like ghosts, hoods up, looking ahead. There are thirteen boys marching—the survivors. Nine from Napoleon's troop. Only four from Karl's. Omaki and Shucks stay close by my side.

It is eerily quiet as we climb the stairs and enter through the immense iron doors. The long table where we feasted has been moved to the wall. The boys gather in the center of the vast room, and the girls encircle us like a wall. I scan their faces and recognize two of them: Jade and Samantha.

Samantha's eyes fix on Napoleon. "Commander, come with us. The Council will meet. Boys, you will wait here."

The ten girls and Napoleon ascend the stairs to whatever room is above us. Where they say Black's leader is. The twelve remaining boys are silent until the Council is out of sight.

"Glad they ain't gonna pick me," Shucks says. "It ain't worth bein' Commander if you gotta be so close to them girls."

A few boys laugh nervously. "I'm with you," one of the

boys says. "Listen, I hear there's a new girl even the Council is afraid of." The boys huddle together like they're sharing a conspiracy. "I hear she's very powerful, very dangerous. Her eyes are all black, with gold flecks. The Council sent two girls to inspect. They went out to her village by the coast. They woke up in coffins."

"See!" Shucks says. "Count me out!"

"I could handle it," Baron says, dead serious.

"As could I," Omaki replies, like it's a challenge.

The other boys—all from Napoleon's side—stare at Omaki like he's a threat, then shuffle away and gather close on the other side of the room, far from the center. They speak in hushed tones. My gaze is fixed on Omaki. Black eyes, gold flecks. This new girl could be Kiyo. I have to find out. Being Commander should help.

"So..." Shucks steps closer to me, rolls his eyes toward Baron. "What's your bet on who they'll pick?"

The words come out cold. "I was Karl's Deputy."

"You sure was. Maybe they gonna pick ya. Hey, nice knowin' ya, and don't forget about little ole Shucks."

"I was Napoleon's Deputy." Baron faces us with his usual granite expression, made all the more emotionless without his memories. "We were the victorious team."

"So you were," I say to him, and leave it at that. There's no use arguing with him or telling him that Napoleon promised me the spot. He'll learn soon enough.

Omaki moves closer to my side, as if on guard against Baron. We may not be allowed to fight in here, but only an hour ago Baron and the rest of Napoleon's soldiers were trying to kill us.

"Karl is gone," Omaki says softly. "It does not feel as good as I had hoped. Still I am...empty."

I put my hand on his shoulder. "Memories will help," I say.

He shakes his head, but Shucks chimes in, "Hey, that's right, and we're as close as we gonna get to rememberin' somethin'."

Dread fills Omaki's face. "Why's that?"

"Well, after a melee like this," Shucks says, "the Council is gonna pick a Commander *and* the next ten boys for the Scouring. And ya know what boys who survive the Scouring get…to wear the crown!"

"I've seen enough of the past. May they pick others…" Omaki shakes his head, then sits cross-legged on the floor. He closes his eyes and goes still.

"What'd I say?" Shucks asks with a shrug. "Just tryin' to tell it like it is."

"Not everyone wants memories," I say. "Some are hard."

"I don't doubt it! But hey, it's like them stories ya let us tell. Anything to get our minds outta this place can't be all bad."

"I disagree," Baron says. His gaze is tilted up, toward where the Council meets, as if he will not deign to look us in the eyes. "We must focus always on what is before us. It is the only way to victory. If your Commander had shared wisdom such as this, he might have stood a chance against Napoleon."

"Bah…" Shucks says, but then he sits and goes quiet, too.

We wait in silence. I feel more and more sure that my time has come. I did what Napoleon asked. Jade recognized me. They will convince the others. They will choose me as Commander. Then I will join the Council and learn how the Colorless One has corrupted this tower.

The Council finally descends, in the same solemn march as before. The boys gather again before the ten girls and Napoleon. The Commander steps forward. The robed girls loom behind him like puppeteers pulling the strings. Samantha stares at me like a cat playing with a mouse. Jade keeps her hooded head down.

"We have chosen the new Commander," Napoleon says. "He will be my new enemy. A worthy foe. He is—" Napoleon's eyes fall on me, then shift. "Baron."

My stomach drops. I rush forward without thinking. "You said it would be me! I'm the one who killed…"

Napoleon faces me calmly. "You will make it someday, I'm sure. You have what it takes. The Council has decided to give you a different assignment."

He sounds sincere, but he didn't make it to his position by kindness. Anger twists inside me. I should have known. He'll do anything for power. Maybe he doesn't want me as the rival Commander because he thinks I'm a threat.

I growl out the question, "What do they want?"

Napoleon looks to Baron. "To be Commander, one must have complete loyalty to the Council and the Black Tower." His voice is sweet, almost caressing, as he glances to Samantha then turns back to me. "You can prove your loyalty in the Scouring."

15

THE GRAY STONE of the Scouring feels hard after training on mud. The shield and spear weigh heavily. Our troop stays tight, close enough to hear each other breathe, smell each other's sweat. The girls, Samantha and Jade, have space between them, in the middle of our square formation. Omaki is to my right, Shucks to my left. Napoleon holds the front corner of the square. Here we all look like old, hardened comrades. Shared enemies can unite anyone. But the other towers are not my enemies.

We will face Blue's wind, Red's fire, Yellow's healing, Green's invisibility. Their powers could rip right through our shields. Our formation is papier-mâché without the smoke. No wonder the Black boys fight so hard to protect the girls.

Samantha commands us to go left around the shard of darkness that looms in the center of the Scouring, a black void where the White Tower should shine. We march in lockstep toward Blue. I'm at the back of the square, seeing only the two robed girls and the backs of the boys with their shields up.

The air suddenly feels cool. Wind caresses my moist brow, then whips at me. The boys ahead divide, flung to the ground by the force. Samantha sends out her smoke. It collides with the blue ribbons and suffocates them. The boys spring back to their feet and into formation and we march on, with a cloud of smoke obscuring my view.

Fighting clangs out behind, shouts of struggle.

"Turn!" Samantha yells.

A helmeted boy with an axe is almost on me. He swings it down hard.

My shield meets the blow, the force shooting into my arm as vibrating pain. I stagger back, but Omaki grabs me and keeps me up. The boy leaps high, axe coming down at my bare head, when Omaki's spear takes him in the throat. He falls on me in a heap.

I try to rise but take a foot to the head. Instinct makes me curl, fetal, hands over head. Footsteps thud around me. Glancing through the struggle, I see our troop has split. Jade leads most of Black's fighters to hold off Blue's assault. Closer to me, Napoleon holds back two red warriors. Fire singes his shirt. He screams, unable to run. Samantha stands behind him and her black smoke snuffs the fires.

The flames come again. Dark wisps pour out of Samantha like ink from an octopus. But blades slice through it, unaffected by the power. Now there are four helmeted boys from Red against Napoleon. They wear collars. But where are the girls they're paired with?

All around us, even through the dark smoke, I glimpse thousands of delicate, tantalizing blue ribbons. They have been out of reach, but now they are close. The cloud has somehow lifted from my mind. Samantha's block is gone.

My gaze swings to her and I see why. One of the Red boys has grabbed Samantha, blade at her throat. The dark shard is only inches behind them. So she's distracted. Her green eyes are furious and afraid.

"I'll kill her," the boy says.

I know him. It's Marcus, the boy who was my friend in Red, who once fought in the Roman Coliseum.

Napoleon goes still. His spear lowers to his side, parallel to the ground. The other two from Red look ready to attack. Two more of my friends, Jafari and Khan.

Samantha meets Napoleon's eyes and mouths the word, *Now*.

She leaps back, toward the shard, just as Napoleon leaps for her. It's the last thing Marcus expects. The three of them plunge into the darkness. Their shadowy forms fall like rocks dropped into a well.

I weave the threads without thought, grabbing them and lifting and setting them on their feet at the edge of the shard. It must lead to the pit. Not even Samantha deserves that.

Marcus looks at me in shock. "Cipher?"

Smoke spills out of Samantha, severing the threads that hold her. She steps away from the shard, toward me. "Knock them in," she commands.

Napoleon turns and in one smooth motion kicks Marcus in the chest so hard that he flies backward into the pit. I weave threads to save him, but Samantha's smoke forms a wall between us. His screams echo as he goes down.

"The others, too," Samantha says, glaring at me. "I'll even let you use your power. Throw the other Red boys in." When I don't react, too stunned to speak, she adds, "It's you or them."

I shake my head, barely controlling my anger, my fear.

"You don't know what it's like down there."

"Oh, I know," she says. "The pit's master showed me what you saw. And he has shown me the way to stop all this. He requires more in the pit, so more we will send. Throw them in."

It's a lie. It has to be. But Samantha has given me an opening. I glance at the two other boys from Red, thinking fast. I wrap them in threads of air and lift them.

"No, Cipher, please…" Jafari's familiar face pleads to me from his helmet. Khan looks frantic beside him. They will understand soon enough.

"Good, good," Samantha says to me.

Just as the boys float to the edge of the shard, I whip them back and fling them at Samantha. But the threads suddenly fail. Jafari and Khan slide along the ground and stop helplessly at Samantha's feet. Her black smoke consumes the blue ribbons like a whale swallowing a ton of krill. And now the smoke surrounds me—not inside, like before, but suffocating all the same.

"Boys of Black!" Samantha looks past me. "Knock them in."

Metal clangs as others from Black rush past. Napoleon forms them into a wall of shields. They advance like a scraper across the gray stone, trapping Jafari and Khan. The two Red warriors, my old friends, rise to attack, but the phalanx is too strong, too relentless. I watch helplessly as Jafari and Khan are pushed over the edge and fall into the shard's black hole. Their collars blur silver as they fall.

Around the Scouring bodies are littered from the fight. Not everyone. Some from the other towers must have made a capture and gotten out, but at least ten did not. Five from Blue, three from Green—in addition to the ones from Red. I see no one from Yellow. Did they even enter the Scouring?

"Clean up time," Samantha says. "Go in pairs. Paul, I'll be watching you."

She stands with her arms crossed by the edge of the shard, as if guarding it, while the boys start collecting bodies. In the distance Jade stands by the Black Tower's gate. Her robed stillness only worsens my despair. She hasn't tried to help.

Napoleon comes to my side and tells me to stay close, spear ready in case someone is only pretending to be dead. He leads toward Green. We come to a small, motionless girl. Her blonde hair against the gray stone makes my heart clench. Napoleon barely pauses as he scoops her up and slings her body over his shoulder. I glimpse her pale face. It's not Emma.

"You get one of those," he says, eyeing two other bodies beside each other.

I go to them and see a familiar face. Apple. She paired with me in Red. She became a friend, even when we found each other again in Green. I scoop her up. I follow Napoleon back toward the shard, thinking of a plan.

Two other boys drop two bodies in and turn away. "Only one more on that side," they say to Samantha as they pass.

Napoleon drops the girl like a bag of trash into the hole. He looks to me. Samantha is watching. Her smoke no longer surrounds me, but she will be ready.

I stand there, sick with myself for obeying this far, and knowing that if I don't stop now it could keep on going and going. The plan is worth a try. Maybe it's useless, maybe it's stupid, but I'd rather be both of those things than colorless.

I kneel and lay Apple's body gently on the ground, several feet away from the shard.

"What are you—?" Samantha begins.

I'm already summoning my every ounce of power I've got. Her smoke floods toward me. But I had a head start.

Apple's small body soars toward the Green Tower. It takes a heartbeat, maybe two. I lower her gently over the wall. Then the smoke severs my weaves.

Samantha storms toward me, fuming. "Have you learned *nothing*?"

She has smothered my power again. I have nowhere to run. The hole looms just behind me.

The other boys from Black stare wide-eyed at me. They saw what I did. This could be my chance to spark defiance.

"You can't do this!" I shout at her. "It's evil! The hole leads to the pit. And down there—"

"*Enough!*" Samantha moves so fast, so unexpectedly, that I can't react. She shoves me in the chest. I stagger back into the shard. My heel finds no ground. I grab for her but she stays back. Her green eyes watch coldly as I fall.

The hole pulls me down me like a nightmare.

16

THE GREEN AND red lights of the machine give the hospital room an eerie glow. I watch the lines of my heartbeat. Up and down in long intervals. It's slow, weak. I've lost track of how many days I've been in this hospital bed. The rough sheets don't bother me anymore. The medicine dulls the pain, the visitors dull the loneliness, but nothing dulls the dim march of cancer through my body.

I sit up in agony. *To be or not to be, that is the question.*

The tube into my arm. The circuit in my brain. These are the only things prolonging the suffering. I could pull the plug. Two or three quick motions and I would sink underwater. First my lungs would struggle. They are so weak. They'd fight for air and lose. Then my heart would placidly pump hollow blood, without oxygen. My brain would go last. That would be the worst. Even after everything I've learned, it could not survive without this body. No transplant, not even of mice, has worked. All my research and experiments have only enhanced neurons. They have moved me closer to machine, but I was always machine, trapped in this body. My brain has been a slave of my body. I want to be free.

Choose this day whom you will serve, that is the question.

The words flash into my mind. I look around the dark

room. I am still alone. Who I serve? I serve myself.

"Daddy."

I jump back, as much as I can with my tubes and wires. A boy stands by my bed. It's Benjamin. His wide eyes study me innocently. But he's dead.

"How did you get here?" I demand.

"Someone sent me. That's not important. I see what you are thinking." His gaze falls to my right arm, where my left hand has gripped the tube going into my veins. "It is a very selfish thing to think."

"Leave me alone." It comes out as a terrified whimper.

"Mom is outside. She has never left you alone."

I glance to the door. Susan is sitting outside. Her vigil has been tireless. This must be a dream. "I know. She's a good woman."

"She's more than that." Benjamin puts his small, pale hand over mine. It doesn't feel like a dream. "Daddy, you don't have much time. Do you know where you are going?"

My heart hardens. "To the grave, son, just like you."

"No." He shakes his head somberly. "It is somewhere far worse. But you still have a little time. It is enough. It is your choice."

"The universe put me here," I say.

"The universe was created. It does nothing of its own."

"What do you want from me?"

"Love, Daddy."

"You know I love you. Look at what I've done for you."

"You were not there for me." His lower lip quivers. He looks down. "You can't make up for that."

My heart softens. "Then what can I do?"

"Let go, Daddy."

"Of what? I have nothing left. I'm dying."

He puts his hand to my heart. It is so small against my chest. "This can do everything," he says.

"The heart is only a muscle. It pumps blood, until it stops."

"There's more than a muscle in here. There's a soul."

"Sounds nice." I sigh. "Hasn't helped me much."

"Your mind keeps getting in its way."

"My mind is the only thing keeping me alive."

Benjamin's brow furrows. He looks angry, and frightening. "There is the lie. You must uproot it." He presses his finger to my forehead. "Unplug your technology."

"Then I would certainly die. Are you a ghost or a demon?"

"I am a gift to you. Maybe your last one. Let go, Daddy, please let go. Get out of your own way. Look to Mommy, look to me. Get outside of yourself and repent and beg for mercy."

"I've never had to beg."

"I know." His puppy-dog eyes are moist. "It's time you tried. Unplug and repent."

"Maybe, I'll think about it."

His small hand lifts. He drifts backward. "Don't think. Love."

"Wait. Where are you going?"

His form fades into the dark corner of the room. I suddenly feel more afraid, and more alone, than ever.

My hand moves to the wire connecting my mind to the machine. One quick yank and…

17

THE BRIGHTEST LIGHT. I can barely open my eyes. There are voices nearby, whispering. There's a smell. Fresh. Warm. Bread. My stomach rumbles.

"He's coming to," whispers a girl.

"Just in time," says another.

An open window lets in the brilliant light, shadowing the two figures beside me. The hospital room was a memory—the distant past on Earth. The memory feels twisted, like a knot in my mind. I couldn't have pulled the plug.

I'm in the Five Towers. I'm alive.

One of the shadowed figures kneels close, and the way she touches my hand, lingering on the scar, sends familiar warmth into me. My heart nearly explodes in joy.

"Emma!"

"You remember!" She laughs lightly. The sunlight makes her hair more golden than ever. "We were worried. You were hurt badly. I healed your body, but it looked doubtful your memories would survive. You landed quite hard."

"Not so good for memories," says the other girl. Her face is still shadowed, but I recognize her silky strong voice and long dark hair. It's Joan, the girl who was queen before

Emma, and who helped us take over the Yellow Tower.

I rub my head. It feels fine. Other than being sleepy and hungry, I seem perfectly well. Samantha knocked me into the pit. The vision came in midair. I must have landed on the pile of bones, but somehow I got out.

"How did I make it here?" I ask.

"Ever since you went to Black," Emma says, "the leaders have stood guard by the entrance to the pit. They look out for you or for any threats or for any bodies that fall. It is too dangerous, even for them, to stay in the pit long. That means some who fall are lost, only to awaken with the Colorless One's tainted memories. This time the guard was Joshua. He saw the bodies falling and managed to rush in and save several. He brought them to their proper towers. He brought you here."

"And Emma healed you," Joan adds. "It was the most impressive healing I've ever seen. You were barely alive. If you'd died, we hoped you'd wake up in Yellow, but we weren't sure."

"I could not take that chance," Emma says.

"So she sapped herself of nearly her own life," Joan replies. "She's quite a friend. She slept for two days to recover. You've been out for three."

"Three days!" I say.

"Yes, but I knew you would be okay." Emma squeezes my hand. "I could tell you were close to waking. You talked in your sleep."

"About what?"

"I didn't understand it all. You spoke of collars and brain enhancements."

"Weird. Mixing the past with this place."

"What happened in Black?" Emma asks softly.

Where to start…the coffin, the troops, Samantha? I struggle for words. "It's bad," I say. "It didn't go well."

Joan lets out a laugh. "We figured that much."

"Is it infected?" Emma asks. "Like Yellow was?"

"It's worse. There's nothing but fighting, a constant battle for power. Boys fall like flies and wake up wiped, in coffins beneath the tower. They have to kill to get out, where they join troops and kill even more." I shudder, remembering how my spear stabbed into Karl, admitting to myself I became no better than the rest of them. "It's the only way to rise. I led a troop. We fought and…killed. I had no other choice. I couldn't use my power. There's a Council of twelve, led by girls. They control everything. One of them, Samantha, knew me on Earth. She hates me. Her smoke was in my mind, totally shutting down my power. But I still managed to rise in the ranks. I came close to becoming a Commander, maybe to changing things, but I…failed."

"You did your best." Emma's hand touches my cheek tenderly. "If you could not change it, no one could. The taint sounds very dark indeed. Do you know how the Colorless One has done this?"

The true enemy. My focus sharpens. "I have some ideas. He might have locked up the missing leader at the top of the tower. Or the memory device, a crown, could be corrupted to show only bad memories. He might be manipulating and twisting the Council this way. I was so close to finding out more. Whatever it is, I have to stop it."

"Not alone," Emma says. "*We* will find a way. But first, you must be hungry."

"Starving." Encouraged by her words, I swing my legs out of the bed. "Is Seymour still a chef here? It smells amazing."

"Yes, the head chef now." Emma grins. "He cooked a feast for you."

We leave the room and follow the smells down the stairs of a turret and to the courtyard. Tables have been set up. They cover the grid pattern of the courtyard, with its squares indicating the initials of each tenant of Yellow's plots. A platform has been built along the wall between the Yellow Tower and the Scouring. It blocks the gateway. Bright yellow banners hang on either side of the gate, hiding the tally of each tower's numbers.

The people stand as we enter. Emma glides forward in her yellow dress, wearing a regal smile. Joan looks serene. We approach a table in the center, just before the platform.

Many familiar faces await us. Emma's son from Earth, Oliver, rises to greet us first. He has her same blue eyes and flaxen hair. He had mastered survival in Green and once saved me there, but he looks like he belongs in Yellow.

"Old chap," he says, embracing me. "Jolly good to see you."

"Same for you." I glance at his hand. No tribal mark. "Had enough of Green's Snakes, I see?"

"Oh indeed. Much as I miss skulking through the swamps and dining on reeds and pythons, the smell of this food summoned me here." He smiles brightly toward Emma. "Not to mention my Mum."

She beams back. "We have traded several with Green. "It has been most useful."

"Our family has had much to scour," says another boy. It's Neville, who competed with me for a golden coin. "You might say we have polished away a deep tarnish of fear and found a luster of courage. Even for me."

"For all of us." Emma's father from Earth, William, steps toward me. My first reaction is to wince. He was the boy-king who ruled the tower before. The Colorless One had corrupted him. But he was healed. Now he smiles warmly as he greets me.

"Cipher, I have heard so much about you," he says.

I shake his hand. "Likewise. I trust you serve your daughter and the Yellow Tower well?"

"Better than ever!" he says.

"We all serve the Healer," Emma says. "Now, let us sit and enjoy the performance."

A group emerges with steaming trays of food. I spot Seymour among them. His freckled face looks buoyant as ever. He bounds toward us and sets a tray down at the center of our table. He comes to me and sweeps me up in a friendly embrace.

"You're alive!" he says. "How was Black?"

"Pretty bad. I missed your cooking."

"Oh, you can't imagine how much better it's gotten." He glances to Emma with a wide smile. "The queen here, she let the serfs in the field go without collars. They've gotten much, much better at growing their crops. We still have our nine grains, but now there's so much more. Li Min has the best vegetable garden. Sally and Camille have teamed up to raise a herd of goats. Don't look at me like that! This is no goat meat. This is steak! But the goats provide the best cheese. In this dish it's paired with the figs. Simeon planted an orchard with figs and apples and…well, what are you waiting for? Try it!"

I study the spread of food. "What first?"

"This one!" Seymour says, pointing to a cracker with a thin cut of red meat, a crumble of white cheese, and a drizzle of dark sauce.

I take a bite, chewing awkwardly as he studies my face for a reaction. It's delicious. I smile approvingly.

"See! Please, enjoy it. I'm sure you're hungry after all you've been through. Now I must get to serving the others. Come visit the kitchen sometime!"

He moves away with a bounce to his waddling step. We take our seats and turn to the food in earnest. I eat until my stomach says it can handle no more.

Midway through the feast, a boy goes to the platform. He wears an amused grin and a hat adorned with a large feather.

"Tonight," he announces, "in honor of our special guest, the queen has requested a performance of *Hamlet.*"

He bows dramatically and glides off the stage. Another boy takes his place, then another steps onto stage. The whole courtyard goes quiet, attentive as the two actors begin a lively banter. The play's unfolding scenes tickle at my memory.

I lean close to Emma. "Why a play? And why *Hamlet?*"

"It was always a favorite," she says softly. "And I think it speaks to where we are. Look, this is the ghost of his father."

On stage, the actor playing Hamlet speaks to another, the ghost, wearing tattered clothes dusted to be pale grayish white.

The ghost croons: "*I am thy father's spirit.*
Doom'd for a certain term to walk the night,
And for the day confined to fast in fires,
Till the foul crimes done in my days of nature
Are burnt and purged away. But that I am forbid
To tell the secrets of my prison house,

The ghost continues his monologue, and gives Hamlet the task of revenge. The play reaches its climactic duel, weaving revenge and remorse and culminating in tragedy. As so many stories on Earth ended.

When it is finished, and the actors have bowed, Emma rises to join them on stage. They stand behind her, resolute as soldiers.

"Remember why we perform!" Emma's voice carries over the courtyard. "We recall the past to be grateful for the present, and hopeful for what is to come. Now, sleep and dream of your own stories. Whatever stains you have will be burnt and purged away. The light beckons, if only we press onward and upward."

The crowd applauds again.

The actors and Emma disperse from the stage. She joins our group at the table, and we depart from the courtyard.

Seymour stops me as I leave. He presses something into my hand. "The nights can be long and cold here. If you wake in a fit, have this. I never go to bed without one."

I look down at the delicately wrapped item in my hand.

"It's chocolate," he says, his voice lowering to a whisper. "Don't you worry about how I get the ingredients…a chef's little secret." He steps back and beams as he announces: "It keeps the ghosts away!"

18

EMMA AND I enter the Yellow Tower's throne room. It has been rebuilt in the same grand scale. Candles glow in the center of the room, but their light hardly reaches the top of the room. The night is dark outside the ceiling of glass.

"Stay there," Emma says to Joan and three other guards, who stop at the doorway. "And please, allow no interruptions."

"Yes, of course," Joan says.

Emma strides to the throne at the center of the long table that divides the room. She motions for me to sit beside her. It's the first moment we've had to talk without others nearby.

"I like what you've done with the place," I say. "But why put on a play like that?"

She raises an eyebrow. "Were you not entertained?"

"Oh, it was good. The food, the show, all of it. The words never had such meaning for me on Earth. But you know what's really going on in the Five Towers."

Emma smiles patiently. "It takes great courage to seek beauty in the face of darkness."

"But it won't defeat the darkness," I say.

"If we do not have beauty, is the darkness worth

defeating?"

"Okay, but we can't ignore the danger. You seem to be hiding in Yellow—even distracting people. Wouldn't it be better to prepare them?"

"For what?" she asks.

"To fight! The Colorless One blocks the White Tower. He stains Black, and they are throwing people into the pit. I didn't even see anyone from Yellow in the Scouring…"

"We stopped going."

"*How?*" I do not hide my surprise. "The leaders allow this?"

"It was their idea."

"Really? Where are they?"

"Protecting us." Her gaze swings to the floor. "They are beneath the tower, in the tunnels."

"How do they protect you?"

"A lot has changed since you left," Emma says. "I told Elijah and the Widow about what we had done in Green—winning over the tribes by freeing everyone and sending the collars back to the Green Tower. I asked them what would happen if the collars in all the towers were gone. They agreed that I could try it in Yellow. We gathered up the collars. Elijah confirmed what we learned in Green—the collars cannot be destroyed. So we locked them away, underground and out of reach. It's never been right, forcing people to be servants and spying on their feelings. And it's much safer without going into the Scouring. The walls protect us in Yellow."

I agree with her, but something still seems off. This is Emma. She's as brave as they come. She gave up wealth and nobility in England to marry a man she loved. She worked and stole to survive. She repented, then faced execution with dignity. Fear served its purpose. She's been a lioness at my side every step of the way through these towers. She's earned my trust. But now she hides behind walls?

I choose my words carefully. "How does Yellow work without its plots of land, and the trading for nine grains?" I can hardly imagine Red without the pairing, or Blue without the servants. "There is an order to this place. Abram said that all of these things work for our scouring. We have to be scoured before we can leave, right, so what if the collars are necessary for that? And the Scouring battle, too?"

"Maybe they *were* necessary, but things have changed," she says. "The White Tower has gone black. No one is leaving now. We have to try something different. We have to unite if we are going to fight against the Colorless One. The leaders told us we have to use our powers together. Only the brightest light will be enough to defeat the Colorless One."

"So this is why you stopped going to the Scouring?"

"It is part of it. Listen, Cipher, you cannot let Black's way of thinking twist you. Not everything can be solved by a fight."

Her words sting with truth. I can't approach this problem like Napoleon. We can't just conquer the enemy.

"Okay, then what should we do?"

She smiles. "Come, we will talk to Elijah and the Widow. They will tell you more."

She doesn't wait for me to answer. Sliding off the throne, she crouches under the large table. I join her, feeling as childish as I look. She places her scarred hand on a stone with a dazzling sun carved into it. Her eyes close, concentrating in the usual way when she uses her power. The sun glows slightly, then sinks and reveals a staircase going down.

She descends the first few steps, then looks back at me. "What are you waiting for?"

I hesitate. "Your father, when he was king, had a secret path down to the tunnels…to the Colorless One…"

"This is different," she says. "The leaders are protecting the way. My father had locked them up."

I don't like it, but I trust Emma. She leads the long descent through the spiral staircase. A few candles along the wall provide the only light. They are spread so far that it becomes nearly dark before we reach the faint light of the next candle.

When we finally reach the bottom, it feels like we've entered another world. It smells musty as a cellar. The stone floor extends to darkness in both directions. I have not missed these tunnels.

Thankfully, Emma does not go far before we see Yellow's two leaders. They shuffle toward us like an elderly couple out for a stroll. Each of them holds a candle. They wear yellow robes and weary smiles.

"It is good to see you well," the Widow says.

"Thanks to Joshua, Emma, and the Healer," Elijah adds. "And I see your mind is intact."

"Yes, it was close," Emma says, smiling at me. "Your questions?"

I study Elijah and the Widow. "Why have you stopped Yellow from entering the Scouring?"

"It is corrupted," Elijah says. "You should know that better than anyone, having seen the dark shard. Who threw you into it?"

"Black," I say. "And Samantha."

"Most wretched," the Widow says. "The Colorless One uses Black to throw the defeated in the pit. We believe they target those who wear collars."

I remember my friends from Red who were thrown in. They wore collars. "Why target them?" I ask.

The Widow and Elijah exchange a glance. "We do not know for sure," Elijah says. "The enemy may plan some vile way to use the links, to twist their purpose."

A shiver runs down my spine. The collars are bad enough outside the pit.

"What about the people who fall?" I ask.

"Many are wiped and awaken in another tower, without a collar," Elijah says. "Even those who are not wiped are infected by false memories that bring despair. The enemy seeks to stop all progress. To hold you here forever."

False memories. Despair. As I fell I saw myself in a hospital bed, with my son Benjamin at my side. But he was not alive then. He couldn't have been. I hope it didn't happen like that.

"How do you know the memories are false?" I ask.

"We restore those we can," Elijah says. "When they fall, some can be caught and brought out. Joshua risks everything for this. We try to help them remember the truth. It takes much time. They need to see more of their true past. They need friends or family who are here to confirm it. False memories are the hardest to purge. Stained minds are prone to distorting the past."

"How can we stop this?" I ask.

"That was my question, too," Emma says, looking from me to the leaders. "The answer is the same, I assume. We must keep fighting for equilibrium and overthrow the powers in Black."

"But how?" I meet Elijah's calm eyes. "Is there really a leader there? The Council controls everything. I tried to rise through their system. To find the leader. I failed."

Elijah clasps my shoulder. "Even we do not know about the leader. You were brave to try."

My gaze drops. My hands slip into my pockets and find something—the chocolate from Seymour. *A chef's little secret*, he said. I wonder if he traded with other towers for the ingredients. It gives me an idea.

"Maybe next time I shouldn't go alone," I say.

"Hm, yes." Elijah strokes his spindly white beard. "Separating people has long been the Colorless One's tactic. Though he might prevail against one who is alone, two will withstand him. And a threefold cord is not quickly broken."

"So this time I'll go with others," I say. "I'll lead an army, the same way we took over the Yellow Tower. We'll attack by surprise from the coast."

"You know a way in?" Emma sounds excited.

"I think so. With my powers, and a little help, we could sail to the shore and soar over the cliffs. Like we did when we escaped from Black to Red. You remember?"

She grins slightly. "We barely made it."

"I know. This should be easier. They won't see us coming, and the mountains of Red are not as friendly as Blue's ocean."

"Blue might not be so friendly," Elijah says. "Without Abram, Sarai cannot keep all the darkness out."

"What do you mean, *without Abram?*" I ask.

"We do not know, not exactly," the Widow says. "He has not been seen in the Blue Tower since you left for

Black. And yet, I still sense his presence here. He will hold back the Colorless One as long as he can."

Elijah sighs. "Do not fear for Abram. He will do what he has always done—pray and obey. But no longer from the Blue Tower, it seems."

I rub my temples, grappling with their words. Blue without Abram would be like a body without a brain. But if the cryptic leaders can maintain their steady confidence, I will try to do the same. We have to find a way.

"So what if we sailed around Blue?" I say.

Emma smiles. "We have done it before."

"But not again," the Widow says to Emma. "*You* cannot leave."

"Why not?" Emma and I ask at the same time.

"The risk is too great," Elijah says. "Black already has two marked ones. If you were both captured, they would have four. I fear we might pass a point of no return."

"Which two marked ones?" I ask, suddenly remembering what some boys in Black said before the Scouring, about a powerful new girl with gold flecks in her eyes. "Baron and Kiyo?"

"Aye, and only she belongs," Elijah says.

"Purple needs Kiyo, as Yellow needs you," the Widow says to Emma. "The boys and girls here trust you. Their collars are gone. They are very close to equilibrium, with only a few to spare. Perhaps Cipher could take two companions. We must preserve what we have already won."

"But Cipher needs me more." Emma crosses her arms defiantly across her chest. "We must fight together against the Colorless One."

"Yes, you must," Elijah says. "But only when all are

united. You two are no match for the Colorless One."

The leader is right. I've felt the Colorless One's power, twisting my past. But even if Emma can't join me, I need more than two extra people to defeat the Black Tower.

"So let me take an army," I say. "Anyone who fights with me can return. I need as much help as I can get."

"Wise words," Elijah replies. "Yet a few loyal friends can be stronger than any army."

"A *few?*" I shake my head. "Black has dozens. All armed."

"You will not defeat Black by force alone," Elijah says. "The Colorless One wins when he fights on his own terms."

"Better to approach undetected," the Widow suggests. "Find Kiyo and work together, from the inside. Not everyone in Black stays locked in the tower, eh?"

"Most of the soldiers are in tents outside," I say. "Others are out in the hills, farming rice. They're all under the tower's control."

"But some have swords!" Emma says. "Remember when we were in Red and snuck into one of Black's villages? Max was its lord. He had a sword."

"Yes. And he was loyal to the tower."

"He was *afraid* of the tower. So were the girls in the villages, treated like slaves." Excitement fills Emma's voice. "With them, and with Kiyo, you could start a rebellion! Like we did in Yellow!"

"I like the idea," I say. "But there's a problem. The girls in Black still have the smoke. They'll shut down our powers."

"If you find Kiyo and get others on your side, it will be black against black. And Kiyo is a marked one. You know how powerful she is."

"Maybe it's worth a try." I look to the leaders. "What do you think? Can I convince others in Black to join us?"

"Aye, but not by force," Elijah says.

The Widow nods in agreement. "Light and love never appear as threats, yet their power always prevails over force. Power is made perfect in weakness."

"It risks too much, with little gain, to take an army from Yellow," Elijah adds. "But gathering help within Black, this is possible. Many in Black are where they belong."

"How do you know that?" I ask.

"We leaders have long orchestrated the towers' movements, and they are close to equilibrium—one hundred forty-four each. Scoured. Pure. Five colors fusing into white. The marked ones must lead *whole* towers. I believe the process would be complete if not for the Colorless One's dark meddling. His powers have only grown since you arrived, Cipher."

Elijah's words echo Abram's from long ago. "So the towers are close?" I ask.

"Only a few boys and girls still need to find their proper towers." The Widow speaks with a grandmother's tender care.

"How did you orchestrate all this?" I ask.

"Each tower had its way," Elijah says. "You are of Genius. It can be deduced."

"Through the Scouring…" I think of how each tower chose its teams. The classes in Blue, the pairing in Red, the tribes in Green, the hierarchy in Yellow, and the battles in Black. They all made us shuffle and move, putting new people into the Scouring. It explains a lot, but not everything. "The leaders never had control over the fight," I say. "So how could you control who was captured in the Scouring?"

"Why did you capture Emma?" Elijah asks.

"Abram assigned her to me."

"Ah, and why did you catch who you did in Red?"

"Many were from Black."

"Red stands close to Black for a reason."

"We just captured whoever happened to fight for Black…"

"I did not say the process was perfect." Elijah gazes down at his flickering candle. "Believe me, this place is far from perfect. But it is a process that works, long and slow, like—let's see, how would Blue put it—like sand tumbled smooth, wave after wave after wave. And now the end of the process nears. We will hold back the darkness as long as we can. You must finish our work of equilibrium. Then the light may shine purely."

His words give me hope. The towers are close to one hundred forty-four each. It's getting each person to the *right* tower that seems impossible. "How do we know who belongs in which tower?" I ask. "Why does it matter?"

"Each tower is part of a single body," the Widow says. The parts must work together, as designed. The brain needs the heart, the feet, the hands. It would do no good to have part of the brain in your hand. Each part must be in its proper place. Emma, you belong here. Cipher, in Blue."

"And yet I have to sail to Black?" I ask.

"Aye, with help," Elijah says.

"Very well," Emma says. "I will go with Cipher and return."

"No, you will stay." The Widow looks to me. "But

surely you can find others who need to visit Black's land."

"Who?" The question fires out of Emma's lips with a twinge of frustration. Even jealousy.

"A few here in Yellow have been scoured of their fear," the Widow explains, "but they have other stains needing the unique scouring of the Purple Tower."

"Ah, yes. You think they will agree to this?" Elijah asks.

"We shall find out." The Widow places her wrinkled hand on my cheek. "Choose two companions, and choose wisely. Seek those who have a soldier's heart."

19

THE KITCHEN BUSTLES at dawn. It smells of bread and fried eggs. Seymour stands at the center of the action. He is so focused on his work that he doesn't notice me as I approach. A tray is on the table before him. There are a dozen or more identical stacks—bread on the bottom, an egg on top of it. Seymour leans over them with a pot and a spoon. He delicately uses the spoon to drizzle a creamy yellow sauce over each stack, then he places a sprig of something green above it all. When he finishes the last one, he steps back and admires his work.

"Ready for delivery!" he calls out. "Next!"

A boy rushes up and takes the tray to another table, where a stack of plates waits. Moments later a girl comes to Seymour with another tray full of identical stacks of bread and egg.

He studies the tray, then turns to the girl. "Not bad," he says. "These two are not centered, and this one's yolk is cooked too firm. But hey, nine for twelve on day one! You have potential!"

The girl's cheeks go pink as she moves the three offending stacks to a separate plate. She turns to go, but Seymour stops her. "Wait, this one that wasn't centered, it needs a tasting." With a smile she holds the plate out to

117

him and he places one of the stacks on his hand. He spoons some of the creamy sauce on top and takes a large bite. "Mmm, yum." He nods with a grin and the girl rushes away. Seymour chews as he continues his careful drizzling work, then sends off the tray and calls for another one.

I watch all this in a sleepy daze, wondering how I'm going to find a soldier's heart. Something about the chocolate from Seymour beckoned me to see him again. I move to his side.

"Quite an operation you have here," I say.

"Cipher!" Seymour wipes crumbs from his lips. "You're up early. Oh dear, we just sent a delivery to your room. It may grow cold. You'll have to eat here. You will, right?"

"Yes, of course, sorry."

"Oh nothing to worry about," he says. "We chefs rise before the suns. Gotta make sure everyone is well fed, eh? Memory is like the stomach of the mind."

"What's that supposed to mean?" I ask.

"Think about the feelings you once felt. Gladness, sadness, fear. They are like sweet and bitter food. You tasted them when you lived—they were on your tongue— but now those feelings are only in your memory, as if transferred to your stomach, where they cannot be tasted any longer."

It's classic Seymour. I smile. "That's kind of ridiculous."

"Got a better way to describe memory?"

"Well...no."

"Stomach of the mind it is! This breakfast is Emma's favorite. I call it Eggs Benedict. Heard of it?"

"Yeah, the name survived until my time."

"As it should! A dish fit for a king. If only we had ham. Hard to get to Red from here."

"That's one of the reasons I wanted to talk to you," I say.

"You want to go to Red?"

"No," I say with a laugh. "But I was wondering how you got the chocolate."

"Always the curious one!" Seymour says. "Well, here in the safety of my kitchen, I'll tell you. In Yellow it gets too cold at night for cacao beans to grow." He steps closer to me and lowers his voice. "So I set up a little trading post beside Green, right by the wall. We use ropes, lower bread in a basket, and they send back cacao. I use that for the chocolate, then sprinkle on a little sea salt from Blue."

It's creative. Even impressive. Seymour bends the towers' rules for food. "How do you get the salt from Blue?"

Seymour glances around furtively. He draws closer to me and lowers his voice. "I found a boat."

"Where?"

"There's a cave hidden underneath one of the huts. Max told me about it. He does the trading for me."

Max. I should visit him. "Does Emma know?"

He shrugs. "We haven't talked about it."

A boy approaches with another tray full of stacked bread and eggs. He waits eagerly by Seymour's side. Seymour turns and dutifully studies the delivery.

"Yes!" he says. "Egg-celent work, Vincent. Get it?"

"I get it," Vincent says dryly. "But do not make light of an artist's work."

"Oh, don't be so serious. I was just having a bit of fun. You're a chef now, remember?"

"I do the work that I must." Vincent spins away and strides out of the kitchen with his tray.

Seymour turns to me with a nervous grin. "He's a moody one, always intense, but what a chef! If only he'd stop wanting to paint every dish. What he really wants is to do the drizzle, like me. But you have to work up to that, you know?"

"I guess so," I say, half-listening. My mind has already moved to wondering about whether Vincent has a soldier's heart. I know he was a famous painter, van Gogh, but there could be more to him than I recall of history.

"Well, sorry Cipher," Seymour says. "But I can't let this batch get cold. Here, take this one, and come by later to try our newest treat."

"You got it," I say. "Thank you, Seymour. This has been helpful."

"Hey, helpful and delicious. That's my goal." He bows playfully. "Always at your service."

Outside the kitchen the Yellow Tower has come to life. Servants bustle about—managers with tasks to assign, things to deliver by dog or cat or goat or whatever animals are roaming around. I spot Vincent crossing the courtyard.

I catch up and fall into stride as he strolls into one of the turrets. "Hey, Vincent. Mind if I ask you something?"

"Fine." He does not slow down. He focuses on holding his tray steady as he begins to climb a spiral staircase.

"On Earth, were you ever a soldier by chance?"

He pauses on the steps. "Look out this window."

The window is a narrow slit. I peer out and see the light of the three rising suns spreading across the Scouring and the Red Tower and its mountains in the distance. I turn back to him. "It's a nice view. What am I looking for?"

"See how the red spreads over the dark surface?"

"Yes?"

"It is like oil paint over my canvas, like blood over the wood floor. I know what this means. This blood is life. It is spilling out of me."

"I don't understand," I say.

"I was wounded, but the battles were in my mind." His voice is dramatic and dark. "I remember a nurse beside me, checking my pulse. It all hurt so bad and I gave into the hurt and never hoped it could be healed. But I survived another day. I begged for forgiveness through lips that would not part. The nurse said, *You're awake!* She rushed out and returned with my brother. Later another man came and said I could have forgiveness." Vincent glances down at my hand. "Around his neck he wore a symbol shaped like your scars. I told him I wanted beauty. He said beauty awaited that was beyond my imagination. Then I woke up here. A little beauty, sure. But I'll admit, when I was poised over a blank canvas, I always expected more. Instead I'm serving someone's breakfast."

He turns from me and climbs the stairs.

"Hey, wait," I call after him. "Thanks for sharing that...does this mean you weren't ever a soldier?"

He laughs. "A true artist can never be a soldier."

20

THE HORSE, SERENITY, nuzzles my hand fondly. She remembers me. Her big chestnut eyes gaze into mine. Lucky animals. They don't have to fight in the Scouring or infiltrate the Black Tower or face the Colorless One. But then, they probably don't have memories to unlock either. Lucky me.

I ride off across Yellow's golden fields, toward Max's hut. I think of Emma. We said goodbye, knowing—or hoping—we'll see each other again. Surely we will. We're marked ones. No one leaves until we find a way out.

Yet more than ever it feels like a burden. Going back to Black. Finding a way out. Holding onto hope. As we parted, Emma said to me: "You have some quality, Cipher. You give us hope." She sounded so sincere. I don't understand it. How can I give others hope when it's so dim inside me? I'm one of the smallest boys here. And as Dr. Fitzroy, I was selfish and arrogant—one of the worst on Earth to even make it here. It all makes me uncertain, not hopeful. I failed in Black. Samantha shoved me into the pit. I might still be stuck there, tormented, if not for Joshua saving me. Where is Black's leader? Where is Abram?

Horse hooves clap behind me. Hair stands on the back of my neck. Someone follows.

I don't turn. I listen. It's a single rider on horseback. Far enough away to not draw my attention. But there aren't many riders in this place...

I veer slightly to the right, ride a bit further, and glance back. The rider has veered after me—not drawing any closer, but following at a steady distance.

The Yellow Tower should be safe now. Why would anyone trail me? Better to confront this head on.

I turn back and bring Serenity to a gallop.

The rider stops and watches me approach. Her form comes into focus. Long black hair, straight posture, like a natural on horseback.

I call out to her, "Joan?"

She salutes as I ride closer. "Hey Cipher. Nice day for a ride."

"It's usually nice in Yellow. Much better than Black."

Her wide-set hawk eyes study me. "I hear you're going back there."

"That's right. Duty calls."

"As duty tends to," she says.

"Were you following me?"

"Emma told me you were searching for someone with a soldier's heart. Someone to go with you to Black."

"So she sent you to keep an eye on me?"

"No, that was my decision."

"Why?" I ask, even as I sense the answer in her rigid demeanor. She's been a guard in Yellow for a long time. She led the charge when we defeated the boy-king, Emma's father. If anyone here has a soldier's heart, it's her.

"I want to find out who you are riding to meet," she says, her gaze tilting down. "You could have come for me first."

"I see that now," I say. "But would you really leave this gentle land for Black? You could be wiped, or worse."

Her stoic expression allows a grin to peek through. "I've faced the worst the world could muster. When duty calls…"

"Ride with me?" I invite.

Our horses fall into a gentle canter beside each other. I ask Joan about her past and her soldier's heart. She tells me she lived in France in medieval times. She talks of her modest childhood. She was a faithful girl. She saw visions, even angels. They told her to raise her banner and join the battle to save her country from English domination. Though she was only a young girl, she led men into battle. They rallied under her banner. They had victories, and losses. She died for her faith and her country. "Not in battle," she says. "But as a prisoner of war. They called me a heretic. Sentenced me to death. It is a regret. There is no greater glory than death in battle. I did not earn that."

I listen in amazement. She's Joan of Arc. *The* Joan of Arc.

"Why didn't you tell me this before?" I ask.

"It did not come up." Her voice is meek.

She has not spoken of it, but history books told of her horrible death…burning at the stake.

"You became a legend," I say.

She shrugs, brushing off the idea. "Emma said something similar. Her country and mine had a long history on Earth. It has drawn us together. But I was no legend. I was only a normal girl. A tragic death should be no cause for celebration."

"It's not just your death, but your life."

"You cannot assess a life until it has ended. If I had

died in battle, yes, celebrate. It is unique for soldiers. In no other field does a person so completely agree, upon entering service, to give up the matter of life and death."

"But isn't being a soldier drudgery? And war is terrible."

"War is terrible for cowards and villains, not for all," Joan says. "To bright souls war is a continual remembrance of death. This is fertile soil. There is cruelty and hatred and horror, to be sure, but such evil calls for an answer, and that answer is courage and charity, even at the cost of limb or life."

"You should tell that to the Black Tower."

"I intend to." She grips her reins tighter and gazes ahead. Max's hut is in sight. "So, who are you taking with us?" she asks.

"Any guesses?"

"I see where we're heading," she says. "Max has never fit well here. He prefers the hut furthest from the Yellow Tower."

Her response gives me confidence about Max. "I first met him in Blue. We fought against each other in the Red Tower. He has even been to Black before. I think he has a soldier's heart."

"He does," Joan says. "But that doesn't mean he'll agree to come. He will not want to leave his daughter, Li Min. And he refuses to talk about his time in Black."

"I can understand why," I say. "But I think he'll come. I know something that may change his mind."

The suns are low behind us when we reach Max's hut. The land ends at a cliff overlooking the sea. The last time I rode here Max snuck up on me and put a knife to my throat.

We tie our horses to a post and knock on the door.

Max opens it. He squints at me. "I heard you'd come back."

"It's good to see you too," I reply.

In the light of the setting suns, he looks like a combination of every version of himself that I've known. He has a scraggly beard as he did in Red; sharp, penetrating eyes as in Blue; bronzed skin as in Yellow; and a stiff, disciplined stance as in Black. There's even something calculating about him—like the Max I'd known and dealt with on Earth.

Instead of welcoming us in, he moves past us and says we should talk outside, where the air is fresh and the view is nice. The three of us sit beside each other at the edge of the cliff. The sea is high on the horizon, filling half the sky. Crashing waves drum far below us.

"So what do you want this time?" Max asks.

There's no point in hiding it. If he's going to come with us, he should come willingly, loyally. "I was wrong about Black," I admit. "It's too messed up for me alone to fix it. They chewed me up and spit me out."

Max grunts with amusement. "Could have told you that."

"I won't make the same mistake again. This time I'm going with help, and not head on. The plan is to sneak onto Black's land and start a rebellion."

"They'll find you all the same," Max says.

"Maybe, but I know something I didn't before." I turn to him, ready to play my trump card. "There's a girl in one of the distant villages who is rumored to be very powerful, very dangerous. The Council sent two girls after her. They woke up in coffins."

"So…?" Max asks. "It's happened before."

"They say she has long black hair and golden flecks like stars in her eyes."

His eyes press closed. "Kiyo."

"Yes. We have to get to her." I knew this would affect Max. Kiyo is his ancestor. He changed, even softened, after talking with her. "You know Black's land," I say. "You have a soldier's heart. Will you help us?"

He sits quietly for a long time. The suns drop below the horizon. The sky spills out color, lighting the clouds, but then darkness encroaches and swallows up every hue. The first stars have appeared when he answers.

"I know a village by the coast," he says. "It has a path to the sea. It's far from the tower."

"Will you show us?" I ask.

He turns to me. His eyes are hard but moist, like wet steel, as he nods. "I need say goodbye to Li Min."

<h1 style="text-align:center">21</h1>

THE OPEN SEA protests our passage. The boat leaves the cave beneath Max's hut smoothly enough, gliding out as a wave retreats, and before the next one crashes in a spray of white. We gaze back at the cliffs looming behind us. Figures stand at the top, small as ants as we sail away. Emma, Li Min, Seymour, and dozens of others. They gave us enough food and supplies to survive a month. I expected the voyage to take a day, maybe two. One should expect nothing of the sea.

The first storm comes at midday and drops like a black curtain around us. The sea sucks us out beyond the sight of land. Waves swell twice the height of our mast. Wind spins us, rocks us, even with the sails down. We would sink if not for my power over the air.

The second storm comes at night and is even worse. Steeper waves. Violent wind. Lightning strikes the sea like molten javelins. One bolt hits the boat, the thunderclap flattening us. The mast splits down the middle and burns. It cracks, already falling, before Joan, Max, and I weave enough power together to raise it up again.

The next morning everything is still. The suns rise brightly. There's no cloud in the sky, no land in sight, no wind. The waves roll up and down like a lullaby. It could be as deadly as a storm to be stuck in the middle of the sea like this. But I have my power.

Max sets our direction using the suns. He feels sure we're closer to Black than when we left. I trust him and follow his direction—weaving a steady wind into the sails, carving across the smooth sea.

"Ever seen it this calm?" Joan asks.

"No, not close," Max says. "But I've never been this far out. How about you Cipher?"

"I've lost sight of land before. Storms have dragged me out." I remember the first one well. It wrecked our boat and nearly drowned Emma and me. That was when I discovered how our powers could work together. Blue and Yellow. We've come a long way since then. "Last night's storm was the worst. But this calm air, it's unnerving."

"Says Blue's chosen one." Max gazes over the water. "By the way, two of your friends from there say hi."

"Who?" I ask.

"Tom and Shelley."

Tom was Thomas Jefferson. Shelley was a famous author. It's hard to imagine them talking to Max. "How did you see them?"

"I traded with them," Max answers. "Bread for salt. They say Blue is darker now, with Abram gone. No one uses the Sieve."

My thoughts go to the pedestal of water atop the Blue Tower. It's the only way to see memories there. "Why not use it?" I ask.

"No clue," Max says.

"So they're stagnant…No memories? No scouring?"

"Heck if I know." Max shrugs, then holds a small loaf out to me. "Better eat while it's fresh. It won't be long before we'll be dining on nothing but rice."

I take the cue and stop asking questions. I focus on my power, drawing more of the still air into a steady wind against the sails. We glide across the water. We are making quiet progress. And the bread tastes good. Seymour baked it for us. "With extra salt to keep it fresh!" he said. Gazing around at the empty sea, part of me misses the warmth and ease of Yellow. But I have to admit, I'm more comfortable here, on the water, even with the risk of storms.

I finally spot something in the distance. There are two dots against the infinite blue—the tips of the Blue and Black Towers. They hover in space, solid as ever, while we sail ahead. Soon the black cliffs appear on our starboard side. They look like a purple mirage above the water.

"That way," Max says, pointing toward the edge of the cliffs, far from the Black Tower ahead. "The village should be close to there."

We tack following Max's direction. The boat carves over the smooth waves. They have grown. But no sign of another storm.

"You know the Black Tower used to be Purple," I say.

"I heard," Max replies. "No one in Black knows, or remembers."

"Emma told everyone in the Yellow Tower," Joan says. "But I know little about it. How was Purple different?"

Staring at the tower's sharp edges in the distance, I can still hear the clash of spears against shields. The grunts of battle and pain. "I imagine there was less fighting."

"I doubt that," Max says. "I bet it was just for a better purpose, in the right time and place and way."

"Sounds right." Joan's eyes look distant. "On Earth there was always a time and place for battle. No reason to think it's different here."

"I'm not so sure." They seem to be forgetting the blood and brutality. "Maybe when it was Purple there was peace."

Max laughs grimly. "What, peace like the Scouring?"

"Peace only works when there is no evil," Joan says, taking Max's side. "You know centuries more of history than I do, Cipher. What would it look like if good people had surrendered?"

I think of the world wars. Emma's heir, Neville, conceded too much to evil forces. It wouldn't have gone well in Europe if Britain had surrendered to Hitler, or if my own country had stayed out of the war. It wouldn't have gone well in Greece if the Spartans had surrendered to Xerxes.

"Very bad," I admit.

"I expect the same here," Joan says. "It's different, of course. We've learned there are stains in each of us. They're meant to be scoured, washed clean. That is why Purple must have fought, too. I think they would champion honor and discipline and justice. They would scour ambition and unbridled power."

"It's not like that now," I say. "They say their facet, the Judge, rewards power. It's unending, ambition against ambition. Each person seeks to rule over others, or die trying."

"The vices of Black become its virtues," Max says.

"That's what we have to change. The Colorless One darkens the stains that need to be scoured white."

"And you think we can change that?" Joan asks.

"It's the only way. We have to gather support and overthrow the Council. The first step is finding Kiyo."

22

THE HIDDEN COVE fits around our small boat like a glove. There is no sandy beach, no tranquil pool, only a slight bend tucked within the oppressive black cliffs. We sail straight onto a shore of pebbles, hardly as wide as the boat. We disembark. My sea legs wobble on the firm ground.

"Better tie it up," Max says, eyeing the boat.

"You think we're coming back?" I ask.

"No, but I prefer to believe there's a chance."

We take as many supplies as we can easily carry—food, water, and blankets. I summon the wind to drag the boat closer to the base of the cliff. The hull grinds in protest against the rocky ground. Water still laps at its base. We tie it to a couple boulders. A large wave could sweep it out, but it's the best we can do. Even if we don't expect to come back, we can hope.

Max leads the way out of the cove. The path is entirely hidden from view. It rises steep as a ladder, each step slippery with moss and the moisture of the sea. We scramble up and up. I make the mistake of looking down only once. An inch separates my foot from a terrible fall. I keep my eyes ahead, my focus on Kiyo and Samantha and Napoleon. We didn't come this far to slip and wake up in a coffin.

We reach the cliff top. I breathe in the fresh, salty air. The boat is out of sight below. The Blue Tower looms far to the right. The path to it would be smooth by sea, but treacherous along the jagged, vertical cliffs. I long to go back there, to where I began in this place.

"Beautiful, isn't it?" Joan says.

She gazes toward storm clouds that have billowed up like violent purple bruises on the horizon. Lightning flashes in the distance.

"We should hurry," Max says, already climbing away from the coast.

Joan and I follow up a terraced green hill. Other hills with others stretch to the left and right. The Black Tower is blocked from view. It makes me feel better.

"The village is just around this hill," Max says, glancing back at us. "Remember, the girls in the fields are no threat. We go straight for the village leaders, the Lord and the Rice. Capture them. Question them. If there's a girl with Kiyo's level of power out here, they'll know."

He marches ahead. This plan was his idea, and he's been confident about it all along. I'm not confident about much of anything in Black. I keep my power ready.

We move along the base of the hill to the right, keeping the Black Tower out of sight. We're half way around when we see the tiny village. It looks like a ghost town at dusk. There are only six huts gathered between rice paddies. There are no lights, no movements, no sounds.

We approach the largest hut in the center. A boy comes out as we reach it, as if he's been watching us all along. His dark skin is drawn taut around his bony frame. He introduces himself as Lord and demands to know why we've come.

I seize him with the wind.

Smoke suddenly billows around him, swallowing my power like it's nothing. It swirls toward me.

Max and Joan charge at the boy. He draws a sword.

"Stop!" It's a girl's voice. She appears before me, out of nowhere, with a spear leveled at my throat.

I swallow in shock. It's Jade.

She used Green's power. She was invisible.

"Take another step and Cipher dies." She glares at Max and Joan. They stand still.

Jade turns to the boy who called himself Lord. "Invite them inside," she demands.

His face goes pale. "Welcome to our village," he says rigidly. "Come, we will talk over tea."

The smoke clears. I focus and glimpse the slender threads flowing around me. If only I could…

Jade stops me with a gentle touch on the arm. "Wait."

I open my mouth to object, but her expression is calm and controlled. She remembers. Even though she's on the Black Council, we were allies in Green. It gives me enough hope to play along. For now. She could be an asset.

"It's okay," I say calmly to Max and Joan. "Do as they say."

My friends look uncertain, but both nod in agreement. We follow the boy into a dim, quiet room. Dark wooden floor. Low ceiling. Still air. The floor is recessed in one corner to fit a table with black cushions around it. Mats for sleeping are rolled up in the corner.

It's exactly like the room I visited before, when Emma and I came to Black to bring my mother back to Red, when Max was Lord and Kiyo was Rice.

"Sit, please," the boy says.

Jade moves to the table as if this is all normal ceremony. Max, Joan, and I take our places at the table. A small white pot rests in the center, with tiny cups arranged perfectly around it. The porcelain sticks out like white barnacles on the dark wooden table.

Moments later a girl enters. She wears a black robe with the hood up, hiding her face in shadows. She kneels by my side and takes the white pot and begins to pour a pale liquid into the cups. If this is like last time, she is called Rice, as the most powerful girl in the village. The boy is the Lord. We will have tea, and we will talk. I pretend like this is normal—just folks getting to know each other.

"Lord," Jade says. "I understand you have a problem."

"These visitors were not expected," he says defensively.

"Not that problem," Jade replies. "I will deal with them. You know why I was sent."

"Yes." The Lord bows his head. "Another village has seized half of our land. They will not allow us to harvest there. Their Rice is…powerful."

Jade studies the tiny white cup clasped between her dark hands. "I have not come to hear excuses."

"It's not an excuse. It's a fact. You know I can't leave my land. What do you expect me to do?"

Jade sets her empty cup down firmly. She turns to the hooded girl, the Rice. "You, what do you know?"

The girl shakes her head.

"What have you seen?" Jade asks.

"Smoke." The girl keeps her face down as the word escapes her lips. "Their Rice's smoke is…beyond me."

I exchange a quick glance with Max, who nods in understanding.

"I see," Jade says. "If this is true, I will correct it and you two may remain as Lord and Rice here. We will take the other Rice back, if we must. But if there is some other cause, Lord, you bear the blame."

He bows his head. "Yes, of course. But we have done our best, I swear. We have produced—"

"Enough," Jade says, with the emphasis of a guillotine severing the conversation. "Both of you, stand guard outside. I must speak to these intruders alone."

23

JADE PULLS HER hood back the moment the Lord and the Rice leave the dim little room. Her green eyes pass over Max and Joan, then find mine. Her stare is predatory, like it was in Green when she was the Eagles' leader.

"You seem to remember," she says. "But seeming is not enough. Tell me what you know."

My first thought is about myself, about how I was Dr. Paul Fitzroy and now I'm Cipher, one of the marked ones. But if I've learned one thing in the Five Towers, it's that I'm not the center of the universe, and that means Jade's question is not about me. So I go to the heart of what we share.

"We were Americans, on Earth," I say. "We both lived in Chicago. Only a few decades separated us. We died and came here. We were both Eagles, in the Green Tower. Baron was our enemy, the leader of the Wolves. But he changed. We learned that he was John D. Rockefeller and that he gave part of his fortune to start a college that you attended. So he helped you become a judge on Earth. Giving set him free."

"Until Black trapped him…" Jade sighs, but a white-toothed smile spreads across her face. "I'm sorry you're here, Cipher. When you didn't come back from the

Scouring, I thought you had escaped. Now tell me, why have you come back?"

"To cleanse the Black Tower," I say.

"Ah, simple as that." She glances to Max and Joan. "And you've brought friends from…Yellow?"

I nod. "Max and Joan, meet Jade."

"Jade," she breathes the name out, a slight smile returning. "It's been a long time since anyone called me that. Well, Joan and Max, welcome to the Black Tower."

"You're on the Council," Max says, his voice hard. "Why would you help us?"

"So you've been in Black before…" Jade muses. "I suppose I'm helping for the same reason you agreed to come back."

"I doubt that," he says.

"Would you be here if Cipher hadn't asked?"

He hesitates. "Maybe not."

"If any intruders other than Cipher and his friends had showed up in this village, I would have had you executed and sent to the bottom of the Black Tower. I still might…"

"We're no threat to you," I say.

"Oh? As a member of the Council, I can expect my actions will be reported. Anyone can be a spy." She looks to Max. "What do you know about the Council?"

"There are twelve of you," Max says. "Ten girls, and the two Commanders of the boys. You meet at the top of the Black Tower and decide everything that's important."

"So we do," Jade replies. "But for too long one person ruled the Council with her iron fist."

"Samantha?"

Jade gives me a questioning look.

"Red hair," I say. "Green eyes. Temper like a storm?"

"Yes. It seems she has gone by many names here. Monica, Khadija, Samantha." Jade studies me. "How do you know her?"

"It's a long story. We knew each other on Earth. She's been tormenting me here. She used her power to stop my powers. It's like her smoke was implanted in my mind."

"I wondered why you seemed almost…normal." Jade sighs. "So you got your memories, but not your powers."

"I had them. She blocked them."

"Then how did you remember? Without the crown?"

I hold up my hands, revealing my scars. "I'm a marked one. I've been in every tower now. And in Yellow, Emma sealed her healing power deep in my mind. I think it protected my memories, even against the Black Tower and the coffin."

"No one has done this before," Jade says. "But I should not be surprised, not after what you did in Green."

Her words give me too much credit. "I still failed last time I was here. Now I have help. We're going to start a rebellion. Will you join us?"

Jade leans back and crosses her arms. "I like you Cipher, but that's bold. You really think a bunch of villagers can take over the Council?"

"We'll do whatever it takes," I say.

"It's been tried before," Jade replies. "Nothing has worked."

Max leans forward, his jaw set, studying Jade. "We're looking for someone. A powerful girl. She'll help us."

"More powerful than I am?" Jade grins. "Well, it just so happens the Council sent me to investigate a village that has not been producing enough. Two other girls from the Council came to inspect this Rice. They didn't return. I think Samantha picked me to get rid of me."

Concern fills Max's eyes. "Kiyo?"

"I don't know her name," Jade says. "Sounds like she could be the one you seek. Whoever she is, she's gotten too powerful. That's why I brought this."

Jade reaches into her bag and pulls something out, gripping it like a viper. The metal hangs. The chrome gleams.

"A collar," I whisper.

"We don't have many here," Jade says, slipping it back into the bag. "But they help with rebellious girls."

I shudder as I remember the collar's power. It requires complete obedience. The Widow and Elijah believe the Colorless One has been stealing them. Not good.

"Don't worry," Jade says. "With this the two of us should be able to manage her without much trouble."

"The *two* of you?" Joan challenges. "What about us?"

"I'm not staying here," Max mutters.

"You once were a Lord?" Jade asks him.

Max doesn't answer. But the knowing look in his eyes is answer enough.

Jade says, "You need to be one again."

"I didn't come here just to let Cipher run off without our help," Max says. "He needs us."

Jade leans forward with a wry grin. "What he *needs* is to avoid the Council's watchful eyes. Think you could help with that?"

"You want us to create a distraction," Joan says.

"Smart girl," Jade replies. "You know how to fight?"

Joan only smiles in reply.

A faint laugh slips out of my lips. "She's Joan of Arc," I say. "She can lead an army."

"Perfect." Jade has awe in her eyes as she looks at Joan. "That is exactly what Cipher needs. Stick with your bold plan. Build an army. Lead a rebellion. Attack the tower. In the meantime I'll help Cipher and this other friend of yours get inside the tower."

"But we need Cipher's powers, and this Rice, to convince the villagers to join us," Max says. "Otherwise no one will fight against the tower."

"Anyone will fight for what matters most," Joan says.

"Hey, I like you!" Jade flashes a smile at Joan. "The villagers are used to obeying. Rally them and march toward the tower. When you get to the next village, capture their leaders, the Lord and Rice, and those villagers will follow you too."

"By force?" Joan asks. "Is there another way?"

"Tell them the Council has been trapped inside the tower and needs to be saved. Tell them the Council will reward them." Jade sighs. "They'll do anything for the Council."

"Is there anything *true* we can say?" Joan presses.

"Oh sure…" Sarcasm drips from Jade's voice. "Tell them the chosen one has returned to the Black Tower to emancipate the slaves and restore freedom and hope." Jade rolls her eyes toward me. "Tell them Cipher comes to cleanse Black of the Colorless One's taint and lead everyone in the Five Towers to escape through the light."

"Much better," Joan says. "People will rally behind that."

Max groans. "Not here. It'll never work in Black. They'll only follow power."

"For once I agree," Jade replies. "This is why it's better to take charge and raise an army by force."

There's a moment of quiet. I look from Jade to Joan to Max. This is not what we planned, but we didn't expect to find Jade. I believe what the Widow said: we will not win by force alone. Our best chance is if Kiyo and I can get inside the tower, and Jade could make that happen. A distraction could be useful. But it's not worth the risk if I lose Joan and Max to Black. Maybe it would be better to keep them with us.

Max breaks the silence. "Cipher, she's on the Council," he says, talking about Jade as if she's not even in the room. "You really trust her? Even with a collar?"

My gut says yes, but it's a good question. Jade could lead me straight into a trap. With this plan, everything rides on her not betraying us. She's been in Black long enough to be corrupted. Yet she remembers her past. We fought together in Green. And she could have collared us but didn't. Despite all that, one question gnaws at me. She was there, on the Council, when they picked Baron over me as the new Commander to replace Karl. Napoleon said it would be me. It wasn't fair. It was a shock.

I study Jade's dark eyes. "Last time I was here, before the Scouring, who did the Council pick as Commander?"

"Baron. The Council chose him over you." She pauses. "And I voted for him."

That's a surprise. And yet she admits it. "Why?"

"Don't give me that look," she says with a grin. "There was no way Samantha would let you become Commander, and I have to pick my battles. Besides, you've seen what happens to Commanders. They are betrayed and killed and reset, sooner or later. You were safer without that rank."

Safer. That's no consolation. "Napoleon said it would be me."

"He lied," Jade says. "He supported Baron. Remember, the Scouring came right after that. As Napoleon's new rival Commander, Baron couldn't go. Napoleon said he'd pick you for the Scouring. I figured something good could come from that. At least you'd have a chance to fight out there."

"Something *good* from the Scouring?" I challenge.

Jade shrugs. "Look, I'm sorry. It was a calculated risk. It's the one place where Samantha and the Council don't have control. And hey, it got you out of the Black Tower, didn't it?"

Samantha shoved me into the pit. But Jade's right. That's how I made it to Yellow, which was better than being stuck in Black. And now we could have Jade on our side without Samantha knowing it.

"All right," I say, turning to Joan. "You think you can raise an army. Cause some trouble?"

Joan nods. "You found the right girl. Max, are you with me?"

"Fine, twist my arm," Max sighs. "Do I at least get the Lord's sword?"

"It's yours," Jade says.

He holds out his hands and clenches them into fists. "It'll feel good to hold a sword again."

"Then it's settled." I turn back to Jade. "We'll follow your plan, on one condition."

"What's that?" Jade asks.

"You let me have the collar." I reach out my hand.

She eyes my scarred palm doubtfully. Seconds pass in tense silence. She takes a deep breath. "Fine."

She hands it over.

Collar in hand, friends by my side, plan in place, we're ready to take on the Black Tower.

24

IT'S NIGHT, DARK and cloudy, when Jade and I set off on foot. Our goal is to be clear of this village's land by dawn, well on our way to the rebel girl. Kiyo.

Jade leads the way up a steep hill. She moves fast and focused, hood up, face ahead, like a hawk pursuing prey. Terraces line the slope and hold countless green shoots of rice in flooded paddies. I follow close as she stays to dry paths between the flooded fields. Her sandaled feet stay dry. Her calves flex with each step.

My legs already ache as we reach the first crest. I bend over, hands on my knees. Jade does not pause or glance at me. She says between heavy breaths, "A few more hills before dawn."

She presses ahead, swooping down the hill's other side. The valley bottoms out in a small clearing, like the base of a cup covered in mossy grass. Then we climb again.

It begins to rain. The mist is pleasant at first, soft and gentle on my skin. But soon the drizzle soaks through my clothes, making my shirt stick to me and weigh me down. I slip going up the next slope. Jade seems to know every firm spot of ground. I stay right on her heels, placing each step in the exact spot where her foot lifted a moment before. Like that, we climb another hill.

Jade stops just over the next crest. The canopy of rain shrouds us, but the sky has brightened from black charcoal to dark gray. The suns must have risen. It's hard to tell.

"How far do these hills go?" I ask, catching my breath.

She crouches, elbows on her knees, resting. "I hear no one's ever found the end."

It's odd. The territories of Red and Blue and Black reach as far as anyone knows. But Green and Yellow have coasts as borders. Their lands are confined. Maybe greed and cowardice are more confined than passion and pride and ambition. Whatever the reason, there's something more harrowing to these lands that know no end.

"Do you like coming out here?" I ask.

"It's better than the tower." She points down the hillside. "You see that?"

At first, through the heavy rain, it looks like a formless dot. But as I gaze closer I realize it's a small cluster of buildings at the base of another valley. "Is that our village?"

"No, we are avoiding it," she says. "It won't be too hard. I doubt they can see us through this rain. And we'll go around the next hill the other way. That's what I like about this place. You can avoid people. The tower puts us on top of each other, where we inevitably fight."

"You mean the boys?" I ask. "The girls seem to have it pretty good."

"Oh how little you know!" She laughs like a mother with sympathy for her ignorant child. "The girls are not so different. We wake in coffins as boys do. There are two identical rooms. Like the boys, we advance only through discipline and the will to power."

"So you fight?"

"Yes, but usually with words. The rule is, first one to

cry, or die, is reset in the coffin again. We tear each other apart with words from the moment we wake, and it can get worse. The Council votes on more than the new Commander. We vote on anyone who needs to be assigned a position. And every single time we meet, we vote on the ten girls who will be on the Council."

"Why every time?" I ask.

"Samantha requires it. I'm telling you, she's twisted. I was a judge. I know how to spot a deviant and a thug."

I had forgotten how stern Jade can be. But I also know Samantha. She might be vengeful against me, but she was nothing like this on Earth. "How did she get this way?"

"Everything out of her lips is about the will to power. She says the voting gives us more chances to show our will. It means treachery and hate breed like flies. No one's position is safe. Factions form and rise and fall. Every girl out here in the fields has a chance. That is one of my tasks during this journey—to visit these girls in the fields. And, perhaps, to find one who is ready for the Council."

"What makes them ready?"

"Someone who will join me and vote against my enemies."

"So it's like a popularity contest?"

Jade smiles darkly. "In a terrible sort of way…"

"How often do girls get voted off the Council?"

"It depends. It takes only five votes to remain. The vote is usually quick. We vote for each other…until a majority changes its mind. It starts with little grudges. A sharp look. A half-hearted hello. The tiniest of slights add up, and then all of a sudden, six girls will agree to vote against one girl. Then boom, she's gone, wiped, and back in the fields."

"I thought you woke up in a coffin?"

"Oh, we do. But surviving only earns us a direct trip to a village to grow rice. It's grueling work. The most promising girls are named Rice, the first among equals. All must obey the village's Lord. If we disobey, the Lord sends us back to start again."

"How?"

She raises an eyebrow. "Who has a sword?"

"Oh, right."

"The Lord's job is to make the villagers produce rice, and to identify girls with power."

"How does he do that?"

"He rules with an iron fist. Most village girls detest it. Their anger becomes fuel. Eventually rage spills out in smoke, even rebellion. Our smoke cannot stop a sword, but one with enough power can drag a body down straight to a coffin."

I swallow. "I remember…"

"You are right to fear this. As is the Lord. He reports any disobedience to the Council. They take the girls who are most powerful to be candidates for the Council. That's the way of Black."

"So the girls who disobey and rebel are the ones who join the Council? It doesn't make sense."

"The strong shall rise," Jade says.

The mantra makes my fists clench. "How is that fair?"

"The Judge rewards power. So it's fair that the strongest rise."

"I don't believe that."

"Then take power yourself and change it…" Jade smirks at the irony of her words.

"Maybe I will." She's partly right, but wrong too. It's

what we *do* with power that matters, not power itself. Kiyo will understand. "So this is why you were sent to inspect this rebel girl," I say. "How will you know who she is?"

"The power will reveal her," Jade answers. "Black's power. The smoke. The first sign is usually a huge burst in a village's output. When a girl uses her power out here, she can threaten others. Take their rice. And if she has this level of power, she is ready to join us." Jade eyes the bag at my side. "That's what the collar is for. To bring her back."

"But doesn't the Council already have ten girls?"

"One will be voted off," Jade says. "And this time it will be Samantha, no matter what it takes. I've been waiting for an opportunity like this. I don't think it's a coincidence that I found you. I need your help as much as you need mine. I can get you into the tower without a fight."

"Fortune favors the bold," I say.

"That's right, and now your luck continues. You get to sleep first while I keep watch."

The chances of sleep seem slim in the rain, but as I lie on my side and close my eyes, with the steady thumping of drops against my hood, it takes only moments.

Jade wakes me with a gentle shake. The rain continues. It looks like no time has passed at all.

"How long was I out?"

"Hours," she says. "Can you watch a bit?"

"Sure. When should I wake you?"

"Before the suns set."

I agree to try, and she sleeps soundly beside me. The rain stops in short order. The clouds even lift.

I stand and stretch and take in the emerging view over the lush, terraced hills. It makes me breathe easier. I climb a few feet to the top of the hill. The familiar rod of iron juts up in the distance. Jade is right. It's better out here, far from Black's battleground and war camp, far from Napoleon and Baron and Samantha.

I turn away from the Black Tower. A smile spreads over my face as I glimpse a steep mountain ridge to my left, dividing these endless hills from Red, and the infinite sea to my right. I've been through these hills and survived. I've been in every tower and survived. We may be hiking away from the Black Tower now, but soon I will be ready to return. Maybe Joan and Max will have an army to join me.

A violent sunset comes. The three suns fall like fireballs behind Red's mountains. I wake Jade.

She yawns and gazes around. "Time to move. We should make the village by dawn. Maybe the rain will hold off."

As we descend, the sky grows dark. The flooded terraces turn violet in the dying light. A murder of crows swoops over head, cawing. The Black Tower dips out of sight.

We trudge up the terraces and down, three or four hills worth. I lose count. I grow terribly tired. We pause only a few times through the night.

The sky finally begins to brighten into gray. I plod sleepily after Jade up another hill when she stops so suddenly that I bump into her.

She stares along a terrace. A girl glides toward us, knee deep in the water of the flooded field. She looks like a ghost emerging in the morning mist. Her hair is shoulder length and blonde and straight as straw. She wears the plain dark garb of a peasant. Her pale eyes are the faintest of green, like a shimmer of algae on water. Her back is so straight that it bends, convex as a bow, ready to fire something at us.

"You're up early," Jade says.

"Go back to the tower," the girl replies. "And please take me."

Jade cocks her head. "Why?"

"You seek my village?" She points toward the next hill. No village or other buildings are in sight.

"Yes," Jade says.

"Then you seek death," the girl says. "The Rice has taken over. She is all powerful, but dangerous and…unstable."

"*All* powerful?" Jade asks. "I'd like to meet her."

"She will not like to meet you." The wispy girl eyes Jade up and down, then glances dismissively at me. "The last ones who came from the tower…they didn't return."

"What happened to them?" I ask.

The girl shivers despite the humid air. "The smoke swallowed the boy, sucked him into the earth. The girl lost her mind. I tell you, this Rice is not like any other. She has…immense power."

"How do you know?" Jade asks.

"I remember my past, and that should tell you everything. Her smoke brings memories. Dark memories." The girl's pale eyes flit past us. She seizes my arm and Jade's, gripping tight. Her fear makes me doubt that the Rice is Kiyo. How could my friend invoke such terror?

"Please, please, take me away with you," the girl says.

"What is your name?" Jade asks.

"Villager 9."

"No, your real name, from before."

The girl scans the surroundings nervously, as if searching for spies. "Jessica," she whispers.

"Thank you for the warning, Jessica." Jade shakes free of the girl's grip. "Now return to your work."

The girl tries to protest, but Jade refuses to speak more and moves on. I ask Jade what this could mean, but Jade is stony. Her only response is, "It's as I thought."

As we crest the hill, Jade speeds up. First a jog. Then faster.

"What are we doing?" I call after her.

"Running."

"Why?"

Jade glances back over her shoulder. Her voice is breathless. "Can't you keep up?"

I try. My body feels tired and stiff, but it warms up as we sweep down the gentle hillside. Blood pumps. Muscles loosen.

Then we begin going up. The next hill rises steep as a mountain. Soon we are climbing stairs between the terraced fields. We crest the hill. Jade stops.

"Discipline is patience," she pants between breaths. "The longer you control yourself...the greater your reward...over time. And when the horizon...is eternity, the rewards are infinite...if you master self-discipline."

Hands on my knees, I suck in more air, blow it out. I finally manage a response. "Sounds...hard."

Sweat moistens her smile. "Patience takes practice."

The first sunlight creeps toward the horizon. Then the second, and third. I spot the village below us. A dense fog hangs over the cluster of huts.

"Almost there, and barely late," Jade says. "We slow down now. Be on guard."

Jade leads down the hill, through the morning mist.

The girl's words haunt more with every step forward.

The smoke swallowed the boy, sucked him into the earth. I've seen it before. The boys go back beneath the Black Tower, wiped and forced to fight their way out. It could happen to me again. The coffin. Samantha shutting down my power. The fight for survival.

I shake away the thought, remembering what I learned in Yellow: fear serves a purpose. My true fears—of the pit, the Colorless One, and the threat of never leaving this place—these fuel me forward. I'll find Black's leader. And we'll cleanse the Black Tower, no matter what it takes. It's the only hope.

<h1 style="text-align:center">25</h1>

JADE STRIDES STRAIGHT into the village. She's a member of the Council, expecting obedience. But no villager greets us. Fog obscures the dark buildings. Through the gloomy dawn I spot two eyes peering out of a doorway. How many are watching us? It's too quiet.

Jade stops before the main hut in the village. I come to a halt by her side. She pushes the door, and it swings open without a sound. She takes a step forward but freezes.

It's pitch black inside.

"Rice," Jade demands, stepping back. "Come out. Now."

There's no motion or sound from within the hut. I glance back. More faces peer at us from behind other huts, trying to watch but not be seen.

Air rushes past me, sudden as a spring storm. Black smoke billows out of the building. It clouds everything. It blocks my power like an eclipse.

A figure appears in the doorway, shrouded in smoke, almost within reach. She is tiny, with her head down and long black hair hanging almost to the ground, like a waterfall of ink.

Jade whispers to me, "Be ready."

I finger the collar, hidden within the bag by my side.

The girl stands motionless. Her head stays bowed.

"We come from the Black Tower," Jade says, her voice regal and clear. "Kneel before a member of the Council."

A soft sound comes from the girl. Quiet at first, then louder and louder. It's laughter, wild and insane. Her body trembles with it. Her hair ripples. Smoke suddenly billows around her like she's on fire, but there are no flames. No heat.

The cackling stops in an instant. The smoke goes still.

She lifts her head slowly. Her face looks cold as ice. Her eyes are black, entirely black. They bore into me. I shrink back, terrified, even as a distant part of me recognizes her. But no, not with these eyes. This is the taint. This is evil…

"You have no right to—" Jade's voice chokes.

She grabs at her throat. Her face twists in fear, mouth gaping open, trying to speak, making no sound.

Smoke solidifies into a thick shackle at Jade's neck, connected to a black rope that drags her forward, toward the girl.

Through the fear I manage to say her name: "Kiyo."

Her black eyes turn from Jade to me.

I stop breathing. I can't bear to look at these eyes, but they won't let me turn away.

She draws in a deep breath, back arching, then unleashes a scream like death made into sound.

I fall to my knees. Hands over ears.

Her scream pierces into me and makes me curl like a fetus on the ground, trying to hide, to be anywhere but here.

The sound stops, leaving silence.

The girl, Kiyo, kneels in a cloud of smoke beside me.

Her face leans close. Her eyes are onyx discs. She presses a finger to my forehead, cold as ice, then blinks as if surprised. She puts her hands to my temples, prodding and feeling for something.

I see the familiar scars. She is still a marked one.

I force myself to remember her, who she really is. Her story was the first I heard in the Five Towers. She suffered so much. She was cold, fleeing through the snow-covered mountains of Japan with her five children. She lost one of her sons, Omaki. She'd seen that in Blue, but it was here in Black where she discovered the rest. Her loss was only the beginning. She grew hard and cold and vengeful. She was samurai, but ronin, a rebel leader. She fought with discipline and power. She killed a wicked shogun, took command of his castle through strength of will. But still a depth, a softness, remained inside her.

"Kiyo," I say desperately. "It's me. Cipher."

She blinks again. My hand slips into the bag, feeling the smooth metal of the collar.

"Are you in there?" I ask.

She must remember. She greeted me in Blue. She came with me to Yellow.

"*Kiyo?*"

She jerks back. Her hand flashes forward, palm facing out.

I follow her gaze and see Jade, frozen in a crouched position, like she was ready to pounce on Kiyo. But it feels like an opening. I have to try something, even without my power, anything to get through to her.

"You're my friend. My first friend here." I take her scarred hand gently. "You lived in Japan, the mother of five sons, a samurai, a warrior, a leader. You were in the

Blue Tower, and later in Yellow, where you met your descendant Max. And your son, Omaki, is here in the Black Tower."

"Omaki…" Her infinitely terrible eyes have closed. She looks almost normal, like the Kiyo I knew.

I slowly draw the collar out of the bag.

"Whatever happened, Kiyo, we can fix it." My voice is calm. The collar is open, inching closer and closer. "We're marked ones. We won't let the Colorless One—"

Her eyes flash open.

I swing the collar.

The instant the metal closes around her neck, she screeches again. The sound hits me like a tidal wave, knocking me back, shattering my thoughts.

Kiyo leaps onto me. Her knees pin my shoulders down. She grabs the sides of my head as if she's going to rip it off.

But the collar is on her. I have command.

Kiyo—

Before the thought can form, black smoke swallows me. I see nothing, hear nothing, but I feel a force pour into me like a dense liquid through my mouth and nostrils and ears. It surges over my mind and my thoughts, drowning everything in darkness.

The pressure grows and grows and concentrates around a single point, trying to smother a dot of light that I somehow know is my memory of Kiyo and her story.

I focus on this light. It cannot mix with black. The smoke cannot shadow this. The light pulses gently and the darkness groans, almost cracks against it.

My thoughts move through the darkness to Kiyo, sensing her presence and rage through the link.

It's light. It's still in you. Kiyo, please, let go!

The black liquid rushes out in an instant, tumbling me like sand in the undertow. As consciousness fades I hear a word deep inside, and it's Kiyo's voice, distant and small, saying: "Cipher."

26

KIYO CLUTCHES A BLANKET tight around her small frame. She is huddled like a lost child desperate for her mother. But, as I come to and push myself up, I remember there are no mothers here. Even my own mother, when she was in the Red Tower, looked my age. We're all the same—trapped in these youthful bodies—no matter what our memories hold.

Jade places a cup before me. "Welcome back."

A candle flickers on the low table, the only ward against the darkness in the small room. It looks just like the room from the other village—dark wood and still air. Jade, Kiyo, and I are alone.

I study Kiyo's pale, solemn face. Steam drifts up from a white porcelain cup in her hands. Candlelight flickers off something at her neck—the collar.

"What happened?" I ask.

"You've been out a while." Jade glances to Kiyo. "She hasn't spoken since whatever you did. She's your servant now."

"I was trying to save her," I say. "Kiyo?"

She raises her head and a sudden fear grips me—the terror of her all-black eyes, her rage, her power. But the eyes have changed back to normal—her normal. There is a pupil, dark against white, and flecks of gold around the iris.

She blinks in recognition, then takes a deep breath. Through the link I feel her composure. She's quiet and cold inside, even as a powerful force lurks within her.

"I am marked to lead this tower." Her voice is quiet but solid as steel. "I have escaped many times, only to be dragged back, caught and wiped, again and again. I remember every detail now. I have come to put an end to the Council. I will rule alone."

"That's impossible," Jade says. "The Council has never changed. We must share the power to maintain control."

"It was not made to be this way," Kiyo says. "Moses and Joshua once ruled here, when this was the Purple Tower."

"*Moses?*" I ask. "He's the missing leader?"

Kiyo nods. "This was a regal place, of honor and justice. Hard, yes, but fair. The rules were clear and applied equally. We had justice and love at the top of their energies. Ambition was scoured. Wrath was disciplined and contained. Now the leaders are gone. There is no love. The Colorless One reigns."

"That's a lie," Jade says. "Moses is in the tower."

"Have you seen him?" Kiyo challenges.

Jade hesitates. "No, but—"

"He's gone," Kiyo says. "The Council is corrupted. *It* is the lie. The lawgiver has been taken. Perhaps to the pit. I've been there."

"You were in the pit?" I ask in surprise. The last time I saw her she was as happy as she could be in Yellow, under Emma's protection, with Max in her neighboring field. But the ashen look on her face tells me it's true. "How did it happen?"

"I was in Yellow, as you know. I grew strong in healing. I became a guard, and so I fought in the Scouring again." Kiyo groans lightly, as if the memory hurts. "Black came for me. They were recklessly focused on me. It put all of the Yellow team at risk. I refused to play this same story over again. I had a plan. I lured the Black team toward the center. As they approached—" Kiyo glances to Jade. "You were one of them, weren't you?"

"Yes, I remember." Jade's voice is tense.

"As you should," Kiyo says. "The Black team came for me with their backs to the others from Yellow, who had agreed to work with Green. Black charged. Their spears were nearly on me when I spun and dove into the dark hole in the center of the Scouring."

"Incredible," I say, amazed again. Yellow must have scoured all of Kiyo's fear if she *dove* into the pit. "What happened?"

She takes a sip of tea. "It worked."

"Our boys were captured," Jade says. "Samantha and I fled through the smoke. We were the only ones who returned to the Black Tower."

"So it went even better than I thought…" Kiyo replies.

"What happened in the pit?" I ask.

"I fell into complete darkness. A vision overcame me." Kiyo shudders. "It transported my mind, as with other memories here. But this was odd, because I was not in this vision…"

Her voice trails off, and I see pain in her expression. It's a pain I've felt. The pit shows what could have been but was not, because of our mistakes. The leaders say it's a lie the Colorless One uses for guilt and shame.

"Whatever you saw," I say softly to Kiyo. "It wasn't

true.”

"No, it was real. As real as anything I've seen.”

"What was it?"

Kiyo hesitates, glancing at Jade, then continues. "You know my story, Cipher, so you will understand. There was a wise old woman who lived with a man I knew well—the man who had been my husband on Earth. They had five sons and dwelled in a gentle valley by the coast. The hills rose steep and green around their home. They had more rice than they could ever eat. The sea offered its bounty too—more fish, clams, and crabs than you could need. The family traded with a neighboring village. They had peace. The oldest son married a beautiful young woman. The wedding was pristine. It was perfection. The silk gowns, the delicate paper lanterns, the flowers. The couple built their own house in the valley. The young wife became pregnant and gave birth to the most wonderful son. I looked into his eyes and then into the grandmother's eyes. She was like me, but not me. My husband had married her instead, as if I had never existed, and it was so much better for them all…”

Her story pulls me like a magnet back into my own visions from the pit, of what might have been if not for me. First it was Samantha, her red hair gone gray, her green eyes still vivid. She had married a genteel husband. They lived in the country, peaceful, with children and grandchildren gathered around. In the second vision I saw my wife, Susan, with a daughter—the daughter who never lived because I put my work before my family. They sat on a park bench while the most beautiful three little children—the ones who could have been my grandchildren—played in the sun. But instead their bones are in the pit. They never lived. They never got a chance because of me.

"You okay?" Jade clasps my shoulder. "You look like you saw a ghost."

I try to shake out of it. I turn to Kiyo and put my hand gently over hers, my scar pressing against her scar.

"It never happened," I say, more confidently than I feel. "What we saw in the pit, it was a lie. Shame is the Colorless One's most powerful weapon."

Kiyo shakes her head. "It felt more real than my memories. Maybe *they* are the lie."

"No, we can't think that," I insist, as much to myself as to her. "The pit is behind us. You made it out. You got here somehow. That's what matters."

"Someone dragged me out," Kiyo says. "It was a man. He took me to a tunnel and tapped against the dirt ceiling and said to me, *Go up here.*"

"Abram?" I ask.

"I never saw his face. But I don't think so. He had no staff."

Jade leans forward, as if noticing us for the first time. "Was he old or young?"

"He wasn't a boy like the others. Maybe middle-aged? Why?"

"Impossible…" Jade trails off.

"Was it Black's other leader, Joshua?" I ask. He and the Hunter are the only two middle-aged men I've seen here.

"I don't know," Kiyo says. "It wasn't Abram or Daniel or Elijah."

"Joshua." There's hope in Jade's voice.

"It hardly matters," Kiyo replies. "I did as he said. I wanted to get away, no matter what. I summoned all my power and bored a tunnel through the earth. It came up in a field not far from here."

"And then you took over this village?" Jade asks.

"Yes. I wanted to bait the Council. I never imagined I'd meet Cipher here. Now we have the advantage."

"For what exactly?" Jade asks.

"I told you. We will put an end to the Council."

"But why?" Jade looks from Kiyo to me. "I'm sorry, Cipher, I support you taking over and changing things, but we can't just get rid of the Council. We have to find Moses."

"No, he is gone," Kiyo says. "He would never have let things become so twisted. The Council *rewards* ambition instead of scouring it. They force boys to fight and kill for no reason. The time has come." Kiyo fixes her intense gaze on me. "Together we will destroy the Council. Black will fade. Purple will return. And then we will fight the Colorless One."

"Look, I agree there are problems," Jade says. "But the Council sent me for a reason. Cipher, your friend is…unstable. We can't even remove the collar. Imagine what she would have done if you hadn't snapped her out of that…blackness."

"I would have killed you. Then whoever came next from the Council. Then all of you." Kiyo slowly sips her tea. "I may not have been able to fight all the Council at once, but after I eliminated a few—ones like you who came to inspect—I would storm the tower and take complete control. My goal is the same, but the way is different. The rage is gone. I feel normal." Her eyes meet mine. "We can do this together."

Maybe it's true, but her quiet intensity makes me glad

she wears the collar all the same. It's safer this way. She hardly sounds like the meek Kiyo I first met in the Blue Tower. I'm not sure I can trust either her or Jade completely.

"How did your powers grow so strong?" I ask.

"The scars, the different towers." Kiyo shrugs. "We are marked ones, right?"

I bow my head, remembering what Rahab once told me in the Red Tower. Our power comes from the gap between what we were capable of on Earth, and what we actually did.

"My failures make my power strong," I say, "but I cannot stand against Black's smoke."

"Yes you can," Kiyo replies. "You stopped me."

"That was different. It was something inside me that worked without even focusing on it, like light against the darkness. But I can't summon the wind against the smoke. I can't go invisible or heal. Before, Samantha had blocked all of it."

"She is very dangerous," Kiyo says.

"On that we agree," Jade replies. "Samantha is the only one who speaks to Moses. She controls the crown, the memories, everything."

I look from Jade to Kiyo. I want both of them on my side. We have to unite around this. "Jade, you said you wanted Samantha off the Council."

"Yes, but the Council must remain," Jade says. "Its leader speaks with Moses."

Kiyo shakes her head. "I told you already. Moses is gone."

"I don't believe that, but..." Jade sighs. "If he *is* gone, then we have bigger problems."

"So it's agreed," I say. "We can work together and find out about Moses. But first, we need a plan to defeat Samantha."

Kiyo puts her scarred hand to the collar at her neck. "I have an idea."

27

JADE BANGS AGAINST the immense iron door. Kiyo cranes her neck upward. Her silver collar looks dull under the Black Tower's shadow. Kiyo is my servant, not Jade's, but no one can see that. No one can know that I feel Kiyo's emotions, raw and unfiltered through the link. She's quiet, controlled, and intensely focused. Her smoke swirls around me, blocking my power for any girl in Black to see. It doesn't feel good, but at least Kiyo's not insane, not anymore.

The doors swing open with a metallic groan. Four guards—boys my size armed with helmets and shields and spears—escort us inside. It's midday, so most of the boys train outside. A few girls work to prepare for the evening's feast.

"Stay here," Jade commands loudly, then moves to the stairs winding up into the Black Tower.

Kiyo and I wait in silence, as ordered.

Jade will go to the Council. She'll tell them of a threat in the villages. She'll say intruders have come from another tower, plotting dangerous things. The Council won't know that, as we traveled here, we met with Joan and Max. They had already gathered dozens of bitter villagers to our side. Rumors of the rebellion will surely have spread by now.

They will attack after we enter the tower.

Our job is to make the Council believe that Kiyo and I reported the threat, and that Kiyo—as Jade's servant—has shut down my powers. Then, when the attack comes, Joan and Max will lure the Council and troops out into the hills, leaving Kiyo and me inside.

And if it doesn't work, we won't go down without a fight.

So we wait. And wait.

The smell of cooked lobsters and rice begins to fill the tower. The first boys from outside file into the vast room for the feast. Jade should have returned with the Council by now. Joan and Max should have attacked.

Napoleon and Baron enter separately. They look as confident as ever. Baron's gaze swings over me without a second glance. Napoleon approaches with a dozen hard-eyed troops.

"So Karl's little Deputy is back?" He glances at Kiyo, then back to me with a smug grin. "And you brought back Rice. Think that will make you a Commander?"

There's no benefit to arguing with him, only risk. I bite my tongue and shrug him off.

"The pit turned him stoic!" Napoleon laughs as he walks away, trailed by his troops.

The feast begins. Lobster shells crack. The boys toast each other and banter around the table. All seems normal.

My doubts unnerve me. What if Jade turned against us? What if Joan and Max were caught? Kiyo and I have little choice but to stay at the foot of the stairs, exactly where Jade commanded us to wait. I ready myself to fight, if it comes to that.

The feast suddenly falls silent.

The Council comes. The hooded girls descend the path coiling around the tower's inner wall like it's a funeral march. Jade is with them. She catches my eyes and flashes a wink. I release a breath, but my heart still pounds.

The boys rush into formation, standing at attention in a straight line facing the girls.

Samantha walks straight to me. "How did you get back?"

"Is there any way but the coffin?" My voice comes out quiet but steady. It's not a lie.

She moves closer, studying me. Her emerald eyes stab into me. I don't blink. She can't feel my thumping heart. "You told Jade about this rebellion?"

"Yes."

"You believe it is a serious threat?"

"Yes." I hold her gaze, trying to reveal nothing, until she finally turns away, to Kiyo.

"You serve Jade well," Samantha says. "Shutting down this boy's powers. Reporting rebellion in the village. You may be rewarded. Would you like that?"

Kiyo stands motionless. She does not respond. Through the link she feels nervous.

"Answer her," Jade says.

"If it pleases you," Kiyo answers, with a deep bow.

Samantha appraises Kiyo with an intrigued grin. "I sense your power. But it is…different. Jade, let's test her loyalty, shall we? Order this Rice, without a word, to take this boy where the last Commander was sent."

Not good. Jade is expressionless, but I know her well enough to see the fear in her eyes. We had not planned for this. Kiyo and I don't know where the last Commander was sent. And Jade can't tell us. She's supposed to order

Kiyo through the collar.

So I have to guess…Karl was Commander when I was last here. That was days ago, but he died as any other Commander might have. They would be sent to a coffin, to start over beneath the Black Tower.

Go to the center of the room, I tell Kiyo through the link. *Take me with you like I'm your prisoner. We will go down the stairs there.*

Kiyo turns and grabs my arm with her careful precision. We walk away, not looking back. Guards fall into pace beside us, spears at the ready.

I feel Samantha's eyes on my back. She doesn't believe me. So why is she letting me go?

"Attack!" a boy shouts.

Air gusts into the room as the massive tower doors swing open. Metal clashes in the distance. The faint sounds of battle.

"From the hills!" the boy shouts again. "Villagers! Dozens of them!"

"To the fight!" Napoleon commands.

Boys rush to their feet. Weapons rattle as they dash outside.

Kiyo and I keep walking. Behind us, Samantha yells out orders. I risk a glance back. The black-robed girls are charging toward the door.

Joan and Max. They've done it.

A smile of relief spreads across my face as Kiyo and I reach the center of the room and descend the stairs. The rebellion has started. Jade can keep up the ruse. She'll fight with other girls of the Council. Joan and Max will harry Black's troops, ever retreating into the hills, to distract them as long as possible.

It doesn't mean this will be easy. Jade expects the Council will leave at least a few girls behind. Kiyo and I can handle them with our powers combined, even if one is Samantha. Her time as leader—whether Moses is here or not—will end.

Kiyo and I go a short way down the stairs to wait as we listen to footsteps above, racing out to the battle. The air becomes thicker, humid and nearly as black as ink. It feels like the pit, with the same gloomy aura of despair. I imagine the dueling ground below, with the coffins on the sandy floor. The noise above us fades to silence.

"Let's head back up," I whisper. "I hate this place."

"Yes, and be alert," Kiyo says, already climbing.

My skin feels electric as we move toward the great hall. It's time to free the Black Tower.

28

THE GREAT HALL of the Black Tower has gone quiet. Almost everyone has cleared out. Only a few boy-guards stand around, with spears raised, still as statues. There are no black-robed girls in sight.

Lead on, I tell Kiyo through the link.

She strides across the hall to the stairs that coil up along the tower's inner wall. A few guards eye us as we pass, but no one tries to stop us. Maybe they're afraid of Kiyo. Or maybe it's a trap.

We climb the stairs steadily, rising higher and higher. The path reminds me of the one in the Blue Tower— nothing to separate us from a fall to the ground many stories below. I force myself to not look down.

We come to a stop at an iron door with a shield emblem at the center. Kiyo leans close and whispers, "Be ready to fight."

"How many do you expect?" I ask, with a sinking feeling, thinking of a room of robed girls and their smoke.

"Enough to be dangerous." A sly grin touches her lips, even as her golden-flecked eyes radiate with intensity. "Here. No more need for this."

Her smoke scatters and parts, lifting the block over my power. The weaves come into focus.

"Thanks," I say. "Much better."

I consider offering to remove the collar from her neck, but I remember what happened the last time she used her power. The darkness was wild and overwhelming. Maybe it's better this way, just in case.

She presses her hand to the shield on the door. Her face concentrates. The door swings open, and she slips inside. I follow closely after her.

The door slams behind us and cuts off the light. It is pitch black.

A hand finds mine, squeezes. Kiyo is by my side. I sense her emotions through the link. She is controlled and focused. There is slight surprise, but no fear. She leads me forward silently. She is too calm, like she knows what's coming.

We need light, I command through the link.

Kiyo flashes annoyance, but she inches ahead in the same careful way. We have moved ten steps when she stops and leans forward. A tiny flame appears above a pale finger and lights a candle. The candlelight fills the room slowly, like a faint yellow balloon expanding with air. The table is immense and black and round, in the center of a round room. The room is smaller than I expected—only about thirty feet wide and mostly filled by the table. Twelve empty chairs surround the table. No one other than Kiyo is in sight.

She studies me, calm as a still lake inside. She points to a steep staircase on the opposite side of the room. "If Moses is here, he'd be up there. Better for you to go alone." Her voice is a feather's touch.

I study her. She's Kiyo, my first friend here. I want to trust her. But just a day ago she tried to kill me. And through the collar I still feel a force, almost like a dormant rage, buried deep and quiet inside her.

Tell me what you're hiding from me, I command.

Her lake of calm ripples. "It's too quiet here. This could be a trap. She might be up there."

Samantha? We're ready for that.

"She has always guarded that room," Kiyo whispers. "She will do whatever it takes to keep her power. You need some element of surprise. It's better if she doesn't know I'm here. I'll be close, ready to help."

The collar tells me Kiyo feels relief saying this. I ask her, *You expect me to go up alone?*

"Yes."

As bait?

"Every trap needs bait," she says.

If Samantha attacks, defend me with everything you have, I command.

She nods and a smile—a sad smile—spreads across her face. "You didn't have to command me."

"I know." I smile back, comforted all the same that Kiyo and her power will be on my side.

29

"MOSES?" I WHISPER.

Only the wind answers. I step slowly up the final, steep stair and into the room. It feels like entering a different universe. It's so cold. The wind howls through a hole in the stone wall just behind me. The room's darkness swallows the faint starlight. I can see only a few feet ahead.

"Is anyone here?"

No answer. My body tenses. Kiyo waits a few stairs below, listening, ready for my command to come.

I take a deep breath and move toward the center of the room. I don't make it far. Something clinks at my feet, tripping me. I fall to my knees on the hard stone.

Feeling around, I find a heavy metal chain. Its links are thicker than my fingers. I lift it slightly and tug, but it catches. It's connected to something. I begin to feel my way forward, hands groping along the chain, crawling on hands and knees, breathing heavily. The wind is deafening.

The chain comes to an end. It is linked to the wall. I feel around it and detect four large metal shackles attached in the same way, positioned as if to hold two arms and two legs.

But the shackles are open.

No one is here.

If Moses was ever chained up, he is gone now. Kiyo was right. Has it been a sham the whole time?

I hear something move. I go rigid, then start to back away.

A hand touches my arm.

I twist violently away, but too late.

Someone shoves me forward. Falling, off balance, I slam into the wall. My head hits stone. Stars flicker in my vision. A shackle closes around my ankle.

"That should be enough for now…" It's Samantha's voice, slicing through the howling wind. Her smoke clouds my mind and smothers my power.

Help! I command Kiyo, trying to keep a straight face as I ask, "What did you do to—?"

There's a loud crash from below. A shout.

Kiyo?

I sense nothing.

The link has broken. My power is blocked. It's over.

The smoke dissipates, and Samantha steps forward, within a few feet. Her red hair spills like blood down the front of her black robe.

"It was a bold plan," she says. "Use a rebellion as a distraction. Then send you up alone, with a girl behind you ready to attack. You underestimate me, Paul. I rule this tower. I always will. And now I have three of you little marked ones under my control."

Panic grips me. I try to buy time, to think.

"What's that to you?"

"Oh I know all about Baron," she says. "The other marked one. Don't give me that innocent look. He told me of your time in Green. He's on my side now, not yours. He's the one who just stopped Kiyo. By now he has opened her collar and closed it again, so she's under his control. You marked ones get to open collars. Who knew? Useful, at times, but it's nothing special. Not at all like my powers."

"We're marked for a reason," I say. "We can lead the way out of this place." I move forward, trying to get within reach of Samantha, but the shackle holds me back by the ankle. "Where's Moses? What did you do to him?"

"What he deserved," she says. "But the real question is what will I do to *you*, now that you know my little secret."

"What secret?"

"It's amusing when a genius plays dumb."

Her taunting tone tells me what I had missed. "There's no leader here. Moses has been gone this whole time…"

"That's better," she says.

"Where is he?" I demand.

She shrugs. "Not my concern."

"But it is! It's all of our concern. The leaders are the only ones holding back the Colorless One."

"Oh, is that what you call the one who speaks in the darkness? He is our only hope."

"*Hope?* He will never let us leave."

Samantha laughs. "You really think we can leave? This is hell, Paul!"

"No, that's a lie!"

"Think about it, Dr. Fitzroy. There is no escape. There is only temporary relief from the pain. We can hope for numbness, maybe revenge, nothing more."

Her words remind me of what happened in Yellow, of how Emma's father had been corrupted by the Colorless One and trapped Yellow's leaders in the mine beneath the pit.

"No, no, none of this is true."

She looks amused. "You sound so sure...the Paul I knew was never so sure of anything."

"I've seen people leave," I say. "I met my mother in the Red Tower. She left through the White Tower."

Again Samantha laughs, and this time it's even more chilling. "If there is a lie about this place, it's the White Tower. If you want obliteration, by all means, go up through the light. Give up yourself and exist no more. Not me. I will not give in." She peers at me, sees the emotion on my face. "What, you think it leads to some kind of paradise? That your mother is happy? She no longer exists!"

"No, the leaders, Abram, Daniel, and others, they told me—"

"The leaders lie! They are here only to guard us and keep us suffering. Think about it, Paul. Who makes us send teams to fight in the Scouring? Who keeps the order? Who makes sure the collars are used? Who really has the power?"

I look away. Each of her questions is a blow to my confidence, because there's some truth in it. I've shielded my own thoughts from this. The leaders have been kind to me...but they have always seemed to hold information back, to keep us in the dark. My mind swirls downward, until it finds rest before a blue light emanating from a staff. Abram's light was the first light I saw in this place.

I take a deep breath and turn back to Samantha's emerald eyes. "Please, listen," I say. "The leaders told me the way out. Each tower has to be in equilibrium. Each marked one has to lead the right tower. Then our powers will be enough to fight and overcome the darkness. Then we can leave."

"If you want oblivion, then by all means," Samantha says. "Not me. I prefer to continue existing."

"The light does not obliterate. The White Tower is a gateway. It's the way we reach a place that's far better than any existence here. It's better than we can imagine." Daniel's words from long ago speak to me, assuring me. Even though I can't prove it, I choose to believe. "You have to trust me," I say.

"Oh, I trust that you are deluded. The leaders have tricked you, that much is clear." She holds out her robed arms and motions to the tower around us. "In Black we've managed to free ourselves from them. Soon we'll set all the towers free."

I shake my leg, making the chain and shackle clank loudly against the ground. "This is not freedom. It's terror!"

"No." Her eyes blaze. She pulls something from her robe. The tip of a spear, dark and hard. "For terror you need pain."

I hold my head up. I won't beg. I won't cry. The worst she can do is kill me. Back to a coffin. Wiped. I've risen before.

She lunges. The point stabs into my side. Deep. Just below the ribs. The spearhead sticks even as Samantha moves back, standing over me.

I stare down. Blood spills. Pain sickens.

I reach for the wound. The chains stop me.

Samantha laughs. "Now *that's* terror! And no escape, ooh, how it hurts. Let's make the most of it, shall we? You will serve me, Paul. You will awake below the tower, and you will rise. As you always do. I will name you

Commander. You will fight for me again and again in the Scouring. But first…"

Smoke billows and gathers tight around me. My stomach twists in agony. The spearhead stays wedged in my flesh. Vision begins to blur. Samantha holds up something I've heard of but never seen.

The iron crown.

It comes into focus. No jewels, no luster. Tips jagged as teeth.

"Before you fade I must see something from our past," she says. "The one who speaks in the darkness, the true ruler of this place, he told me we should do this together…"

She lowers the iron band. I try to twist away, but it only makes the pain bite harder. There's no escape. The crown feels heavy as a cage as it presses down.

30

THE HOSPITAL WINDOW is black at night, reflecting the green and red iridescent lights of my life machine. Susan has gone home. Not even she, ever faithful and strong as she is, can or should stay in a hospital for a month. The doctors and nurses are on call, but my condition is stable. My physical condition. Otherwise I'm as unstable as ever.

There's no lonelier place than a hospital room at night. It's solitary confinement without justice. No one deserves sickness. No one deserves death.

Or do we? One thing a deathbed is good for: perspective. I was always smart, always driven. But I lied to get ahead. I married Susan for money. I was an absent father, a cheating husband, an arrogant surgeon.

I got better, I must sadly admit, after my son died. It shook something in me. I gave up a fortune to pursue my quest. I would fight death. I would discover the secret to eternal life.

It started at the National Institutes of Health. Our team found ways to fight cancer, even beat it most of the time. But the discoveries and inventions went deeper than that. We implanted circuitry on human brains. We animated their minds as never possible before. The government authorized the research, but tried to hold it back, to control it.

Then I found my business partner from China. Max and I signed a contract to introduce the technology to the masses. It started with the elites. They bought it for their kids, to ensure success, and it worked. Smart phones moved from inside pockets to inside skulls. Much more convenient. Much more effective. Much more dangerous.

I glance at the two stacks of letters by the hospital bed. It's only a small subset of the thousands I receive. My assistants comb through them and pick the best each day to deposit here, for my casual reading. I lean to the side, tubes straining in my arm, and take the top letters from each stack. I lay them on my lap and read.

The left one is from a hater. The right one is from a lover. I never let myself read from one stack alone.

The lover's letter is ironic, written as it is on paper. So few write on paper anymore. This one's from a mother. It praises my "world-changing" invention and says I made all the difference in her son's life. He'd been hit by a car, nearly died, paralyzed from the neck down. But thanks to a grant from the government, she'd been able to buy my technology—the model called the "fusion"—and it enabled her son to learn to walk again. Digital circuitry fused to neural activity. A handicapped life made whole.

The hater's letter is typical. Another mother. Mothers always write because they always care. My mother cared, but she's been dead a long time. I feel like I barely remember her. "Dear Devil Fitzroy," the letter begins. Ouch. Must they be so harsh? This mother's son had the highest-level technology called the "precept." He had been a middling student. The precept changed that. His average test scores turned gifted with the flip of a precept switch. It was a common story. So, unfortunately, was the next paragraph the mother wrote:

"He was a junior when he first started playing the game. The addiction was worse than drugs. After a week he was gone. At dinner his mind was in the game. In class his mind was in the game. We made him turn it off. We talked to him. *But all my friends are on it*, he'd say. We gave him one last warning: play during school and we're uninstalling the precept. He ran away that night. We haven't seen him since."

I lay the letter back on the stack.

"It wasn't my fault," I say softly into the empty room. Of course technology could be used for good and bad. I didn't make the rules. I only invented and shared a tool. Her son connected with his friends. Millions found freedom like this. Even if things didn't go as some people had planned.

Enough letters. I focus on my own precept. I find an old sitcom I used to like. It projects before me, playing in high definition in the quiet, dark hospital room. It only makes me feel worse. I should sleep. I put the precept on sleep mode.

I toss and turn but sleep doesn't come.

I pick up a book Susan left for me. It has real mass, even golden edges on its pages. No wonder, it says "Holy Bible" on the front. I flip it open and read a few lines near the front. It's about killing goats. Doesn't make any sense to me. I turn toward the back. There's a book called James. It's short. I read it. One thing sticks out: whoever keeps the whole law but stumbles on one thing is guilty of breaking all of it.

That hardly seems fair. I hope it's not right. I've stumbled on more things than one.

I close the book and turn on the precept again. I find another show, a newer one. I laugh shallowly. I hurt inside.

I'm on the third episode when the door opens.

A woman strides in and stands beside me, looking down, not smiling, waiting.

"You don't recognize me," she says.

But then I do. Her voice and green eyes are the same, though her hair's gone gray. It's Samantha, my old fling.

I haven't seen her since Chicago. It's been twenty years, more. Last time she threatened to kill me if she ever saw me again. "Why are you here?"

"I heard you're dying from a brain tumor."

"True."

"Does it hurt?"

"Not since they stopped the treatment." I motion to the chair in the corner. "You want to sit?"

She shakes her head, glances to the show projected from my precept. "Could you turn that off?"

"Sure, sorry."

"Thanks, that's better." She adjusts the purse over her shoulder. "How long do you have?"

"I don't know. Weeks, maybe a few months."

"I made a promise…" Her voice fades. She starts to cry.

"What do you mean? What's wrong?"

She wipes her eyes, smearing black mascara down her cheeks. She reaches into her bag. The gun is small. Her fingernail on the trigger is red against black.

I panic. "No, wait. Please, listen. I've changed."

Her arm extends. "You will never change for me."

"Don't do this, Samantha," I beg. "Look at me. I'm going to die anyway. Please. My precept is recording this. You'll go to jail!"

She shakes her head, face grim. "You first, then me. We'll go where we're going together."

"This is crazy! Why now?"

"You think time has helped? You have no idea how much I've suffered."

"I'm sorry," I say. "I really am."

"Too late," she says.

"It was my fault." My voice is pleading. "I was the one who led you along, I know. But I've changed, I swear it. I'm still with Susan."

"Don't say that name!" She jabs the gun forward, presses it to my forehead. The metal hurts against my skin. It all hurts.

My eyes moisten. "I'm sorry, Samantha."

"Oh, don't cry," she moans, her own tears carving channels through her smeared mascara.

I place my hand gently over hers. The gun moves back, retreating, then lowers.

Samantha sighs and collapses over me, her head against my chest. I lay there a moment in shock, feeling her closeness and warmth. She is hurting. I am dying. Her presence is a painful reminder of my mistakes.

The tube in my arm swings as I put my arms around her. "I'm sorry. I'm so sorry." I say it to myself and to her as we cry together.

The vision freezes. It rewinds.

"Only in your dreams," rumbles a deep voice.

Samantha is still. The gun held steady. And in that moment, from beyond the hospital window, from the black, the voice comes again.

"You deserved it."

It is a voice I have heard before, in the pit. "Who are you?"

"You know. I control her. I can stop her. I can make her shoot. Your fate is mine."

No. The Colorless One. This can't be real.

"I did not create this," he growls. "You did."

"You lie. Let us go. All of us."

"The enemy would like that very much…"

In the vision, from the hospital bed, inside myself, I summon my power from the Five Towers. As much as I can hold. I unleash it like an explosion against the formless void behind the hospital glass. The power flashes uselessly, like heat lightning in the distance. The darkness absorbs it, drains all of it. My power is gone.

The sinister voice laughs and laughs. Cruel as death.

"Your power is nothing to me," he says. "I could crush you with a word. You could die and die and die, but back you would come, and this would grow tiresome."

"You can't kill me," I say.

"And you can't leave. Your mother was the last. Never again, not without payment."

"You're the one who blocks the White Tower. You're…the Colorless One."

"A silly name your leaders use. Call me what you wish. Only black has the power to conquer light. Black is basal and nonnegotiable, the source of shadow, line, perspective and mood. It defeats white. It hides stains, and God doomed all his creation to stains. He allowed this. Blame him. Not me."

"That's a lie," I say. "The leaders said we are being

scoured, washed clean."

"Do you really think *you* can be cleaned?"

His question strikes like a blow. I've always questioned this. I've come far, but the more light I've found, the more stains I've seen. "What do you want from me?"

"There's that brain of yours! I want no more than what I wanted from the enemy. A trade. You give up yourself, and the others can go."

I don't believe him. But I have to know. "What do you mean, give up myself?"

"If you stay with me, the others can go to the White Tower."

"Why should I trust you?"

"Because I'm going to let you go now. Do whatever the leaders have asked. The darkness will grow, but I will release my hold over the Black Tower. Only the Scouring will remain black. When the time comes, the others may leave. You will stay with me. In the pit. Forever."

Dreadful deal. Cold sweat on the hospital bed. The lines on the machine show my heart racing.

"Why me?"

"Consider it my way of saying thanks," the Colorless One sneers. "You are the one who gave me the world. You invented the technology. You connected the world's minds. It was the final tool I needed."

"If you won the world, then why are you here?"

"The enemy is a sore loser. He burned the world to nothing once it was mine."

"I don't believe you."

"Oh? He flooded it once. This time he used fire. He wanted a new earth. He's never satisfied. Blame him. Not me."

The lies coil around me. They squeeze. I pretend to stop fighting. "How did you come here?"

"It's the gateway. It's the furthest I could come. The enemy won't allow me through."

"But he would let me?"

"I will speak truly. All of you were *meant* to leave, but I stopped that. You have seen my powers here. The gateway is gone. The enemy does not like this, so we have reached an agreement. I will open the gateway again *only if you stay*."

No, no, no. "Why me?"

"Must I explain even this? The enemy chose you. He made you number 720. He gave you the scars. And now I want to take you from him. You know your own failures. You belong with me."

"What if I don't agree?"

"Then everyone stays in the Five Towers. Forever."

"And if I agree? What will happen to me?"

"I make no promises, except that the others may leave if you stay. What's your decision?"

It's too much, too heavy. I'm still in the hospital room, with Samantha's gun leveled at me, frozen in time and space. "Did she shoot or not?" I ask.

"Stay with me and you'll find out every possible ending, except one."

It makes me shudder. The Colorless One twists my past and present. I remember the visions in the pit. The one with Samantha happily married if she had not had the affair with me. The one with my beautiful grandchildren who never existed.

I fear the answer but ask anyway: "What ending won't I see?"

"The one after the White Tower. The enemy's ending."

I think of the others, all 719 of them. I see the faces of Emma and Kiyo and Baron and Hank and even Samantha. They deserve to be saved from this place. Even if I don't, I could still help them escape.

"So you'll let the others go through the White Tower?" I ask. "All 719, and the leaders?"

"The leaders will abandon you. They know they cannot withstand me, so they are fleeing already. Their fates are beyond my control. But the others, yes, all 719. It's simple. They leave if you stay."

Is this real? I am Paul Fitzroy, inside his frail body on the hospital bed. I look into the barrel of Samantha's gun. It is blacker than black, a hole into oblivion.

And it's my fault that she's here.

"You see," the voice rumbles. "You can never be scoured of what you've done. You don't deserve to leave."

The words hold me like a vice. I'm not like the others. I'm the worst failure who made it into the Five Towers— capable of so much on Earth, but never living up to it. That's why my powers are strong. That's why I'm chosen.

If this is my fate, and I can still save the others, so be it.

"Okay. I'll do it."

"You were always so smart." The Colorless One chuckles darkly. "This is our little secret. Tell no one. If others know, the deal is off. You will know when the time has come. Until then, do whatever you wish. Obey the leaders. Fight me. It doesn't matter. You cannot win."

I gaze into the hospital window, reflecting my pale face and Samantha's gun, hollow as death. Is there no other hope?

"Until then..." The voice makes the black glass tremble and the reflection fade.

31

"I SHOT YOU!"

Samantha's scream shatters the vision. Her face, twisted with rage, is inches from mine. Wind whips her hair into a frenzy of red. She clutches my shirt by the fist. Her other hand holds the crown. Her smoke still smothers my power. The shock of her anger almost makes me forget the pains—spearhead wedged in my side, deal with the Colorless One. Almost.

"I did it. I killed you," she growls. "That vision's ending was a lie. I would never be so weak, so broken. I would never cry over *you*."

Laced within her anger there's fear and uncertainty. I can hear it in the shrill vibrations of her voice. I can see it in her flitting green eyes.

"I'm sorry, Samantha." The words come out in a painful whisper. I taste iron. Blood in my mouth. Life spilling out. My body might be timeless here, atop the Black Tower instead of in a hospital, but it dies before it comes back. "I'm...sorry."

"Don't you *dare*," she cries out. "*I* am in control here."

"You didn't pull the trigger." I grit the words out. "I...deserved it. But you did the right—"

She swings the crown and slams it into my head like a

club. Pain explodes. Something wet pours down my face.

She twists my shirt tighter in her fist. She pulls me closer. The angry snarl of her lips is blurred. She rears back with the crown to strike again.

But she doesn't. Her face goes white with shock. A hand has grabbed her wrist. Smoke presses in around us.

"Let him go," says a voice from the smoke. It's Baron.

"*Kill them!*" Samantha shrieks. Her grip on my shirt releases, and I fall to the side, flat on the stone ground.

I try to push myself up. Through the pain I hear intense fighting. Metal clashing against metal. Grunts. Shouts. A scream grows faint, like someone falling.

Power erupts everywhere. So many colors. Blurring. Fading.

Yellow threads suddenly surge into me. They shock my system like a dive into icy water. I come up for breath.

I rise to my knees. The pain is gone.

An object falls. I catch it. The spearhead that stabbed into me. I clench it as my vision clears. The weaves are thick and vivid. Black, yellow, blue, and green.

My power. It's back. The block is gone.

In the darkness I focus on the thousands of intricate blue threads. They were invisible, but now they are close. The cloud has lifted from my mind. Samantha's darkness fled.

The wind bends at my command. It funnels together and scatters the smoke. The light of dawn fills the room. Several bodies are motionless on the ground. Two black-robed girls. Three boys in helms. The smoke surges up to take them.

Four others are locked in battle before me. On the far side of the room, before the hole in the wall, Napoleon and

Baron face off with spears and shields. They jab and thrust, block and evade, ever turning and shifting. Closer, in the center, Kiyo and Samantha stand motionless but fight with even more intensity. Their powers collide like atoms in a nuclear reactor, threatening to explode and kill us all.

"No!" Baron shouts. Napoleon has pressed him back, toward the gaping hole. Baron's heels are on the edge. His arms swing wildly. He's going to fall.

But I won't let that happen.

I grab him with the wind and yank him back. He slides across the stone floor. I seize Napoleon next, wrapping him in air tight as a caterpillar in a cocoon.

When I glance to Samantha and Kiyo, my stomach sinks. Kiyo has fallen to her knees. Still her power is there, but Samantha's black weaves loom over her like a tidal wave. Worse, Samantha's eyes are locked on me.

The wave shifts and rushes at me. I lift my power to try to hold it off, but I know it will fail. Black smoke will smother my weaves.

Her power enters my mind. She shuts me down again.

Knowing I'm finished, I meet her green eyes. I mouth the words, "I'm sorry."

Samantha flinches, and in that moment of hesitation, Baron lunges behind her. His spear stabs, and she falters.

Napoleon comes at Baron from behind.

Kiyo rises and steps forward with outstretched arms. Wind blasts from her and whips into Samantha and Napoleon. They are flung back, through the hole in the wall. The rushing wind drowns out their falling screams.

32

I PEER OVER the edge, down the length of the Black Tower. The bodies of Samantha and Napoleon look like ants on the ground. The smoke comes quickly. It swirls up and over the bodies, like a vicious morning mist. When the smoke retreats it leaves the ground bare; it leaves me somber.

Samantha and Napoleon led the Council. Now they will go to the bottom—wiped and, I have to hope, scoured of something. All else is quiet around the tower. There's no sign of the rebellion. Joan and Max should have retreated far into the hills by now.

I turn to Kiyo and Baron. Seeing their familiar faces brings warmth back. They saved me—Kiyo, who nearly smothered me with her power, and Baron, who was once my enemy in Green. My hands go to my side, where the spearhead stabbed into me. I feel something. I pull away the fabric.

A scar. My fifth.

I quickly lower the shirt. Daniel said I would get five scars. He said it would mean the end nears. But how? The dark deal with the Colorless One? My chest tightens. I desperately want the deal to be a lie. It goes against what the leaders have said. The light would never agree with the

Colorless One. The light wouldn't abandon me.

Or would it?

I clench the black spearhead, then pocket it as a reminder. It's my fault Samantha is here. I can cling to a faint hope that there's another way, but if I must stay so the others can escape, I'll do it.

"You okay?" Baron asks. "You look pale."

I meet his eyes and nod. He and Kiyo have scars like mine. We are the marked ones. I will fight with them until my time comes. We have to take control of what we can.

"Thank you both," I say. "I would have died."

"You would have come back," Kiyo says softly. "But this was our chance. She knew you had help, and expected it would be me. She did not know about Baron."

He bows his head in acknowledgment. His granite eyes are steady as ever. "Napoleon made me his Deputy. He thought the crown would make me stronger. But the crown, even among its twisted visions, helped me remember who I was, and what happened in Green." He flashes a boyish grin. "Giving sets you free, right?"

I smile back. "You've saved me twice. When I was in Green and we fought together in the Scouring, you gave yourself up to Black so I could escape. I never had a chance to thank you for that. So…thank you, Baron. And thank you again."

"Hey, we're family. You married my granddaughter, after all."

"I was lucky to have her." The vision in the hospital room comes back to me. Susan had stayed by my side for weeks. Samantha came, too. I glance again over the edge, to the bare ground where her body and Napoleon's were a moment ago.

"We have to help them," I say.

"No need," Baron replies. "They will go to the coffins and fight to get out. They deserve no better."

Kiyo shakes her head. "We might all deserve that. It was not always this way."

"What do you mean?" I ask.

"I arrived in this tower first." Kiyo gazes out of the tower and over the hills as she speaks. "In other towers I have remembered the truth of what happened here. Once, long ago, when this tower was purple instead of black, waking here was gentler than in Blue. Moses and a troop would *welcome* the newcomers in the pit. There was no fighting. The troop would invite them to join. Joshua would train them, with padded weapons, for the Scouring. For unity and order. There were no Commanders, no Deputies, no Lords, no Rice. All were equal under the Judge."

"Who is this Judge?" I ask.

"That is what we call Purple's facet of the prism," she says. "Like the Genius in Blue. The Healer in Yellow."

"Can we go back to that old way?" I ask.

Kiyo shakes her head. "Moses is gone."

I glance around the room. Light floods in with the rising suns and the lifting mist. Dust covers everything. The open shackles hang like distant memories on the wall.

"Do you think he was ever bound here?" I ask.

"Perhaps," Kiyo says, "but he has long been gone. Samantha said she alone talked to Moses. She used this to strengthen her hold on this tower. She did everything should could to maintain power. She lied about Moses. She changed the laws. She hid *this*."

Kiyo lifts a simple, metal chalice before us. Her gold-flecked eyes gaze upon it like it's a holy grail. Her fingers are pale against the dark purple surface.

"What is it?" Baron asks.

"The cup of judgment," she says. "When this tower was purple and the leaders were here, they would invite others to join them in the room below, at the round table. They would pass the cup. We would drink and see the past. The true past."

I look from the chalice to the crown, still lying on the ground near us. I'm amazed Samantha changed even this. Maybe it was the Colorless One's doing. He tainted the crown.

"If this happened here," I say, "the Colorless One could try the same thing in other towers. We need to find out how it happened. Maybe Samantha could remember…"

"Better if she does not," Baron replies. "The past is dangerous. Her past seems especially so for you."

I think of Samantha in the hospital room, with her gun leveled at me. I think of her in the Black Tower, with smoke smothering me. It was the same wrath. But it could also become the same remorse. And she alone might know how the Colorless One has infected this tower.

"What if we could control the crown?" I ask. "Kiyo, do you remember how we last used the Sieve in Blue?"

"Yes, you used your power," she says. "It directed the memory to what had happened in the Black Tower. But the Colorless One's taint was even there, in the Sieve. It dragged you into the pit. The taint will surely be stronger here."

"We'll try the chalice first, but then the crown," I say. "You two will be with me. Two marked ones to drag me

195

back if the Colorless One tries to suck me in. We will direct Samantha's memories to this tower and whatever the Colorless One has done."

Baron rubs his chin, considering it. "Controlling the past could be more dangerous than the past itself."

"We have to learn what the Colorless One has done before we can undo it," I say. "And we have to start somehow giving Samantha and Napoleon their memories back."

Baron grins as his gray eyes meet mine. "All right. Worth a try," he says. "Giving sets you free."

"If this is our plan, we should go now," Kiyo says. "They could already be waking."

We move fast from there. I carry the crown. Kiyo takes the chalice. Troops eye us curiously as we descend the stairs and pass through the great hall. No one tries to stop us. They don't know that their Commander and the leader of the Council have died.

The door to the cavernous battleground is sealed, with its emblem of a metal shield. Kiyo presses her hand to the emblem. The door swings open.

"This one is for boys," she says. "The next one is for girls."

"Baron, will you go to Napoleon?" I ask.

"Seems right," he says. "I was his Deputy, after all."

I weave my power to lower Baron to the sandy floor, and then Kiyo and I hurry to the next cavern. Two coffins lay like black monoliths on the sand. There is a faint tapping from one of them. I rush to it and unclasp the buckles holding it shut.

Samantha rises up on her elbows, yawning.

"Welcome," I say.

Her vivid green eyes are amazingly calm and innocent. "Where am I?" she asks, rising to her feet and stretching her arms and yawning again. "Who are you?"

"I'm...Cipher. And this is Kiyo. It's safe here." I force myself to smile, to soften my voice. "We have a lot to tell you. You died...but you're born again. This is the Purple Tower."

33

SAMANTHA'S HAIR RIPPLES like a red banner in the ocean breeze. Waves crash at the base of the cliff, dark blue against black rock, foaming into white. The suns must be high overhead, but blocked by the clouds. The Blue Tower is shrouded in mist. The Purple Tower is lonely and dominant behind us.

Samantha drank from the chalice, the cup of judgment. She saw fragments from her past, but mostly gaps. Kiyo believes that the Colorless One's hold over Samantha, through the crown, still blacks out things the chalice should reveal. Samantha didn't see me or anything about how the Colorless One twisted her and this tower. So she agreed to test the crown.

Now, on a ledge perched over the sea, the time has come. I lift the round iron band, wary of its jagged tips.

I look to Kiyo. "Ready?"

She nods and places a hand on Samantha's shoulder.

I turn to Baron, whose granite eyes steady me.

He clutches an open collar in his white-knuckled fist. He clasps Samantha's other shoulder with his free hand.

Samantha gracefully bows her head. I've told her that we will put the crown on her, and that she will see more from her past. I have not told her that if this goes wrong, if the Colorless One tries something, Baron will snap the collar around her neck.

I summon the blue threads first. They flow like glistening ribbons, feeling smoother and clearer this close to the sea. The threads pass in and through Baron, drawing dense cords of green, then through Kiyo, taking on purple and red and yellow. Invisible to Samantha, our powers weave into an intricate five-colored tapestry that covers the crown as I lower it onto her head.

We are yanked away from the Five Towers.

Samantha studies herself in a mirror. She looks young and stunning, exactly as I remember her from high school, but only a few years older than she is in the Five Towers. Inside she feels nervous, insecure. Her parents are gone, busy with work. Johnny will be here soon. It's their first date. She wants to be wanted. Her hand trembles as she rubs lipstick onto her lips. The red is a dark, unnatural crimson.

A doorbell rings. After a final glance at herself, she turns from the mirror and flicks the lights off.

I feel the vision yanked again.

This time I fight it.

I pour every thought and power into the Five Towers, away from Earth. A force like gravity fights back, tugging me down, but I pull harder and blast away from the terrestrial sphere.

A stately old man stands alone before Samantha. He holds a crown in his aged hands. His beard is white as snow. His eyes like lively coals. He looks concerned.

"I know the memories can be hard," he says. "But you must see before you can be scoured."

He lies.

The voice is a hiss in Samantha's mind.

He manipulates you. Put the crown on him. See what happens!

The words coil around Samantha like a serpent around its prey. She pretends to cry. She shudders as her hands cover her face.

The old man places a hand on her shoulder. "There now, it's going to be okay. The light will come. It will be worth it, more than you can imagine."

As he continues, speaking comfort, the serpent squeezes tighter and its words fall like black ink over a violet canvas. Samantha strikes like an asp. She seizes the crown and twists and yanks.

The old man's wrist pops. The crown comes free.

Samantha sweeps it up and down, hard, onto the man's white hair. He falls to his knees. The look on his face is not pain, not even surprise. It is sadness.

"Your end comes soon," the old man says.

"No, this is *your* end. I control this domain now." The words come from Samantha's mouth, but they sound like the same dark hiss that was in her mind.

"Light will prevail," the old man groans. His form flickers and fades. As his body vanishes, his last words come like an echo, "The light…"

The crown clatters against the ground. Samantha kneels and picks it up. She does not think of the man. She does not think of herself. She moves like she's under a spell.

Put it on, the voice says. *Your eyes will be opened. You will be like a god. You will rule this place.*

Samantha lifts the crown and gazes at it. The metal is cool and lifeless. Black cracks pulse across the surface like a virus. She hesitates, almost drops it.

Will you let men rule you?

Samantha hardens inside. She raises the crown. It fits flawlessly, weightlessly.

She is no longer bound by time, or by the past. She sits on an iron throne near the center of the Scouring. A gaping black hole is on the ground to her side. A long line of boys and girls stretches before her, coiling around and around and covering the Scouring's flat gray stones. Five towers loom over the Scouring. They have no color. Each one is black against a charcoal sky. There are no suns, no stars.

A boy steps to her throne and kneels. He wears a collar around his neck.

"Color?" Samantha demands. "Tell me truly."

"Green," he says.

She shakes her head. "There are no colors here. Go."

He shuffles, obedient to her command, toward the black hole in the ground. He steps over the edge and falls into the darkness.

Another boys steps up. He and Samantha have the same exchange. He says, Yellow, and she sends him into the hole.

On and on it goes, until a girl comes forward without a collar.

"Color?" Samantha demands. "Tell me truly."

"Black is the absence of light," the girl says. "Without light there is no color."

"You speak truth." Samantha points to the hole. "You may go freely to your peace."

The girl moves listlessly to the hole and steps over the edge and falls into the darkness.

Another girl comes forward. And another and another. For every person that falls into the hole, one emerges from outside the Scouring and steps to the back of the line. They do not talk. They do not eat or sleep or dream. The line never ends. Samantha will judge each boy and girl forever.

But then a light flickers from beyond the Scouring.

Samantha looks up to one of the towers. It has the shape of a tree, a dead tree with no leaves or green. Near the top, a figure stands gazing down on the Scouring and on Samantha. He flashes a light. It blinks green.

Anger swells in Samantha.

Get out of here, the voice hisses.

Another flicker makes Samantha turn to another tower. It has tall, intricate turrets. A figure blinks yellow atop it. The light is only a flash, like the beam from a lighthouse spinning around.

The next tower's light is brighter still. It is blue, like the ocean and the sky. When it flickers, I come into the vision. My power is there, faint but visible.

When our different colored lights meet above the Scouring, we fuse into a greater, whiter light. This force beams down to Samantha. It touches her crown.

She clenches it tight, holding it down.

No! the voice shouts.

But our light is too strong. We grab the crown and yank it free and hurl it as far as we can.

34

OUR FEET DANGLE over the cliff's edge. Samantha, Kiyo, Baron, and I gaze out over the sea. The crown is somewhere down there, maybe smashed against the rocks, sunken to the bottom, out of reach.

It worked. Our powers guided Samantha's memory. But the memory in the Scouring has not happened. May it never. Even if it means I go through with the Colorless One's deal.

"You were on a throne," I say. "How did you get there?

"That was his promise." Samantha breathes fast, shallow breaths, like an accused under interrogation. "He showed me it. I don't know how."

"Who is *he*?" Kiyo asks.

"The voice in the darkness," Samantha says. "I don't know what he looked like. I don't remember. My memories are all jumbled. But his voice was power. He warned me about this place, gave me this vision as a hope if I would serve him. He would make me the judge of all."

"What did he want you to do?" I ask.

"You saw it." She shakes her head, gazing blankly at the crashing waves. "He wants to remove the colors. He wants endless repetition. No change. No color. My part was to lead the Black Tower, to gather everyone here and drain the light from their pasts."

"How?"

Samantha turns to me. Her eyes are moist. "The one who promised me the throne, he said he knew the pain I felt from my memories of Earth. He said he could remove the pain. I don't know how exactly, but in the memory on the throne, it no longer seemed to hurt. With the crown on my head, I couldn't feel much of anything. There were no colors. I was numb."

"This is evil." Baron, who had been silent, speaks with quiet confidence. "Draining the color from our past only drains life. I have seen hard memories, too, but now they are flooded with vivid light. The enemy wants to trap us here forever, in a cycle of despair and shame, until we are robbed of what makes us who we are."

"I'm sorry," Samantha says. "I don't know how it came to that. I just wanted to stop hurting…"

"It could have happened to any of us," I say. "You were deceived. We won't let it happen again. I think your vision showed how we can fight back. It ended because there were lights from the five black towers. I was the light from Blue."

"I was Green," Baron says.

"Purple," Kiyo says, running a finger along the scar at the back of her hand. "Three marked ones."

"Yes, and three small beams of light. We need more light than that." I gaze hopefully at the Blue Tower, remembering what Abram and Sarai once told me. "If we bring the towers to equilibrium, with each person in the tower that best reflects his or her light, the prism would be complete."

"That is the opposite of the vision we just saw," Baron says.

"Yes, the enemy wants to twist everyone's past," I say. "He would eliminate our unique colors and make us a colorless mass. And he has been gaining ground. Just look at the White Tower gone black. He is tainting our memories, draining them of light. He blames us." I meet Samantha's eyes. "He shames us."

"So I'm not the only one?" Samantha asks.

"No, not at all." Kiyo gently places her hand on Samantha's. "We all confront difficult pasts."

"I'm sorry. I—" I start to apologize to Samantha again, but I don't know where to start. Her memory is so confused. She doesn't even know about me yet.

"It's okay," Samantha says, her voice innocent. "You didn't know the crown would do this. At least I know something of my past now."

"Something, yes." I smile as my heart aches for her.

"Kiyo," I say. "Will you help Samantha as she gains her memories back?"

"Of course," Kiyo replies. "We all will."

"How?" Baron asks, his gray eyes peering down at the foamy sea. "The crown is gone."

"It was the Colorless One's device," Kiyo says. "Now his taint should be fading. We will drink from the cup of judgment to see the past. It may take time, but those who belong in Purple will see the truth. We will all be scoured."

"And then what?" Baron asks.

Kiyo and Samantha look to me expectantly.

My hand finds the spearhead in my pocket. I look toward the black shard that rises from the center of the Scouring. A blade stabbing into the sky.

The darkness will grow, the Colorless One said, *but I will release my hold over the Black Tower.*

And so it has happened. One step closer to my deal with the enemy. Whether it's true or not, we will keep fighting him with everything we have. Abram's words come to me again.

"We need equilibrium," I say. "Only then will our light be pure enough. The darkness will continue to grow. We must move quickly."

"You sound as if you plan to leave," Kiyo says.

I nod. "We've cleansed Black. Kiyo, there's no one better than you to lead here now."

"Yes, I am marked for this." Kiyo folds her scarred hands. "I will restore order to the Purple Tower. We will allow more light in."

Her quiet strength reminds me of our time together in Blue. The memory makes me smile. "Do you remember when we first met?"

Kiyo looks up, her eyes like galaxies. "Yes. In Blue."

"We were in a class together," I say. "Sarai was the teacher. She wanted us to get a piece of paper without rising from our desks. Max mocked you for trying to summon the air."

"And then you blew him out of his desk." Her hand covers her mouth as she laughs. "So funny to think of it now."

"We've all come a long way," I say. "You helped me. You shared your story. I've always been amazed by you."

A touch of pink colors her cheeks. "Thank you, Cipher. What will you do now?"

I look back toward the Scouring. I point past the dark shard to the immense tree in the distance. "Baron, we need to get you back where you belong, as soon as we can."

"The Green Tower," he says. "And what about you?"

"I'll visit the other marked ones." I think of Emma in Yellow, and Helena in Red. "We need to fight together."

"It is a good plan," Kiyo says. "Will you go back to Blue?"

"Yes." I look over the sea, to the familiar tower rising above the clouds. I'll go back to where I started, where Abram first greeted me. I repeat the words that he said when I last saw him beneath the towers: "The final battle comes."

35

KIYO STANDS BEFORE the gate to the Scouring. Her hair is black as a raven's feather. Her robe is vivid purple, like a first spring flower. Hers was the first robe to be changed. Then our Scouring team. Soon they will all be purple, dyed with indigo from the fields. They will no longer grow only rice. They will no longer fight out of the coffins and the pit. They will join troops. They will learn discipline, with honor instead of brutality, humility instead of ambition.

The boys and girls surrounding Kiyo stand alert as sentinels along the base of the wall. So many familiar faces. Max and Omaki, close by Kiyo's side, her heirs, wear quiet dignity in their expressions. Napoleon and Karl, the former Commanders, stand among the others like equals. They are emperors wiped clean. The exalted brought low.

Shucks, Crispus, and Birger fall into step behind Baron and me. They will march with us into the Scouring. They have drunk from the cup and seen their pasts. Shucks was a homespun American who died in the First World War. Birger was a medieval king of Sweden. Crispus was a Caesar of the Roman Empire. He asked me again to tell his grandmother from Earth, Helena, that he forgives her. She advised her son Constantine in ordering Crispus' execution,

208

over a sordid family affair involving Constantine's wife. "She won't accept the forgiveness," Crispus told me. "She's iron. Tough as nails." But Crispus is tough, too, and I'm glad he's scoured and on our side.

In all these faces, focused and determined, I glimpse what this tower was meant to be. They are a royal banner, a monarch's glory. Loyal and disciplined by choice, not force.

"You fight for the Purple Tower," Kiyo announces, raising her scarred hands. "You fight for the Judge and the glory of the light. Deliver Baron safely to the Green team, then return. Capture no one. Defend as you must."

This is our plan. Kiyo and Baron convinced me it would take too long to sail, especially when the Scouring is the straightest path to Green. I agreed to let Joan take the boat without me, and with a few others from Purple. She and Max created the distraction we needed. Dozens from the villages had rallied behind them, with the promise of hope and freedom. Yet Joan found several villagers plagued by fear. "They need healing," Joan told me. "I will bring them, gently, to Yellow. I will report everything to Emma."

Yellow will not be in this Scouring. But the other towers will, and it's time we use the battle for something good. We will approach the twelve from Green. We will offer Baron to them, without resistance. The rest of us from Purple will make sure he gets there. Then I will go to Blue.

I bow before Kiyo. "Protect this tower," I say. "May the light be with you."

She bows back gracefully. "And with you."

The Scouring gate opens.

I once craved this moment, to escape from this tower. But now the tower has changed. It is not as easy to leave as

I expected, especially when the dark shard rises like a knife in the center of the vast battleground.

A grip on my shoulder steadies me. Baron's granite eyes meet mine, grinning slightly. "You ready?"

We just need to get him to Green. "Let's go," I say.

Our troop of twelve marches forward onto the gray stone of the Scouring. We stay tight together, moving in well-timed order. Jade and another girl I hardly know stay within our block of spears and shields.

I eye the other teams, readying my power. Yellow is not here. Blue and Red are charging. Green is…invisible, I hope.

We veer to the right around the dark shard in the center. The air suddenly feels hot. Flames erupt around us. Jade and the other girl block it with a wall, smoke suffocating the fire and obscuring my view. Fighting clangs out a few feet ahead. The boys from Red are on us.

Grunts and clanging metal are all around. Glancing through the struggle, I see the flames again. We don't need to capture any of them. But we need to get past them.

I blast with the air, flinging several boys back. Others are engaged tightly with Purple's boys. Blunt force would hit my own team. I begin to pull Red's fighters away, one by one.

A power collides against mine. Fire.

It comes from a girl in a red dress. She has auburn ringlets and moves with a saunter I'd recognize a mile away. Helena. The girl who mothered a Roman emperor. The girl who is a marked one.

"Helena!" I shout, but the words drown in the noise of battle. She won't recognize me behind the shield and helmet. But she might recognize my power.

"Cipher!" Jade yells, rushing to my side. "You and Baron go. I'll hold Red back."

She's right. This clash is a distraction. I nod as Jade's smoke snuffs Helena's flames.

Baron meets my eyes and grips my arm. The moment he does, we vanish. He pulls me away from the fighting. Our team will have to hold without us.

The two of us sprint, unseen, toward Green's gate. We are running full on, putting distance between us and the shard, when the blow comes.

It hits me from the side, like a freight train out of thin air. I fall into Baron and we both go down. Our cloak of invisibility is lost.

But so is the other boy's. It's Fugger. The boy who killed me once in Green. He glares at me like a nemesis.

We all rush to our feet. I scan around but see no others from Green. "Fugger, where are the others?" I ask.

"How do you know me?" he demands.

"Where are they?"

He spits. "Ready to take you, runt."

"Baron will go with you freely," I say, forcing calm into my voice, holding out my hands innocently.

Fugger's eyes dart to the side.

"Cipher!" Baron shouts.

My friend is knocked flat, sliding quickly away. He grabs at the ground but can't stop. A weave of power has coiled around his ankle, yanking him toward the center of the Scouring.

I summon enough air to—

The next hit comes from both sides. It knocks the power away. I'm down. Invisible figures take form around me. Green.

I glance up and see Baron hanging at the edge of the shard. His body is half consumed by blackness, his hands grabbing desperately to pull himself up, his face wrenched in fear. The coil of power has released his ankle. But before him stand two red figures, Helena and Marcus.

Baron yanks himself out. He is rising when Marcus strikes like a snake. He kicks Baron so hard that he flies backward into the pit, arms flailing. His yell echoes as he goes down.

Around me iron spears and shields slam into the Green team. Many go down, wrestling invisible forms. The heat of fire presses toward me. Smoke billows to meet it. Blue weaves drop like a net overhead.

Anger funnels into focus. Baron, the marked one, my friend, has fallen into the pit. The Blue Tower will have to wait. I can't let the Colorless One can't take him.

I draw more and more of my power, as much as I can hold, like a diver filling his lungs before plunging underwater. I weave the countless threads around myself and, in a single release of concentrated power, blast out like an explosion of air. Bodies fling back. None are spared. They slide across the stone like iron filings rejected from a powerful magnet. They hit the wall.

I move to the shard and glance down into the darkness. Baron saved me. It's my turn to try to save him.

I take a deep breath. I leap.

36

I TUMBLE THROUGH complete darkness. I try to focus, to summon my power, but fail. Wind rushes up. My arms flail. A skull flashes in my mind. Bones litter the floor of the pit—the bones of those who never existed. They will break my fall, unless I land on Baron...

Questions whip at me. If I die where will I wake up? Or will the Colorless One trap me down here?

Blue light suddenly glows. The wind takes shape, like a net catching me, slowing my fall. The air turns me upright. I land gently on my feet. On a pile of bones.

A tall, robed man stands beside me. He stares up into the darkness, with a raised staff emanating blue light. Intense, gloomy blackness presses around us, but his light holds. He looks like an old wizard. He looks like hope.

"Abram?" It comes out faint as a whisper.

He doesn't look down. "Are more coming?" His voice is strained. His fingers flex and extend like he's pushing against a massive weight.

"I don't know. I leaped in."

"Cipher?" Baron steps from behind Abram.

"Go now," Abram demands. "Both of you. Follow the light."

"But we can help—"

"No. Get out. *Now.*" Still he strains, gazing up. The intensity of his eyes and his voice make me feel very small.

"This way," Baron says, tugging at me.

I turn and see a slender tunnel of pale light leading away. Baron and I move toward it, scrambling as the bones shift beneath us. At the bottom of the pile the darkness feels colder. The ground is bones. The dark eye sockets of a skull stare at me. They pull me in.

My vision goes black, then shifts.

My mother and father are together, like I've never seen them. Their eyes have gentle wrinkles at the corner. A fresh breeze rustles their gray hair. Their hands clasp. Their bare feet press onto soft sand.

"Do you ever wonder what it would have been like if we'd had kids?" my father asks.

Hey! I shout. *I'm here!*

My mother ignores me. She smiles patiently. She eyes a seagull swooping overhead. "It would have been hard on us."

"I know," my father says. "You're right."

"It's better this way." My mother squeezes his hand. "A child could have come between us."

My heart sinks. This can't be true. I try to shake out of it.

"Yes," my father says, "and the world has enough people already…"

No, they are my parents. Surely they wanted me…

"Cipher! Baron!"

The vision blinks away.

It's Abram's voice, firm and loud. He still stands atop the pile of bones, but now he holds his staff out toward me. The blue light pulses forward and pulls a tentacle of darkness out of my head. The relief is like an ear popping, only a thousand times more. I sag from the sensation of release.

"Go!" Abram commands.

He swings his staff and jabs it up so that the blue orb seems to touch the blackness, prodding it back again. Where his staff was before, darkness drips down like tar. He swings the orb from place to place, pushing the deluge back, his blue eyes intense.

I force myself to look away, to obey. Baron is on his knees beside me. I pull him up. He glances to Abram and the dripping black around us.

"What I saw..." he hesitates.

"It was a lie." I clasp his shoulder. "Let's get out of here."

We move forward over the bones, steadying each other as femurs, tibias, and skulls rattle and scatter beneath our feet. There's no telling how deep the bones go. I try to keep my eyes up, looking toward the ceiling of light against dark.

We've gone maybe a hundred steps when the bones thin and reveal bare ground underneath. The solid stone feels good underfoot. The ground slopes up away from us, like we've reached the shore of a lake filled with bones.

A distant grunt makes me turn. The ceiling of light dips as if unable to hold the weight of the darkness any longer. Abram's blue orb is gone. He has fallen to his knees. The black ring around him closes, smaller and smaller.

He looks to us, and even from the distance, his ashen face is resolute. "Go!" he gasps as the darkness engulfs him.

Blackness collapses over all light.

It's quiet. Dark.

The only sound is our heavy breathing. Baron's hand finds mine. He pulls me away.

"It's okay," I whisper, more to myself than to him. *If that happened to Abram…*

Hand in hand we run. We go up an incline, not slowing until the feel of the air changes. It is musty, but lighter. We must be out of the pit, maybe in a tunnel. But I have no way to know which direction we are heading.

"Who goes there?" calls out a voice ahead. It's familiar.

"Cipher."

"Ah, yes. It's me, Daniel." He approaches, hobbling on his gnarled staff and emanating a faint green light, like life itself breaking through the darkness.

Baron sighs with relief. "I made it."

"So you have." Daniel's beard sways as he takes each of us in. "What of Abram?"

"The darkness, it…it closed around him," I say.

"Hm." Daniel's mossy eyebrows droop as he blinks. "Come, come, shelter is not far."

He limps away down the tunnel, his green velvet robe rippling with shadows. We reach a wooden ladder and climb up after Daniel into a room smelling of earth and mushrooms. A door beside us bears us the emblem of the giant tree—the Green Tower's gateway to the Scouring. Beside the doorway is the familiar tally, with updated numbers:

Purple 175

Red 149

Green 144

Yellow 138

Blue 130

The numbers are better than I expected. Not so far from equilibrium. Not that it will be easy to change. How will Yellow get more without even going to the Scouring? The battleground is more chaotic than ever. Maybe Green should stay away from the Scouring.

"Green has equilibrium," I say.

"Aye. Come now." Daniel leads us away from the doorway.

Each step distancing us from the pit feels lighter. The path is familiar, along the inside of a root. We reach a small group of wide-eyed boys and girls. They look like they have been wiped. Three wear Red, two Blue. None from Purple or Yellow. Daniel tells the group to follow.

He leads us up the long stairway through the trunk of the Green Tower. It is narrow and makeshift compared to the stone precision of the tower I've left behind, but this feels much more tranquil. Fairies flutter in glowing blurs around us. The smell is thick and earthy. In the somber quiet of the group following Daniel, I feel like I've made it somewhere safe.

But my shoulders sag as I consider the cost. If Abram's gone, just so we could make it here, nowhere will be safe for long. The darkness that he held back will be unleashed in the Five Towers.

37

WE STEP OUT onto the Jubilee platform. It is just as spellbinding as when I first saw it. The wide plank floor. The lush green canopy above. The gentle floating fairies. It overwhelms my senses after the dark underground world. Tables are spread for a feast. Smells of roasted meat and baking pies fill the air.

"Nebuchadnezzar?" Daniel calls out.

The Hunter suddenly appears beside Daniel, standing twice the old leader's height. His grim, bearded face is mostly hidden under a hood. The long knife still hangs at his hip, the bow at his back. He looks over our group like he's surveying sheep for slaughter.

"They'll need leathers," the Hunter says. "And food?"

"Aye, all but Cipher and Baron," Daniel answers. "They'll come with me."

Daniel leads us up a broad staircase set into a thick tree branch. We ascend toward a small wooden building. The old leader enters first, then Baron and me. Above the small room there is no ceiling, only lush leaves and drifting fairies. Daniel motions for us to sit.

The room is quiet and serene, but what happened in the pit haunts me. "Is Abram okay?" I ask.

Daniel sits cross-legged, studying me calmly.

"It looked like the darkness took him," Baron says.

"It is not so simple," Daniel replies, with each word as delicate as a drop of dew. "We have told you it is different for us, the leaders. Our souls do not dwell fully here. We are meant only to shepherd this place. It is why we cannot defeat the Colorless One. He knows this. He also knows that you—all seven hundred twenty of you—are the true threat. We leaders have long worked for the equilibrium that would bring an end to the Five Towers. Our enemy is no doubt pleased with today's outcome."

"What do you mean?" I ask. "Is Abram gone?"

"Abram has always been willing to sacrifice, to give up what he loves most." Daniel sighs. "Such great faith."

"Is he coming back?" Baron asks.

The thick brush of Daniel's beard turns up in a grin. "We each play our part, until our part ends. The Provider saw fit to entrust me with the wrangling of royal courts, sorcerers, and tyrants. I have faced lions before. Are you ready?"

"Ready for what?" I ask. "If the Colorless One can defeat Abram, what chance do we have?"

"Your assumption is wrong," Daniel replies.

"So Abram *is* still here?"

"What do you think?"

"There was a story, from my time on Earth," I say. "A great wizard was taken down into darkness by an evil creature. But the wizard returned. He even grew brighter."

"Most interesting!" Daniel presses his hands together. "What was this wizard's name?"

"Gandalf."

Daniel shrugs. "Never heard of him. Sounds like a fine tale though. I'd like to hear more of it sometime. But

Abram is like no other. Stories repeat over and over on Earth. This is not Earth. The Colorless One is not simply an evil creature."

"I believe that." I shudder at the enemy's name, remembering my agreement with him—to sacrifice myself to save the others. "I saw what happened to Abram. And the visions…"

"The pit is terrible," Baron agrees. "Maybe we should have stayed in the Purple Tower."

"No," Daniel says. "The darkness may have lifted for now from Purple, but the Colorless One taints every tower."

I remember Helena and Marcus in the Scouring. They knocked Baron into the pit. Could they be tainted? But *every* tower? No, that's impossible.

"We cleansed the taint from Purple," I say. "And surely Green is safe. You and the Hunter are here. You have equilibrium. And I was in Yellow not long ago. Emma and its leaders protect it."

Daniel leans closer, his eyes timeless. "What have you learned of the Colorless One's tactics?"

"He twists the past," I say. "He shows us things that never really happened. He uses our fears and regrets against us. He stops us from being scoured."

"It's shame," Baron says, looking down. "Resentment."

"Hm, yes," Daniel replies.

"He had completely twisted Samantha," I say. "She *hated* me. She wanted to torment me. That's why she shut down my powers and tried to make me suffer. With help we defeated her. She was wiped clean, and I think she'll be okay. Kiyo, one of the marked ones, leads Purple now. Isn't that what you leaders said we should do?"

"Hm, yes. It is good that Purple respects the true Judge again." Daniel breathes deeply, his chest rattling. "What evidence of the Colorless One did you see there?"

"Moses is gone," I say. "The Black Tower had a Council. Samantha used it, and the Colorless One used her, to rule like a tyrant. They called it justice, but it was only power. Everyone fought from the moment they woke, until they died and started again. We've changed that. We destroyed the crown because it tainted everyone's memories."

"I see." Daniel strokes his beard. "As the Sieve has been blocked in Blue. Even here…"

"Is the sap tainted too?" I ask.

"Traces of darkness leak into it. Oh how I fight it, ever I fight, but a leaking dam *will* fail. It is only a matter of time." Daniel sounds grave. His shoulders slump. "All are vulnerable. None of you would be here if your pasts were white. But the Scouring is breaking down. Yellow no longer fights. You've asked Purple to stop. The Colorless One would love nothing more than stagnation…"

"Why go to the Scouring if the White Tower is blocked?" I ask. "There's only the black shard. There's the pit. It's not worth the risk."

"Hm, but fear serves a purpose," Daniel says. "Elijah told me you learned this in Yellow. The Colorless One fears, too. Ever since he fell, the Morning Star has been dark and alone, with no equal and no true companion in his domain. He may overpower a single soul, but not those who unite. We were not created to work alone. We each reflect facets of the prism. Together we make pure white. Together we burn the darkness. Together we overcome the Colorless One."

The hope of Daniel's words washes over me. "So I will return to the Blue Tower?"

"In time, yes." Daniel takes my hand and Baron's. He pulls them together and gazes down at our matching scars. "You represent two of the facets. Three other marked ones represent the other three towers. All are in their proper places, except you, Cipher. If each of you were to lead a tower, ripe with its share of the harvest, one hundred forty-four each, then the prism would be complete. The light would shine through you with such force that the Colorless One would flee and the White Tower would supplant the darkness and take all of you at once."

He makes it sound possible, even easy. "Why didn't you tell me all this in the beginning?" I ask.

"You were not ready. Now you have five scars sealing in your memories. Even with four scars you could discover your past in Black. Emma enhanced this. With her power she sealed light in you, Cipher. The Colorless One cannot take it. No dark deal can remove it. Not even the pit can eliminate it."

I keep my face blank. The spearhead's weight is dread in my pocket. Does Daniel know of my deal with the Colorless One? Is Daniel right? Maybe there is hope…

"So what's to fear?" Baron asks. "Let's attack."

Daniel laughs lightly. "This is why you have not visited Yellow, eh? Fear serves a purpose, as Cipher has learned. It would be foolish to attack without unity. Only together. Cipher, you have done well, bringing Baron here. But you have also seen the consequences of going alone. We lost another leader."

"Another?" I ask.

"You said Moses is gone. I have long suspected this."

"But what if he's in the pit, or locked away, as Elijah and the Widow were?"

"Perhaps, though Joshua surely would have found him by now," Daniel says. "Do not worry about us leaders. We will continue to save those who fall into the pit as long as we can. Those who fell are no longer Black. They have been taken where they belong. This is why Purple's numbers have fallen. Elijah has taken up the task for now. Baron, you will lead here. Your prime facet is the Provider."

Baron holds up his scarred fist before his granite eyes. "Green's tribes will be strong together."

"Yes," Daniel says, "And Cipher, you must visit the other marked ones. Helena in Red, Emma in Yellow. Tell them what I have told you. Each person must be in the proper tower to complete the prism. Then you and the other marked ones can lead the towers, harnessing the light to attack the Colorless One. But beware. The enemy's power grows in desperation. He will taint any memory he can touch. Even now he reaches into Red."

I don't like the sound of this. It's no good if the darkness has only moved from Purple to Red. "How do we stop the taint?"

"Same as ever," Daniel says. "Those who are tainted must be wiped cleaned."

"But what will protect their new memories?"

"What protected Samantha's?" he asks.

"I guess...we did. We helped her remember the truth about her past."

"Aye, you need each other. You must share your stories. Light can shine through everyone here, if only you can find those who know of your past and can guard its truth from shame and vengeance."

Everyone. It sounds right, but it won't be easy. "I'll talk to Helena about this."

"And I will handle Green," Baron says.

"Hm, yes. Helena needs you, Cipher." Daniel's bones creak as he rises. He steps to me and clasps my shoulder. "But in time you must return to where you began, in the Blue Tower. Remember, giving sets you free…"

His words echo in the small room even as his body vanishes.

"Wait…" Baron says, but the leader is already gone. Some things haven't changed. Daniel likes a dramatic exit. "I was going to ask him about the collars."

"What about them?" I ask.

"There should be more. Look." He moves to a bag in the corner of the room. I hadn't even noticed it. He opens the top and pours it out. "This is only a couple dozen. Some could be missing, as they were in Black."

"What if the Colorless One…?"

"Exactly. He could be stealing them somehow. That's what Yellow's leaders told you, right? This will not end well."

"We'll try to find out more," I say, thinking of how Emma hid Yellow's collars away. I hope they're safe. "Until then, we should make the most of it. We need the Green Tower to unite, and the collars only divide us. If we didn't use these, it would be easier for the tribes to share. There would be no leaders who abuse them, like…"

"I know," Baron says, looking down at the lifeless metal on the floor. "Like me. I used them for power. Before I changed. But I'll admit, there's still something tempting about them. We could lead a powerful force against the Colorless One."

I shake my head. "You know that's not the way."

"Right, we have to fight freely."

"You're ready for this," I say. "You will lead the Green Tower in freedom. Unite the tribes and tell them of our true threat. When the other towers are ready, we will attack."

"Sounds fun," Baron says. "Green will be ready."

He looks more confident than ever. This boy was once John D. Rockefeller, the richest man in the world—the one who gave so much of his wealth away that he forever changed human existence, from education to science to industry. His fortune is why I married my wife, Susan, and had my son, Benjamin. It funded the purchase of my mansion, and my research. I can't express the magnitude of it, so I say, simply: "Thank you, Baron."

A grin cracks his granite face. "Only doing my part."

"And you can keep Green's numbers at equilibrium?"

"I think so," Baron says. "I'm strong enough now, with all the good memories I need. But after you leave, Green will need another person. By the way, how are you going to get to Red if we stay out of the Scouring?"

"I'll ask Daniel," I say. "He'll know a way."

A murmur of voices rises from below us, like a chattering of birds. The rich smell of food fills the air.

"It's the Jubilee," I say.

"Good." Baron smiles. "I've missed the feast."

38

THE TRIBES CLIMB from the forest floor to the platform high in the Green Tower. Their clothes are in tatters. They are gaunt and worn down. They look hungry. I know how they feel. I survived here, but I nearly starved before I made it fifty days to the Jubilee. As the crowd sees the tables loaded with food, their faces light up. They come together and heap portions onto their plates and sit in groups and eat like there's no tomorrow.

Baron and I move together through the crowd. They are too focused on the food to pay us much attention. We see the familiar marks on everyone's hands—Wolf, Lion, Eagle, and Snake. The tribes stay together, segregated from each other, showing that the wild struggle in the forest has resumed. There was a temporary peace when Emma and I were here. Our power was enough to stabilize the tribes. But now they are back at it, fighting for every scrap of food, fighting for survival. Giving has not yet set them free.

Daniel stands on the stairs before the crowd. It goes exactly as I remember it. He announces the good results of the Scouring—three captured from Red, two from Blue, and two from Purple, Baron and me. Only two from Green were lost. Next Daniel names the four tribe leaders. They join him on the stairs. I recognize two of them: Violet and

Hank.

Finally Daniel invites the crowd to drink deep of the sap. As the crowd shuffles toward the trough of amber liquid, I remember the things it showed me. Growing up poor. Vowing to be rich. Marrying Susan for money. Inheriting a Rockefeller fortune. Buying a mansion. And then driving away from it all.

"Cipher!" the shout pulls me out of the past.

It's Hank. I smile. He looks like a kid first glimpsing presents on Christmas morning, and in three long strides he's swooped me up into a bear hug.

I pat him on the back, struggling for air. "Hank, Hank, that's good…you can let go…"

He releases me and flashes his boyish grin. He has the same flop of sandy hair, the same broad shoulders. "I can't believe it! When did you get here? How?"

Daniel, Baron, Violet, and two other tribe leaders gather around us. I consider how to explain it. "You know where I went from Yellow?"

A shadow crosses Hank's face. "The Black Tower."

"We've cleansed it," I say. "Now it is the Purple Tower."

His eyes open wide in surprise. "Purple? Imagine that! Seneca and I found our way back here. We belong in these woods. But…does this mean we can leave this place now, through the White Tower?"

"No, sorry…" I shake my head. "Darkness still blocks the way. Baron and I just passed through it. The leaders saved us. That's the only reason we made it here."

"Don't worry," Baron says to Hank. "Green will not enter the Scouring again. Too dangerous. The center is a hole straight down to the pit."

"The pit, " Hank repeats. "I remember…"

Hank went with me once, when I traveled from Yellow to Blue through the tunnels. He has seen the taint of the Colorless One, the twisted visions of what never was.

"Baron's right," I say, clasping Hank's shoulder. "You're safe here. We'll find another way to bring equilibrium to the towers. We must help everyone discover and scour their pasts."

"You sound like a leader," Hank replies. He turns to Daniel, looming like a large adolescent over a bent grandfather. "Why haven't you told us any of this?"

Daniel smiles patiently up at Hank. "Hm, you wanted to know that the Colorless One threatens the Scouring? That his touch darkens even our forest and our memories? How would you feel about the tribes' struggle if you believed that?"

"It would be pointless," Hank says softly.

"I assure you it is not," Daniel replies. "Green has four tribes and the Jubilee for a reason. We must ever be churning, struggling, scouring. This is how we grow, eh? Life stagnates here without trials and tribulations."

"I'm tired of fighting," Hank says.

"As am I." Violet speaks up for the first time. Her weary amethyst eyes meet mine. "Have you come to bring peace to Green again?"

I don't want to tell her no. She and Lily saved me when I first fell out of this tree into Green's vast forest. She was loyal to me when Emma and I united the tribes. She collared Helena, who was once her master in the Roman Empire. And now she's a tribe leader, with the coiling Snake mark on her hand. No wonder she's tired if she's been fighting with the tribes this long.

"I cannot stay here," I say. "I'm going to the Red Tower next. I need to talk to your old friend, Helena Imperatrix."

"Helena." Violet says the name like it's a spell.

"She is a marked one, like us," Baron adds. He holds up his hands, showing the scars to the four tribe leaders. "I will stay to lead this tower. I will work for peace. We must all fight together to defeat the Colorless One."

"Aye, but first you must drink deep of the Provider's bounty," Daniel says, pointing his staff to the sap.

We say goodbyes and goodnights. Hank wraps me in another hug. Violet wishes me well, but she remains distant. All of us move toward the trough at Daniel's direction.

I kneel and dip my hand into the amber liquid. The sap tastes bittersweet.

The aftertaste is banana smoothie.

The butler takes the empty glass, leaving me alone on the veranda. Susan still sleeps inside. She likes the house. It's smaller than the mansion we once had in Chicago. The trees of Rock Creek Park look like dark fingers trying to pull down the sky. A light blinks at the top of the Washington Monument. It's an hour before dawn. An hour to analyze.

The inputs flow seamlessly between neurons and silicon in my mind. This wasn't my goal. I wanted to find a cure for what killed my son, Benjamin. I wanted to live forever. We stopped some forms of cancer but didn't get much farther than that. Instead we found a way to make this connection of human and machine. The best inventions come by surprise.

I test every model personally. They were very expensive

at first. Only the richest could afford it. But we've trimmed down the size, streamlined the production. We bought some of the tech from a Swedish inventor. We will buy out others, whatever it takes. Max, my business partner from China, shipped this prototype yesterday. It is cheaper than champagne. It will take the world far more places, and far faster. Max says governments won't be able to stop it. I say disease won't be able to stop *us*.

We call it the *precept*.

The interface opens. Data streams in. News from around the world processed in nanoseconds. Customized. Arranged. The results appear, perfectly curated to my tastes. In the last twenty-four hours over three million people have accessed one of our products. 3,140,666, to be exact. Not bad given that our earlier models cost more than a car.

The users have viewed a dizzying array of information. Lots of news, sports, lewd things. Whatever. I'm not the judge of how people use my technology. I only give them freedom. And doctors give them cures. Most users have high blood pressure. Their prescriptions can be given and delivered automatically.

I search among all precept users for anyone with early signs of a tumor like Benjamin had. There are seventy-four people. One of them flashes, pulling my attention to my own data.

It's me.

I swallow. No fear. This is the point. Now I know. Now I can fight it. I will see a doctor later today. The precept schedules the meeting automatically, 2 pm with Dr. Neimeyer, one of the nation's best neurologists. I smile. He was a classmate of mine in medical school. He never had what it took for surgery, but he'll be fine for an assessment. He'll be impressed I found it so soon. The world will be impressed. Precepts will sell like bananas.

An alert from Max. I look to it. His face appears.

"Perfect, isn't it?" he asks.

"Just as good as the last one," I say.

"Something wrong?" he asks. His dark eyes peer through the holographic screen. "You look like you saw a ghost."

No reason to hide it. "The precept showed me a medical issue. I'll get it checked out. No big deal."

"See!" Max claps. "No more secrets."

I laugh. "Aren't you the one who led a secret plot against your government?"

"That was different," he says, suddenly defensive.

"Right, sorry." I shouldn't have mentioned it. It's true that his rebellion succeeded, changing a whole country in the blink of an eye. But it's also how he lost his daughter. He doesn't like to talk about that.

"The point is," Max says, "we'll never let any authority have control. Our systems have made sure of that."

"What if someone tries to buy us out?"

It's his turn to laugh. "Have you checked the value of your shares lately?"

"You know it's not about money for me." But I have. In five years Max and I have gotten beyond rich. Susan doesn't like all the attention. She helps me give it away, but we can't do it fast enough.

"No, not money," Max says. "But this will protect us, and the world. We must preserve this power. The precept is too dangerous otherwise. The safeguards will be built into the system. A government can never own it."

"I'm with you," I say. "We'll keep the precepts free. But shouldn't we control some of the content? Are we really going to give coders and celebrities free rein? They could hack people's minds."

He smiles. "Hey, that's not our job. We can't change human nature. People flock to the stars. Who are we to stop them?"

It makes me uneasy. This wasn't the purpose. I created this to preserve life, not for more distractions. "What if it's more than people can handle? Like neon."

"Neon?" Max sounds confused.

"You know, too bright, unnatural. It could make people forget real color, real life."

"Come on," Max says, "you're growing a conscience now?"

I sigh. "No, you're right. Not our place to judge. We only give them the precept, at a fair price."

"Exactly. We will set the world free."

39

THE HUNTER WAKES me. It's still dark. He kneels by my side, hand pressed firm against my chest. "You were tossing and turning. You wouldn't get up," he grumbles. "Daniel says you must go now."

I follow him out of the great tree in a daze, taking nothing but a bag of food, a walking stick, and the clothes on my back. There is no ceremony, no goodbye. The tribes have not even awakened when we slip away.

The Hunter stays silent as we make our way through the forest. We pass through sentinel pines, dark as obelisks in the night. It's too quiet. No birds, no bugs. The air is still.

We cross a creek. We pass a huge, familiar tree. It's where long ago Violet and Lily first took care of me in the Green Tower. They told me about the Hunter. They said he was once a great king.

"Your name is Nebuchadnezzar?" I ask.

"Was." The Hunter pauses, glancing back at me. "I had power. More than those of your era could know. But it was only when I became wild, like an animal in the wilderness, that I saw my error. I worshiped my throne, so it ruled over me. Now I'm free to serve you…"

Leaves rustle in the distance. The Hunter listens for a

moment in silence. His eyes find mine.

"Quiet now," he whispers. "Let's move."

He turns away and moves deeper into the forest. I rush to keep up, ducking under branches and leaping over roots.

The darkness presses closer. Shadows grab at us. Hairs rise at the back of my neck. I can't shake the feeling of eyes watching me. It could be nothing, I tell myself. It could be an innocent nocturnal creature. An owl.

But the Hunter has slowed. He moves forward in a crouch. His footsteps make no sound on the soft pine needles. My breathing and pounding heart thunder in my ears.

He stops behind a tree and motions for me to stay right behind him. He presses a finger over his lips. Tension tightens his face.

He draws his bow. Then he disappears.

I know he's here, only invisible. I reach out but do not feel him. He's already moved ahead. I hide at the base of the tree, back pressed to its large trunk. I summon weaves of air, trying to steel myself for whatever might attack.

The sound is faint but close. A rattle.

I peer around the tree. A gleam of metal slices through the darkness. A shadow moves with it, like blackness taking form. It rushes straight at me.

I freeze in terror. *Run or fight?*

An arrow suddenly stabs into the shadow. The white-feathered shaft quivers just beneath the metallic gleam.

A scream shatters the night, full of rage and hate. My hands press over my ears as I back away.

The shadow staggers. Then it flings the arrow down and charges again.

It's too fast. I have to fight.

The creature is almost within reach when my wind blasts at it. The gale bends trees back. But the shadow slows only for a moment. It presses through my power.

I can't stop it.

Another arrow hits, this time above the metal gleam.

The shadow screams again as it falls at my feet. The forest goes silent.

The Hunter appears, kneeling where the shadow fell.

I move slowly to the Hunter's side. The shadowy form is gone. Lying before us on the pine-needle ground are two arrows and a collar. The chrome band is closed.

The Hunter snatches it, studies it for a moment, and places it in a bag by his side. "Got one back." His face is grim as he turns to me. "Better keep moving."

"What was that?" I ask. "One of us?"

"No. Nothing I've ever seen in this forest," he says. "One of the Colorless One's creations. His power grows."

The fear in his voice—in the invincible Hunter—fills me with dread. "It was wearing the collar. Where did the body go?"

He shakes his head. "It's gone, that's what matters."

"Did you kill it?"

"Two arrows to the head," he says with grim satisfaction. "Nothing to celebrate. We'll see worse things yet."

"Like what?" I try to sound calm, but my voice breaks.

His large hand finds my shoulder. He looks like his usual strong and guarded self—except his eyes hold less wildness. They are comforting in the dark forest. "Here, take this." He holds out a small acorn. "Save what's inside for when you most need it."

It must be sap. I take the acorn and pocket it beside the

spearhead. "Thank you."

"End this soon, okay?" he says tiredly. "I've had enough wilderness."

"I'll do my best."

"That's all we ask," he says. "In Green we keep moving. We fight. We survive." He glances beyond me. The first hint of dawn touches the forest. "Now let's get you to Red."

40

THE SHADOWS HAVE faded when we emerge from the pine forest. The trees come to an abrupt stop before the edge of a canyon. A river carves through the deep gorge. Rapids churn a hundred feet below, glistening in the light of the three suns. On the other side of the canyon dusty orange foothills rise to steep red rock mountains. Only a few low and twisted pines cling to the reddish slopes. This is the border between Green and Red, separating the lush Provider from windswept Passion.

"Ready to cross?" the Hunter asks.

"How?" I expect a secret path or bridge to cross.

A rare smile tugs at his bearded face. He pulls his bow from his back and draws an arrow from his quiver. This time he does it slowly, joyfully, with none of the tension or urgency he had when he shot the shadow in the night.

He sets his gaze on the hills across the chasm. As he shifts his bow, aiming, I notice a small moving shape. It is a horned animal, like a deer but smaller and with twisted antlers and a white streak across its reddish side. The animal leaps just below the far edge of the canyon. It jumps an incredible distance and lands perfectly on a cleft that looks no wider than my hand. Then it jumps again, and again, climbing steadily. A larger animal, maybe its mother, waits patiently for it. The movements of the Hunter's bow reveal that he is targeting the smaller animal.

I put my hand on his arm. "There's no need..."

"Just watch." He shakes my grip off, then in one smooth motion fires the arrow with perfect form. The missile streaks over the gorge, soaring straight at the little animal.

A shadow swoops and blocks the arrow. When the immense shadowy form turns, I recognize it.

The dragon, Behemoth.

Behind it, the little animal leaps again, as if oblivious of the arrow and the dragon. It lands beside its mother, who gives the fawn a friendly lick.

"See?" the Hunter says, grinning.

"You..." Behemoth's growl echoes over the canyon, making stones shake loose and scatter down the steep slopes.

The dragon soars at us and lands on the canyon's edge, only twenty feet away. Its claws perch on the stone like giant grappling hooks. Its teeth are iron swords. Its breath carries a sickly sweet smell and the heat of fire.

The Hunter doesn't flinch. "You're on Green land."

"You may not hunt Red creatures," Behemoth growls.

"I wasn't hunting," the Hunter says. "If I was, I'd bring back a trophy. Maybe a dragon tooth."

"Why do you come?" Behemoth asks.

The Hunter looks to me. "Our friend wants to visit. Not sure why anyone would leave the forest for all that dust..." the Hunter motions to the mountains with a grimace. "But Daniel says Rahab expects him today. I figure he needs a ride."

Giant yellow eyes study me from the scaled creature's

face. "Cipher, you are welcome. Climb on." The dragon stretches its neck out and stays still, waiting.

I hesitate. Behemoth saved me once before. But his eyes still invoke terror. They greeted me when I first arrived in the Red Tower, in the cave underneath. Emma said the dragon was chaos. I've never liked chaos. And another dragon's fire burned my friend, Seymour. It showed me the past. It showed me Samantha…

"See?" the Hunter says to Behemoth. "It's hard to leave Green. And you stink. Ever brush your teeth?"

The dragon ignores him. His eyes stay fixed on me. "If Rahab expects you, do not keep her waiting."

I move forward slowly. The dragon remains still. I climb up the scales along its neck. They are smooth and warm, like stones pulled from a fire. I mount the creature and grip the horns on its back.

"When will I get a ride?" the Hunter asks.

"In paradise." Behemoth's voice rumbles.

Muscles flex beneath me. Wings unfurl. The dragon leaps.

"Till paradise!" the Hunter calls out.

Behemoth flies low along Red's foothills. Wind whips at me as I get a harrowing glimpse straight down the gorge. I press as close as I can against the scaly back and clutch the horns tighter.

In only moments the Hunter is a mere dot standing at the edge of Green's vast forest. We rise higher and higher to the first ridge of rocky peaks.

When we crest the ridge, the Red Tower appears in the distance. The other towers, and the dark shard, loom beyond it. In the other direction mountain ranges stretch to the horizon. Behemoth swoops over the ridge toward the tower.

As we soar over the rocky crags, we fly faster and faster. It is not far—the same distance the Hunter and I had trekked through the night and morning—but something about Behemoth's flight makes it feel urgent. The dragon is not gliding or swirling as it did long ago. It flies like a jet, propelled toward the Red Tower. My grip threatens to slip in the battering wind. I summon a shield of air to keep from blowing off. With the shield in place, a smile spreads over my face. We're flying. The view is otherworldly.

A mass of dark shapes wipes the smile away.

They appear as we cross another ridge. There are five, no six, flying forms, like dragons but made only of darkness. They come straight at us, cutting off the path to the Red Tower, only one ridge away now.

They're on us in seconds.

The collision happens in a blink, jarring Behemoth and knocking my grip loose. Just as I slip off, I weave the air to fling myself on. I hold tighter than ever. My head spins as I glance to the ground, a million miles down.

There's a deafening roar above. A black form claws at Behemoth's face. He bites and swipes his claws, knocking the shadowy dragon away, but another strikes Behemoth's wing. It's no mere shadow. It slices open a gaping hole.

We jerk and plummet.

Behemoth twists his neck back and bites and snaps another dragon in half. The black form vanishes. I blast one away with the wind, its darkness shattering like a thousand pieces of black glass.

Another lands behind me, on Behemoth's back, claws stabbing into scales. Its black face fixes on me. It coils its neck back, as if ready to breathe fire.

The flames come out in a black surge. There's no red, no heat. But the darkness burns and smells of sulfur, making me wretch.

Behemoth snaps around. His own fire meets the blackness, pushing it back and knocking the creature off, roaring in pain.

Still we fall. Wings flap violently, but the gashed wing catches no air. I glance ahead. The Red Tower is so close.

But another dark form slams into Behemoth's good wing. It claws mercilessly. The blows are devastating. We are knocked back. Down.

We drop like a boulder. I stare at the ground in horror.

We're going to die.

Muscles ripple and flex underneath me, like a coil gathering up all its tension. Behemoth suddenly bucks. I fling off his back like a marble, flying out into open sky at an incredible speed.

"*Go!*" Behemoth shouts like a dying breath, before blasting fire at the dragons around it. They strike the ground like flaming meteors.

The explosion is instant. The force of it propels me faster, away and away. Soaring in midair, body spinning, I glimpse the Red Tower ahead. With every ounce of mental energy I focus and summon the wind. It buffets my fall, but gravity yanks me down. Momentum yanks me forward.

I fly, out of control, straight at the closed iron gate of the Red Tower. It welcomes me like a club to the head.

41

I HURT EVERYWHERE. My head hangs over nothing. Red, rocky ground is far below. I scurry back from the ledge and bump into something.

Legs. Red dress like fire in the light of the setting suns. Long auburn hair. Amber eyes. Rahab. She's brighter than the torches blazing to her sides.

"Welcome, Cipher," she says, hands on her hips. "You're a bloody mess. This is quite an entrance."

"Behemoth..." I mutter, standing slowly, wincing at the pain. "We were attacked."

Her eyes go wide in surprise. She looks past me, toward the mountains. She hurries to the edge and gazes down. I join her. A large dark shape lies motionless at the bottom. The shadowy forms are nowhere to be seen.

"Who attacked?" she demands.

"They were like dragons, but only black forms, like shadows. There were five or six of them. Behemoth fought as we went down. He flung me here. He saved me."

"Shadows can't do that..." Rahab eyes Behemoth's body far below.

As I follow her gaze, I see something shift. A form darker than shadow rises from a crevice. It soars up at us, letting out a shrieking roar.

Rahab grabs my arm. Her grip is so hot it sears my skin. "Inside," she demands.

We hurry to the gate. The moment we step through, the iron chains begin to lower the heavy metal door. Something slams into the door, like a hammer against steel. A black claw squeezes under the gate. It no longer lowers.

Rahab blasts a stream of fire at the claw. There's a screech on the other side. The claw yanks back. The gate slams closed.

The creature pounds against the gate. Claws scratch over the iron, like fingernails on a chalkboard. The sound is terrible. I back away, expecting it to break through any moment.

"We're safe in here," Rahab says, though she sounds uncertain. "The towers can hold back the gates of hell."

"And dragons?"

"If only these were dragons…"

The scratching has stopped outside. There's a sudden roar, then a rush of wind. It goes quiet on the other side of the gate. Rahab looks almost as relieved as I feel.

"What *are* they?" I ask.

She shakes her head, hair flowing. "Dragons have long been tied to Red's land—the way the sap is tied to Green, the grains to Yellow, and the boats to Blue. But they've been corrupted, blackened. Not even Behemoth could withstand them. The Colorless One grows desperate…and bold. He is ripping at the fabric of the Five Towers."

"We have to defeat him," I say. "We're close to equilibrium. Daniel and Abram and the other leaders, you've all said we can do it. We just have to summon our powers together, fusing them into light that will pierce the darkness."

"Yes, yes. Hope. It's needed here." Rahab's eyes blaze. A grin turns up on her red lips. "I've missed you, Cipher."

I blush. "I guess…I sort of missed…"

"Oh, don't bother." Her laugh is sultry. "You were always meant for Blue first. I take no offense. Even after Red, you've stayed cool. Too cool for Red's taste. It's quite something you became the Alpha while you were here."

I hold out my scarred palms. "No credit for me. I just happen to be a marked one."

"The strongest of the five," she says. "And you remember why?"

"You told me." And as many times as I've been wiped since then, her words hurtle back to the top of my mind. "Of everyone here, I had the greatest gulf between what I was capable of and what I actually did on Earth."

"It's no reason for shame." She places her hand gently on my cheek. "It is cause for celebration. You were allowed to come here, after all. So much has been scoured in you. The passion in your eyes has, well, *matured* since I last saw you. The same is true of the other marked one here. She truly belongs in Red."

"Helena?" I last saw her in the Scouring.

"Yes," Rahab says. "You'll see. The feast has begun. But you must promise me something."

"What's that?"

"No word of this attack or of Behemoth. Not yet." She swallows, as if holding back sadness. "The Red Tower will not take this easily."

I agree and we walk away from the gate. Torches glow orange and ocher on the red stone walls. Warmth tingles on my bruised skin. Ahead comes a steady, familiar drumbeat. Boom. Boom. Boom.

The doors of the Feasting Hall swing open as we approach. Inside there's a rush of chaotic action. Flames blaze in midair. Pairs of boys and girls sing and dance to the pounding drum rhythm. There's no other place like Red's Feasting Hall.

Rahab leads me toward the raised dais with the thrones. The crowd parts naturally, like fish around a shark, as we advance. I smile inside. It's a Blue metaphor. I've never fit in well in Red.

On the throne sits Helena. She looks like she belongs, like only a slightly diminished version of Rahab. My old friend Marcus—the one who kicked Baron into the pit—stands close by Helena's side. She wears a ring. It looks like they are paired, and he is the Alpha. It reminds me of what Helena once told me in Green: she has a thing for power. But something about it seems off.

Helena and Marcus both bow to Rahab.

"I've brought a new competitor for the Arena tonight," Rahab says, stepping aside and motioning me forward.

I didn't expect this. "Wait, that's not necess—"

Rahab silences me with a fiery hot squeeze on the shoulder. "We always have time for the Pairing," Rahab says. "And we lost two strong boys last time in the Scouring. What do you think, Helena? Will one of our girls want this one?"

Helena looks me up and down. A grin plays on her pretty face. "Good to see you, Cipher. You look rough. But don't worry, there's one girl in particular I have in mind."

"He smells like the Black Tower." Marcus looks to Rahab. "What task will you give him?"

"Hm, something special," Rahab says. "But that can wait. Now then, to the Arena."

42

STEEP RED STAIRS lead down to the Arena. Helena sits front and center, with Marcus to her left and me to her right. Rahab has not entered yet. She stands above, watching everyone as they enter. I was once a wide-eyed boy passing by her, scared out of my wits. Now I'm a wide-eyed boy who knows who he was on Earth, and what he has to do. It doesn't make it easier. Only clearer.

The crowd fills the rows of benches that ring the Arena. I glimpse many familiar faces. Jafari and his sister Jacana sit close to us. They look stronger than ever, like panthers among lemurs. Seth, my old sheepherder friend, is with Zelle. They laugh like they have no cares in the world. Khan, the horseman, looks serious with his long dark hair pulled back. But he smiles when he spots me. Boleyn sits beside him. She was once mixed up with British royalty, King Henry VIII. Now she looks like a friendly girl ready to watch a play.

Nearly everyone sits together in pairs. Boys wear collars. As before, a few girls—the most powerful ones—wear rings. They are the ones who fight in the Scouring.

It's so different from Green. It's almost…stable. Despite the flames and the passion, it seems not much has changed. Maybe the Pairing, unlike the tribes, does this over time. Maybe Helena has helped. Maybe the Scouring. Whatever it is, down in the Arena the dangers outside the tower seem far away.

The vast room falls quiet. Rahab has appeared on the opposite side of the Arena. She raises her arms. Flames burst forth from her open palms.

"The performance begins!" she announces.

All eyes turn to the center of the sandy ring. For a moment it makes me shudder. The sand, the fighting—it reminds me of waking under the Black Tower. The two coffins rested on sand like this. A crowd looked down on the two boys as they awoke and fought to the death. They chanted and cheered, as Red will.

I shake myself out of it. The Black Tower is Purple now. And the Arena is not a fight to the death. This is a competition, a *voluntary* one, for boys to pursue the girl who performs. Still, some connection lingers between the two places. Red and Black, now Purple. There's a fine line between passion and power, and wrath lives in the middle.

Amidst flames a figure appears in the center of the Arena. She faces Rahab, with her back to me. The memory of my first time in the Arena rushes back. It was my mother who appeared. She performed and we raced for her. She chose me as the victor. She took care of me. She answered so many of my questions, before she was taken up to the White Tower.

The flames begin to fade around the girl in the center. Her figure takes clearer shape. Her red hair, her bare shoulders, send electric currents through me.

Rahab lowers her arms. The flames vanish.

The girl turns. Her green eyes meet mine.

It's Samantha.

Her lips curl into a smile as she begins to sing.

Maria, gratia plena

Ave, ave dominus

Dominus tecum

Her voice is achingly beautiful, lifting me beyond this place and this moment. I feel suspended, hanging on each clear note.

Then she summons her fire.

It starts small. Intricate ribbons of flame flow out from her hands and encircle her. They spin around and around, delicate as silk. Thread by thread they expand into a vast tapestry a thousand shades of red and orange. It all emanates from Samantha, the dazzling heart of the web.

The flames grow until they fill the room, rising above us, glowing with warmth, pulsing with each note Samantha sings. It could go on forever. Music makes time eternal.

But eventually her voice gently releases us. The final notes echo, *Ave Maria*. The flames dim and burn no more.

Hushed silence settles, soft as a dandelion's round white seed drifting in the wind. But a sudden gust of applause blasts the delicacy away.

"Now," Rahab announces. "Let the race begin!"

Boys spring into motion. They drop over the wall that rings the Arena. They land on the sand and charge.

I hesitate. The first one to reach Samantha may pair with her. I can't imagine it. Even if she's scoured of whatever afflicted her in Black, we have too much history.

"Go on!" Helena says, and Marcus gives me a shove.

I shake my head. Marcus pushes me to my feet.

"It's not right," I protest.

But Marcus presses forward until I have no choice. He's too strong. I'm on the ledge, falling back, when I summon the wind. It catches my fall and I land in a crouch.

The other boys are close to the center. Samantha's green eyes are locked on me, as if I'm the only one in the room. Her face flickers with passion like I first saw in Red, not the rage she had in Black.

Something turns in me. Maybe there's something we need to see together about our pasts.

I blast the air forward and hurl the boys back. I stride toward the center as my wind restrains them.

Rahab appears in a burst of flame just ahead of me. Her lips form a severe line. "You've forgotten the rules."

Now I remember, too late. No powers in the Arena, or anywhere inside the Red Tower. I made the same mistake the first time I entered the Arena, when my mother performed.

It's déjà vu as Rahab reaches out and places her palm to my forehead. My power slips away. There's only heat.

So much heat. Burning.

Past Rahab and through the pain, the last thing I see as I collapse is Samantha's green eyes.

43

SAMANTHA RECLINES BEFORE a crackling fire when my eyes blink open. Still in a daze, I feel warm all over except for coolness at my neck. I sit up and touch the collar. I try not to panic.

"I chose you," she says.

The Arena. Rahab stopped me. "We're paired."

"This is what we do in Red."

"But you were in Purple." My hand moves to the scar at my side, where she stabbed me. She was wiped after that. "How did you get here?"

"Captured in the Scouring." She speaks calmly, as if this did not bother her at all. "The Purple Tower's numbers have fallen since you and Baron left."

"He fell into the pit. I went after him. Then we were in Green. It hasn't been long."

"Long enough for me to see a lot in these flames. I know now what we did." Her eyes meet mine. "I've learned about…the passion."

I look away, toward the fire. "I saw that here, too."

"That's what led us to the hospital room. When we were older, and you were sick."

My throat tightens. This was the vision we shared at the top of the Black Tower, when the Colorless One spoke to me. He could have twisted what we saw.

"Do you know how it really ended?" I ask.

"No. I have so many questions. Did I come to you like we saw? Did I really have a gun? Did I...shoot?"

I meet her uncertain gaze. "I don't know."

"Rahab told me we could see the truth together. She said your mother learned how she died here."

"Yes. She did." It was after Emma and I escaped with her from Black. We saw the vision together in the fire at the top of the Red Tower. My mother helped me move into my college dorm—the one named after Emma's son—and she had driven away. The cop called. He told me there had been a car accident. I never saw my mother alive again, until I came to Red.

Samantha rises from the floor. She holds out her hand to me. "Will you join me?"

She could command me. Instead she asks.

I take her hand. "We're paired."

"You already said that," she says with a faint smile.

Samantha leads the way up through the Red Tower's maze of tunnels. We reach the door leading outside, to the stairs going to the very top of the tower. The first time I came this way I was with Seth and Khan, carrying Jafari's lifeless body. The weight of it all wore me down. This time I feel light on my feet, almost eager to see what the flames will show.

Once outside, I summon a thin barrier of air to block the wailing night wind. We climb steadily up the stairs. I gaze up, hoping for stars, but the cloudless sky is black. It unnerves me, almost worse than looking down.

When we reach the top, Rahab is there. She sits on the parapet ringing the large signal fire. She is bent over, face in her hands. She looks up as we approach. Tears glisten in the firelight.

"He's gone," she says. "Behemoth controlled the chaos. He was this tower's ballast. He balanced what was in me."

"What's in you?" I say.

She doesn't speak but the answer flashes in her blazing eyes.

"Passion," I say.

"Chaos is a wellspring of passion." Rahab turns to Samantha. "In Purple some tried to use ambition and power as a shield against chaos. But passion is not so easily controlled."

"I see that now," Samantha says.

"Good. All must learn this. Chaos can only be tamed by controlling passion." Rahab gazes past us toward the mountain ridge looming above, and the tower beyond it. "Even now there is one in Purple who must still come to Red."

"Who?" I ask.

"Helena should know," Rahab says. "Talk with her."

"What about our vision?" Samantha asks. "You said Paul and I could see the truth here."

"All who come must be scoured of passion's excesses. The first step is to see it for what it is." Rahab motions toward the fire. "Look now, together."

Samantha and I exchange a glance, then turn to the flickering flames. They reach high into the air, bright orange and red against the night. They pull me in.

My vision shifts.

Red and green lights reflect in the dark window of the hospital room. I'm on the bed. I'm alone. I'm dying.

The nurse enters. Her red hair has gray at the temples. Her green eyes look more alive than I remember. It's been twenty years since the affair. And still Samantha wanted to be my nurse.

"Good evening, Paul." She walks to the window and draws the curtains closed. "It's dark out there."

"I don't mind the darkness," I say. "It reflects the lights of the medical equipment—another reminder that I'm a dead man without machines."

"Your inventions save a lot of lives, including your own." She stands by my side, reviewing stats on a tablet. "Everything looks stable. Except your heart rate has jumped a little."

I study her. She is calm and professional. Yet her presence haunts like a ghost, even after all these years.

"Why did you want to be my nurse?" I ask.

She smiles. "You prefer someone else?"

"No, but after…you know, our past, I thought you'd…"

"I've told you, Paul, we have to get over it."

"You say that like it's easy."

"It was a long time ago. And who better than an old friend to care for you now? Hey, did you know Johnny was just accepted at your alma mater?"

"Congratulations," I say flatly, hoping to avoid her showing me pictures again. At first it was interesting enough. Her husband—former captain of the high school crew team that I tried out for and didn't make so long ago—now he teaches high school math and coaches track. Her three children are great kids. She has a happy family, a good church, blah, blah. It's almost sad how boring and normal her life became. Looking into her green eyes, I remember how she was once so…passionate.

She pats the foot of the bed. "Mind if I sit a moment? I've been on my feet for hours."

"Go ahead."

She moves closer. She sits by my side. "There's something I've been wanting to tell you."

I swallow nervously, feeling awkward and trapped. I'd scoot away, but my body hardly listens to me anymore.

"I've been thinking about your son," she says. "Benjamin."

"Benjamin," I repeat. It's been a lifetime, but the name still hurts. I failed him.

"I know he was in a room like this. He had a similar tumor."

"So?" My hand moves to my head. "That's why I invented all this. To stop this terror. This *death*."

She puts her hand gently on mine, pulls it slowly down from my head and places it on my chest. Her hand remains there, over my thumping heart. "Susan told me what Benjamin told you."

I wince. "You talked to Susan?"

"Of course, she's here every day," Samantha says. "You're so lucky to have her."

"Yes." I can't deny that. Susan has been loyal through it all. Another thing I don't deserve.

"Well, I've been thinking of what Benjamin told you."

"He told me lots of things," I say.

"In the hospital he said something very important. He forgave you. He said he wanted you to be with him, but you had to change."

"So?"

"He was right. You still have a chance to change, just as

I did. That's why this is easy for me. The past doesn't hurt liked it used to."

"I'm not like you."

"But you can be," she says. "We all have the choice to allow the light inside, if only we get out of our own way."

"And how do we do that?"

"It starts with repentance. So, Paul, I'm sorry. I said I forgave you, but I was bitter for a long time. I resented your success, your wealth. I resented *you*. But I'm working through that. I care about you, Paul."

"Thanks. But I'm not apologizing."

"I can see that." She smiles patiently. "I will be here if you change your mind. But it's not about me. You have too much good in you to go down like this."

Her hand still covers mine, which is clenched into a fist. Her gentleness makes my fist uncurl. She leans closer and, soft as a feather, kisses my forehead. She steps back.

I take a deep breath. A smile touches my face despite myself. "Thank you," I say. "I don't deserve it."

She laughs lightly, her buoyant joy filling the room and lifting me. "That's the good news, Paul. This isn't about what we deserve."

44

DAWN CRESTS OVER the mountains. The morning sky is textured crimson, like the inside of a blood orange. The signal fire burns low. The vision has released us.

"Nice sunrise," Samantha says, her gaze distant.

"Red sky at morn, sailors take warn," I mutter.

"It was red last night, too," she replies. "Red sky at night, sailors delight."

"There are no sailors in Red." Rahab's voice surprises me. "But we should take warn. Look."

I'd forgotten she was here. She sits behind us, in the same place as the night before, like a beautiful gargoyle on the parapet. I wonder if she even moved. Her red dress offers no protection against the cold morning air. Her bare arm points toward the ridge of mountains that separate us from the Purple Tower.

Above the ridge the suns rise. My stomach sinks. The sun in the center has gone completely black.

I point to it, my arm trembling. "What's that?"

"Sun black as sackcloth, moon like blood," Rahab says.

I don't understand. There's no moon here. "What's that supposed to mean?" I ask.

"The Colorless One's power grows. He eclipses more of the light." Rahab fixes her amber eyes on me. "The final battle comes. All must be scoured. All must join the right tower. All must fight together."

Daniel said the same thing. Does she also suspect the deal with the Colorless One? Would they know and say nothing? I doubt it. And if the deal is real, I must keep it hidden to give the others a chance to escape. Part of me still clings to hope that I can leave, too. But the hope feels fainter than ever, after the vision with Samantha. She was so kind. I was so harsh. *All must be scoured.* Maybe all but me—these stains are too much.

I turn to Samantha. "About what we saw last night…I'm sorry."

"Now we know the truth," she says softly. "I didn't shoot. I didn't even have a gun."

"No. You were gentle. And I—" I probably deserved the alternate vision, the one where she shot. "I have no excuse. What we did on Earth, it was my fault."

She puts her hand over my clenched fist, just as she did in the vision. "I stand by what I said. It's not about what you deserve."

"Sounds nice," I say, failing to hide my doubt.

"It's true," Rahab says. "This is what the Colorless One would hide from you all. He darkens the past with shame."

"But the past can't change, can it?" Samantha asks.

"Not the *true* past," Rahab says. "But in the pit the Colorless One creates entire visions that are lies. They prey on us, tainting perceptions of what is true. Beware of any shame. It has no place in the light."

As I look to Samantha's gentle eyes, I feel a weight lift. But it's her weight, not mine. She forgave me. The passion faded. Now she should be ready to leave this place. "Samantha, do you think you belong in Red?"

"Maybe," Samantha says. "It feels better than Purple."

"Hm, yes." Rahab gives Samantha a warm smile. "And others must come to Red soon. One is in Green. She was one of Helena's servants on Earth."

"Violet," I say.

"Good, you know her. Talk to Helena. She will be in the Alpha's quarters."

Samantha and I agree and descend the spiral stairs into the Red Tower. We wind our way down through tunnels to the Alpha's quarters. We reach the iron door with a flame emblazoned at its center. Samantha presses her hand to the flame. The door opens.

Marcus greets us as we enter. He escorts us past the openings to the Scouring far below, and into the Alpha's room. Helena sits on the throne as Max once did, with a leg casually draped over one of the throne's arms. Two collared servants are by her sides. One holds a plate of grapes, the other a fan. She's comfortable as a queen. But this throne was meant for a king.

"Isn't that the Alpha's chair?" I ask.

She flashes a severe look, but takes a deep breath. "Things have changed since you left." She holds up the back of her hand to me. A pale scar runs down it. "You know better than anyone, rules bend for marked ones."

Our scars entitle us to nothing. It's not a privilege. It's a burden. Rahab taught me that.

"Do you know why we are marked?" I ask. "The real reason why we are more powerful?"

She rolls her eyes. "Strength out of weakness. Blah, blah."

I turn to Marcus. "Are you the Alpha?"

"Yes." His hardened face reveals nothing. I can't help

but see remnants of the Purple Tower in him. An iron will. A soldier's heart.

"I saw you in the Scouring," I say. "How could you knock anyone into the pit? Don't you know what's down there?"

"Only those from Black," he grunts. "As they deserve."

I shake my head in disbelief. "Not anymore. We've cleansed it. It's the Purple Tower now."

"Black or Purple, still the enemy," he says.

"Marcus fought in the Colosseum." Helena's voice drips with disdain. "Romans of his era had little refinement, and no faith. Such brutal games they played. It's a mercy that I've paired with him. He's nothing like the emperor I once loved." Helena idly plucks a grape off a stem. "But Rahab suggested this, and I obey the leaders as you do. You did well last night, Cipher. You always seem to do well. I trust your Pairing has gone smoothly?"

"We saw an important vision together," Samantha says, squeezing my hand.

"Boys often need to learn from girls." Helena drops the grape into her mouth. "Oh Cipher, don't look so serious. I heard you met your mother here. Did you not learn from her?"

"I did. She went up to the White Tower. She was the last one who made it out before the white turned black."

"Very interesting," she says. "It is a special thing, what a mother teaches her son, *and* what she can learn from him. You remember who my son was?"

She told me this in the beginning, in Blue. Now I know what he did to his own son, Helena's grandson. She and Crispus have the same curls and olive skin. "Constantine, the Roman Emperor," I say. "But he—"

"Yes," she cuts me off. "My dear son seems to have skipped this place. I understand yours did the same."

"How do you know that?"

"Girls talk," she says with a playful shrug. "The truth is, we're the sorry lot left to fight endlessly here. Why not make the most of it, eh? Find a little pleasure where we can?"

This is not going well. There's shadow in her words, a subtle twisting of the same kind that infected Samantha in Purple. Helena needs a jolt of light. We all do.

"I found your grandson," I say. "Crispus."

She winces like she's been poked by a needle. "Where?"

"In Black. You know about him?"

"I've heard he was among these towers."

"Why didn't you tell me? This could be important."

She scowls. "We will talk no more of this."

"You can't avoid it!" My own intensity surprises me. I calm my voice, but I feel flush with energy. "We have to face the past, all of it. There's no other way to scour it, to be done with it, to be ready to leave this place."

"It's his story. Not mine," Helena replies coldly.

"But they're all connected," I say. "Everyone has connections here. We have to discover them, to find out why they matter."

Helena's gaze swivels to Marcus. "Lead everyone but Cipher out. Prepare dinner. We will not be long."

Marcus obeys. Samantha leaves my side. The servants take their grapes and fans and follow after them. Helena and I are left alone in the vast room.

She glares down at me from her throne perch. "My story is enough, Cipher."

"Oh? You think so? You think it doesn't matter that

your grandson Crispus was executed? Or that you and your son, Crispus' own father, approved it?"

"Stop…" She has looked away. Voice like faint embers rather than a raging fire. "I'll admit, things are connected. I've found other kings and queens here. I've found their servants. One girl was Queen Elizabeth. She was the niece of another girl here, Boleyn. British monarchs. Feudal lords. Oligarchs. Servants. Slaves." Helena's scarred hand grips the arm of the throne tight. "And I speak only of those in Red. We suffer equally enough here. You don't have to rub it in."

"Look at me," I say. "Please, look at me."

Helena turns slowly. Her eyes are moist. Her lips tremble in anger. "Happy now?"

"Crispus told me he forgives you," I say.

Her jaw clenches. "I won't accept it."

"He said you would say that. *She's iron*, he said to me. *Tough as nails*. Can't you see how your guilt is hurting you?"

"It's not guilt when it's deserved."

Her words hit me like a punch to the gut. It's exactly what I feel with Samantha. "I get that," I admit. "But the leaders say this is shame, a weapon of the Colorless One."

"Call it whatever you like. We are stuck here. And if you really want to know, I think it is *your* fault." She holds up her scarred hand. "Why else would we have these marks? And you have the most."

I swallow. I won't deny it. "Did you talk to Rahab about this?"

"She told me I am wrong. But I disagree."

"What about Daniel?"

"We barely talked. I did not stay in Green long."

"He told me that there are five of us, the chosen ones with scars. He said that when each person is in the proper tower, we five can lead the towers, harnessing the complete prism of light to pierce the darkness."

"How grand. Then what…we somehow escape?"

"Yes, through the White Tower. I think we are very close. But we have to share what we know of the past to keep our memories from being tainted. It seems hardest for us, the marked ones."

Helena leans forward. Her almond eyes look deep into mine. "Why are we scarred? What have you learned?"

"This could take a while. Besides us, the three others are Emma, Baron, and Kiyo. I've learned a lot from them."

"Tell me all of it."

Helena listens as I pour out what I know. I tell her about Kiyo. In medieval Japan. Losing her son had made her harder than steel. Colder. I tell Helena about Emma. British royalty under Queen Victoria. Fled home with a man she loved. Lived in poverty. Lost everything. Stole. Forgiven by her father, but executed under the law. Her family produced one of England's leaders, Neville Chamberlain. In Yellow he is scoured of cowardice—of fear that had passed down since Emma herself. Fear served its purpose. Now Emma is the bravest person I know.

"And you know Baron," I say. I tell Helena he was America's titan, John D. Rockefeller. The richest man in the world. Power emanated from his wealth. Some of it even came down to me, when I married his granddaughter. He brought none of his wealth to the Five Towers, but he came bold and proud and hungry. He accumulated collars—the closest thing to money in the Green Tower. Time after time he became the tribal leader. With Emma's help we defeated him. After that he saw a vision of giving away his money. He had done that before, many times, but this time it was different. The money was to start a school. The women who accepted it wanted to name the school after him. He told them no. *Don't mention me, but I'll give you what you need.* That memory gave him peace. He fought by my side in the Scouring. He sacrificed himself to save me. Giving set him free.

"And you know about me," I say to Helena. "American doctor. Genius, liar, cheat. After my son died, fear of death nearly drove me mad. I tried to live forever by transplanting the brain. The technology went a different way, to neural enhancements by nanotechnology that—"

"Wait," Helena says. "Neural *what?*"

"Sorry, it was like a computer in your mind. The point is, I tried to fight death, and I lost."

"So what is your point?" Helena says. "That we all died? And we are all stuck here? This is nothing new."

"There must be a common thread," I say. "It could be family or history. I think we can figure it out if you share more of your story."

"You have always been curious." She blinks slowly, as if lost in thought. "My story may be interesting, but it changes nothing."

I sense her opening slightly. If only I could get her started. "You were an empress. And you are a marked one here. There must be something unique about your past. What harm could it do to tell me?"

She sighs. "When we met in the Blue Tower, I told you I was Helena Augusta Imperatrix."

"Yes, I remember."

"You might also remember I was not born that way. I

was a servant girl. I worked in an inn where soldiers often stayed. Constantius visited one night. He had a twinkle in his eye. I liked him. Everyone liked him. But he came to love only one person—me. So when he rose in the Roman ranks, from soldier to officer to governor to Praetorian Prefect, he brought me with him as far as he could. It was not far enough. To make his final leap, to Caesar, he had to marry a woman of nobility. My past meant I could never be noble. He found another woman who was—the daughter of Emperor Maximian. She was his ticket to the throne."

"That's awful," I say. "What happened?"

She waves off my comment. "It gets worse. He never loved her, but I raged all the same. Oh, how I raged. He had to send me away. He could not bear it. But by then I had borne his child. I told you how I raised him—knowing his destiny as the Caesar's firstborn, as the heir. Eventually, once Constantius' power was secure, he brought me back. He still loved me. He let me build a palace. And what a palace I built. I dealt with that in the Green Tower."

"Green showed me a mansion, too," I say.

"I am not surprised. It must be in our nature to ever want a bigger home, as if it makes us more secure. It did not work for me. I stayed bitter until my son Constantine taught me to seek the light. But I was never secure. This is what drove me to suggest the execution of Crispus. I did it to protect Constantine and myself. It was a terrible mistake."

She falls silent, studying her hands in her lap, and this time I don't speak. Her story and her tone have shaken me. It's shame. I know it well.

"I grew old," she continues. "I was past seventy when I had a vision of the Holy Land. Violet told you of this in

Green. We trekked there and found the temple of Venus covering the holy site. I ordered them to tear it down, stone by stone. We found treasure. Three decayed wooden crosses. One had an inscription. We pieced together the letters to find one, powerful word: *King*."

"Why?" I ask.

"This was the relic I had been searching for. I saw its power with my own eyes. Soon after our discovery, a cobra bit a woman and she was dying. Someone rushed her to us. We pressed small pieces of wood from each cross into her hand. The first did nothing. The second did nothing. The third healed her. Completely. The moment she took the small piece of wood into her hand, warmth came back to her cheeks. She stopped shaking. In moments she was smiling and singing, alive as ever. I ordered a church to be built on the spot. More churches, too. I felt in my old bones that death was near, so I tried to give away everything I could. All the treasures, all the relics, I gave them away. On my return to Rome, my son Constantine held a great feast to celebrate what we had done. He vowed to carry on my work. I went to sleep, and I remember nothing after that. I was over eighty years old, a life fully lived, pains fully felt, and—at last—passions set at ease."

Helena sighs. Her expression is more tranquil than when she began. It's as if telling her own story, the good and the bad, lifted some of the shadow that hung over her.

"Thank you for sharing this," I say.

She rubs her scarred hand. "I still do not see how it helps us escape. How could we be connected? And why do you have the most scars?"

"Rahab says my power comes from the gap between what I was capable of on Earth, and what I actually did. It was a huge gap for me. Doesn't sound so bad for you."

"Oh I do not know about that," she says. "I had plenty of failures."

"Maybe all of us marked ones did. Maybe that's what connects us. The leaders say we can escape if we harness the light together. We have to try it. I'm going to lead Blue. Can we count on you to lead Red and fight with us?"

She hesitates. "How will we fight?"

"We'll gather together and…find a way." I try to think of a better answer. With the light. Against the Colorless One. But her question is troubling. I still don't know exactly what we'll do. "We have to open the White Tower again. But the pit—"

A loud pounding at the door interrupts me.

It repeats, louder.

"Enter," Helena calls out.

When the door opens, Jafari's hulking shape shadows the room like a man before the opening of a cave. His boyish face looks intense. Behind him are Samantha and Marcus and others.

Between heavy breaths, Jafari says, "We're under attack."

"*Attack*? How?" Helena asks.

"From the bottom," Jafari says. "They're…bones."

45

WE RACE DOWN the Red Tower with Jafari in the lead. Helena and Samantha and Marcus stay close. Others fall in behind us. Dozens and dozens, until it seems we have the whole Red Tower joining us.

The passages are familiar. Rahab took me this way when I first arrived in Red. She showed me the cavern underneath. She locked me inside, with Behemoth. I was terrified. There was so much I didn't know. Now Behemoth is gone. Now I have worse things to fear.

When we finally reach the iron door with the flame imprinted in the center, Jafari turns to us. "Only a few defenders are inside," he says. "They won't hold long. You have to help. My sister is in there!"

"You have done well to bring us." Helena speaks like an empress. "Where is Rahab?"

"No one has seen her."

"She was at the top, by the signal fire," I say.

"Go there," Helena says to Jafari. "Fast as you can."

He spins and sprints away. Helena presses her hand to the door. Samantha stands by my side. We're still paired, and her fiery weaves of power pulse through the link. I wear her collar, but she has not given me any commands.

I summon the wind.

Helena catches my eyes, then looks to Samantha. "Be ready to control him and use his power."

"Yes," Samantha says, with a slight bow of her head. But as Helena turns away, Samantha takes my hand. Her power weaves into mine. She's given me control.

The door swings open. The stench of sulfur spills out.

Fire explodes before us, flashing light into the immense cavern. A small group from Red faces a horde of skeletons. The bony figures surge up through a gaping hole in the center of the room. The firelight fades.

"You, more light!" Helena commands a girl behind us.

Boleyn. She casts out a web of flame that lights up the cavern in flickering red.

We charge forward to help the others. I blast with the weave of blue and red power, knocking skeletons back. They are heavier than they look—too much to lift all at once. I focus on the closest ones. The searing wind slams into a handful before us, flinging them against the rock wall. They shatter into a thousand fragments of bone.

But more come. The skeletal shapes emerge from the dark hole in the center, from the tunnels and pit below. Metal collars gleam and jangle at their bony necks.

They surge at us, straight into the fire. Dozens burn and collapse, but more come. And more and more. The first line of Red defenders falls back, exhausted.

Helena and I press forward. Fire brings light, but the skeletons bring wave after wave of darkness. Bones pile up around us.

My power sweeps away another onslaught like a giant swatting flies. When they shatter against the wall, their collars fall and clink against the floor. More come.

A shout makes me turn. Skeletons have broken

through the first line. They charge straight for Helena. Like she's their target.

I surge after them, but my foot catches. My hand slips out of Samantha's as I tumble head over heels.

"Cipher, here!" Samantha reaches out for me.

I take her hand and spring up, but something snags my ankle again. The bones of a hand, connected to nothing, gripping. I shake at it, blast the power at it, but the finger bones hold like they'll never let go.

Behind us, more skeletons charge. They scurry and scrape across the stone. Too many to hold back.

"Go!" I shout to Samantha.

She backs away, looking for help.

I twist frantically, but the hand on my ankle yanks me down. Another hand crawls onto my shoulder. It shoves me down with immense force.

Across the room I spot a beacon of red. It's Rahab.

I shout to her.

But more bones scramble over me. They cover me like a wave. They pin me down. A small skeleton, like a child, leans over me. The empty sockets of its eyes look into mine.

I scream. Everything goes black.

I'm on the hospital bed. My head is shaved. Tubes are in my arms. Benjamin stands by my side. Pale as a ghost.

He leans over me. His eyes look into mine. "Remember when I was on this bed?"

I've relived it over and over since I stood beside him. But he died. He can't be here.

"Answer me," he says.

It comes out like a death rattle: "I remember."

"I knew where I was going then, but you didn't. I asked

you, what would you believe if you were on this bed instead of me?"

His voice tremors, almost sinister. I can't bear his gaze. I have to escape, to get out. But I can't move. I'm trapped.

"Now you're here," he says. "What do you believe?"

"I don't know."

"You should. You've had a lifetime to consider it."

"I'm still alive," I say, defiant through the fear. "I'm fighting it. I've learned a lot since you died. Death won't have the final say."

He shakes his head in disappointment. "Then you deserve what's coming."

46

SOMETHING SHAKES ME. It's dark. My vision is blurred. A woman commands: "Get up!"

I scramble to my knees. Hands against my temples.

"It was a lie." Rahab's amber eyes come into focus, pulling me back from the vision. "Whatever you saw, it wasn't true."

What I saw. A child's skull and a vision.

My heart clenches. It was my son. This vision happened before, in the pit. A figure of light came then. He was the one in the room with Benjamin, when my son was dying. *You are not finished*, the man said to me. *Wake up.* This time there was no light. I was trapped.

"Cipher, we need you here." Rahab clasps my shoulder, bringing my attention back again.

"Right, thanks." I stand and take a deep breath.

I'm in the Red Tower. A battle raged in the cavern. Bones against us. Collared skeletons.

Now the cavern is quiet. Torches flicker along the walls. The battle is over. The others from Red have all left. Only Rahab and Helena remain.

"You must resist the Colorless One," Rahab says. "He tried to invade your mind. If he gets hold, he might never let go. Then everyone here will be stuck."

Everyone. No, the deal with the enemy is that the others can leave. *You deserve what's coming,* Benjamin said. Maybe this what he meant. Maybe it was a reminder from the Colorless One. Even if I must stay, I'll do what I can to help the others escape. Emma, Samantha, all of them.

Rahab leans closer, studying me. "What did you see?"

"Nothing new. Something from my past, but twisted."

"It's the enemy's lies," she says. "It's shame. Don't ever listen to him, Cipher. Don't ever lose hope."

"Yeah, I know." My fingers go to the collar around my neck. "Where's Samantha? And the others?"

"Safe inside the tower." Rahab reaches to me and unclasps the collar. She drops it into a bag by her side. "We have to block them. They won't stop."

I stretch my neck, feeling free. "Block what?"

"The Colorless One's creations," Rahab says.

Helena approaches, her usual saunter now a weary shuffle. Her face is drawn tight in controlled fear. She places a few more collars into the bag. "This is the last of the ones we found."

"Good. Come with me." Rahab picks up the bag and moves to the hole in the center of the cavern. "We must stop them before another surge attacks."

I follow after her. "Why is this happening?"

"You saw the black sun," Rahab says. "The Colorless One grows bold. He has been stealing collars. Now he uses them. I'm going to destroy what we can. We have to slow him down."

"The bones could…return?" Helena breathes out.

Rahab pauses at the edge of the hole. "Yes. You've both survived the pit. You know its terror. The bones are shame put to life, and now this evil seeps into the towers."

"I felt it." Helena rubs her arms, shivering. "Even before that skull looked into me. Now Crispus is stuck here and..." She turns to me. "Cipher, I'm sorry about what I said. It's not your fault that we're stuck here. We're all to blame."

I nod, but I'm not so sure. She might have been right. I'm the only one with five scars.

"No. Both of you, look at me." Rahab's eyes blaze like fire. "You are marked ones. The Colorless One will do anything to steal your hope. Shame can undo everything, but only in darkness. We must never doubt the light. No matter what happens. We defeat shame by exposing it."

I've never heard her this intense. I want to believe her. "How?" I ask.

"We take the fight to the Colorless One. We light up all that he controls." A flame bursts into life above Rahab's hand. She looks down into the dark hole beside us.

The pit. Not again. "What do you want us to do?"

A sad smile spreads over Rahab's face. "The leaders can't hold back the darkness much longer. Soon *you* will lead the towers. Cipher, you've told what Helena what she needs to know?"

"I think so," I say. "The marked ones will lead the towers. Once we have equilibrium, we can use the light to pierce the darkness."

"Yes. And now we must get you to Blue," Rahab says to me. "Helena, your tower needs one from Purple, and one from Green. We will find them below."

"*My* tower..." Helena whispers. "Isn't there some other way—perhaps above ground?"

"I'm afraid not," Rahab says. "Without Behemoth, nowhere around the Red Tower is safe. And someone will need to lead the newcomers back…" She steps toward to the tunnel going down, kneels, and picks up something. It is dark and the size of her hand. She studies it, then holds it out to me. "Here, take this."

It's heavy as iron and cold as ice. "Why? What is it?"

"A scale from Behemoth," she says. "You never know when you might need a little piece of passion and chaos."

A deep rumble rises from beneath us. Helena and I stumble back. Even Rahab takes a step away from the hole. Yet she says, "We must hurry."

She moves quickly to the tunnel and descends, with the bag of collars slung over her shoulder. Helena stays on her heels. I pocket the scale. It scrapes against the acorn and spearhead, almost forgotten.

As we advance into the tunnel, the last flickers of torchlight battle the shadows along the walls, but eventually lose. Rahab's flame gives just enough light for me to see her a few feet ahead. The path begins to level out. The air grows thick. We near the pit, the bones.

The tunnel walls open into immense darkness. A sickly wind whips at us, harder and faster. Helena staggers back into me. We are pressed flat against the rock wall. Helena's hand finds mine.

"Steady now," Rahab whispers. She kneels beside us, setting down the collars with a faint clang. Her candle-sized flame is miraculously still in the gusting wind. Its light shines only a few feet before the blackness of the pit swallows it.

Bones rattle in the darkness ahead. More skeletons. More terrible visions.

A man suddenly steps toward us, appearing out of the darkness. A body hangs over his shoulder, like a limp bag of potatoes. His grim face glows violently in the candlelight, but his eyes look softly on Rahab. It's Purple's leader, Joshua.

"Sight for sore eyes," he says. "It's worse than I feared."

"How so?" Rahab asks.

"The bones fight like the damned. Mindless slaves, but worse. They have no life, no souls. Never did. But the Colorless One keeps digging them up through the pit. More and more bones. There's no end to shame. It could fill the pit. It could cover the Five Towers. The Colorless One discovers new depths and builds his pile of horrors, his own towers rising in the darkness. Now he is sending them out, each skeleton twisted into a custom nightmare to attack someone." The mighty warrior shudders. "Don't look into their eyes."

Rahab glances to me. "One almost took Cipher."

"Same for this boy. We barely made it from the Purple Tower. Kiyo leads them well, holding the darkness back, but the passage here was treacherous." Joshua sets the body down gently. The boy faces us with blank eyes. "He was wiped."

It's Crispus, stoic and quiet. Helena rushes to him. Looks deep in his eyes. Wipes away tears. Neither of them says a word. They have the same eyes, the same auburn curls.

"All will be well," Rahab says to Crispus. "You are entering the Red Tower. Helena will take you."

"All right," Joshua says. "Ready?"

Rahab nods. "I will distract them. When I say go, you and Cipher run right along the wall. Enter the first opening."

"But that goes to Green, not Blue," I say.

"Daniel will meet you," Rahab replies. "Stay with Joshua. Don't stop running until you get there. Understand?"

"Yes." If anyone could fight off skeletons, it's Joshua.

Rahab places her hand gently on his cheek. She leans forward and kisses his forehead. "See you soon."

Joshua flashes a rare smile. "The walls will crumble down."

Rahab steps forward, her red dress shimmering in the darkness. She slings the bag of collars over her shoulder and glances back to us. "*Go.*"

Joshua takes my hand and charges along the wall into pure darkness. I race beside him, trying to keep up. The wind is biting. My eyes tear up.

Within moments flames erupt. Joshua doesn't slow, but to our left I see Rahab igniting everything around her as she strides over the bones, like a moving bonfire. Yet more and more bones from the pile tremble and form into skeletons surrounding her.

Joshua stops. "Quick," he demands.

"Hm, so bright." Daniel's wrinkled face shows a thousand shadows in the flickering light. "Here is Red's final person. Take her. Be safe."

Violet stands by his side. She meets my eyes and smiles. Her face is serenely beautiful. "I'm ready," she says.

Joshua releases my hand and scoops up Violet, gently cradling her in his arms. He turns without a word and dashes back along the wall.

Rahab's blaze has grown so bright that I can see the entire pit. It makes me stagger back in horror. Joshua was right. The stack of bones rises almost to the ceiling above.

In the center is the dark shard, rising from the depths and surging out at the top, into the Scouring and the sky. Not even Rahab's fire can penetrate its blackness.

"Come now, Cipher." Daniel pulls at me.

But I can't look away. Rahab climbs the mountain of bones. At the base, far to my left, Joshua reaches Helena and Crispus. He leaves Violet with them. They rush into the tunnel to Red.

Joshua turns and charges into the pit. A purple cloak streams like a banner behind him. The wind doesn't slow him. He barrels through the skeletons like a bull.

He reaches Rahab as she nears the top. Skeletons attack but do nothing to slow the leaders. Rahab and Joshua blaze forward. The bag of collars flashes like a wild spark. It glows and melts, dripping silver. The molten metal rises above the leaders. They hurl it forward at the shard. It hits the darkness like a drop of mercury into a black hole.

The wind suddenly shifts. It reverses and yanks me toward the pit. The force is too much. I slip and start to slide. An arm grabs around my chest. It drags me back into the tunnel, holding me steady.

"Goodbye, my friends." Daniel's voice is somber by my ear.

Rahab and Joshua advance the final steps up the mountain of bones, burning skeletons as they go. Their inferno sucks into the dark shard. Red and purple touch black. There's a moment of delicate, silent stillness, like an intake of breath.

Then the pit explodes.

47

THE TUNNEL COLLAPSES. Dust and heat and darkness billow out like a mushroom cloud. I would die. I would be trapped. But Daniel saved me, his weathered arm still wrapped tight around my chest.

"There now." His voice is velvet. "Come, Cipher."

He leads me by the hand. I shuffle forward in shock. My eyes close. It's so dark it wouldn't matter if they were open. The explosion brought down the roof of the tunnel. No one inside the pit could have survived.

"Rahab and Joshua. They sacrificed themselves," I say.

"Hm, they gave up life here, such as it was," Daniel replies softly. "Is there anything greater we can do for those we love?"

I shake my head, still feeling the loss. But the leaders aren't like us. They're not fully present here. "How did their sacrifice help?"

"They slowed the Colorless One. They have bought time, eh?" The leader's staff taps with each step. "Yet his power will return like another wave, surging ever higher and stronger against the towers."

More skeletons. More twisted visions. They were too much for us to stop without Rahab.

"He collars the bones," I say. "How can we defeat

them?"

"You can't," Daniel says. "Not if you fight in the dark. But in the light, well, that's a different matter."

We ascend a steep slope. The stone turns to dirt underfoot. An earthy smell overtakes the dust and decay. The ground levels. There's a faint, fluttering glow of fairies in the distance. The root of the great tree.

"Ah, light." Daniel stops and turns to me. "Look."

He points behind me. It's Green's gateway to the Scouring. Numbers are written on the wall:

Purple 147

Yellow 146

Green 145

Red 144

Blue 138

I stare in amazement. "We're so close."

"As is the Colorless One," Daniel sighs.

My gaze snaps to the old leader. "He's close to what?"

"Hm, forever darkness. He has found a skeleton, a vision, a forbidden fruit—whatever you want to call it—for each of you. He readies his final attack to trap you here. And now you must proceed without the Scouring, and without the tunnels." Daniel turns and walks down the dimly lit root, his green robe swaying. "If shame taints you, the light will not overcome our enemy."

I follow after him. Despite Daniel's words, hope rises after seeing the numbers. All we need to do is move six people to Blue—one from Green, two from Yellow, and three from Purple—then we would have equilibrium.

"Who should leave Green?" I ask.

Daniel stops again, now at the base of Green Tower's trunk. The thick wooden door with its vivid tree emblem is closed behind the old leader.

He smiles as he taps my chest. "*You*. The others rely on you, the boy with five scars, number 720, to bring the towers to equilibrium. You must pass through Yellow and go to Blue. Your passage will come at great cost. You will not return here. That is why we send you off like this."

The wooden door swings open. A rush of sound and fresh air make me step back. Daniel's hand gently prods me forward.

"Go on now," he says.

I step forward into a dense crowd. Dozens are gathered in the glade beneath the great tree. They're gazing at me in wonder. So many familiar faces. Hank. Seneca. Even old foes look on me like a friend. Fugger. Polo. And above all, Baron.

"Welcome back, Cipher." Baron grins as he comes to my side and takes my hand. Scar against scar. He raises my arm with his own, high in the air.

The crowd breaks out into cheers.

As I scan their joyous faces, it strikes me that I've never seen the Green Tower quite like this—not even at the Jubilee feast, or when Emma and I brought a temporary peace here. Green has always separated into its tribes. Now no one's hands show marks. No Lions, Wolves, Eagles, or Snakes.

"What happened to the tribes?" I ask.

"They dissolved without the collars," Baron says. "We are one tribe now. We are the Green Tower."

The crowd parts ahead of me. A figure moves through it, like a prowling lion approaching through tall grasses. He stands twice as high as the others. The Hunter.

He stops before Daniel. "The wall is watched." His

voice is a low whisper, like leaves rustling in the wind.

"Hm, yes." The old leader's mossy beard bobs up and down. "Every path between the towers is watched now. The final battle comes."

"I will do what I must," the Hunter says.

Daniel nods and embraces the larger man. "Goodbye, my friend, until the other side." He speaks quietly, barely loud enough for me to hear beside them. "The light will reveal mysteries."

The Hunter almost looks relieved when he steps back. He reaches down to clasp Daniel's shoulder. "Goodbye."

"Where are you going?" I ask.

The Hunter turns to me. "I will take you to Yellow. It's time to go, Cipher."

I hesitate, concerned by their formal goodbyes.

"All will be well," Daniel says. "Light be with you."

The Hunter leads me through the crowd. Their hands reach for me, patting my shoulders, squeezing my hands, as if they're celebrating a champion. I'm not worthy of this, but it warms my heart all the same. I try to keep my head up for them.

Hank messes my hair like a big brother. Seneca grips my hand fondly. "Remember the tribes," she says. "Giving sets you free."

We walk out of the crowd and into the open glade. The Hunter slips into the forest ahead. I turn for a glance back, thinking it may be my last. My hand slips into my pocket, and I feel the acorn beside the spearhead and dragon's scale—three mementos from three towers. I stare in wonder at the tree shading us overhead. I fell out of that tree once. I fought against these tribes. But now they are united, cheering me on. I wave goodbye and turn into the forest.

The Hunter is nowhere to be seen. But among the dense trees stands an amazing stag, antlers rising like trees from its handsome head. It bounds into the woods and I race after it.

I lose sight of the beautiful creature many times, but always it reappears and bounds off again. It leads me toward the wall that separates Green and Yellow. Baron led me this way once before. We feared the Hunter then, and for good reason: he killed Fugger when we hunted the stag. So much has changed. Now, based on what Daniel said, I feel like the Hunter is my only hope of reaching Yellow.

The forest comes to an end. I step out onto the soft grass, hoping for sunlight but still in shadow. The massive stone wall looms above. And above it, high in the sky, the three suns have all gone black, like a total eclipse. It's dark as dusk.

A twig snaps behind me. The Hunter steps forward. "Fear not," he says. "Night leads to day."

"You led me here," I say. "You're the stag."

The corner of his bearded lips turns up in a grin. "We all have a bit of the wild in us. Some more than others." He looks past me to the wall. "This is where you will cross."

I gaze up. "What about Yellow's archers?"

"Green and Yellow work together now," he says. "But there's no dragon to help. Can you fly over?"

"Not alone." It makes me feel vulnerable. With Emma or Kiyo or others I could do this, but my power is not enough by itself. And I can't take anyone from Green without losing its equilibrium.

"There's another way," the Hunter says.

He draws his bow. With a swift motion, he fires an

arrow up into the sky, soaring over the wall, with a rope trailing behind it. The arrow lands in Yellow's territory. The Hunter pulls the rope until it catches and holds. He tugs hard at the string, the muscles of his forearm rippling.

"Use your feet against the wall." He puts a boot against the vertical stone beside us. "Like this."

I take the rope from him. "You sure it will it hold?"

He nods. "Use a little wind if you like."

"Thanks for your help," I say.

He clasps my shoulder. "Green will be ready. I've waited a long time for this. See you on the other side."

It sounds like another goodbye. We part and I start to climb. The rope holds as I pull and then lean back, testing it with my weight. It's hard work, going straight up, but I summon the wind as a gentle lifting hand. Soon I reach the top, thirty or forty feet above ground. Standing, I gaze down toward Green's forest.

The Hunter is gone. No stag in sight.

The wall extends in a straight line toward the sea in the distance. In the other direction is the Scouring. The dark shard is gone. The smooth gray stones have cratered in at the center. There's only a lifeless hole.

But then the jumble of stones suddenly moves at the edge of the crater, as if sensing my attention. My heart skips a beat.

Two huge blocks tremble and shift toward each other and fuse. Other stones move faster, piling one on top of another, twisting in midair like feathers. The stack takes shape as a massive creature, like an unnatural golem. Two legs. Two arms. It steps toward me. Then it bounds across the Scouring, shaking the ground like an earthquake.

The stone creature leaps onto the wall. The impact of

its landing knocks me to my knees. Its head has no eyes, no mouth, no expression, but a chrome band rings its neck.

I summon the wind and blast with everything I have.

The stones do not budge. The golem charges.

Just as I consider leaping from the wall, the stag appears beside me. It's so close, so huge. Twice my height. Smell of the forest. Its dark eyes blink knowingly before it turns away.

Its head lowers. Its antlers aim. It charges.

The stone golem and magical stag race at each other along the top of the narrow wall. There's no retreat, no turning away. I cringe, expecting another explosion like the one Rahab and Joshua set off in the pit.

But this is pure physical force. The stag hits the golem like a freight train. The momentum propels both creatures back toward the Scouring. Antlers stab clean through the stone. Boulder fists crash down against the stag's back. A breaking sound, loud as an oak tree snapping in half, makes me sick to my stomach. They slam onto the stone ground like a meteor, landing with a deafening thud.

I stare in shock. Neither creature rises.

The Scouring is still and quiet again.

The Hunter saved me. He and Daniel knew something like this was coming. But what was that golem? Another minion of the Colorless One. It was collared like the skeletons. Could anything become his weapon? Is anywhere safe?

"Ho there!" calls out a voice.

I turn toward the golden fields and the Yellow Tower. The tower's turrets and parapets glow like a fairytale castle.

"How'd ya get up there? Wait a sec, is that you Cipher?"

I breathe easier as I see the boy below me, leaning on a hoe. It's Drew, my neighbor when I first arrived on my little square plot of Yellow's land. I wave to him and take hold of the rope, still connected to the arrow below. I climb down, buffeted by the blue weaves of air. I land in a field of ripe corn.

Drew approaches through the tall stalks and greets me with a hug. "Cipher's back in Yellow! How 'bout that!"

"It's good to see you, Drew." I notice he doesn't wear a collar. "You're free now?"

His chest puffs up. "Free as day. And I ain't never grown such a beautiful crop. Now if only I can keep them crows off of it."

"I need to talk with Yellow's leaders," I say. "Want to walk with me?"

"Heck yeah! It's a fine day for a stroll." He squints up at the charcoal sky and the three black orbs. "Well…fine as we gonna get these days."

48

THE YELLOW TOWER no longer gleams in sunlight. It glows from inside. Standing in the central courtyard, turrets rising high around us, we are the source of light under the three black pearls in the dark sky.

Emma glows before me. Her power emanates and interlaces with the powers of the many others from yellow, golden strands like strings of light. Her family is close around her—father William, son Oliver, descendant Neville. Dozens of other familiar faces gather near us. Drew leans on his hoe. Li Min holds a flower in her clasped hands. Seymour moves through the crowd with a smile and a tray of food. Joan stands by the Scouring gate as if ready for battle. The golden armor is long gone, hurled into the pit after Emma and I won here, but I've never seen the Yellow Tower so strong. I've never seen it so bright.

"You say Rahab and Joshua…exploded?" Elijah's gentle eyes show no fear, only wonder. The Widow stands by his side, with her yellow robe looking bioluminescent.

I've told them how I came from Green on my way to Blue, about how the pit and tunnels imploded, and about the Hunter saving me on the wall. "Sort of," I say. "Joshua and Rahab touched the darkness like an opposite charge, and it caused the explosion. They sacrificed themselves."

"Passion to the end." The Widow flashes a kind old smile. "And Daniel?"

"He's still in Green, I hope." But so few leaders remain. I miss them. Even Joshua. He was a physical force, as was the Hunter and Behemoth. They're gone now. So are Abram and Moses. In the dark vision the Colorless One said the leaders were beyond his control but could not withstand him. They're leaving us. Yet we still face skeletons, shadows, shame…and maybe worse. The next sacrifice could be me.

"Are you okay?" Emma asks, peering into my eyes.

She knows me too well. But I can't tell her of the deal. My hand slips into my pocket, finds the reminders. My hope of leaving is faint but alive. And if I can't, it's for her good. It's for everyone.

"I'm fine," I say. "Just worried about the leaders. Elijah, who's next?"

Elijah studies me but doesn't answer.

"None of us is enough." The Widow places her frail hand on my cheek. She gazes at the others gathered around us. "But together, scoured and purified, you can shine whiter than the suns once did. Do not fear the darkness— either in the sky or in your own pasts. The light shines in the darkness, and the darkness has not overcome it."

"We are ready," Emma says, taking my scarred hand in hers. "How do we do this?"

"I've talked to the other marked ones," I say. "We'll each lead our towers and attack the Colorless One in the Scouring. We'll try to open the White Tower again."

"Aye, once the towers are ready." Elijah's eyes stay fixed on me. "We will make sure Cipher gets to Blue safely, along with two others. It will be our final act in this place."

"Are you coming with us, then?" I ask.

Elijah and the Widow exchange a glance. "No," they say together.

"But you'll come when we need you?"

"Our power is not our own," the Widow says.

"We simply serve and obey," Elijah adds.

His tone is like the Hunter's, like Rahab's—like a goodbye. I can't bear losing more leaders. And I don't want to leave Emma so soon. I squeeze her hand.

She faces me solemnly and holds out a handful of golden grains. "Take these," she says. "All nine grains. They may help us connect. We will need to coordinate our attack."

"Thank you," I say, pocketing the grains. Her words remind me of how we once spoke through the stars. "How will we do this? The stars have gone black. And Daniel said every passage between the towers is watched."

"As marked ones you are linked," Elijah says. "Anything that helps you remember can help the five of you find the way. Cipher, once you are in Blue, draw on these memories and use the Sieve. Sarai is there. She will guide you."

"I will be waiting," Emma says. "Call for me however you can. The Healer's light be with you."

Her warm smile encourages me more than ever. We will enter the fight together. We'll try to open the White Tower for everyone, even me. But if my faults mean I have to stay so she can leave, it will be worth it. I would give myself up for her.

"It is time, Cipher," the Widow says. "You must go to Blue now."

"How?" I ask. "The tunnels are blocked."

"And the sea is not safe," Emma adds.

"Aye, only the towers are safe now," Elijah says.

I meet Emma's eyes, thinking of our power together, of how we once soared over Green's forest. "If two others are going with me, maybe we could fly. Blue is close to here."

The leaders smile in agreement. Elijah looks to the crowd. "As for who goes to Blue, you know who you are."

Nervous silence falls. Boys and girls exchange glances. No one speaks. It seems no one wants to leave Yellow's safety and warmth. I can understand that. Danger follows me.

But then a girl approaches us. Li Min, Max's daughter, the one who had the perfect score in China. Her long black hair hangs like a veil. "I'll go."

"You show courage," Elijah says. "Who else?"

Only one other person steps forward. It's Sally, another of my neighbors when I first arrived in Yellow's land. She was the folksy wheat grower who once lived in colonial America.

Elijah and the Widow seem satisfied with these two. "You must go now," Elijah says to me.

"Stay safe," Emma says, embracing me. "We will be ready. Yellow will have equilibrium now."

"Yes," the Widow says. "If we can hold back the Colorless One. Cipher, you must move quickly."

49

LI MIN, SALLY, AND I soar like eagles away from the Yellow Tower. Hands clasped, our combined powers propel us, thick blue threads woven into braids of yellow. The power drains fast, but we don't have far to go. We stay low over the ground, with the Scouring wall to our left. We must be ready for anything.

Li Min looks stoic at my side, wind blowing her hair back like a black ribbon. She lived in my time on Earth. We knew of people flying—one way or another. Sally did not. Her tense face is exhilarated as she gazes down at the golden fields below.

We approach the steep cliffs that separate Yellow and Blue. They drop straight down to the sea. We'll soar over them and land on the dock by the base of the Blue Tower. I do not expect it to go smoothly, not after what happened to the Hunter.

Just as we reach the cliffs, a dark shape surges over the wall to our left, from the Scouring. The huge form is made of countless black dots. It reaches for us like a fist.

"Higher!" I shout, lifting us fast as I can.

Up and up we rise until we've flown higher than all of the five towers. Only then do I risk a glance down, steeling myself against the heights. The towers are dots, but the attacking shape reaches up like a geyser of ink. There's no sign of help. No Elijah or the Widow.

I blast the air against the force. It's too late. The shape swoops over us. It's a flurry of countless birds. Each one is a dark crow, and they're like a monster together.

They batter at us like black hail. I hold tight to Sally's and Li Min's hands by my sides, trying to weave the wind into a shield. But I can't hold enough power to keep us flying and protect us at the same time. We fall in fits, like a plane with a blown engine.

We spin down toward the cliffs. Far below, jagged rocks jab up through the ocean spray.

I shout for help, but there's no answer. We're alone.

The crows come again. This time they bend into the shape of a scythe. The crescent strikes down at us. The countless blows spin, knock, and batter us.

They break my grip on Sally's hand. She plummets, screaming, down toward the sea.

"No!" Li Min shouts, gripping my hand like a vice.

I try to catch Sally with the air, but the crows swoop at me again. Vision blocked. Body battered.

When they clear again, I don't see Sally. I summon a flicker of wind, hardly enough to slow the fall.

"Look!" Li Min points to the ground behind us.

A blazing shape races across Yellow's golden fields. As it rushes to the wall, it surges up. There are two horses at the front, drawing a chariot with two radiant figures. They leave a wake of white-hot yellow flame.

The chariot takes off. It soars toward us. Above, the countless crows swoop down again. The forces will collide.

The chariot reaches us first. As it races past in midair, I hear a whisper of voices, like Elijah's and the Widow's, through the whirlwind. "For the light!"

The chariot stabs into the dark flock like a golden javelin. The crows part and press ever down. But moments before they strike again, a golden web swoops around them. It pulls up and up, like a net drawn tight behind the chariot.

Li Min and I land on the edge of the cliff and stare up. The chariot rises faster. It soars at the three blackened suns, with the mass of crows towed behind in the golden net. The strange shape shrinks in the distance, going small as a star, soaring further and further until it vanishes into the suns. There's a moment of stillness, and then a bright burst like the blink of a galaxy.

Dusk quickly falls again.

"Our leaders." Li Min's voice is soft, her gaze still locked on the dark sky above. "They saved us."

"Yes, and we're on our own now," I say. "We have to keep moving. Let's look for Sally on the way to Blue."

Our powers have drained, but we have just enough for the descent. We leap from the cliff and soar down. I study the roiling sea as it crashes into the rocks. Whitecaps everywhere. No sign of Sally. No one could survive that fall. I have to hope she wakes in the Blue Tower.

Li Min and I land smoothly on the dock. Boats bob up and down, tied to the wooden pier that leads to the tower. I take a deep breath. Fresh sea air. Salty breeze.

Through my despair, I feel a rush of relief. It feels like coming home.

50

A GIANT SEA TURTLE drifts behind me. Its immense shell and ancient eyes shadow all of us at the table, making us look young and small. Beneath our feet flashes a school of silver fish. A blurred shape darts after them. They fade into the midnight blue beyond the glass.

"Luther here thinks faith was our ticket to the towers." Tom sips from his bowl of squid soup. "I say that's nonsense. The Sieve and Scouring have shown it's what we did that matters, not what we believed."

Luther's blunt eyes glare like a rival across the table. "What you *did* only showed what you *truly* believed. This is the effect of faith. It isn't magic."

Tom waves off the comment. "Meh, talk to Cipher about magic. He's the marked one, returned to lead us and all that."

All ten faces around the table turn to me. Luther and Tom said Sarai would come here, so I have waited. And they have been debating through the whole meal. I figure they've been debating the whole time I've been gone. What else comes from geniuses cooped up together in a tower? Tom says God's words are all that matters. Luther says Tom never would have made it to the towers if not for faith. I don't have answers to their questions. What I know is that we were all messes, and that the Colorless One wants to trap us here forever. But maybe it will be only me, the worst of the lot.

"Cipher, what do you think?" Li Min asks. She's spent the meal gazing out the glass walls in wonder. "Was it faith that brought us here?"

"Yes." The confidence of my answer surprises me.

"See!" Luther winks at Tom.

"Cipher has faith only in himself," Tom says. "Now, I can understand that. We have to believe in ourselves."

"What do you think faith is?" Li Min asks.

"It's what faith *was* that matters," I say. "Tom's right. I believed in myself—too much. It took five towers and all the scouring I could get to strip that away."

"Same here." Tom's voice has lost its challenge. His pale eyes are soft as he studies me. "So what did you believe in?"

"There were good things." I think back through the visions, pulling out scoured remnants. "My son's love, even in pain. My wife's devotion, even after my betrayal. Samantha's forgiveness, even after my lies." And the man who came to my side on my deathbed. He told me I wasn't finished yet. He believed in me. "It was the faith of others that almost changed me. They tried to persuade me, over time and over a life of mistakes, to believe in something greater than myself. I just didn't deserve saving."

"Ah, imputed righteousness," Luther says with a smile.

Tom sighs. "Here goes the theologian…"

"Your words cut, Mr. Jefferson, because you strike true." Luther shrugs. "But what's life without theology?"

"Wait," I say, as something from history clicks. I peer closer at the large boy. "Were you Martin Luther?"

"No, I was a nobody, a privateer," he replies.

"That's fancy for pirate," Tom quips. "Why don't you tell him why you call yourself Luther?"

"I don't deny it," Luther says. "I took the theologian's name. It seemed to fit here. I learned a lot from his books—they kept me company as I sailed the high seas. Luther never allowed for a place like the Five Towers. Nor did I. I was sure faith was all I needed. I admit, much as Mr. Jefferson savors, that I was wrong."

"Why?" I ask.

"I believed death brought a simple up or down. Sheep go to heaven; goats go to hell."

"Livestock again?" Tom mutters.

Luther ignores him and speaks as if lecturing to everyone around the table. "If what Abram said is true, and I believe it is, the real Luther may still be right. We died with the 'up' fate—sheep by grace—but the work we built on the foundation couldn't survive." Luther glances to me. "Paul wrote something like that."

"You mean me?" I ask, confused.

Luther laughs. "No, the apostle. Ever read his letters?"

I shake my head. I don't remember.

"You missed out," Luther says. "He wrote that if anyone's work is burned up, he'll suffer loss but still be saved as through fire. I figure that's us. Until we enter the White Tower." He sighs and gazes past us, as if looking beyond. "I can't wait to talk to the real Luther there."

"You forget, the White Tower is blocked," Tom says. "We don't deserve it, apparently."

"We *deserve* far worse than this," Luther replies. "But it's not about what we deserve. It's about faith."

Tom grins at me. "There he goes again…"

I study the former President, wondering about what he really thinks. "You've been in the Green Tower, Tom. What was scoured there?"

"I didn't make it long in Green." He shrugs. "It figures. I died bankrupt on Earth."

"You were with Seneca and me," I say. "We hid in the mangroves by the shore. Blue came in their boat. You walked right out to them. They brought you back here."

"I belong in Blue," he says.

Li Min points past Tom. "Your friend agrees. He likes you."

The turtle has drifted back and pressed its nose against the glass just behind Tom, who looks uneasy.

"Weird," he says. "Sarai should be here by now. Cipher, are you finished with your soup?"

"Almost." I have a few sips left.

Tom pushes his empty bowl to the center of the table. A servant comes within moments.

My mouth falls open. It's Sally. Did she die and awaken here, or somehow survive? She wears a white robe and a silver collar around her neck. She leans over the table to pick up the bowl. As she moves away, her eyes catch mine.

Hope sparks. "Sally?"

She stands frozen in place, the bowl held idly in her hands.

"You know her?" Tom asks.

"Yes, from Yellow," I say. "Sally, do you remember?"

She nods but her lips stay pressed tight. She looks from me to Tom, with anger and excitement in her eyes. She suddenly goes rigid, then turns to leave.

After a few steps it hits me: she's Tom's servant. "Wait," I say. "Tom, tell her to come back."

"Why?" he asks, too casually. He's hiding something.

"I want to talk with her," I say.

"There's no point," Tom snaps. "I tried this morning to convert her. She refuses to join Blue. It was merciful to let her wear the collar. She'll be wiped soon."

Sally has left the room. I have a nagging doubt about Tom's explanation. "How did you capture her?"

"I didn't. It was odd—she just showed up under the tower, but unlike the rest of us who work our way up from the bottom, Sarai brought her to me. I don't mind. She does her job well enough, and she's cute."

Sarai. She must have had a reason. And Tom's words stir something inside me, something thick from the past, like a spoon through molasses. Behind him, there are now two turtles. They watch us curiously.

"Ask her to come back," I say.

Tom sighs. "Whatever, you're the marked one."

Sally returns, walking stiffly and quickly, and stands before us with her hands clasped. She doesn't look at us. She looks past Tom, where there are now four turtles. Each one presses its beak to the glass, like people huddled around a television screen. It's unnerving.

I force myself to turn away from the aquatic spectators and face Sally. "How much do you remember?" I ask.

She does not respond. But she blinks and flicks her eyes toward Tom.

"Tom, release your commands," I say. "Let her talk."

"Fine," he mutters.

Sally turns to him and snaps, "How am I supposed to follow an order like that, *Mr. Jefferson?*"

"That's enough!" he fires back, surging to his feet and knocking his chair to the ground.

"Oh, I'll call you Tom!" In a sudden motion, Sally grabs Tom's robe in her fist, twists it, and pulls him close. For a moment their eyes lock.

Tom, even with complete control through the collar, looks afraid. Sally leans forward and gently kisses his forehead. Then she jerks back and slaps him hard right across the face.

He clasps his cheek. He shouts, "*What the—?!*"

"Both of you, stop!" I summon the wind, pulling them apart and fixing everyone around us in place. I can't let this get more out of control. We have to be united.

Sally and Tom fall silent and face me, looking chastised.

"Sally," I say. "Are you able to speak freely now?"

"I sure am," she says, holding her head high and casting a glance at Tom. "*Now.*"

A faint memory clicks into place. "When we met in Yellow, did you tell me your full name?"

"I sure did." She glances to Tom, whose face has gone white. "It's Sally Hemings."

Hemings. The realization unsettles me. Thomas Jefferson and Sally Hemings. Master and slave. Lovers. Here in the Blue Tower.

"I remember now, about your…history," I say, trying to find the right words. "I'm sorry I forgot. I guess it took seeing you two together."

"Well, it's been a while," Sally says, with a slight nod of satisfaction. She turns to Tom. "Sounds like our story got told in the end."

Tom does not meet her gaze.

"Cipher, I can't move," Luther grunts from across the table. "How about releasing that wind?"

"Right, sorry." I scan the group around us, feeling bad

for holding them. They look confused. "I just wanted to keep things calm," I say. "Tom and Sally had a complicated past on Earth."

"What do you mean?" Luther asks.

"I was his slave," Sally almost spits the words. She grips the collar around her neck. "Almost as bad as wearing *this*."

"Tom, you should take the collar off," I say.

He shakes his head warily. "Not a good idea."

"It was your best idea!" Sally says. "Life, liberty, and the pursuit of happiness, you said. All men are created equal, you said. Fate would have my people be free, you said!"

I recognize her words. Tom was famous for them. "They carved these things on your memorial," I say to him.

"They built him a memorial?" Sally asks, as some hint of pride comes through her frustration.

Tom has backed up to the glass wall. He slides down and stares blankly at the clear glass floor, where a bright fish flashes past a sea turtle.

Sally kneels in front of him. For a moment I worry that she's going to slap him again, or worse. But she gently takes his face between her hands.

"Set me free," she whispers. The words flow like they've been spoken before, like they're running through worn grooves.

Tom shakes his head as if torn. He looks past her to me, with a plea in his eyes. "I can't take this. It's better to wipe one of us. Or send her back to Yellow."

"No, we're too close to equilibrium," I say.

"But she loves me *and* she hates me," Tom says. The link through the collar would tell him that. It would tell him everything she feels.

"I hate what you did, what you left undone," Sally says.

"But not *you*. No, you were in my dreams in Yellow, Mr. Jefferson. Healing dreams. I could almost forgive you, if only you'd let me."

Tom buries his face in his hands. "I can't. I'm sorry."

"Why not?" Luther asks. "Just take the collar off."

"If he does it here, it'll be admitting he should've done it on Earth." Sally stands and gazes down at Tom, with a hand on her hip. "And Mr. Jefferson sure can't do that."

"It wasn't that simple!" Tom protests.

"Nothing ever was. But that didn't stop us."

"You know I couldn't just—"

"Oh I know. The President ain't always free to do what he wants. What he knows he should."

Tom does not respond. The pained look on his face says he's had this argument before.

"See?" Sally says, glancing around the group. "He knew the right way, but he chose the easy way. Heck, I let him. Maybe that's why we're here and not someplace better."

The easy way. I want to deny it, but her words ring true. I'm the only one with five scars because I chose the easiest ways of all.

Luther brushes past me and clasps Sally's shoulder. "No. That's not right. I see how it is now."

"How what is?" Sally asks.

He doesn't answer her. He squats before Tom on the glass floor. He takes Tom's face with one of his large hands, forcing their eyes to meet.

"This is your chance, Tom," Luther says. "It's like I said. Build a better foundation."

Tom looks back at him, eyes red-rimmed.

"That you may pass through the fire," Luther says.

Tom gazes into Luther's eyes for a long moment, then

to Sally. I sense something passing between them, through the link.

"Set me free," she says again. It is a plea.

Trembling, Tom rises. He moves to her with halting steps. The rest of us are silent, watching.

"Put your hands to my collar," Sally says, and he does, his hand shaking.

"Now funnel your power into it," she says.

I see Tom's threads coil with Sally's, the colors weaving together, and the collar falls and lands with a clink against the glass floor.

Sally begins to cry first. Warm tears run from her eyes, then she throws her arms around him. She kisses his cheek. Soon they are both weeping, holding each other close.

Li Min touches my arm gently. "Let's sit," she says.

The others from our group return to the table, giving Sally and Tom space. We feel lightness in the room, a weight lifted, as the two of them eventually join us.

"All things work together for the good," Luther says, grinning toward Sally and Tom. "But you have to tell us more. Who *were* you?"

Sally and Tom explain everything. They say Sally was Tom's slave in colonial America. Tom's wife had died. He was in Paris. He was famous but lonely. Golden fixtures and the finest sheets were little comfort. Sally was close, and beautiful. She was smart and obedient. She even looked like Tom's late Martha, as her half-sister.

And so Tom found his companion.

They tried to keep it secret. He was a public figure, a potential president. This sort of relationship between master and slave couldn't be brought into the light. The shame and guilt lay too heavy over it. Still, over the decades, these dark clouds lifted whenever Tom and Sally were alone together.

Tom weeps through much of the retelling. But Sally forgives him again and again, her mercy ceaseless. She came from Yellow. She knows how to heal.

As their story comes to a close, there's one mystery that still baffles me. "How did you get to Blue?" I ask Sally. "The last I saw, you were crashing to the sea."

Sally smiles and gazes out the glass wall, toward the turtles that still drift lazily near us. "I sure was falling fast, but a rush of wind from something—hard to believe, but it looked like a chariot—slowed my fall. I landed smack on the water. I hurt too much to swim long, and the Blue Tower was way, way off. I figured I'd die and wake up wiped. But then, I'm telling it true, a turtle came. It floated right beside me until I grabbed its shell, then it hauled me straight toward the tower. On the way I healed a wound on its flipper. Maybe there was something we shared, surviving like that. So I reckon the turtles have watched while Tom and I came together, like they're celebrating with me."

"Everything serves a purpose here." The voice, Sarai's, comes from close behind me. I didn't hear her enter. Now she stands by our table, a tall sage with gray hair and wise, ocean-blue eyes. She holds Sally's open collar in her hand like a dead snake.

"Another shame scoured," Sarai says. She puts a hand on my shoulder. "Cipher, it's time to come with me."

51

SARAI LEADS ME along the familiar path up the Blue Tower. It coils along the wall, open in the center. We pass many doors. We pass blue-robed students. Candles light the way until we reach the door with the imprint of a large raindrop.

Sarai stops and kneels by a bag on the floor. She places Sally's collar inside, then draws the bag closed. Metal rattles lightly.

"Last one." She turns to me, looking satisfied. "You remember what happened last time in here?"

It was on my visit from the Yellow Tower. I looked into the Sieve with Emma, Kiyo, and others. We saw into the pit. "The Colorless One had tainted the Sieve."

"So it was," Sarai says. "Abram has purified it."

She speaks of Abram like he's in a room down the hall. I perk up, excited. "Is he here?" I ask.

"No, he has moved on."

"How? I saw him in the pit…"

"He gave you all the light he had to bring here. As each leader does. We have guided you."

"How can you guide us if you keep leaving? The Colorless One is getting stronger. We can't fight him without you."

"But you will. The Scouring washes your stains clean."

"Even if we're scoured, aren't we stuck without the White Tower?"

"Scoured souls shine with pure light. Genius would not design a place where this light could not overcome dark."

"The Colorless One doesn't seem to care about the design," I say. "He's using this place against us. Shadows attack. Bones and birds attack. Even the stones of the Scouring…they took out the Hunter."

Her hand gently grazes my cheek. "No victory is won without sacrifice. You have earned your scars. Now you know all the marked ones. And you know their towers."

I reach into my pocket and feel the acorn, the dragon scale, the spearhead, and the grains. "Yes."

"Use the tokens that you have gained," she says. "They will help you speak to the other marked ones."

"How?"

"Focus on the memories you share and summon your power as you look into the Sieve. The others will come. You have done well, Cipher."

It sounds like yet another goodbye. "Can't you stay? Just a little longer?"

She shakes her head and glances past me, out the opening in the wall. "I must tend to the sea. Someone must hold back the storm for a while. The enemy would flood this place. He was never one to create original ideas. He only copies and corrupts."

Outside, clouds the size of mountains darken the already dark sky. The sea looks more black than blue, with whitecaps of raging waves. I peer down. My chest tightens. The boats are gone. Only bare pylons and scattered fragments of wood remain of the dock. A wave swells and crashes over the broken pier. The crest hits the tower so hard the stones shake. Foam splashes halfway up the tower's immense height.

"The deep laughs as I once did," Sarai says.

"I don't understand."

A smile wrinkles her weathered face. "No one can fathom the power of the light without seeing its true source. May the hope of light sustain you."

She squeezes my shoulder and turns away. She lifts the bag of collars. Slings it over her shoulder. Her dark blue robe sways as she strides down the path.

The stones tremble again under my feet. Another wave.

I lean back against the wall and slide down. I sit on the floor and hug my knees, feeling empty and alone. Abram and Sarai were the ones who welcomed me to the Blue Tower. They and the other leaders guided me every step of the way. How can we stand against the Colorless One without them? The tokens from the other towers weigh heavily in my pocket. The other marked ones wait for me.

I gaze up at the door. I must go to the Sieve.

I force myself to stand and press my hand to the emblem and summon the wind. When the door swings open, a gust of cold, stale air greets me. It is darker inside than I remember. A fine layer of dust covers the floor. The Sieve stands like an otherworldly portal in the center of the room, alluring as ever.

I approach cautiously. Nothing stirs beyond the chilling breeze. Silence surrounds me.

I lean over the water in the Sieve. It gives no reflection. It looks solid, like a block of black ice. I summon the air and blow it gently over the surface. The water ripples.

A voice whispers, "Look."

I tremble as I glance around the room. I am alone.

"Look."

"Who are you?" I ask aloud.

No answer.

I back away from the Sieve.

"Look," says the voice. "*Look.*"

It comes from the pedestal, from the water, soft but insistent. The tone is almost familiar.

I take a step forward but stop.

It could be the Colorless One.

My hand slips into the pocket of my robe. I pull out a handful of grains, tumbling them between my fingers. Then I retrieve the other items—acorn, spearhead, dragon scale. Sarai said this would work. I trust her.

I hold fast to the tokens, envisioning the other towers and the marked ones. Emma in Yellow, Baron in Green, Helena in Red, and Kiyo in Purple. And I'm in Blue.

I summon the wind and stare down at the still water. Deep below the surface, through the darkness, there is light. I plunge my head in.

52

"WELCOME, CIPHER," EMMA says. Light blurs her golden hair, but not her blue eyes. Their sapphire gleam fills me like fresh oxygen in the lungs.

Emma sits to my left at a pearl white table. Beside her sits Baron, then Helena and Kiyo going around. It's the same arrangement as the towers. The table stands dead center in the Scouring, where the stones collapsed into the pit, where the White Tower should be. The vast stone battleground is empty and quiet around us, shrouded in mist. No tower is visible. It feels like a dream.

"How is this possible?" I ask.

"The leaders showed us before they left," Emma replies. "I found my way here as I slept."

"The sap brought me." Baron's granite eyes spark with life.

"I see you through flames," Helena says. "You look good with a shade of red, Cipher."

I can't help but smile at her fiery banter. "Have you all been waiting for me?"

"Some longer than others," Kiyo replies. She looks regal in her purple robe. "What have you learned?"

"It's not good," I say. "The darkness has grown. The Colorless One is turning this land against the towers.

Stones rise up. Birds attack. Even the sea assaults the Blue Tower. We have little time left."

"Our gate trembles against the dragons," Helena says.

Kiyo leans forward. "We have three in Purple who must reach Blue. Joshua had been helping move boys and girls to the right towers, but he never came back after he took Crispus."

"It's up to us." Emma's eyes are icy and intense. "Elijah and the Widow left the Yellow Tower like a blazing chariot. They haven't returned."

"I don't think they will," I say. "They helped me reach Blue. And now Sarai has left."

"Rahab and Behemoth are also gone," Helena says.

"I think Daniel left too," Baron says.

"Daniel? How?" I ask, feeling a final hope extinguished. It seemed that Daniel, of any of the leaders, might remain.

"Soon after you left," Baron says to me, "leaves started to fall from the tree. Dead leaves. Green decaying to brown. Daniel said he would stop it. The last thing he said to me was, *Giving sets me free*. He had that cryptic look in his eye as he disappeared. The decay has stopped. For now."

"And the Hunter is gone," I say. "He took one of the enemy's powerful minions down with him. So…that's all of them. The leaders have left. It's only us."

"I don't think we can hold without them," Kiyo says, her voice haunting. "We were attacked last night. They came like shadows. Skeletons clambered over the Scouring wall, dozens of them. We fought them back, barely. They retreated at dawn, pale as it was. If they come again, we might not make it through another night."

"We must move fast," I say grimly. "I will bring the

three from Purple to Blue. We'll finally reach equilibrium."

"Great, and then what?" Helena moves her hand as if she's waving a magic wand. "*Poof!* And the Colorless One's gone? No way. I've seen his skeletons. He'll fight. He'll torment."

I meet her almond eyes. "You're right. That's why we must attack, together. Abram told me long ago that with perfect equilibrium we, the marked ones, can harness the purest white light of the Five Towers. He said we could stab it into the black heart of the Colorless One."

"A fine idea," Baron says. "But how exactly are we supposed to do that?"

"In the Scouring, at the very center," Emma replies. "We must restore the White Tower. It is the only way out."

Emma's quiet dignity, as ever, steadies me. We glimpsed the White Tower together. We came so close.

"Yes, we'll lead the towers into the Scouring," I say. "Baron and Kiyo, remember the vision we saw when we put the crown on Samantha? Even as the Colorless One blackened everything, our light stopped him. A ray of each tower's color met above the Scouring and fused into white light. So let's get as close to the center as we can. We'll harness everyone's powers to attack the darkness there."

"Can we really harness so much power?" Baron asks. "Others here are stronger than I am. There are seven hundred fifteen of them, only five of us. What do these scars even mean?"

"They connect us," Emma says.

"I have no connection to any of you," Helena says. "Other than this place."

"I'm not so sure," I say. "It's hard to trace ancestors that far. Maybe we're connected by blood. Maybe more.

Emma's son is here, and he gave a bunch of money to the school I went to on Earth. I married Baron's granddaughter. I did business with Kiyo's heir."

"So what?" Helena says. "My son was the Roman emperor. As far as I can tell, none of you were heirs to the throne."

"Your empire crumbled soon after you died," Baron says. "No offense. It's only the truth."

"Did any of you know the descendants of Helena, and her son Constantine?" Emma asks.

"How would we know?" Baron says. "It was centuries before our time. We all come from Adam and Eve, but so what?"

"The whole world is family," Kiyo says. "But Cain killed Abel. Maybe it's not our families that connect us."

"It could be our genes," I say. "That's part of family."

"Family must matter," Emma agrees. "Cipher's mother was here. My father and son and grandson are all here."

"As are several of my descendants," Kiyo replies. "It matters, yes. But I think there's something deeper to our connection."

"Oh?" Helena eyes Kiyo. "Fire away, cold one."

Kiyo smiles. "We are the most extreme, I think. What if we are the ones most *un*worthy to have arrived at the Five Towers?"

"Makes sense to me," I say. "Rahab said something like that. She said my power came from what I could have been on Earth, but failed to be. Genius is capable of great things, but I was a scared and unfaithful man, and an arrogant doctor." I look to Emma. "I wasn't a true healer."

"You are now," Emma says. "This could be right. I was never brave on Earth."

"I like this idea." Helena sounds surprised by her own words. "I've met no one who rivaled my passion."

"Or anyone as rich as I was," Baron says. "Maybe it's true. Maybe I'm the biggest camel ever to squeeze through the eye of a needle."

I look around the table, taking comfort in the familiar faces. "We are the worst the Five Towers has to offer."

"And our failures passed down," Emma says softly. "My heir Neville inherited his fear from me and, from what he has told me, this fear allowed the most terrible evil to spread." She closes her eyes and shudders. "We are responsible for so much pain and loss. I've seen it in the pit. Millions and millions of bones…"

"No, Emma." My voice is gentle but firm as her sad eyes meet mine. "Whatever you saw, it's a lie." I feel like I'm trying to convince myself as the words come out. "The bones are the Colorless One's weapons. They are shame."

"Cipher's right," Kiyo says. "We can't blame ourselves for what was beyond our control."

Baron and Helena nod in agreement, but Emma doesn't flinch. "We must be responsible for what we did," she says.

Her somber words are hard to swallow. "If so, then I am responsible for bringing the whole world down. I invented the technology that allowed darkness to penetrate every mind on Earth. I don't deserve to be here."

"None of us do," Kiyo says.

We fall silent. Uneasy glances pass around the table. Furtive eyes, looking down, not meeting for more than a moment. Dreamlike mist presses close around us.

Words drift into my mind: *When the time comes, the others may leave. You will stay with me. In the pit. Forever.*

My deal with the Colorless One. If anyone deserves this, it's me. I'll fight to get out if I can, but I'll stay if it's the only way to save my friends. Otherwise we'll all be lost in this gloom. It feels worse than any nightmare.

Emma names it, softly, as if breaking a spell. "Guilt. Shame. It's still here."

"It always will be," Helena says.

"No." Baron presses his scarred hand against the table. "Not always. There have been moments here. I remember giving on Earth. It set me free, as it does here. Only memories of darkness bring the guilt and shame back. But those memories are dimmer than they once were."

"They're scoured," I say.

"Mine are also burnt away," Helena says. "Like ashes in my mind. The memories that remain have been refined by fire. They are like gold."

"I think it's like that for everyone here," Kiyo says. "The Judge will punish evil. This is not our burden, but justice requires that the wrong we did be wiped away."

"And what's left must be healed," Emma says.

"So we focus on this goodness," I say. "We draw on everyone's powers together. That's our only hope. We must explain this to our towers and lead them into the Scouring, to fight the Colorless One, to reopen the White Tower. All of our prior battles have prepared us for this."

"I like it," Baron says, and Kiyo agrees.

"You make it sound too easy," Helena says. "We must not underestimate the enemy. But...I don't have a better idea." She sighs, her grim expression turning to resolve. "Okay, I'm with you. Red will bring the fire."

"Then our plan is settled," Emma says. "But Cipher, we still need to get the three from Purple to Blue. How?"

Not tunnels. Not boats. Not flying. Cliffs separate Blue and Black. Sarai said she would tend to the sea. If we could go along the base of the cliffs… "Kiyo, do you remember the ledge where we sat with Samantha, after we took over the Purple Tower?"

"Of course," Kiyo says.

"Find the three and take them there. I'll come soon."

"Good. I need to show you something." Kiyo sounds nervous. She glances around at the empty Scouring. There's nothing to see beyond the pale mist.

"What is it?" I ask, feeling uneasy.

Kiyo shakes her head. "You can't see through Blue's clouds. We should not speak of it here. But…Helena's right. The path to the White Tower will not be easy. We must be ready for anything. Come quickly, Cipher."

53

WE GATHER AT the base of the Blue Tower, by the door to the docks. It's a small group of fourth-class kids. Luther looking blunt and pensive. Tom sharp and wry. Shelley distant and sad.

I open the door. The group gasps at the dark scene of destruction. The docks are gone. No boats remain. There are few signs that a long pier ever stood here. Scattered fragments of wood drift among the gentle waves. Short splinters jut out from beneath the door, where stairs once led into the Blue Tower.

"Sarai left for *this*?" Tom quips. "Perhaps she was late…"

I've told them what Sarai said, but they don't understand. They haven't seen the shadows, the bones, the birds. "No, it would have been far worse if she hadn't gone," I say. "The tower still stands. And look at the water. It's calm."

The group stares at me. They are waiting, hoping for a plan, wanting action. I lean out the door and peer to the left, in the direction of the Purple Tower. It's not far down to the base of the cliffs. With the sea this gentle, we should have enough power over the air to fly down and hold the water back. We can still traverse beneath the cliffs. Maybe stay under the radar.

I turn back. I hold out my hand to Li Min. "Ready?"

She eyes my hand uneasily. The scar looks like a wicked groove in the pale light. "So sorry," she says. "Our last flight didn't go well."

I scan the group around us. "We'd be stronger with others."

No one moves. Maybe I don't inspire enough hope.

Shelley steps forward. "I'll go with you. We're stronger together. I once wrote about solitude as consolation—deep, dark, deathlike solitude. I've learned better now. Besides, I still owe you after how you saved me in Green."

"Thank you." I smile at her, the once famous writer. She's right. Every mistake I've made here has been because of trying to go it alone. "Genius can work together. Respect the mind, right?"

"Respect the mind," Shelley responds with a grin.

"Fine, twist my arm," Tom says. "I'll go, too."

"And I," Luther says.

Even Luther, the boy who once bullied Emma, who threatened to punch me in the jaw. It's enough to make me feel embarrassed. I don't know what to say.

"Who will stay to keep the tower in order?" Tom asks.

"The rest of us will," says a boy from the back of the group. It's Pierre. He was my rival for the Hunting, so long ago. "You will be back soon, yes?"

"Yes, before nightfall, if all goes well," I say.

It's agreed. Luther, Tom, Shelley, and Li Min stand with me at the edge of the doorway. The sea is far below our feet. I summon the wind. Blue threads coil with mine. Plus yellow from Li Min, green from Shelley, and red from Tom. Each of us is stronger than ever. Together, we form the invisible stairs as easily as we would swim.

We descend away from the others. At the base of the mist-shrouded tower, black rocks grip the smooth stone walls. The waves rise and fall only a few feet. Each ebb and flow reveals tiny crabs nestled into the rocks. A silver minnow the size of my hand is stranded in a small pool, only to be swept out with the next wave.

Around the tower, along the cliffs, we move slow and steady. The trek passes quickly. It's uneventful. It unnerves me all the same. Something should have happened. Some challenge, some fight. It's as if the Colorless One watches us in quiet amusement, ready to spring an attack when our guard is down. And what did Kiyo want to show me?

I force myself to stay focused. I'll be ready.

Ahead I spot the ledge on the cliffs above. We summon the air and climb invisible stairs. The sea stays tranquil beneath us. Even the wind is only a slight, warm breeze.

Kiyo waits on the ledge with six others. There are two other robed girls and four boys. Kiyo's son Omaki stands by her side like a guard. Her other descendant, Max, rushes forward and embraces Li Min by my side. He and Omaki have swords strapped to their backs. Shucks, the freckled boy who once welcomed me to my first troop, gives me a toothy grin.

My fists clench as I stare at the final boy. Napoleon.

He's the ruthless commander who rivaled Karl. He prodded me to put a spear through the former Holy Roman Emperor, then he broke his word by choosing Baron instead of me as commander. He would do anything for power. He threw away lives like discarded peanut shells. Now his smug face looks noble as he stares at me. He was wiped. Maybe he has changed. I have to accept that even he will be scoured.

"Goodbye, Max." Kiyo steps toward him. Her scarred hand grazes his cheek. "It's hard to let you go, but I know you belong in Blue, with Li Min."

His hard eyes look up, to the tower looming over the cliffs above. "This time I join a tower freely," he says. "But can I keep the sword?"

"Yes, you have earned it." Kiyo turns to me, then glances at the group from Blue behind me. "Why do you bring these others?"

"For safe passage," I say. "They will return to Blue with me."

She nods. "You will take Max, Napoleon, and Jade."

"Jade?" I say.

She steps forward and pulls back her hood. Her dark eagle eyes meet mine. "Are you so surprised I belong in your tower?"

"No." I'm not. Jade's sharp mind and quick feet saved me in Green, and in Purple. It will be good to have her by my side in the final battle. "But it's not my tower," I say, motioning to the others behind me. "It's ours."

Jade and Napoleon cross the ledge to join us.

Napoleon stops in front of me. "My apologies for what I did," he says, bowing slightly. "It was a bit of my old self coming through. I've drunk from the cup of judgment. I've seen the errors of my ambition, but also the gifts of my mind. I will serve Blue well."

I clasp his shoulder. One of the greatest tacticians of history. "It's good to have you."

"Come, Cipher," Kiyo says. "I must show you something you could not see through Blue's clouds. The rest of you wait here. Omaki, you have command."

Her scarred hand takes mine. She summons her power—an intricate weave of five colors. The thread moves through me, and I add my own thick strand of blue to hers. She has control.

The air stirs at our feet. She lifts us.

In an instant, before I can warn of crows or shadowy dragons, we soar along the edge of the cliffs. Kiyo veers right, toward the Purple Tower.

Below us the soldiers' camps cluster around the tower's base. Their campfires light up the tower like a gleam of oil, violet against the dusk.

We land atop the tower. Kiyo leads the way down into the uppermost room. This is where Moses was supposed to be. This is where justice should have been dispensed, instead of the Colorless One working his tyranny through Samantha.

"Come, look," Kiyo says by a window.

There's a distant hammering sound. Beyond the soldiers' camps and the wall, dark shapes move across the Scouring, like animals prowling the night.

"What are they?" I ask.

"Bones. Let's get closer. I'll show you." She squeezes my hand, as if readying to leap.

I step back. "Wait, the sky's not safe."

She motions out the window. "The way is clear now. That's why I brought you here first, to be sure we could go safely. Come, not much further."

She doesn't wait for a reply. We fly again.

This time we land on the wall around the perimeter of the Scouring, at the midpoint between Blue and Purple. Here the wall the stands at the edge of the cliffs, dropping to stone on one side and far down to the sea on the other. The Blue Tower is completely enveloped in clouds, masking it from view.

Kiyo crouches and pulls me down. I summon weaves of green to cloak us in invisibility. What I see in the Scouring makes my stomach turn.

"There's no need," she whispers. "Since the last attack, they have ignored us. They only dig and dig and dig."

Across the entire Scouring countless skeletons—thousands or more—hack at the stone ground. The bones come in many sizes, like vestiges of lost souls. They wield pickaxes. Shovels. Scythes. Swords. Every tool imaginable.

In the center, where once there was a white disc leading into the White Tower, now there's only the rubble of imploded stone. The skeletons concentrate there. They scramble and fight over each other like ants clamoring for the same crumb of food. Through the chaos all seem to serve the same purpose: digging and clearing away whatever holds back the Colorless One.

The ground trembles. A stone falls near the center.

Where the ground was solid, now a hole gapes. A deep, terrible groan rises up. A line of blackness emerges from the hole. It stabs straight into the sky.

The dark shard returns. Larger. Worse.

With so many skeletons at work, the whole Scouring will soon be gone.

Maybe this is why the passage from Blue to Purple went without challenge. Maybe this is what the leaders feared most all along. Now they're not here…

Kiyo puts her hand on my arm. "We must hurry."

"Gather Purple. Send up a beacon," I say. "I'll take the others to Blue. We'll have equilibrium. We'll fight our way to the center, to the White Tower."

Golden flecks sparkle in her dark eyes. "For the light."

54

WE STAND BEFORE the closed gate to the Scouring. The tally on the wall shows the perfect equilibrium. Max, Jade, and Napoleon have joined us in Blue. Now each tower has its one hundred forty-four. The Five Towers have their seven hundred twenty. The leaders said this is what we needed to win. And now the leaders are gone.

We, the marked ones, lead in their place. We're as scoured as we can be. It will have to be enough. We'll charge into the familiar battleground. We'll weave our powers together and fight the skeletons, the darkness, and the Colorless One.

Everything has led to this. It's time to fight. And time to face what I deserve, if that's what it takes. I summon my power and weave it into the gate.

The thick door shudders. It rises an inch, then another.

No light enters from the Scouring. Only the sickening sound of metal and bone pounding against stone.

I turn to face my friends of the Blue Tower. We fill the tunnel leading to the battleground. Before, we looked small in this narrow passage, when twelve of us would fight against a dozen of each tower's best. Now we look like an army. We wear robes. We wield the mind and the wind.

But as they peer past me and spot the skeletons, their

expressions change. Determination slips. Focus fades. Faces go pale. Mouths twist in uncertainty and fear.

"Respect the mind!" I shout.

They look to me. They answer. "Respect the mind!"

I don't deserve their loyalty. But my failures somehow qualify me to lead. My power has emerged like dawn out of night, and it has earned their respect. It gives them hope.

"For the light!" I shout.

"For the light!" they echo. The chant continues, louder and louder.

The gate has lifted halfway up. The legs of skeletons are almost within reach. Dozens of them bend down. Eyeless skulls stare at us. I won't let them suck me in. Not this time. I look past their hollow gazes to the black shard. Abram told me what to do. *You must unite the colors and stab light into the black heart of the Colorless One.* Now the time has come.

The first beacon appears. It comes from the right, from Kiyo and the Purple Tower. And around the Scouring the other hues of light flash up and hold, like signals to the heavens. Helena and Red. Baron and Green. Emma and Yellow.

They are too far away to make out their faces, but thinking of the other marked ones fuels my hope, my power. I draw more and more of blue, and the threads of others weave into me. The Blue Tower gives me control over its vast energy and light.

I cast it vertically, knowing what it means.

Our beacon rises. The Five Towers have the Colorless One surrounded.

I use the weaves to project my voice like a thunderclap across the Scouring. This is the final signal. The time for the marked ones to lead the charge.

"FOR THE LIGHT!"

I step forward, knowing Emma, Baron, Helena, and Kiyo will be doing the same. We are united. We are ready.

We surge out of the gate into the Scouring. The others from Blue follow close, funneling their power through me. I weave the pulsing force together and blast into the skeletons. The creatures bend back like palms in a hurricane. Some of them manage to hold their ground. They are stronger than humans, as if rooted down by darkness.

But we are relentless, pressing ever forward. Dozens of skeletons are flung back. Bones clatter against the hard stone. Others are mowed over. Bony hands grab at me, but my friends fight them away.

We are making it. I carve a path straight toward the center. Around us I glimpse the other towers doing the same, in their own ways. Yellow moves together, plowing ahead at Emma's lead. Some of them fall, but they are healed by allies behind them. Green's team is invisible, but their presence is clear. Skeletons collapse and fall under their attacks. Red blasts fire, burning a path like ours. And Purple's steady phalanx marches forward, a uniform line of shields and spears, blocking and thrusting, as the girls cloud the battle in smoke.

We are over halfway to the center when my power suddenly hits something hard. Blue threads billow around it like wind around a boulder. Unmovable.

It's a figure in golden armor with black seams. There's a silver collar around its neck and a sword in its gauntleted fist. Out of its helmet stare the empty eye sockets of a skull.

More armored figures emerge around it. Dozens. They form a ring around the black shard. A wall.

I blast the wind harder, blowing other skeletons into them. Bones crash against the golden armor. The skeletons shatter, but don't make a dent in the wall of armored figures. They step forward in unison.

I stop, realizing what this could be. We melted the Yellow Tower's gold after we defeated the twisted king. We sent the gold into the pit. Collars have disappeared. Rahab melted other collars. The Colorless One has somehow crafted the gold and silver again. But this time there are no boys or girls inside. Only skeletons.

They are more of the Colorless One's lies. They are souls of shame, of those who never existed. They can be defeated.

One of them locks its dark gaze onto me. It lets out a terrible scream, piercing into my mind.

I fight the fear. I form a wall of air between us.

The figure dashes and leaps. Twenty feet at once. Straight through my wall. Fast as a blur. Screaming.

I duck. The sword swings inches above my head. But the mass of armor hits me like a hammer. I'm down, flat on my back. Ribs feel crushed. The figure looms over me.

I blast the wind but it's futile.

The skull's eyes meet mine. "Hello father," it growls.

I jerk my gaze away. It's a voice I've heard before, in a vision in the pit. My daughter. *But I had no daughter.*

Something surges up in me, flooding over the fear. It's more than anger. It's righteous fury at this abomination.

"You're a lie!" I shout.

I try my power again. It gusts viciously, but the wind does nothing to the armored evil. It kneels down on my chest. Heavy as an anvil. Gauntleted hands grab the sides of my head, then try to pull my eyes open.

Deep breath. Inhale.

I refuse to die under the Colorless One's shame. I imagine Susan and Benjamin before me. Their faces smile. They don't judge me for failing. They don't ask about this daughter who never was.

Exhale.

There's a sudden crash. A grunt. The weight on me shifts slightly as my eyes open again. Two boys have tackled the golden armor and are wrestling it off of me. It shrieks and flails wildly at them.

Hank and Max.

As I try to twist away, the skeleton lunges for me. Hank grabs its golden helm and, with a massive yank, rips it off. In a blur Max swings his sword at the exposed bones. The skull and collar clatter to the ground. The armor topples.

"Ha, they ain't takin' Cipher!" Hank says.

"Not over my dead body," Max says, cool as steel. "They can't stop us now."

A girl rushes to me. It's Emma. She holds her hand out to me. "You okay? We need you."

Her blue eyes are a jolt of life. I grasp her hand and rise. The power from her is immense. Yellow threads spool around her, drawing from dozens in her tower, and heal me in an instant. Through our clasped, scarred hands, our powers join.

"One down!" Hank yells. "Come on!"

He charges like a bear into a cluster of skeletons. Seneca appears at his side, protecting his back.

"Almost there," Emma says, eyeing the shard. It's only a hundred feet away. If that.

We stride forward, hand in hand.

Around us I see victory. In the chaos the towers have mixed. Our fighters are everywhere, knocking back skeletons, pressing toward the center.

"Help!" The shout makes me turn.

To the left Joan clashes against one of the creatures in golden armor. She blocks a blow, but the next pierces her side. She crumples forward, clutching the wound.

Emma and I flash our power toward her, but others from Yellow are already there. Neville and Seymour. They kneel by Joan's side, healing her, while others fend off the armored creature with physical force.

A boy slams into the skeleton. He stands facing it, granite eyes bold and confident.

Baron.

Joan is on her feet again. She and Baron and a dozen others charge at the golden armor and knock it back.

As we charge forward, the wall of Purple's shields converges with us. Their spears stab forward, pressing the bones into the hole at the center. The shields part and Kiyo strides out, between Omaki and Karl. She stands still and composed at the edge of the hole, gazing down.

Across the hole Helena appears. Crispus and Marcus stride by her side, axes slung over their shoulders. Ribbons of fire sweep out from Helena, burning skeletons as they fall.

The fighting fades around us.

We've made it. All five marked ones.

Emma, Baron, Helena, Kiyo and I take a stand at the edge of the void. Everyone from the towers gathers behind us. It's time.

I extend my hand toward the darkness, just as the other

four marked ones do the same around the circle. We weave our threads together, drawing on the power of everyone around us, to stab light into this black heart.

Blue, yellow, green, red, purple. Fusing and melding. Brighter and brighter, bending the shard back, piercing…

But the blackness lashes out.

An inky tendril clamps over my wrist like a handcuff, and yanks me viciously down.

55

THERE'S NO GROUND. I drop like a rock. Shouts chase after me from above. They're too slow, too late. I reach for the air, my power, but there's nothing. An irresistible force sucks me down. Terror pumps through me.

Twisting, I glimpse faces far above, peering over a ledge, gazing down at me in horror. The faces shrink. The force yanks harder. I spin out of control, pulled down and down, like I'm caught in a raging dark waterfall. The blackness shakes with cruel laughter. It covers everything.

I scream.

Other screams join mine, faint behind the demonic laugh. I'm not alone. I recognize the voices, one by one. Darkness separates us, but we are the marked ones. All five of us. Falling into the abyss together. We attacked the black shard. Have we lost?

I expect the worst. To crash onto the pile of bones. To be trapped by the Colorless One.

But the falling goes on and on until I simply stop. The force no longer pulls. I lay on my back, still as when I first woke in a coffin under the Black Tower. I try to sit up, but my body is lead.

"You there?" Emma's whisper is only a few feet away.

The other four of us say yes. All are close. All terrified.

"What…is this?" Kiyo asks. "No, no, no…"

A sickly, sulfur stench floods my nostrils. A force penetrates my mind. It wraps around my thoughts like a serpent, and squeezes.

"You…" It's Benjamin's voice, angry. I see his fist emerge out of nothing. His hand, large as a giant's, tightens around me. It grabs me by the chest. I can't breathe.

"You didn't love me," he says bitterly.

I try to answer. I did. I loved him.

"The cancer was a curse on you, for your failures. I could have lived if only you had loved me."

No. It's a lie.

The hand squeezes tighter.

Susan's face appears, inches before me. Her gentle eyes burn with fury. I feel her hate staring into me. "You never loved me. Never."

I can't speak. I'm sorry. I changed. I learned…

"And you cheated!" she shouts. Hate courses through despair and resentment in her voice. "You deserve this."

She slaps me across the cheek. It burns like hot coals. She slaps again, and again. My head twists. Skin sears. I smell burning flesh. Susan's face slips away, but her raging eyes remain. They hover over me like vampires ready to suck out my life.

Another figure slides between us. This one is a voluptuous body with wings like a bat and burning hair like Samantha's.

"You lied." It *is* Samantha.

Her hand extends. Her fingernails are black claws, blacker than the void around me. She presses a claw to my neck. "So did I," she taunts. "I never loved you."

The claw's sharp point pricks my neck. She drags it down my chest, carving a channel of pain into my skin. "You lied. I lied. We lied."

Susan slaps me again. Another claw comes to my neck.

The three of them press their torments at once. Benjamin's hand squeezes the life out of me. Susan's slaps burn. Samantha's claw draws anguish on my pale body.

Other tortures come. My mother. My father. A nurse I worked with. Susan's father. The President. Max. People I don't even know. Each one extracts a new piece of me. Each inflicts unique suffering.

I can't move. There's no escape.

No end to this infernal pit.

I cry out in despair. The tormentors laugh. Darker than black. Worse than pain. Cruel, ceaseless, crushing.

Hell.

A dot of light, infinitely high above, sees me. The light descends in a slow and delicate line, like the glistening silk thread of a spider suspended in morning light.

As this thread approaches the tormenters edge away. The pain relents. I suck in the sweet air of relief, even as the threat of torture hangs heavy around me.

The thread reflects a spectrum—weaves of blue, yellow, green, red, and purple. It touches me. It floods me with hope. Like gazing out of ocean depths through a periscope, I see the other end. First there are familiar faces. Hundreds of them, a source of this light, peering down at me, saving me. They are my friends in the Five Towers. But beyond them, higher than the heavens, is another light. This one is pure light. It is the source of all the strands of color.

The light lifts me, like a weaving spider lifts a bug.

"You see this?" Emma's voice is relief and wonder.

Through the torments I'd forgotten she was by my side. I'd felt completely alone.

"Light," I say. "It's saving us."

"Light," the others echo. Kiyo, Baron, Helena.

But then the void trembles.

"This is my domain," rumbles a voice deeper than deep. The light weakens. It fades so thin I can barely detect it.

"I have made a deal." There's sinister glee in the Colorless One's growling voice. "One of you will stay, or all will be trapped."

The time has come. This was the deal.

The others may leave. You will stay with me. In the pit. Forever.

But I can't bear it, now that I fully understand. It's too much—this ultimate result of my failures, this infinite torture and darkness. There must be a way out.

"It is already done," the voice says, and I feel the Colorless One pulling me down, claiming me.

"No," says Emma's voice. "The light will save us."

I want to believe her, but the light is too far from me. I hurt too many people. I have no defense.

I speak into the darkness. "It's too late. I must stay."

"*No!*" Emma shouts. "You can't!"

"Tell them," says the Colorless One.

"It's the only way you can leave." My voice is grim, defeated. "It's what I deserve."

"No!" Baron yells out, his voice distant from above. "We *all* deserve it but—"

"The deal is done!" The darkness thunders around me. "This one is mine."

True to his dark word, the Colorless One releases his

hold on my four friends. The light lifts them instantly, as I'm dragged down and down.

They call out for me as they rise. They reach down desperately, as if they could take me as they soar away. Their pleading voices fade to nothing.

It is done. I am alone. All is dark.

The tormentors swoop back, shades of onyx, obsidian, and black. They press close. They pin me down and resume their torture. I can't fight it. I give up. I moan. I wail. It's over now. They will be my only company in the abyss. My own personal horror.

56

"BY LAW CONDEMNED. Banished. Cursed. Damned."

The voice hisses in my ear. It needs no introduction. It gives no greeting. It's the Colorless One. The others, my tormentors, have fled. I'm alone, suspended in the void. No air. No light. Nothing.

"He said the last shall be first," the Colorless One hisses. "He lied. The last is mine."

The dark voice, the presence, forces me inward. Out of the void and into myself.

A memory takes hold. Won't let go.

I am on the hospital bed. I am alone.

The shadow starts in the corner of the room. It creeps toward me. Everything it passes over loses color. The blue floor goes black. The blinking lights of my life support go black. Even the small bump of my feet under the sheets— the dim yellow rise of fabric—turns black. The darkness is so complete that no memory remains. It feels like a limb being sawn off.

No, no. Focus. Think of color. Think of blue. Summon the air.

The hissing voice laughs. I can do nothing but watch.

The creeping shadow moves to the next memory. My meeting with the President is blackened away. My moment with Susan on a snowy morning in a car before a mansion…it fades. No snow remains. My mother, her smell, she's gone. The darkness marches relentlessly through my mind. With every erased memory another piece of me crumbles, like an imploding tower.

The shadow comes to another hospital room. This time my son, Benjamin, is on the hospital bed. He has no hair on his head.

It's the memory I saw when I first stepped onto the white stone at the center of the Scouring, before it turned black. Familiar figures stand around my son—Susan, Samantha, me. The shadow slinks toward Benjamin's pale form on the bed. I, Dr. Fitzroy in a white coat, move close to his side.

My son, my little Benjamin, sees the darkness coming. He stares at it calmly. A light brightens from within him.

"You cannot have him," Benjamin says to the shadow.

The shadow comes to the edge of Benjamin's body. It stops. It pushes against the light but moves not an inch. It shakes with fury, then pulls back and coils tight around me.

It shouts in a whiny raging hiss: "*He is mine!*"

"No." Benjamin takes my hand in his. He looks straight at the darkness as the light within him pulses. A sliver of the light extends from him and stabs into the shadow like a sword. The darkness shudders.

"He *will* deal with me," the shadow growls, fainter now.

"HE BELONGS TO THE LIGHT." The voice comes from the light, a voice that could melt mountains.

Benjamin smiles at me and opens his mouth to speak. Weaves of white light carry his soft words to me: "You're not done yet."

He releases my hand. The vision shifts again.

I should be asleep. It's dark and quiet. The bed is soft, the pillows well-placed. Even the medical equipment emits a bland humming white noise. My body is tired and broken. But my mind won't relent. It won't let me sleep. Thoughts run in circles, spiraling through my past.

There's Susan. There's Samantha.

There's Benjamin.

And here I am, on a deathbed like he was, but kept alive. I am proof of the enhanced brain's ability to fight death, long after a body has given out. But no technology can solve my guilt.

I toss. I turn.

My thoughts come back and back again to Benjamin. The day I stood beside his hospital bed. For the first time, within my own painful memory, surrounded by darkness and death, Benjamin's words come to me. I remember exactly what he said. He looked at me, face pale, body frail. Tears welled up in his eyes.

"I forgive you," he said.

Forgive me? I thought. Why? Because I couldn't heal you?

"It's not your fault," he said.

"I know," I said, standing tall beside him in my white coat, admiring my young boy for his courage to speak through such pain, but baffled still.

"You should've been around more," he said. "I heard you and mom arguing about my birthday, about everything. But I forgive you."

Now his words—his forgiveness—reach all the way to my deathbed, all these years later, with more force than ever. They shatter me. Pride. Ambition. Discipline. Things that have kept me alive. None of it holds up, only forgiveness.

But how, how, how could he forgive me? I don't deserve it. He doesn't deserve this.

He told me a name. He said it was his hope. The name enters my mind like a secret treasure. I can't say the name. My lips seal it in. There will be no more words from my broken body.

My breath fades. My heart slows…and stops.

But *I* don't stop.

My soul rises out of the lifeless body, vibrant and pulsing and soaring with joy. I sweep up and down, yelling the secret name over and over, like it's the only victory, the only way out of death and into life, out of darkness and into light.

Time does not exist in this light. Hope exists. I exist. And in the last flicker of consciousness away from my deathbed and Earth, I flash through a flame. It transports me instantly into a pool of blue.

The first thing I know: I'm treading water.

But this time I remember.

I am back in the Blue Tower, and I remember it all, and the memories are pure and good. Benjamin, Susan, and even Samantha forgave me. They helped me find the way here, but this is only a pit stop. A temporary gateway to forever reality.

I swim to the shore. Water drips from my young, bare body as I crawl onto the sand. As before, a light shines there. This time it is white, not blue, not Abram.

The man's thick beard has no gray. He carries no staff. His face beams like the sun. His clothes are white as light.

He approaches and wraps a robe around me. It is whiter than freshly fallen snow. He takes my hand. He has a scar on his hand, but my scar is gone. I glance down at my other hand, my feet, my bare torso. No scars at all.

"You finished," he says, in a voice I know, the voice that could melt mountains, only gentler now. "Your work has been tested and burned up."

He is the man who was beside my hospital bed so long ago. He told me I wasn't finished yet, just as Benjamin did.

"I know you," I say.

The face of light turns up in a crescent smile. "You always have. You needed to remember. Come, the others are waiting."

I follow him in silence and awe. We wind steadily up the Blue Tower and step out onto the Scouring. The ground has returned, but everything has changed. The stones are pure white. There are no skeletons. Only friends. Hundreds of them, beaming. In the center the light shines up farther than I can see.

The White Tower.

The man of light leads me across the vast open space and through the crowd. This is where we have fought so many times. Around the Scouring rise the Five Towers. As my gaze alights on each one, I remember the stains I've seen.

In Blue there was pride. I was a neurosurgeon who touched minds and healed them, for my own glory. Now that pride is gone. The Genius scoured it.

In Red there was lust. I let a spark of desire grow into a wildfire that consumed my marriage, my family, myself. Now that lust is gone. The Passion scoured it.

In Green there was greed. I always hungered for more. I married for money, bought a mansion, and put others down. Now that greed is gone. The Provider scoured it.

In Yellow there was cowardice. I feared death. I hid behind my research, too scared to see relationships for the treasures they were. I refused to accept that I would die, as Benjamin died. Now that cowardice is gone. The Healer scoured it.

In Purple there was selfish ambition. I yearned to have power, to create something that changed the world, even if it meant bending others to my will. It was tyranny of the self, not justice. Now that selfish ambition is gone. The Judge scoured it.

And as I approach the White Tower, I see Abram standing at the edge of the light, beside four of my friends from this strange journey. The marked ones. Emma, Baron, Helena, and Kiyo. Their glowing faces make it clearer than ever that they helped me see these stains and wash them away.

I want to go to all of them and say thank you. I want to look them in the eyes and say, *I couldn't have done it without you*. But I see it in their joyful eyes: they know. And I know. We needed each other. That's how we found balance. Only our unique colors woven together could reveal the light to us—the way to this final Scouring.

"You are ready?" Abram holds his staff with the blue orb up to the light. Unlike me, he has not changed at all. He was not here to be cleaned. He was here to help us.

"Yes," I say. "We see the light."

He smiles and spreads his arms wide, inviting us forward.

When my feet reach the edge of the white circle, I pause. I look down at the stones. It has been so long since Emma and I stood by the White Tower and watched my mother go up. So many towers together. I've been bruised.

I've died and been wiped. I've been scoured. And Emma has been by my side for so much of it.

I turn to her and hold out my hand. "Together?"

"Of course," she says. "You are glowing, Cipher."

"Light suits us well." I take hold of the air and send a gentle breeze to tickle her neck.

She laughs. Then her eyes concentrate on me, taking my power and forging it with hers, the familiar coil of yellow and blue. She looks to her left, and I feel Baron's power join ours, like a green vine growing up around it. Next comes Helena and her fire. Finally there is Kiyo. The first girl I met here. The girl who was so cold when she suffered in the winter in the mountains, and when she lost her son. Now she smiles wide and free as she links her power to our thread. Instead of black smoke there is a ribbon of velvet purple, like the strand of a royal robe.

Light from each of us comes together. Five facets shine as one, brighter and stronger and purer.

The light pours through us, all seven hundred twenty of us, and through everything else. The White Tower expands and fills the entire Scouring like a supernova. All is bathed in this light. No trace of darkness or shadow. The purity feels like paradise.

As we rise up and up and up, we reflect every hue of this pure light like a peerless diamond shining down on the five towers, blue and red and green and yellow and purple. The towers grow smaller and smaller beneath us. They fade in space and time, as everything does, when soaring into eternity.

The rush of light takes us through a gate and releases us. We stand in awe.

A crowd waits beyond the gate. They are countless.

Behind them a golden city rises in the distance, with mountains and birds and rivers and stars and wonders beyond belief.

The crowd approaches us. Several of them come to Emma, still at my side, flanked by her father William, her son Oliver, Neville, and others. There are hugs and laughs and words.

My focus centers on three people before me. They are from my story, and they are perfect. Joy bursts inside me.

Susan smiles a thousand smiles at once. She looks like she did on the day of our wedding. She takes my flawless hand in hers. "By grace." Mirth dances in her voice. "Welcome, Paul."

Benjamin embraces me, then steps back. He has the same inquisitive eyes, but he is older. He is grown. He is a man in his prime, as I now am.

There are no words to describe this feeling. Benjamin. Susan. Love. Wonder. Glory. They overwhelm me.

"There now, take your time." My mother moves forward and gently clasps my cheek. "I'm proud of you," she says. "I knew you would make it."

I made it. I gaze down, trying to remember. An infinitely wide light holds us up, rising from a depth I can barely see. Below are dazzling colors, more than five, more than any rainbow.

"There were five towers," I say. "I was scoured." I look to Susan and Benjamin. "You were with me, in my memories. You helped carry me here."

"We were made to carry each other, Paul. That is love." Susan spreads her arms wide, basked in golden light, gesturing to everything, beaming with joy.

"Love and light," Benjamin says. "What the light fills

no darkness can overcome."

"And now no darkness remains," the man of light says, appearing beside me, brighter than three suns. "The colors were made for delight. In the radiance of every facet, the light shines forever."

THE END

HISTORICAL EPILOGUE

The Five Towers is fiction inspired by fantasy, faith, and history. Many characters grew out of rich stories from the past. This note offers brief historical snapshots for prominent characters, in chronological order. Some names are omitted or changed to protect the innocent.

Helena (248-330 AD): Helena of Constantinople is a legend and mystery of history. Long ago Saint Ambrose wrote that she was a young *stabularia*, which can mean either innkeeper or stable maid. She likely met the future emperor Constantius while he was fighting a campaign in Asia Minor. Some sources refer to Helena as the emperor's concubine, while others say they were officially married. In any case, Constantius eventually left Helena for a woman of higher birth. Helena's son Constantine became the first Christian emperor. Helena found what was believed to be the True Cross and other relics while in Jerusalem. She is considered today to be a saint.

Crispus (295-326): Flavius Julius Crispus was the son of Emperor Constantine and, through many military victories, rose to become Caesar of the Roman Empire. Historians believe he had a close relationship with his father. One historian writes that Crispus was "an Imperator most dear to God and in all regards comparable to his father." Yet, after allegations of an affair with his father's wife, Crispus was condemned to death and executed.

Karl (748-814): Charles the Great, known today as Charlemagne, was born as prince of the Franks and rose to be the first Holy Roman Emperor. Through almost constant warfare, he united all Germanic peoples into one kingdom. He fervently followed Augustine's "City of God" and converted those he conquered to Christianity, with penalty of death to those who refused to be baptized. In 800, Pope Leo III crowned Charlemagne as emperor. Many consider him the Father of Europe.

Fugger (1459-1525): Jakob Fugger was an extremely wealthy German businessman. His decision to loan money to one archbishop and the ensuing events led Martin Luther to publish his 95 theses, which was a catalyst for the Christian Reformation. He funded kings and popes, backed wars, and helped propel the Hapsburgs to become the most important dynasty in Europe. Some historians call him the most influential businessman of all time.

Kiyo (1563-1600): Hosokawa Tama lived in medieval Japan. She married young and had five children. Her father betrayed and killed the Japanese leader, Oda Nobunaga, putting her life in danger. Her husband sent her into hiding in the mountains. In the face of intense persecution across the country, she secretly visited a church where she was baptized and given the name Gracia. Rival lords later invaded Osaka castle and attempted to take her hostage. She died in the conflict; her family household committed seppuku as the castle burned. Fictional context for Kiyo's story can be found in novels such as *Silence* by Shusaku Endo and *Shogun* by James Clavell.

Omaki (1584-1645): Miyamoto Musashi was a Japanese swordsman and philosopher. He was renowned for wielding a double-bladed sword to win 61 duels without a single loss. He authored *The Book of Five Rings*, which discusses the craft of war, strategy, and martial arts. Although he was not the grandson of Kiyo, her son Omaki embodied many of Musashi's principles.

Seneca (1743-1833): Mary Jemison was born aboard a ship from Ireland to America. Her family settled on the frontier in Pennsylvania, where she enjoyed happy childhood days. At age fifteen, however, during the French and Indian War, Native American warriors captured her family. The Seneca tribe purchased Mary. She integrated, married, and took the name Dehgewanus. She moved to a valley near the Genesee River. Her husband died, but she remained among the Seneca people. She became known as the "Old White Woman of the Genesee."

Hank (1743-1805): Many early American pastors lived on the frontier. They were plain-folk itinerants and circuit-riders. A good horse was paramount to their work. Saddlebags often carried no more than a watch, a change of clothes, boots, a Bible, and a hymnal. One such itinerant, Henry Smith, was overtaken by a snowstorm on the frontier. His journal entry recorded that his "lot was hard, and wept," but that the following day he preached to a small town and a person was saved. Other inspiration for Hank's story came from the folksy ballad *Long Black Veil*.

Tom (1743-1826): Thomas Jefferson, the Founding Father and third U.S. President, wrote for his epitaph: "Author of the Declaration of American Independence, of the statue of Virginia for religious freedom, and father of the

University of Virginia." Debates about his views on religion, slavery, and Sally Hemings have lasted two centuries and show few signs of stopping.

Napoleon (1769-1821): Napoleon Bonaparte rose in power like few others in history. Born in Corsica, he led French armies during the French Revolutionary Wars. He became Emperor of France in 1804, at the age of 35, saying, "I am Charlemagne." Many regard him as one of the greatest military commanders in history, and his liberal legal system, the Napoleonic Code, has shaped the modern world. His failed invasion of Russia ultimately led to his exile, and he died on the remote island of Saint Helena. In exile he reflected: "Alexander, Caesar, Charlemagne, and myself founded great empires; but upon what did the creations of our genius depend? Upon force. Jesus alone founded His empire upon love, and to this very day millions would die for Him...."

Sally (1775-1835): Sarah "Sally" Hemings is believed to be the daughter of John Wayles and his slave Betty Hemings. If so, Sally was three-quarters European and a half-sister to Martha Jefferson. As Martha's property she joined Thomas Jefferson's estate. After Martha died, it is widely believed that Thomas and Sally began a long-term relationship and had six children. Controversy and speculation about this relationship began in the 1790s and continues to this day.

Emma (1810-1840): The idea of Emma Chamberlain was born in the works of the Brontë sisters, Jane Eyre or Wuthering Heights, as you prefer. Charlotte Brontë was an Anglican who once wrote in a letter: "if your lips and mine could at the same time, drink the same draught from the same pure fountain of Mercy—I hope, I trust, I might one day become better, far better, than my evil wandering thoughts, my corrupt heart, cold to the spirit, and warm to the flesh will now permit me to be." Emma would have said the same with her royal dignity.

Baron (1839-1937): John Davison Rockefeller was an American titan and one of the richest men in history. He rose from poverty and steadily earned his wealth in the oil industry through shrewd business moves and fortunate timing. He often quarreled with his youngest brother Frank, who had fought in the Civil War, never succeeded in business, and depended on John's generosity. Rockefeller became a frequent target of criticism as a symbol of the robber barons, and he was known to hold a grudge and flame with selfish indignation. But in private he was a kind family man and devout churchgoer. His vast philanthropy has left its mark on the world. Historian Ron Chernow writes of Rockefeller: "What makes him problematic…is that his good side was every bit as good as his bad side was bad. Seldom has history produced such a contradictory figure."

Neville (1869-1940): Neville Chamberlain served as Prime Minister of the United Kingdom at the start of World War II. History remembers him for signing a concession to Germany that preceded German attack against Poland and beyond. Many claim that his weakness and failure to prepare contributed to the outbreak of war. He resigned in 1940, replaced by Winston Churchill, and died only six months after stepping down from his position. One historian observes that expecting Neville's reputation to be restored "is rather like hoping that Pontius Pilate will one day be judged as a successful provincial administrator of the Roman Empire."

Max (1980-2060?): Max and his daughter, Li Min—or others quite like them—live today under oppression. The Communist Party of China represses freedoms and increasingly monitors citizens in every aspect of life, even using a "Social Credit System" to score its citizens. It may not be long before resistance against this authoritarian regime arises, perhaps led by someone like Max. Technology's danger grows dire without freedom.

Cipher (1982-2065?): No one like Paul Fitzroy, the hero of the Five Towers, has made it yet into Earth's history books. But perhaps someone will. Dr. Fitzroy was a brilliant neurosurgeon who used his unique drive and skills to study the mysteries of the human brain and nanotechnology. This sparked breakthroughs for a computer chip that could be installed in the mind, enhancing humans' processing abilities to levels never before imagined. As to whether this was a good thing, and how it might relate to the end of the world, a great place to look is another series by J.B. Simmons, *The Omega Trilogy*.

ACKNOWLEDGMENTS

I might not have much in common with Cipher, but I have my own rough edges. These inevitably find their way into writing. As in life, it's those around me who help polish these edges so light can shine from the Five Towers.

First thanks go to my best friend and bride, Lindsay. These books would not exist without our magic. Thank you as well to Jamison, who asked all the right questions to make the story sing for young readers, and to Eliza and John Ezra for helping me dream of Five Towers movies and amusement parks. Red has the best rides.

Among a host of superb editors, special thanks to Danny Murphy for his brilliance in drawing out the characters, the story's deep threads, and my very best. He's the Tolkien to C.S. Lewis in our modern Inklings. I'm also grateful for wonderful insights and edits from Anne G., Ryan E., Daniel S., Michael A., Laurel S., Sean and Meredith C., and all the magnificent members of the Five Towers Advance Readers Group. When my energy flagged, your encouragement and eagerness for the next book was wind in my sails. And you get credit for the map!

So, you're still reading this? You're amazing. Let's wrap it up: the world would be a much better place if more people spent more time thinking more seriously about what they truly believe will happen after they die. But death is dark and gloomy. The Five Towers, I hope, is a fantastically bright and fun way to think about what comes next. Please share the word about these books. Let's make the world a better place, while we still can.

J.B. SIMMONS is the bestselling author of the
Five Towers series, the *Unbound* trilogy, and *The
Babel Tower*. He lives with his family outside
Washington, D.C. To learn more about J.B. and
his books, visit **www.jbsimmons.com**.

9 781949 785128